# KA HUAKA'I O KA PO

The Marchers of the Night

By
Matthew Guerrero

Graphic Hawaiian Folklore
by Matthew Guerrero.
I dedicate these humble interpretations of Hawaiian folklore to the
Kama'aina who hanai'd me into their lives and shared their beliefs.
'Ohana nui lives on in stories.

# KA HUAKA'I O KA PO

The Marchers of the Night

**MAKA 'IKE**

THE GIFT OF SECOND SIGHT

**KU'I MOE'UHANE**

POUNDING NIGHTMARES

**UHANE KIHEI PUA**

FLOWER MANTLE ENERGY

**KA LELE 'O KA PUEO**

THE FLIGHT OF THE OWL

**PU'UWAI HAO KILA**

HEART OF STEEL

**Hawaiian Fiction**
**By**
**Matthew Guerrero**

1

# Maka ʻIke
## The Gift of Second Sight

From the endless horizon, the deep ocean spawns a tremendous swell before her eyes. The first massive wave thunders across Waimea Bay in the darkness before dawn. White water violently erupts and charges forward from the dead black seascape, exactly when Tiki Mano predicted. Twelve waves stack up and explode in succession, gushing their salty mist into the valley. It consumes the jagged cliffs around her like fog. She sits on the beach, holding his hand tightly in her lap while the shore break threatens to wash them both out to sea.

Just before the first sign of dawn's purple light, Alana secures the spiral notebook in her lap. She sings out a soothing melody, pretending not to be alarmed at the voices coming to pull Tiki's soul out of his mortal vessel. His body heats up from the core. His spine begins to pulsate like a long steel chime. The warmth suddenly vanishes. Alana carefully inserts a pen in his slithering fingers. With one hand, she manages to shake the sand from her long brown hair and twist it into a tight bun. Her other hand holds Tiki's arm steady as he writes neatly in the journal. His legs twitch, kicking sand down the sloping beach. Abdominal muscles ripple and wrestle his coarse back for control. His head shivers back and forth with his eyes rolling under the sealed skin.

Just after the clouds burn through their dawning colors, Alana plucks the pen from his twitching hand before he stabs it into her leg. She tries to keep his airway straight and clear. No melody can soothe the ferocity of his convulsions. Yet, she hums along until he lies still. Alana then notices the entire bay has gone placid as she leans in to feel for breathing. The moment she glances down at the words written, Tiki's body contorts itself completely off the ground. Frenzied splashing violently erupts all across the bay water's smooth surface. When he finally collapses and gasps in a deep, desperate breath, she wakes him for the ride home.

They share a shower and a breakfast with naïve affection. Tiki retreats to sleep and leaves Alana alone in the living room. She never vents her concern about this one thing. It saddens her to silently watch him endure things far worse than what she conceals. He sees what cannot be seen by others. And still, he contains this burden like an incurable virus. She waits until the bedroom light is off for at least two minutes before opening the journal.

# "TIKI'S BOOK OF TRIPS
December 10, 1985

This one creeped up faster than ever. I better write this shit down before I'm completely torn from my body:

Aia i ka opua ke ola- Life is in the clouds. That's what I coughed up before work last night. It came out like bong resin. I coughed and growled so hard, I was seeing stars- living, dancing stars with encoded messages. Considering how much pakalolo (cannabis) I burn, they must have known this one would get my attention. Just now, I realized its intended meaning is that the reader of omens knows by the color and shape of clouds. Lucky thing it was still too dark and I couldn't see these particular clouds while I was driving the truck. Seriously, I just went sat down on the beach, looked up to the morning sky and the buzz hit me like Sandy Beach Shorebreak- a one-peaker-tweaker.

I already know Princess will tell me this trip will be followed by the strongest seizure yet. I don't know what to tell her anymore. My mind aches as if something is trying to break in. And, it's getting more difficult to write in this journal. Each page is like an even bigger wave on the horizon. The swell is building rapidly and I don't know how big it's going to get.

Clearly, this is not something my mind is doing to itself. In the beginning, several trips actually went by before I attempted to document these episodes. Spontaneous self-intoxication sounds like a dream-come-true until it gets scary, mysterious and painful. I dismissed the first couple of trips because the Captain's weed has indeed proven to be killer to the Max. I regret that it took me so long to realize all this needed to be documented. Luckily I was high and made proper sense out of all this. I was in a special state when I was drawn to that pen and a new world was unleashed.

Little by little, I am learning what else is out there in the universe. Just reading the passages I've written over the last few months, few years, makes my brain sizzle like lasagna in the oven. Staring at the words tickles my head like magic shrooms. Sometimes I have to skip over certain words that trigger different states of consciousness, and then there are pages I won't even look at. But it's so hard not to. I'm constantly piecing together the code within the text and discovering new perspectives of consciousness and layers of reality.

But the seizures are totally getting worse, like my body is reacting to something foreign, unnatural. I often remind myself that I didn't dive willingly into this rabbit hole. The more I document, the more nuggets of code appear in my writing. And I'm afraid the next piece of this puzzle will cause me to snap my jaw muscles and pop my eyes out. At that point, I just might go consult a physician- I don't care what Alana says about doctors. She's the only one who understands- and the last person I want to share this with.

I bet her a foot massage that a giant northwest set would meet us at Waimea. I call these rogue waves because the buoys never pick them up. Swell energy diverts from its path and somehow hunts me down, or maybe I'm pulling in strays like they're magnetic to me. It also creates a magnetic field that gives sharks boners, but at least they never try to eat me. I knew the waves would hit hard and fast as soon as we got near the shore. It's a good thing it's too dark for any surfers to be out. This is the kind of clean-up set that makes people vanish.  The crashing waves are shaking the ground.  The rumbling from deep in the valley is making my teeth rattle loose from my skull.  I can visualize the vibrations like sonar.   The thumbnail moon refuses to brighten anything for us.

The edge of dawn is now showing us the racing clouds above. It's the colors going through the clouds that reveal the messages I'm meant to see.  My princess glitters like starlight, even with my eyes closed.  I want to tell her how beautiful she looks but I already lost my ability to speak.  I can hear the chanting getting louder and her singing getting farther away.  There's no turning back now.

It suddenly feels like we're spiraling wildly across space.  But I'm anchored to the pen with my mind.  It's like drawing with one Etch-a-Sketch while you're being dragged across the rocks.  Funny how time slows down for me when I reach this point of the buzz.  While I'm concentrating so hard on moving the pen like a puppeteer from above my head, I'm actually scrubbing words down incredibly fast.  It just seems impossibly fast because the waves are crashing in slow motion- like time is about to stand still and I'm still writing a journal entry.  My vision is getting pulled away from the paper.  I'm being forced to look at the sky.  I've never seen clouds do this before.  Every fluffy little purple puff of cloud instantly became black and menacing.  The slow-crashing waves are sounding further and further away now, spinning into my ears.  I'm not alone.  Something is about to pull me away and take control of my pen.

It has recently become obvious that there is something supernatural walking the earth.  Maka 'ike – if this is the second sight, then it has come to warn me of what is coming.  The sky is now a swirling blur and the intoxication I'm experiencing has reached a new level of intensity. I've lost all feeling of my body but remain anchored to the pen on the paper. Interpreting this sonar as mere images leaves out the fact that I am sharing molecules with everything around me - like the entire world is only a single living organism. I can sense the Bay has filled with a thousand sharks, all staring at me, and the shore break is about to tsunami up the beach and pull me in. All I can do at this point is wait for the spell to end.

The sky has now lit up enough for me to receive the next episode. I am completely out of my body now, staring through my eyes from the distant void. Something of my lost father is fizzling into clarity. I believe energy from his spirit has forced its way into my vacant body and is now taking control of the pen. This is what the dancing colored clouds are transcribing:

'Mai Kinohi a Ho'ike'ana. From Genesis to Revelations – that is all man is meant to know. I fear you are about to learn what is beyond. The fifth world is about to end and your tribe will arise in the next. Lucifer reincarnates himself in each world and leaves traces of his magic behind. My enemy is using that magic and you will need it too if you are to survive what is coming. Without it, you will become his slave. Knowing this is a curse. I have kept that dark secret inside this withering body to protect myself from something no one in this world should ever know. That secret has burned through my veins like lava from Kilauea and scarred my body like Kalapana's molten avalanche. I prayed to Jesus Christ to end my life; but I was tortured, dissected, revived, not able to die. I hoped that after my physical death, the world would find a balance for the abominations that have spawned from my existence. But, there can be no peace. After I soon part

10

from my body, my spirit will remain bound to the world by Kaulike, Justice.

O na hoku no na kiu o ka lani. The stars are the spies of heaven, promising all evil deeds reciprocation. As events grew darker, I found myself delving into the lost mythology of our ancestors and giving this energy context. You will discover how to appropriate the Mana (spiritual energy) as a righteous entity. There is so much I need to tell you, but I finally found a way to escape this world. My previous warnings have been terse, too faint for him to take notice of you. Little by little, my world has been seeping into yours. I'm afraid you are extremely receptive to this spiritual transference. Your mind is already radiating with this ancient spectrum. It is a secret you must protect. It drives men mad. Those who are able to exploit it have conquered enemies, murdered thousands. All have been crucified before finding peace.

Yet, he seeks those who can survive this transference. They are drawn to him by fate. Do not even think his name. Your mind will cast energy out into the universe and he will tune you in. He will take notice and come for your entire tribe, just as he betrayed me. I became receptive to this transference and he drew his evil from my power. He creates abominations from my torture. It is too late for me, but my uhane (soul) bleeds to see what spells I can open onto the world. It has been a curse for me, but it will be a gift for you. All the power I have been forced to conjure will find its way to you. On the last phase of the moon, I will leave this plane of existence and my spells will open its course. Die in battle or by your own hand. Have faith the Lord awaits you.'

I'm seeping back into myself now. I can feel something unnatural surging through my muscles. The shakes from this little episode are about to be horrendous. It felt like someone grabbed hold of my pen and just wrote a whole paragraph. I cannot wait to read that shit later, I hope it's not in code. Actually, I think it would be better if I got Princess to read that back to me. Looking at a ghost's writing is definitely a bad idea at this point. I have never seen my father and know little about him. That was what my mother wanted before she leapt from the Ke'alohi Point, staring into my eyes the whole way down. All that I do 'know' has been revealed in these convulsive dreams. Maybe sleeping from dawn to afternoon makes my dreams more vivid, but I cannot ignore these nightmares any longer. When I stare at the words written in my journal, terrible images seep into my vision from the darkness and burn into my conscious mind. I'll be expecting the Mana (spiritual energy) to manifest itself before my next episode. The sky just came to a complete halt. The trip is over. Here come the tremors. I'll pray she's still not infected with this mana, but who am I supposed to pray to?

- Princess, you're my first and only love."


The words remain illuminated in the back of her eyes as she slams the journal closed, "Tiki? Tiki, are you all right babe? Wake up! You scared me... aw baby, your nose is bleeding."

# Ku'i Moe'uhane
## Pounding Nightmares

"Time to get up. Tiki, wake up. Eh!" Alana hovers over the futon. "You're missing out on surf." Tugging on the pillows blocking the sun, "Eh, not another flake and bake day. Brian called ten times to get you up already. Tiki?" Alana suddenly feels the warmth being sucked out of the room. She releases the pillow and slowly steps back.

Tiki jerks his torso up off the sheets with a growling scream, "Ka lua kupapa'u o na ali'i!" He gasps inwards as if he has been choking on those words since noon.

She flinches slightly, "Wow, never mind. Go back to sleep."

A chunky amount of congestion erupts in several small roars. Tiki ignores the lingering muscle spasms. "Oh da cold! Wow, it's like forty degrees in here or what?"

"Nah. Eighty-five." She sits next to him and smoothes his hair down.

"How come you never woke me up? They was supposed to pick me up early today." He mumbles and breaks through the crust sealing his eyes from the world.

"Look babe, you need rest. You're kind of wrecked up right now. I made you a special ginger tea. I'm putting you on detox today. K? Dee-tox." Alana prepares herself on the edge of the pastel quilt, glowing in the afternoon sunlight. "Eh. Listen. Now, remain calm. A pig got through Brian's fence."

"WHAT!"

"What did I just tell you? Eh? I said stay calm. I need you to take it easy today. Look, you already have a wad of bloody toilet paper hanging out of your nostrils." Alana stands and kisses his forehead. She watches him drag the clean quilt across the floor. He scrambles for the dry pair of surf shorts drooping from the bathroom window louvers.

15

She interrupts his grumbling, "Now, they're going to pick you up at four, and it's already three-fifteen so go eat." Looking over her shoulder as she walks away, "Hurry up you! If you're not ready, they're gonna park that stupid truck in the yard and smoke a smelly doobie with the music turned all the way up!" She detects no signs of convulsions from him, "So embarrassing, those turkey's. Eh, try ask them when they're going to barbecue the pig. Save the ears for auntie Charlotte. Can remember that, or what? No ears, no banana bread. Got it?"

Tiki plops down at the table with his best James Dean impression. This conceals his apprehension as he glances around for his notebook. Alana brings the Spam lasagna from the microwave, "I put it on the desk. You were kicking and saying so much weird stuff this morning, so I got up and did the bills. You sleep better when the book is out of the room. You know what, you've been grinding your teeth so much lately, you want me to get you one bit to sleep with? Or maybe keep that journal in the trunk of the car."

He doesn't respond to grinding his teeth, but smiles at her nice handwriting. "Eh, so what, this paper on my journal, you wrote what I was saying in my sleep? From today? Ya?" He silently thanks her for not writing inside the notebook. "Hmmm, let's see... Well, I can explain this... Pepehi a 'oki'oki mano. To butcher sharks. Lately, I dream about sharks plenty. You know, I would like to be the guy who finds out who is actually killing all those sharks they've been finding washing up. It's a damn shame. Shark fin soup is one thing, but killing sharks just to kill them is kapu (forbidden). Hmmm... Let's see... What's with this kupua (shape shifter)? Eh? Last phase of the moon? Nazi disguised as humanitarian water purification, disease eradication? Sorry, none of this makes sense. You must have wrote it wrong. Sometimes you don't listen because you're plotting for the right moment to gripe about things I was supposed to do and forgot. And do me one favor, try not to touch the book so much. It has one aura of its own."

"What, you bagging on me? Ka leo o ke ola. The voice of life, remember? That entire journal is advice from the spirit world that you've been living with for how long? Eh? Three years already."

She watches him avoid her eye contact. "Yes, it would be nice for you to discover who has been killing all those sharks. They've been washing up all over the island, pretty much since you started getting your dream shivers. Sometimes I think your nightmare is about you being chased by sharks. That would explain all your squirming around, waking me up every two hours. I'm sure that is what the god Kamohoali'i wants from you. Stop the slaughter and let me get a good night's sleep.

And, the kupua will lead you to that path. I wonder which one of your stoner friends could be the shapeshifter, but then, they're all too stupid. So most likely, the kupua will be the embodiment of an ancestor. And the last phase of the moon, what happens on that moon phase? You dream about the dead sharks. But you should pray for health and food. You pray for the god Lono to return and bring the people together. But actually, you wake up screaming about your missing father. Right? And don't worry, I don't read your book. Is that secret code, or is your handwriting just that crappy. What else? What else is going on here? Eh? What else would you like to discuss this afternoon?"

With his pinky rotating the sand in his ear, "Babe, where the shoyu stay?"

With a snap, "Right there. Oh? What, not going to argue today? Too early? Sharing too much before surf?"

"No, I'll give you some confrontation if it makes you happy." He inspects the tip of his little finger.

"Well, let's have it." Palms up, she wiggles her fingers for him to bring it.

He sets his fork down so gently before smiling up at her glare. "What is this right here... right here, child? What child? Our child? Why? You hapai (pregnant) or something? What are YOU not telling me? Eh? We talked about this. We're not ready. That's so irresponsible you know, to let yourself..."

"Eh, shut your furry clam Mano." Snarls Alana. "It was your dream. I knew you were going to crap in your shorts when you read that. If

17

you think getting pregnant is ME not being responsible, then you better keep your filthy paws off the princess. And tell me, why would you name our son Lono? Too much pakalolo? And you are on detox today. Unreal. Keep your hands to yourself for that one. Got it? Now, my turn. When did you plan on writing your paper that is due tomorrow? While you're surfing?"

Shoveling in a big scoop of lasagna buys him a little time. "Nope."

"During your nap before work?" Her fingernails give off a loud tap on the table.

"Uh... Nope."

"Tell me you didn't buy a paper from Brian's sister again. Lani's only in tenth grade you know."

"Nah. I do 'em at work. They keep one word processor in the big supply closet. You know, for the supply inventory." He points in the general direction of that supply closet to distract her glare.

"You know they have security cameras on the cubicles." She taps a loud triplet.

"Ya, but not in the closet. No worries. And they get one printer in there."

"Ya, but the point is, they are really creepy about their work and I don't want it to look like you're snooping around in their business. It's not a good idea. Non-disclosure agreement." She leans in with a few more taps.

"Eh, you know what, fock 'em. Fockin' fockahs. I can type up one 'out-of-order' sign for the lua (toilet), but cannot type my report? Brah, they hired us right from our academic career placement counselor. They know we're students and we need to type shit for school. You know, I would love to actually ask for permission, but no one's ever around to ask for permission." Because she is so close, he keeps his face to the plate. "Not like I'm messing around at the desks. That's your job." He instantly regrets the ending and attempts a smile.

"First, I'm not your brah. Second, they pay us to clean, not type our shit. Third, there's no way for them to tell the difference between typing school shit and snooping in their proprietary research. We signed a contract, remember? It's a cruise job, they pay us more better than the hotel job, and it's a marine biology research center that counts as an internship for school. And, despite how creepy they are, wouldn't you want to get hired on permanently as a marine biologist? Be making bank. Anyways. Do you even know what to write?"

"Affirmative baby. Let me tell you. To again instill the Hawaiian culture as the dominant one in this melting pot, island chain of ours, one of the most profound ways would be through the mandatory use of the Hawaiian language in certain important aspects of our everyday life."

"Oh wow. I'm listening. This blank look is because I'm still stewing over the me-not-being-responsible comment." She lifts her finger and lets it hover without breaking her glare.

"Well, ok then. I'm proposing that in order to own land here, the owner must speak and write in fluent Hawaiian. All land contracts, deeds, mortgages, leaseholds, and rental agreements should be written and conveyed in the Hawaiian language. If they cannot do that, then they have to surrender the property to the Department of Hawaiian Home Lands. Or, they have to hire one Hawaiian Interpreter and pay the Moke (local) a shit-load of money.

That would really shake the shit up in the business world, because the Hawaiians don't own anything anymore. In fact, the fockahs that own our house, our work, our school, the grocery store, not only are they not Hawaiian, plenty don't even speak any goddamn English. I would do the fockin' hula every month for cheaper rent, but the owner doesn't even live in this country. We actually invented a new way to hula-out a big 'fock you, you fockin' fockahs!' It's impressive when several people do it at once.

Too many foreigners own our homes and the locals got no place to live because they set the market price for the rich haole's (foreigners). Now, I'm not saying this is strictly for Hawaiians, but any local who can pass one kama'aina (child of the land) exam. Then, we'll pass out separate menus with different prices and privileges and respect. Fockin' haole charge, gratuity already included, surcharge on all transaction- kind. Any focker that lives here and cannot pass our exam or cannot bother to learn our language and culture will have to pay the price of ignorance or leave like they're supposed to."

"Ok. Take it easy babe. Wow, you put some thought into this. I'm sure you will leave out all the 'fockin' shits and goddamns' from your report, right? Maybe a test with an ID card, ya? Hmmm... that's called, let's see, a driver's license. Except, didn't you write this paper last time? Lolo (crazy)."

"Aw, come on babe. I could write a hundred papers to stand up for the rights of our peoples. But this one, I added the land forfeiture. Ok? No worries." He has a 'go-to' smile that often proves reliable when calming her down.

"And what?" She smiles back, "You're going to go lock yourself in the closet after the perimeter sweep and hack this sucker out before lunch break?"

"That's the plan baby." He huddles over his breakfast.

"Hmmm..." She taps her nails and gives a little scratch on the table. "But, what does that have to do with psychology?"

His fork halts, "Well... we have to change the psychology of the land laws to improve the lives for all Hawaiians." His fork resumes.

The scratching halts, "Seriously? That's what you got? No, that sucks. What else you got?"

He glances at the clock, "Eh, didn't you say Brian-them was picking me up at four?"

"Ya. Hawaiian Time four. I bet they haven't even rolled their doobies and tugged the soggy shorts out their asses yet. I got you for another hour at least. What else you got?" She snaps.

"Well fock." He scrapes up the last bite and cues it up, "Excess in moderation is the key to a balanced and healthy life."

"Eh?"

"They say the key is to take everything in moderation, but the problem I have with that is how do you really know what moderation is if you've never fully tested yourself? Don't look at me like that. What I'm saying is, how do you know where the middle of the road stay if you never swerved out of your lane and plowed into the curb on the other side? And then bounce off and hit the other, other side.

Every person has to hit rock bottom and then bounce back into delusional joy in order to know where their middle of the lane actually stay. You can go out and have a little drink every once and a while, but you'll never know your true potential unless you get totally donkey-piss ripped with your face in the mud. And you go find out who your true friends are when you puke in their car and wake up on their kitchen floor with your boto (penis) in the rice cooker.

Then you stay violently hungover for several days and go to work with a heroic tale and revel in admiration. That's living a life worth living and that's how you actually find your middle of the road. And the key is excess in moderation. Why eat like, one little stem and see funny colors, when you can eat the whole baggie of magic shrooms and see god?"

She sighs, "Um... what the fock?"

He scoops up the last bite. "Well... my teacher always talks about when he tried LSD in college and I have a case study on hallucinogens that I already wrote on three, the kind, four-by-six index cards. I could totally type this shit out in thirty minutes, max."

"That's what you got? Seriously? I admit I'm curious to see if you can pull that one off. What about your dad? How is it you're sensing his spiritual presence without believing he's actually dead?" She places her fingertip on his wrist.

Tiki gathers his dishes but dares not leave the table. "I don't know how I know, but I just know he vanished but didn't die. But I feel like he's near death. The loneliness can be haunting."

"Who's loneliness, his or yours?" She takes his hand.

"Well. There was a void. My mom filled it with drugs. I filled it with surfing, partying, fighting... and then you. You put me back together. But something is reaching out from the void and I know you can tell. I need to figure out what this is without bringing it into your life. I don't want you to see what I see. You understand that, right?"

"It is in my life." She tickles his wrist with her nails.

Tiki sighs, "Ok then. When I say haunting, I mean these episodes are a deliberate feed of clues to a path I'm supposed to find. I know you are kind of tuned in to this kind stuff, but... I just need to find where this path is leading before I can take you along. Please. Let me scout this out first. I almost got it figured out. I promise."

She nods, "Ok. Just promise me you'll figure this out before your head explodes. And smoking that pakalolo until your eyes bleed isn't helping. What the hell kind of weed are you turkeys growing anyways? You're getting your ancestors high with that shit.
Look, I'm not trying to freak you out... but, uh... on the beach this morning, I could hear the voices in your head. Your head was like one empty coconut. When a spirit kicks you out of your body and takes over, it's called possession. They have exorcists for shit like that. I know it may have seemed like it was your father, but you know demons can take possession of other souls, like a hostage, and use them to deceive you. If they can possess you once, there's a good chance they will possess you again. That's what it seemed like to me. Do you think that could be what is happening here?"

Tiki holds onto her hands, "Did you sense evil in my body this morning?"

She stares into his eyes for a spell. "No. What I felt in your body this morning was familiar. Lonely. Regretful. Hopeful. It was sad, but there was no evil. I'm just concerned of the void you leave in your body when your soul is displaced. I lost you for a moment. We've always been connected, but I lost you and I didn't like it."

"But I never lost you. I was out, completely out of my body. But I felt your connection the entire time. You looked like an entire galaxy to me and I could find my way back to you from anywhere in the universe." Tiki closes his eyes and feels her presence, "You know how you told me the atoms in my body also belonged to every other element everywhere else in the universe? I think my atoms absorbed something from the spirit world. From my father. That's what I'm supposed to figure out."

"Wow, stoner." She pulls his eyelid open with her thumb. "You've got a lot going on in there. That's the most you've ever talked with me about these episodes, or your father. The possession shit freaked you out, eh?"

"Totally." He glares comically before he kisses her. "But my father isn't trying to possess me. I think he's trying to make a connection, one bridge. I want you to read to me what I wrote this morning."

"Why, you haven't read it yet?" She taps his chin. "Read it now."

"Nope. I got business to take care of. Sometimes there's code in the writing and it tickles my brain."

She pinches his chin and forces him to look up at her, "What? What do you mean there's code? What does it do to your brain?"

"There's code in the writing. When I look at certain words, my vision scrambles up, like static and makes my brain feel funny. It makes me tune in to something else in the universe. It's taking me somewhere, or bringing something to me." He leans away slowly.

"What the fock?" She flicks the tip of his nose. "Do you think that's normal?"

"I didn't say any of this is normal." He grins, "I think my dad sends me secret code during these episodes. They're keys. I think he's warning me. That's why I think he was abducted, and that he's still alive."

She grins back, "Well, you'll definitely be surprised later I guess. You go brush your teeth and you go take care of your business with your lolo friends. And later, I'll read you the journal entry and you can explain this secret code to me. Hey. But not if it's going to scramble up your little brain because you got a paper to type. Dee-tox."

Tiki ponders now that he has her relaxed. "How come it seems like the gods were actually talking to me today? I dreamed of so much noise, so many different kinds of voices and languages. I feel like I had a representative from every nation in my head, and they left the door wide open. I heard voices from great distances... like from dead languages and shit. Like Latin, Egyptian and Mexican.
Well, maybe this is the last moon phase I will have this dream. I hope I get my sex dreams back. Like the one where I'm the surf instructor at the nude beach, or the bus driver for the airline stewardesses."

Alana giggles in his face, "Oh no. That was so sad. Were you trying to get frisky there, Mano? And, Mexicans from Mexico, they speak Spanish you know. The presence of such great power makes everything else more powerful. If you were touched by the gods, I would know." She attempts to flatten his hair and gives him a lick on the ear.

"Come on now. It's still impossible for you to resist the frisk from the king of the fish. And these Mexicans, they were not speaking Spanish, it was Mexican."

The obnoxious muffler and horn can be heard down the street, "Mano! Let's go! V-land four to six!"

Tiki is already ready, but is slow to leave his princess. "Wow babe, you look worn out. What was I saying? Eh? Touched by the gods."

24

"Ok, that was nice. But I wouldn't call seventeen minutes great power. We'll see if you have some left for later." She watches as he chooses which battered surfboard makes the trip.

Tiki smiles so passionately at her that his eyes water, "Love you babe. I'll be back by dark." He wipes the joy from his face and stomps the screen door open. Tiki drops his weathered surfboard in the back of the truck. Instead of climbing up to the seat, he runs back inside yelling for a pen. "Wait babe, try write this down for me, fast kind! I remembered what I forgot! Ka lua kupapa'u o na ali'i!"

Alana responds from the futon, "The burial place of the chiefs. I already wrote it. Wow, you almost left on the first try. Remember: Detox! Take it easy today!"

"Ya, ok. Love you." He erases the smile from his face as he hoists himself into the truck. "I hope you got that fockin' pig! All those lazy focking dogs are worthless and they shit everywhere! I know you did not leave the gate open! If my plants..." as he slams the door.

"Relax brah. Relax." Grins Brian. "Under control."

Brian's younger brother, Kanoa always has to sit in the middle, "Brah, we're lucky the pig got in or we wouldn't have caught the Chan brothers stealing the plants."

Tiki's eyes burst wide open, "SHUT UP! Are you fockin' kidding me? The nerve! Please tell me right now they got poundings! Brutal fockin' poundings brah! Fockin' Fockahs! Going scrap those fockin' mutts!"

Brian proudly responds, "Chill braddah. Dig this: We kept hearing shit outside. So Kanoa went out to flick on, the kind, spotlight. I was almost to the plants and when the lights went on, I heard those fockin' pussies all screaming and shit. They came running right at me with a knife in their hands. Brah, I stuck my arms out and clothes-lined them both to the ground!"

Kanoa giggles in his part, "So I came running up and braddah's holding their faces down in the mud. Then, out of nowhere, brah, this big 'ole fockin' pig runs out after us! Bambucha (big) kind brah. Tearing up the whole yard!"

Brian has his neck out the window, yelling at whoever is holding up traffic. Re-entering the truck, he explains, "So I still got Dennis and Drew by the neck, using them for block da pig. Then, when the pig got tired, I used the Chans to corner the pig next to the dog kennel. They was all crying brah. You wouldn't believe. Oh, and when the fockin' mutts finally woke up, they started barking and we couldn't shut them up."

Kanoa was waiting for his part, "So, I picked up the knife those two fockers was cutting the weed with and popped that pig right on top of the skull!"

Tiki glares over, "And what, the thing went dropped?"

"Nah, I made those kooks hold it down so we could yank the knife and stab it like, four more times." Brian says as he stares at a big set of waves ripping across Sunset Beach, causing him to swerve off the road. "That was at like, five in the morning. We had those kooks cleaning the mess until nine. We was calling brah. Where was you?"

Tiki squeezes onto the handle above the door as the tires screech, "Oh, interesting. We was at Waimea. We were watching some rogue waves hit right at that same time."

Kanoa holds the steering wheel steady while his brother curses loudly out the window, "Oh, mean eh, the kind, waves went broke at Waimea. Swell's dying already, not big enough no more for Waimea to break like that. Rogue waves is a good sign, ya? Oh, and then. They tried to put the plants back, but the roots was all mangled. Pretty bad kind. We had to bag all the buds."

Tiki suddenly snaps his head towards Kanoa in shock. He reaches across and grabs hold of the wheel after Kanoa turns to dig behind the seat.

26

His jaw drops. His eyes sag and bulge in disbelief. Neither Kau brother will make eye contact with Tiki.

Kanoa turns back around with a large plastic bag stuffed full of flowering green buds, "We've got fourteen more like this one brah. Not ready for smoke yet, still gotta hang 'em up in the garage. Eh, try roll up the windows so I can roll up the joint."

Tiki's hand drops from the steering wheel, his eyes droop. "Uh... excuse me, but... What The Fock! Those plants were like my children, my gift to the island... the only way I can endure my midnight cleaning job... the aphrodisiac, the creative catalyst, the goldmine of hard work and meticulous attention! I loved those plants! Everybody loved those plants. Everybody respected those plants. I had big plans for the herb in that baggie! Brah, this was going to be my final crop!"

Both brothers glare over, "WHAT!"

"Ya, that's it, no more. I have to prove to Alana that I'm mature enough for marriage, and to buy one new surfboard. I mean one wedding ring. I have to buy both. Get that baggie out of my face. I'm feeling... depression, betrayal, anger, sabotage, paranoia and an overwhelming surge of disappointment here."

Tiki turns to the window. "You know how important those plants were to me? The episodes are getting worse. Alana was talking to me about the kupua. She woke me up because my nose was bleeding. You know what she was saying while she stuffed the toilet paper up the nose? 'Ano lani i 'ano honua. A heavenly nature; an earthly nature. Because I stay in two realms. She said the 'aumakua make themselves visible to loved ones by assuming earthly forms. But, they retain the nature of the gods."

The Kau brothers listen intently with the truck drifting slowly towards the side of the road. "Why would she say that to me this morning? Brah, she's already asking me questions about my dad. She thinks this is a case of demonic possession and shit. With such bizarre events brewing, brah, it would be reasonable to believe that the pig you killed could have been one of our ancestors, sent to warn us of something. Ya?"

Brian swerves back onto the road without taking his eyes off Tiki, "Ya, no shit brah!  That shows how vulnerable we are!  We almost lost the whole goddamn operation to a couple of kooks from down the road.  And what, we got six fockin' mutts sleeping right out there and not one of them could even bark for us?  Bark, fart, scratch the fockin' door!  No more nothing!"  Brian hits the horn to amplify his cursing.

Kanoa ignites the end of a massive four-paper confection, "Ya brah, no more security.  But cannot quit on us.  We need your help now more than ever.  Braddah, you're the only one who can raise a whole field from sprouts.  We got the seeds going already.  But, cannot let Bri fock 'em up.  You got the magic green thumb."

"Ya..." Tiki catches himself nodding, "No!  That pig was a sign for me to make a change in my life... before something bad happens.  Otherwise, the slaughter of that 'aumakua would be for nothing."  His face flushes white, "Brah, wait.  Was there one snake in the pig's mouth?"

Kanoa coughs out a lungful of smog, "Snake?  Uh...  Funny you should mention that..."

"Fockin' kook!"  Brian swerves back in his lane, "You said you was gonna keep your mouth shut about that shit!"

"Too late."  Kanoa passes the joint to Tiki and digs around for his notepad.  "We think that's why the damn pig went all lolo on us for.  It got spooked."

"Eh?"  Tiki evaluates the bad omen.

Brian reaches over and snags the joint from Tiki's listless gaze, "Ya.  Uh, there was in fact one snake."

"No!"  Tiki blurts.

"Ya!"  Kanoa confirms.

"No way!"  Tiki is in disbelief.

28

"For reals brah!" Brian reassures. "One mean poisonous snake. Came charging right at us, right behind the focking pig!"

"No ways brah!" Tiki shakes his head. "How you know the fockah was poisonous kind?"

"I don't know, I never seen one snake before." Brian puffs again on the hefty joint, "This was my first snake experience. But while we was stabbing the pig, the snake went crawled up the fat fockah and I threw the plants at the slimy buggah."

"You mean the pakalolo plants? You threw the pakalolo plants at the fockah?" Tiki asks.

"Ya. I threw the pakalolo plants that Dennis stole at the fockah." Brian explains.

"Ya brah." Kanoa interjects, "That gave me enough time for grab the rake and beat the fockah down. Unreal brah. I only seen a snake on that one show before. That's how I know it was poisonous and shit."

"What show?" Tiki demands.

Kanoa snatches the joint from his brother, "Da kind brah. That one show. The one with the focking snakes. Went bit the fockah and the fockah died!"

"Oh. The kind, eh?" Tiki reaches for the joint. "You went killed the fockah with the rake?"

"Ya brah." Kanoa passes the joint. "Make-die-dead. One dead pig, one dead snake. You like barbecue the fockah or what?"

"Barbecue the snake?" Tiki coughs and tries not to fumble the pass. "I'm still tripping on the 'aumakua showing up to confront the snake."

Brian has the joint hanging from his bottom lip, "Shit, that 'aumakua saved our buds. And we're going to have one hell of a barbecue in honor of that pig's sacrifice. 'Aumakua or not, any pig like walk into my yard is going to end up roasted in the imu (underground fire pit made of rocks)! Fockin' Big Island coz! We kill the pig, we cook the pig!"

He stares down the line of stopped cars, "Eh, didn't you say that we can absorb the powers of the 'aumakua if we eat them? Whatchoo think gonna happen if we eat the focking snake? Eh?"

"Eh, is that a joint or a microphone?" Kanoa blurts. "You're just talking into the mic! Fockin' pass that shit! Oh, now you decide to smoke 'em. You nutty fockahs. You guys are getting me restless. Watch the spooky shit already. I no like you fockah's going turn this into one-nother episode, and shit. Can I just enjoy being high for once?"

Tiki seizes the joint and stares out through the dense fog building inside the cab, "Brah, I'm telling you, I had a dream of evil snakes... and zombies. You know what they said to me? They are hunting my bloodline. They are shape-shifters too. You believe that? If I ever find some focker out here with snakes, poisonous snakes, I may have to kill him. Eh, you guys know what eugenics is?"

"Oh, ya. Da punk rock chick with da ehu (reddish tinge) hair." Brian sings, "Sweet dreams are made of these. You and I no disagree."

Kanoa harmonizes, "We go travel da world and surf da seven seas. Everybody go roll 'em and smoke 'em!"

"Fockin' mutts. Don't ever sing around me with your punk rock disco shit. Da kind, eugenics brah. It's racial cleansing- like Hitler's Nazi Germany. They were breeding pure Germans with pure Germans to make the kind, super pure Germans. And, anybody that wasn't pure, or focked up with disease or deformity was exterminated. Or experimented on. Da crazy. Ya? Anyways, I'm not sure what the snakes mentioned that for, but what's really strange... my father mentioned something like that too. Eh, any particular spot on the floorboard the ashtray?"

"Uh... try put 'em in the empty can. That's why they're there. And try pass that thing. Wait. So you was talking to snakes, zombies and your father, in the same dream? Crazy." Brian responds.

"Crazy. It's strange to think about how Alana and me got together. She don't talk about it, but she had the maka 'ike too from before. And she puts up with my lolo shit because she can relate to what I'm going through. I think that's why we were drawn together."

Tiki gazes at Brian puffing away with no regard to the traffic buzzing around them. The cindering cherry is barely visible through the fog within the cab. He ponders, "You know what, I just realized... the snakes mentioned the word eugenics, but now I'm not sure if they knew I was actually listening to them. Like, I overheard them say it. But what's tripping me out is... the marine biology place me and Alana work for is called... Applied Eugenetics. Is that some kind of coincidence or what? Like, why were we drawn to work there?"

Kanoa scribbles away on a notepad without responding. He then holds the pen near Tiki's hand to check if his fingers begin slithering for the pen.

Tiki continues, ignoring the pen. "You know what, this is leading up to something. You're my brothers. So you know I'm not trying to bullshit you. I got the maka 'ike, the second sight, getting more stronger and stronger. All the time, things come out of the darkness to let me know some wicked shit is out there. And that puts you in danger."

Kanoa lifts his pen momentarily and sways it back and forth near Tiki's face, "Is this the maka 'ike right now? Let me see your eyes." He watches Tiki's pupils constrict to tiny dots. "Ho, get ready Bri! I see da iris rippling already. It looks like fire inside his eyes! Fockin' Tiki. Brah, you always wait until the bud kicks in and then you go spook me the fock out. Every focking time. Ok, what can you see right now that's not spooky?"

"That's not spooky?" Tiki closes his eyes. "Ok, I got this one song coming into my head right now. Like one Run DMC, kind rap song. But it's one haole surfer guy playing rock guitar and shit. It's a wipe-out song. It goes: I got rocked, cold cocked, pad lock in the chops, dead drop, belly flop,

31

catapulted from the top, I got slayed, got flayed, the player got played, complete disarray, tossed out by the maid, I got slapped, drop smacked, beat down with the bat, went splattered like crap, when the strap went snap, I got hit, got bit, got tossed in the shit, I could never forget I was grinded into grits, but I paid my dues, I paid my dues, I grew some wings and then I flew, I got thrown in the fire pit, I flew out with the barrel spit."

Brian laughs and skids to a halt at a crosswalk, "Holy shit braddah! That's somebody's song in your head, like that?"

"Ya brah. I been hearing this guy singing at a concert lately. I thought he was one ghost and shit, but I can hear the audience clapping and yelling." Tiki scratches his head, "Unless he's having a concert for a bunch of dead fockahs."

Kanoa stops laughing, "Brah, that was funny for a moment. And then you had to bring it back to dead spooky shit again."

Tiki hands the joint over, "See, you cannot deny the profound energy. You writing this down brah?"

"Trying brah. I cannot write as fast as you." Kanoa continues to scribble.

"It's all coming together really fast. Too fast. That's the mana my brothers. At Waimea this morning, plenty spirits came to me. They were speaking every language you can think of, pidgin and all. I think as the episodes are getting stronger, more and more spirits are tuning me in. And I'm broadcasting the mana out for them to see. I think it won't be long until something bad finds me. It turns out, the god Kamohoali'i is the one who wants me to find the shark killers. I now believe that the mutilated sharks is a trail leading to something evil. It might be a path to whatever happened to my father. And after what Alana said about the kupua, I hope that pig you killed was actually not Kamohoali'i."

Kanoa stops writing, "Now, that's some heavy shit. Brah, we're with you. You find those shark killers, and we're going to kill them for you. But I seriously doubt that Kamohoali'i would have let us kill him in our bud farm with the Chan brothers while getting chased by one deadly snake. Not possible."

Tiki reasons, "Listen to me. When you get the mana, it radiates out from you. Hmmm... ancient spectrum... like, it's in my aura and shit. It's like one contagious disease. Once you get it, you cannot get rid of it and it will drive you mad. And, it's only a matter of time before others with the mana will find you- and that's definitely trouble. Because they're probably mad too. I'm afraid you guys are getting too deep in my shit."

Brian peers out at the ocean, "You know what, it's kind of smoky in here, but... it looks like there's only three guys out surfing. And the waves are going off."

All three try to gaze through the smog at the surf. After a silent moment, Brian abruptly clears his throat, "Brah, I seriously doubt that pig was one kupua. And, if it somehow was Kamohoali'i, then the power was passed on to us. Seriously, I don't think I have ever been this high before in my life. Our bud was the meanest around before, but this is some true power. Ain't nobody going to buy Keolanui's weed after they try our magical shit!

And look at the surf. Have you ever seen more perfect barrels like that with only three... two guys out? Magic pig, magic weed, magic surf; sorry you have the bad dream seizures, but this kind surf makes it all balance out!"

Kanoa's head wobbles as he peers out the window, "Are we still driving? Are we parked already?"

Tiki feels his stomach spiral wildly into nausea, "Balance? Brah, you just made me think of something terrible. All this magical sweetness right now, it is clearly no coincidence. The mana is present. It's building. But, it won't balance out until the mana strikes down with the kaulike."

Kanoa continues to write, "Kaulike. You mean the vengeance?"

Tiki closes his eyes for a calming breath, "More like justice, that's the balance. But, I wouldn't expect justice to be served without some wicked shit going down, with the vengeance."

Brian waves the smog away from his face, "Ah you fockers! Now you're really freaking me out! Open the windows! No can see nothing!"

Brian and Tiki reach for the locked vice-grips and begin rotating the windows into motion. As the pungent smoke slowly begins to billow out, hazy shadows in the smog begin to take shape. The figures darken in the center of both windows as they scrape down into the rusted doors. They remain oblivious to the shadows taking the forms of human heads, only inches away from their own. Kanoa stares down at his lap, shredding the weed into a feathery pile for rolling. Brian and Tiki eventually draw their vision in closely to the silhouettes directly before their eyes.

With a high-pitched screech, Brian and Tiki jerk their bodies away from the open windows as the Chan brothers scream back and flee from the truck. They collide into Kanoa, creating a jolting chicken-skin sandwich. As they gasp with their eyes bulging out the windows, Kanoa squeals at the fine particles of high-grade marijuana floating in the air like green snow.

"There's those fockahs right there!" Tiki screams as the door handle rips off in his hands.

Kanoa holds him down with both arms, "Yo! Don't move! You fockahs made me spill all the weed!" He wrestles violently for a moment, "Chill brah! Let Bri handle it first, then see. I promise you braddah, Bri's got it under control. Now help me pick all this shit up. There's like five grams all over the place."

Brian hops to the ground and smirks into the window, "Try watch braddah, watch them pee in the shorts. Eh, Tiki, no worries. I'm taking care of you. You'll see."

"Try watch what, brah?" Tiki reaches across Kanoa and grabs Brian's tank top. "I cannot see out the damn window!"

"Dood, you're sick!" Kanoa grumbles, "You know how much weed is floating in your nasty spit cans? Clean your damn truck! Tiki, open the damn window!" He grabs Tiki's shirt and pushes him to the side, "Relax.

34

Let Bri handle. Tiki! Eh, I never knew the name of your work was Applied Eugenetics. I thought it was one fish farm." He tugs for a response.

"What? Oh, ya. The damn windows are open but the smoke is too thick! The focking wind can't even blow the smog out!" Tiki peers across the street at Brian. Through the fog, he watches his friend lumber over and pull Dennis out of the driver's seat. Brian walks him to the back of his father's work van and vanishes. "Well, apparently they cannot do their genetic research on humans, so they Frankenstein the fish. They also cross-breed algae and propagate them, like how we clone the pakalolo plants. Eh... I saw Dennis, but where's Andrew? I better go over in case he tries to ambush 'em from the bushes."

Kanoa tugs, "Just relax brah. Bri's got 'em. So what, I thought you was taking oceanography. How'd you get a job in genetic research? Yo, Tiki!" Kanoa keeps a tight grip on his friend while he piles the weed onto the platter for rolling.

"Eh... Brah, it looks like Bri's just talking to them." Tiki hollers out the window, "Ku'i pehi (pummel, pound, abuse horribly)! Ku'i pehi! Pound them like the poi! The fockin' mutts!" He slaps the dashboard, sending the marijuana fluttering to his feet. "Nah brah, they study chemical compounds in sea life and develop medicines that can be used on humans."

"Like what?" Kanoa notices a little tension has lifted.

"Well... like, this one sponge from the Caribbean, the Cryptotethya crypta. It has a chemical they just identified as spongothymidine, and it might lead to a treatment of viral diseases like AIDS and leukemia and anti-cancer compounds. I read their documents so I can learn about their research."

"Wow. Far out man. That's some real Jacques Cousteau kind shit right there." Kanoa gives a little slack on Tiki's shirt. "And you guys are studying these compounds?"

"Nah brah. I just clean the fish tanks like a chump, after everybody leaves. I never even seen the researchers before. In fact, the only reason I know the name of the company is because I help Alana throw the shredded documents in the incinerator. No more sign on the door or nothing. In fact, you could be standing at He'eia Kea Boat Harbor and never even know the building was there. Oh... hold the focking phone, Hawaiian... Remember what I said last week about Kane and Kanaloa (two Hawaiian gods) wanted me to find out who was killing all the sharks? Ma'eli'eli is the cliff right above He'eia. It's literal translation is..."

"Digging!" Kanoa blurts. "Didn't you say those fockahs dug into the rock to put the underwater tanks?"

"That's right, brah." Tiki stares at Kanoa.

Kanoa stares back, "I thought that was weird. I don't understand how they got the permits to excavate like that. Excavate into the rock at the shore to make underground tanks? How's that even possible?"

"For real. That's some shady shit right there. Must've bribed some fockah's to pull that off." Tiki sweeps up and handful of chopped cannabis, "So the mo'olelo (story) of the two gods racing up that cliff, remember that? They dug into the mountain right there. Ke'alohi Point also happens to be where my mom jumped off. Was the last time I saw her."

"Focking shit, brah." Kanoa licks the glue of a rolling paper to stick to another rolling paper, "Ke'alohi point is a sacred leaping point for souls of the departed to leap from the earth and reunite with their ancestors. You know your mom wasn't crazy. She was trying to reunite with your dad after he vanished. Was abducted."

"Ya, reunite with him. Or, find him. Or... rescue him. And now, brah... I think my dad is trying to warn me. That's why that focking pig and the focking snake are tripping me out so much! Shoots. Brah, how high are you right now?" Tiki stares at the four rolling papers Kanoa assembled. He carefully plucks a long, curly hair from his handful of shredded pakalolo and drops it on the silver serving platter.

Kanoa masterfully layers the weed onto the papers, "Brah. What I'm experiencing right now cannot be quantified on any highness scale we've constructed so far. I seem to have entered a new plane of existence and I haven't yet realized how I'm supposed to be working with this reality."

"Hooo, that's ok, brah." Tiki fans the thick smog blocking his clear view of Kanoa's eyes. "Just keep rolling that focking joint. I believe we finally cracked the code and propagated the final level of the Captain's Cannabis. This is the eternal buzz we've always dreamt of. I'm sorry I said I was gonna quit the business. I had no idea we've unlocked the heavens. We gotta get these clones going again."

"Brother Tiki, I'm crying right now." Kanoa stares through the smogless tunnel towards Tiki's eyes, "But I cannot because my eyes are so dry and I need something to drink. Hand me one of Brian's spit cups."

"No, brah. Don't do it." Tiki reaches into the glove box and pulls out a can of guava nectar. "Here, let me open this. You just keep rolling that doobie." Tiki administers a sip for his friend and sets the can on the dashboard. He gazes out the window as his jaw drops, "What the... Bri's letting them go!" Tiki opens the door from the outside handle and snaps away from Kanoa's grip in one slithering maneuver.

"Ah you slippery fockah!" Kanoa yells out the open door. "You're gonna ruin Christmas, dick-smack!"

Brian stops his friend in the middle of the street, "Tiki, let 'em go brah."

"Ku'i pehi! Brah, we can still catch them!" Tiki screams from the middle of traffic.

Brian is big enough to hold Tiki down with one arm, "I knew you was going to trip out, so you get to pick first. See, I promised that you wouldn't beat the crap out of them today if they gave you one of these." Brian points to the side of the road, "They promised to buy three new surfboards for us if I could prevent you from killing them today. So you're not going to kill them today because there's three new surfboards right over there braddah."

Tiki peers over, "Wait, is that one T and C... with three fins... for real? Oh. Well. Fock. Ok... I guess there won't be any beef today. But I can still pound the fockahs tomorrow, right?"

"Nope." Brian stands firm.

Tiki growls as he watches the Chan brothers squeal away in their father's work van. "You're killing me brah! I like go pound them!"

"Nope." Brian waits for Tiki to turn and look at him, "Brah, that's just the first three boards. You're not going to pound the fockahs because next week, they are going to buy us another three boards. And the week after that, guess what, more boards. The twelve surfboards of Christmas. You can pound the fockahs on New Year's."

Brian releases his friend, ignoring the line of cars forming. "So what, no more tripping out, right? That's four brand new boards for each of us, and try look at the perfect waves with nobody out. We're going to barbecue that pig, and we'll even bring you the kau kau (food) delivery at work tonight. How's that, eh? Do you think you can loosen up a little bit on the Chan brothers for a couple of weeks? What do you say Hawaiian?"

"Ya. For sure. No worries brah." Tiki straightens his shirt and watches Brian make obscene gestures to the drivers honking at them. They walk to the side of the road and let a dozen impatient cars pass by cursing.

"Eh." Brian lets Tiki pick first and then he grabs the only board large enough to float him. "So what, no more spooking me out today? For real brah, you keep saying our little sessions are getting too deep. But, if you think it helps you understand this mystery, then we're going to be there for you. Brah, I know you don't want to involve Alana in your episodes, but she knows about this kind of stuff.

And look, nothing bad has happened to me and Kanoa so far. Maybe you can share this with her and things will work out. I mean, what part exactly are you not willing to share with her? I can already hear her say- 'just quit smoking the fockin' pakalolo'. It's not like she's gonna murder your shit like her lolo sister."

38

Tiki stares deep into the polished glass of his new surfboard. "Brah. I see our son growing up fast in a dark world- one bloody, violent world. And then I see how he dies and bleeds into the earth. He dies in the burial place of the chiefs, but in a frozen, far away land. I see this over and over again; and the girl he loves and his entire tribe hunted and slaughtered.

And the part that really makes it hurt- I feel that exact thing happening to me. It's like we are on the exact same path. I see them coming after Alana. That's when I wake up with my nose bleeding.

Brah, let me tell you this. I had the toilet paper jammed up the nose today. When I went yanked them out, brah, was gushing. My blood was gushing out, down the drain and into the ocean. I can feel my living blood absorbing into the earth. The mana will find me by tomorrow. If I share this with her, it will burn in her mind and attract this very thing to materialize before our eyes."

Brian ponders by tugging at the rear of his shorts, "Wow. Well, ok then, no need for share all that brah." He squats slowly to pick up the third board.

"No worries brah. The only reason I share this with you is because you don't feel any pain when you die." Tiki gives him a quick smirk and walks off.

Brian clutches the boards under his arms, "Ho, brah. Wait a minute. What? You never told me that! You saw how I die already? You focking mutt, brah. You're doing this to me again!"

"Nah. One second you're there, one second you're not. I never saw nothing." Feeling confident that he does not die from a vehicle impact, Tiki struts out into the street towards the truck.

"What, you fockah! Tell me! Brah, I like smack your fockin' mouth right now! You tell me shit like that and then cruise off and leave me to shit a squid in the blender? Gonna focking ding your new board, that's what I'm gonna do!" Brian sizzles after him.

Tiki tries to calm him by giggling, "Serious brah, I don't know. Only that you go with no pain. That's a good thing. And your brother too. But no worries 'cuz that's in the future. Trust me, you're lucky. I see what happens to me and my nose bleeds. I see what happens to you and you get a brand new board with perfect V-land all empty. Relax. You got nothing to worry about."

Brian reasons, "Brah, you're fockin' with me. I no like get high with you anymore when you tell me shit like that. Kook. Nah, just focking with you Hawaiian. You know you're my braddah. Very insightful. Well, anyways. I still think Alana has a right to know. Especially before tomorrow. I believe she would tell you and you'd deal with it together. She reads you like one book. Just think about it. But later. Because now we go surf. Just think about it, ya? K-then. Fock the bullshit, brah. We go surf."

"Ya. I'm sure she already knows and she's sick of waiting for me to open up. But we should discuss it. You're totally right brah." Tiki sighs and squeezes the back of Brian's neck. He puts his arm around him and follows his friend back to the truck.

Kanoa ignites the hog-leg sized, coned shaped confection and immediately erupts in a burning cough. "Here! Help me with this." He exchanges it for his new surfboard and reaches for the bar of wax in the back of the truck. "That's a one-hitter-quitter, brah. Don't know why I rolled such a large doobie."

Brian gasps and chokes and hands it over to Tiki, "This doobie is one, da kind, victory lap, and shit. Brah, this stuff is out of control. I'm getting twisted already. Where the wax stay?"

Tiki assumes command and attempts a controlled, easy inhalation. "This batch is really impressive boys. It kind of tunes the whole world out, yet makes you more insightful. And you guys sound like you're coming in on a, a walkie-talkie or something. Wow. Here, take this thing away from me."

Kanoa waves his turn and points to his brother. Brian grabs it and stares at it for a moment. "Fock. I'm tapping out here. I know, I'm gonna

40

hand this to brother Dane when we walk down. I think I plowed the truck over his rock again. Might need his help to get the front axel down. You know, if they never put the big rocks on the side of the road, I might have driven the truck into the side of his house already."

Brian squats down to scrub the wax on his board and peeks under the truck. "I never even noticed hitting the bugger. Did I even put the truck in park? Eh, you guys gotta raise the windows down and get that smog out the truck. It's gonna stink in there."

Kanao chuckles, "They already stay rolled down. The smoke never like leave. Brah, we gotta roll the windows up for go surf. And lock the doors so nobody mess around inside."

Tiki laughs, "Who's gonna mess with your truck? Parked in Dane's yard? Nobody's that stupid."

Brian tosses his tank top on the front seat and grabs his leash, "The fockin' Chan brothers are that stupid. Actually, I think that was meant to happen. If they never snuck into the yard, we wouldn't have found that pig. And if we never found that pig, we would have never found that snake. And what if that snake would have bit the dogs or bit us in our sleep? Eh? Unreal. Come on you fockahs, let's go."

Kanoa slams the door and struts towards the beach, completely oblivious to the crowd surfers pointing and shouting. "Tiki, brah, come here." He extends his arm and waits for his friend to catch up, "Fockin' special day, eh? I cannot believe there's nobody out. How often we get the entire line-up to ourselves?"

Tiki ignores someone tapping on his shoulder and walks up to Kanoa with a high-five, "Brah, this is unbelievable. I don't know if it's the pakalolo, but it seems like we are the only humans left in existence. Nobody around to get in the way, nobody dropping in. Maybe this is an alternate plane of existence. Focking inter-dimensional doobie! I can totally see peoples' electromagnetic aura and shit."

Tiki plows past a group of people as they wave and yell at them. "Too bad nobody stay around here 'cuz I'd like to foretell somebody's future and shit. Oh hey, there's Dane and Mike."

Brian walks past Kanoa and whistles, "Brother Dane, how's it, brah!" Brian's hand smacks Dane's hand with a loud clap. "Brah, sorry, eh, I went rolled my truck over your rock again. Here, try smoke this, da kind, and we gonna figure out how for get the truck down later. After we go surf."

Dane laughs, "Brah, everybody just got chased out the water. Choke sharks, brah."

Brian laughs, "Eh, how your mother stay? She make some more banana bread?"

"Nah, no more." Dane is amazed how red Brian's eyes are, "She made the beef stew today. Brah, did you hear what I just went said?" Dane watches Tiki and Kanoa throw the Shaka's and continue walking toward the beach, "Brian, did you hear what I just said about the sharks? No can go surf today, brah. You better go get your brother."

"Hooo, brah. Cannot stop thinking about that banana bread, coz (cousin). After surf, I like get some. Eh, go grab the board. Try go paddle out with us. Looks like we get the whole place for ourselves!"

Dane snaps his fingers in front of Brian's squinting eyes and dizzy grin, "Braddah, you never heard one word I just went said! I said no can go surf today! There's one hundred focking sharks all up in the channel and all over the reef, brah! I never seen anything like it before!"

Brian smiles, "Hooo, and let me know when she makes the kind, beef stew. Ono (delicious) kind, that's my favorite."

Dane looks over to Mike in disbelief, "Fockin' Hawaiian. Unreal."

Brian clutches onto Mike's hand and gives it a tug, "Unreal, I know. Brah, you seen the waves? I cannot believe you're not getting barreled right now. Nobody gets more barrels than you, braddah."

Mike replies calmly and articulate, "I was getting plenty of barrels, but then we all got chased out the water by the focking sharks, brah.

Hundreds of sharks.  Do you understand?  Cannot surf because there are a shit-ton of dangerous sharks in the water."

Brian nods his head in agreement, "Brah, she went put the ripe mango in the banana bread.  Went broke the mouth!"

Mike looks over to Dane, "Brah, for real, what we gonna do here?"

"Focking go surf, brah!"  Brian hollers and throws a shaka before turning towards the beach.  "Eh, go paddle out with us, brah!"  He smiles back and then jogs away to catch up with his brother.

Dane laughs, "Those lolo Kau-boys brah.  That pakalolo they grow attracts the sharks and repels the sharks at the same time.  If we paddle out there not high, the sharks would totally bite our shit wide open."

Mike is still concerned, "Wait, so the sharks won't attack you if you're high?  Is that right?"

Dane gives a sly smirk and looks down at the giant doobie, "Yep.  It's a special kind of stupid."

Mike nudges him, "Focking spark that thing up and let's go get some barrels then."

Dane yawns, "Nah.  Those waves were meant for them.  Let them have their fun.  Plus, who's gonna call the ambulance for them?"

Mike smiles and leans back, "Did we do enough here?  I feel like we should intervene or something."

"Nah, that's all we could have done.  Tiki and the Kau's stay in a different world, brah."  Dane leans back and admires the craftsmanship of the joint.  "They said they were on the verge of creating an inter-dimensional doobie for the eternal buzz.  I think they finally focking did it."

On the beach and still incognizant of the group of surfers trying to warn them not to enter the water, Tiki leads a chant with the Kau brothers,

"He ka'e'a'e'a pulu 'ole no ka he'e nalu (An expert on the surfboard who does not get wet. Praise of great surfing)!"

Brian plops his board in the shore break, "Brah, Dane said his mom went made some more banana bread!"

Kanoa dives in the channel after his brother, "Right on! Oh, I wish she was cooking beef stew. Ono kind brah, that's my favorite!

Tiki doesn't even feel the group of surfers trying to block him from reaching the shore, "Brah, the barrels are going off right now! I cannot believe nobody's out. I figured this place would be totally packed!" Tiki dives underwater and pulls his new board under his belly. He starts paddling fiercely and catches up with the Kau brothers in mere seconds, "Do you realize how truly blessed we are? This is an amazing life and I'm glad we get to share it together!"

Dane and Mike extinguish the joint after one puff and set it aside. Dane gazes unblinkingly at the surf, "Unreal. What did I tell you? Eh? Anyone else would be dead right now. Those lolo fockahs. I bet they're gonna bring sharks with them everywhere from now on so they can score the good surf uncrowded."

"How the fock are they doing this?" Mike's eyes are too dry to blink, "One puff and I cannot feel my focking legs anymore. Those guys are out there ripping that shit, and the sharks don't even care. I'd like to see them finish the wave off with one big turn or one full-on cut back."

"Nah. It's a total focking shack fest today, brah. No need for turns. Get barreled, hurry back out, get more barrels. I'm happy for them. It's so beautiful. So beautiful." Dane's lip quivers.

Mike sniffles, "I can't believe it, brah. And the sunset? It's so special right now I wish I could cry. But my eyes are so dry they stay glued open. Can pass me the banana bread?"

"Wow. You look happy." Alana smiles at her man prancing in with his new surfboard. "So what, you went bust-up Dennis-them and stole their board?" she asks suspiciously.

Tiki defends, "Hooo. Not even. They gave it to me so I wouldn't pound them. You were talking to loose-lips Lani, weren't you? Moa kani ao (a chicken cackles in the daytime, a woman who talks all day)."

"Ya, whatever. You're funny. She was the one calling this morning because her stupid brothers were trapped in the dog kennel with the Chan brothers!" Alana watches Tiki's smile deflate. "Oh yes. She was laughing so hard at them, all screaming for help. She said the guys locked themselves in with the dogs. And then a wild pig ran into the gate so hard after them, its giant head got stuck between the poles."

"What?"

"Oh, ya, I'm sure you heard a different story, probably a more 'macho' one. But Lani didn't want to go out there and tried to call you for go help. When she told me what was happening, I knew exactly what was going on. We started laughing, yes, uncontrollable laughing at the stupid boys. But then, she had to put the phone down on the window because they were screaming so loud. I listened while she went out there to shut them up. Listen to this: They made her pick up the knife and stab that pig in the neck!"

"Shut up!" Tiki stares at her like this is an impossible tale, but he can actually picture it happening in his mental cartoon.

She continues, "Nah, for real. She was scared to do it, but it was the only way to shut them all up. She said it was the most horrible thing ever. She had to stab that monster like twenty times. Blood was squirting everywhere. Each time, Lani thought the pig was going to bust free and run after her. She would stab and then run, stab and run. I could hear the pig squealing over the phone. But poor Lani was screaming louder at all the nasty blood."

She is humored that Tiki is stunned silent. "So the giant thing finally collapsed in front of the gate, but the boys were trapped inside with

45

the dogs. And then the strangest thing happened. She said one big nasty snake went slithered up the pig and tried to crawl up into the bloody hole on the dead pig's neck. She ran into the house, but those stupid boys started crying even louder than before. So she took the knife, grabbed its tail and cut it in half before it could disappear into the puka (hole). You believe that shit?"

"Was it one poisonous snake?" Tiki asks.

"How the hell should I know? Anyways, little Lani couldn't move the pig by herself. So, you know what she did? She came back to the phone, after she hosed herself clean of all the blood, and told me she had to call Mr. Chan to come move the pig and get the boys out. Oh yes, and since all the boys were trapped in the kennel crying, she was the one who cleaned up the yard by herself so Mr. Chan wouldn't see all your stupid pakalolo plants."

"Ho! Those focking guys!" Tiki scoffs. "Well, that sounds more believable than the crap they told me today." He says while again admiring his new board.

"Did you smoke?"

Her question has a sobering effect, "Uh... small kind." Tiki reluctantly admits.

"What did I tell you? Eh?" Her arms cross, anticipating a ridiculous response.

"Oh, about the detox? Well, shit... Ho'ipi'ipi'i kai (Causing the sea to rise, stirs up wrath)." Tiki mumbles and leans the board against the wall with the others.

"Yes, that's right. You're stirring up the wrath Tiki Mano. We agreed you were on detox today. And, you straggle home at nine o'clock fully baked. La'i Hauola i ke kai ma 'oki'oki (Peaceful Hauola by the choppy sea. Peace and tranquility in the face of disturbance)."

"Uh... What?" Tiki's eyes dart about.

46

"Oh, playing dumb, stoner? You're sitting there peaceful and tranquil in the face of disturbance. Do you not see the storm coming?"

"Babe, take it easy. Everything is totally cool. After I shower, eat and nap, I'll have my shit together in plenty of time for work. I can type my paper in half an hour."

She glares into his eyes, "But you need to clean out. You've been smoking too much lately. Don't you realize you need a clear head tonight?" Her voice trembles at the end.

"Ya, for sure." He opens his eyes for her to see, "The paper's easy. I'm not going to be staring at the blank screen like one doofus. Wait... What are you talking about?"

"What are you talking about?" Alana asks.

"Is your temper the storm coming or what?" He instantly regrets this remark.

Her glare intensifies, "My temper? Oh brother, you haven't even seen my temper yet. What is coming Tiki? You tell me, what exactly is coming?"

Tiki thinks about his response for a long moment. "Ok. Ya, you're right babe. Change is coming. I told the Kau's that I'm out of the green business for good. I know that pig was a sign. I told them I would not sell the pakalolo anymore. All pau (finished). Things will change, I promise you.
And I think I found a balance with the maka 'ike. I had a vision today and never got the shivers. No headaches or anything, just great clarity and power." His expression relaxes, "Just, let me clean up and after I finish my paper, I'd like to talk to you about these things I have seen. Or, actually, what I interpret from the strange things I have seen. It's been a long time coming and you deserve one proper explanation. Then, maybe you can help me figure this out. How about at lunch, I share everything

with you and we go from there. And I mean everything. Ok?" Tiki sighs as he has bottled this up for too long.

"Ok. I'm just afraid your little bean brain will pop, that's all. Your eyes need rest. I'll bring food and we'll nap before work. Go." She holds her relaxed posture until after he kisses her and walks into the bathroom.

Tiki slowly creeps the Malibu over the narrow wooden bridge to the back driveway. Alana opens the passenger door hangs over the road, combing the darkness for the newspaper. "To the right! Can you believe this fog?" Alana strains to reach out far enough and scoop it up.

Tiki tugs her back up to the seat by her belt, "Unbelievable. I usually get the stuffy nose from the voggy Kona winds (fog with volcanic ash from the Big Island of Hawai'i with southerly winds). But this isn't bothering me at all. It's like volcanic ash, but more thick." He stares out through the headlights, "Aia i ka 'opua ke ola (Life is in the clouds. The reader of omens knows by the color and shape of clouds)."

Alana raises an eyebrow, "You mean like you can read omens in this volcanic fog?"

"No, I just thought of that from somewhere. No can read nothing. Cannot see the kind clouds through this fog." Tiki mutters.

"Use your English smarty-boy. You know I don't want to hear that pidgin right before you go write your paper." She waits for an explanation but he scans the parking lot in silence. "Well, at least the newspaper didn't end up in the ditch this time. Or else what would I do all night? Actual work?" She chuckles to herself as he parks the car.

Tiki hides his apprehension as the volcanic fog thickens around them, creeping towards them from the trees. Alana immediately begins the routine, "I'll go clock us in. Hey, look at me. After the perimeter sweep, you better go type that report. When you finish, come get me at the office. You go type that thing in thirty-minutes, ok? Don't make me wait."

"For sure babe. No problem. Eh, let's eat outside so we can talk. The moon makes it more romantic, ya?" Tiki gives her a wink.

Alana walks towards a lone door on a large concrete wall. "Tiki, there is no moon tonight." She presses her code on the number pad and it unlocks with an echoing click. The door pulls open against a vacuum as if she is unsealing some ancient tomb. She vanishes into the building.

Tiki watches the fog seep in after her before the door hisses shut. He plucks rear speakers out from the back seat, through the side window and onto the roof of the car. He cues up the Van Halen cassette and adjusts the volume to blast around the entire building. Coffee cups and cigarette butts are quickly hunted. He stirs the fog with his broom to find the trash hiding along the sidewalk. Tiki begins scouring the ground faster and faster, losing his patience with the mundane work.

An unnatural sensation begins to build against his skin like dense humidity. He feels the eyes of something stalking him from the darkness of the trees around the perimeter. Tiki ignores any trash more than a broom's-length away from the illuminated sidewalk. Rustling grass disturbs the fog and suddenly causes a wild anxiety to pump throughout his limbs. Vibrations in the deep fog roll out in expanding rings, as if from dropping a rock in a pond. His vision starts throbbing from his heart pounding against his sternum. Tiki stares out into the blurry night fog, wishing the loud music would drive away anything hiding in the trees. "It's all in your head, kook." He whispers before dropping the trash bag when his scalp tingles with a nervous itch.

His sight finally locks onto movement. A ripple in the fog emanates out from the trees. The placid lake of fog covering the ground begins to animate before him. "It's all in your head. One puff of that doobie would clear all this up, but you're on detox." The wailing guitar solo from the opposite side of the parking lot is sucked away from his ears by a ringing silence. Tiki's head becomes painfully flooded with a ghostly pounding of drums, screams and chanting. He freezes in a panic as the fog suddenly rises over his head and swirls around him like the birth of a tornado. Time halts. His head becomes dizzy. An abrupt taste of metal and blood penetrates his senses and spurs a wicked sense of dread.

His vision begins spinning wildly as he tries to focus on streaks of colors dancing in circles. Tiki shields his eyes, stinging with sweat. As if this is all emanating outwards from within his own mind, he feels helpless to stop it. Even with his eyes covered, he can still perceive demonic blue and green figures moshing in circles around him with shimmering steel blades. He dares not to reach out and test if the slashing metal is a hallucination. He recalls the bizarre temptation of sticking a hand near a high-powered fan and recoils his arms.

The strobing colored lights vanish silently for an instant and then return with screaming and wild drumming. During fleeting bursts of stillness and silence, Tiki visualizes the unblinking eyes of snakes creeping towards him beneath the fog. He is quickly consumed by a dreadful vertigo. The pounding gyration and flashing silence drop Tiki to his knees. Though crippled with this horrible disorientation, Tiki tries to focus on a blur of darkness slithering amidst the frenzy. He leans forward to grasp at this blur. Blood and shredded flesh appear to spray outwards, covering everything, splattering against his face. Tiki reaches outwards to shield his face. The shadow then appears directly before him, growing as it nears. What lies in this shadow, engulfed by the fog, does not want to be seen. Tiki falls forward to the ground and catches nothing but the damp grass next to the sidewalk.

Tiki springs to his feet and finds the fog completely settled still on the ground. He wipes his face and finds sweat instead of blood. The perimeter lights along the sidewalk flicker and then radiate their ordinary pale glow. The ringing silence subsides and his ears are pierced with the scream of the guitar solo from his distant car stereo, exactly where it left off. Tiki kneels and peers into his trash bag. It is not filled with severed limbs, only coffee cups and cigarette butts.

Tiki's muscles are left pressurized with blood. He feels his body swollen with rage, waiting to be ignited. Tiki yells out to the serene darkness, "What! You like the volcano to erupt! You focking mutts!" He sucks in a cleansing breath to extinguish the adrenaline. "Brah, who you yelling at? No one's there. If someone was there, you would know. You're not going mad, are you? Nah, I'm not crazy." Tiki chuckles at himself.

50

"They say talking to yourself is a sign of intelligence. You hear that, you focking snake in the grass? You cannot sneak up on me! Ok, this is getting weird."

Completely over the perimeter sweep, Tiki runs to his car. He tosses the broom and dustpan inside. He quickly drops the speakers back in their holes with the wires drooping over the back seat. Tiki starts the car, pulls the knob for the headlights and then flicks on the high beams. He gazes out into the fog, searching for movement. "Fock this shit." He mumbles, "Just get the damn paper done already."

Alana is usually immune to the phobias of working alone in a dark building. Considering that her memory is filled with unexplainable occurrences, she relishes this silence. It is numbing for her to mill around the computer stations with her cart, gathering piles of shredded, encrypted documents to incinerate. On this night, with the anticipation of Tiki's most vivid episode percolating in thoughts, a nervous tickle is making her restless. Nevertheless, she embraces her mundane routine. With only the red glow of the exit signs to guide her, Alana scurries down the corridor and plucks the boxes of documents up, into her cart.

She looks down the dark passage and notices her perception has suddenly changed. Chills run down her neck and shoulders. A brilliant ring of refracted light is now encircling the exit sign at the end of the hall. Even with her eyes closed, the eerie ring still glows in its place. Swimming under chlorinated water for too long produces this sort of visual distortion. But they have not swam in auntie Ruby's pool in weeks.

Alana sadly recalls another time her vision was affected like this. It happened the afternoon she watched her mother drive her car off a cliff with her father. An alarming amount of dread swells in her chest before she can diffuse it.

She whispers to herself, "Stop it. Focus on your work please." Alana expels the trepidation with a deep, cleansing breath. The red brilliance remains in her vision, but she clutches her cart and scampers to the incinerator room.

Alana abandons her cart in front of the doorway to the incinerator. Something itches in her mind. She becomes fixated on Tiki's recent revelation. He used to share everything with her, until the day he first spoke of his estranged father contacting him in his sleep. This was followed by grotesque dreams of mutilated sharks. It was then that the newspaper began reporting of dead sharks around the Island. Tiki then went silent- and she let him.

The wicked images of slaughtered sharks continue to haunt her thoughts as she walks to the storage area. The shadows appear like pools of black water, too dark to perceive the images of flayed sharks drifting alongside her. Alana turns on a lamp at the last cubicle and spreads out the newspaper sections. She begins scanning the articles to occupy her mind. She has the ability to endure waiting.

Eventually, patience burns out, "Eh! Tiki! You finished or what?" She listens for his complaint. With no results, "Eh! Lunchtime!"

He barks from inside the storage room at the end of the hallway, "Fockin' pau already!" Tiki hollers over the slamming metal doors. "Wow! It turned out to be eight pages!"

She hears him stuffing the papers in his bag. His body glows to her from across the room. His eyes are ignited like a cat in front of a car's headlights. "How long was it supposed to be?"

"Three. But I wanted to include my thoughts on the Hawaiian bloodline. Is it being diluted for extinction or evolution?" he cups his chin to appear in deep thought.

Alana turns and walks with him towards the dock. "I thought you wrote that on your last report."

"Ya, but it had nothing to do with my last report. This time, it had flow. I think I like the evolution of our people now." Tiki struts proudly towards the time clock and plucks the only two cards from the slots.

"Wait…" Alana questions, "What does that have to do with your 'excess in moderation' theory?"

"Well… um… drug abuse as a coping mechanism to colonization. After our monarchy was stolen, corporations inflicted their laws upon us, and made us slaves to their political system of oppression, they introduced our society to the misery of addiction and robbed us of our ambition to regain our independence. I referenced Native American life on reservations. I had a whole three-by-five index card on that shit, front and back." Tiki halts and holds an awkward pose, waiting for her response.

"Hmmm…" Alana pats him on the top of his head, "And somehow charging full-blast into weekend drug and alcohol binging will make you a more productive and proud Hawaiian during the rest of the week, rebelling, yet assimilating into indoctrinated haole (foreign) norms while preserving native culture as a tourist destination?"

"Exact-a-mundo!" Tiki resumes his shimmy and gets the cards stamped by the clock.

"The only reason you are getting passing grades for this class is because you make your haole teacher feel uncomfortable for giving bad grades to so-called oppressed locals." Alana giggles.

"Exact-a-mundo! Eight pages of subliminal guilt, baby. Easy-A, every time." Tiki makes her laugh with his step-slide shuffle.

On their way to have lunch outdoors in the grotto, Alana wishes she could repress this visual distortion before Tiki takes notice. "Eh, check out what I found in the paper just now: More sharks wash up near Ka'ena Point. It says authorities are investigating; but of course, that's all. You know, I keep expecting some speculation from them. Local fishing boats are the most obvious suspects. But they don't explore how bizarre this actually is.

Or, they don't want to report it to us. I've counted around fifty sharks dead as reported from the newspapers. And some of these are species of sharks that are not found in the Hawaiian waters. It's remarkable. Could the sharks be gathering here, or are they being brought here and dumped?  Are they cutting the fins for consumption or just to make it look like there's a market for shark fin soup?"

Tiki gazes at the constellation reflecting in Alana's soft eyes.  It sparkles of comfort now; but the relaxed, flawless skin around her eyes reveals traces of tension.  He sees stress lingering.  "Ninety-four."  He continues his gaze to show her his permanence.

"Ninety-four dead sharks?"  She is not surprised.

Tiki replies, "According to Pacific Islands Fish and Wildlife Conservation, Ninety-four big ones reported since that 'da kine' when I was spear fishing."

Alana sighs at his reference, "Oh, of course.  Your 'da kine'.  Hey, that fish that the shark gave to you- stupid Brian doesn't still have it in his back window, does he?"

"Ah, da kine.  Yes he does, for three reasons:  It was the first time he ever heard of a tiger shark offering a fish to somebody while spear fishing.  Honey, he's very superstitious like that.  Because of our ability to catch the fish, he believes it was my 'aumakua offering us respect. Second, he cleaned the bones just enough for the stink to keep his sisters from borrowing his truck.  And also, it keeps the cops from smelling the weed. Third, Kanoa thinks it smells better than cans of wintergreen tobacco spit and wet shorts."

"So stupid."  Alana steps out into the placid humidity.  Though the thumbnail moon refuses to enlighten the cove, everything glows for her. Tiki sets up lunch on their flat log in the sand.  Alana gazes up at the stars, "Hmmm...  so maybe the timing of it is another clue.  Not for your admirable abilities as a fisherman, but as a peace offering, a kind gesture for cooperation in helping to solve this mystery of who is killing these sharks. The shark was asking for help.  Maybe you were meant to help stop the slaughter, Mr. Mano (Shark).  Eh, before I forget, I never burned the papers."

"Why not?  No time to finish because I typed my paper so fast, eh?"

"Seriously babe, I type faster with my cute toes."  She is disappointed that he doesn't refute.  "No, I was just anxious.  You know, feeling anxious."

"No worries.  You're my babe.  I'll burn 'em for you after lunch.  But then, you can help me clean the fish tanks, ya?"  Tiki shovels a musubi completely into his mouth, "Weird about those sharks."  He grunts it down with a shoyu chaser.  "Strange... I feel like the sharks are calling out to me.  Like, they're crying for me to help.  You're right, we got sharks that shouldn't be here."

"No kidding.  They got sharks in those tanks that shouldn't be here."  She shakes her head at his mouth jammed with Spam.

He continues, "You know what it's like to dream of these sharks?  I feel how it feels for the sharks to get hunted and tortured and mutilated, like on a personal level.  And their ghosts stay with the body.  The hunt is for sport, the rite-of-passage.  They hunt the biggest, and the most exotic.  They want them all.  There's an aura of ghosts from those that consume the sharks.  And it makes me wonder... if the Nazi consumed the ghosts of the Jews from the holocaust.  I think I would be able to see if a person's aura had imprisoned ghosts."

"For real?  That is so horrible, don't even.  Eh, maybe a shark bit some fisherman and this is how he gets his revenge, this vengeful extermination."

Tiki digs into her pretzels, "What?  Eh, not kidding babe.  I was about to feel like the kind burden had been lifted by sharing this with you.  Eh?"

Alana arranges her neat lunch, "Well, I think that you're dreaming if you actually consider these episodes to be like a dream.  It's more like getting your boto (penis) plugged into one electrical socket.  Isn't it, stoner?"

"Ya, what ever. The weed is actually helping me process this stuff. It's calming. I just tell you it's a dream so I don't have to tell you that I'm communicating with the spirit world. Just think how mental I would be if the pakalolo didn't calm my shit down."

Alana shakes her pretzels onto the towel so Tiki won't dig into her bag, "Calm your shit down? Ya. I appreciate how sweet you always are to me. But calm? You're funny. You know what, Mrs. Chan called this evening to tell me that you idiots had her boys duct-taped to her tree. Ya, and that you were spraying them with the water hose from her flowerbed. Oh, and also, she smelled you boys smoking your pakalolo."

"Actually, before we left, Kanoa knocked on the door and apologized to Mrs. Chan for the flowerbed. And he explained that her boys came over and tried to sell us a bag of pakalolo. She was upset to find her boys with a joint in their mouths and a bag of marijuana taped to their ass. She took the dang bag. Guarantee they're grounded."

She scoffs, "It's not funny."

"Ya, well, they got caught pulling Brian's plants. That's dirty cracks and they deserve worse. Of course, you know I stayed in the truck and told them to stop. But, ya, anyways... I wake up with the feeling that somebody is going to hunt me like that. Like the sharks, not the Chans."

The juice snuck in with her breath. She growls out, "Excuse me. What?"

"Ya, um... babe, this I need to tell you. I feel like somebody wants to have the spirit of Tiki Mano imprisoned in their aura. You know, like how I was saying with the ghosts of the dead sharks. I feel like I have a stalker sometimes."

"Ok, thanks for warning me. Tiki, would something like that actually conjure up one of your, da kine, episodes? The maka 'ike? The seizures?" Their eyes pierce into each other's.

He responds calmly, "Nah, nah, nah. If somebody was hunting me, I would get the maka ʻike and I would sense them coming. And I would destroy anyone that even came close to you. You seen how I get.

Like when I surf, I go rip as if the ocean empowers me. When I go battle, I feel the power of my ancestors giving me their strength. I was having seizures because the spirit world was giving me too much power and my body could not handle. That's why I was getting the shakes and the nose bleeds.

But don't worry babe. I promise you, now I can take all the power I need to protect you. Just today, when we was surfing, I learned how much power I can take in and how much power I can use. You wouldn't believe what is out there in the spirit world for me to use. This is my rite-of-passage. This is actually a gift from my father."

"Eh, did you happen to read your journal entry from this morning?" She continues observing his eyes glowing from the building's pale perimeter lights.

"Uh, actually, no. I didn't get the chance. I was waiting for you to read it to me."

Alana smiles and shares her passion-orange-guava drink, "Really? Because that's kind of the gist of it, right there."

Tiki sips. "Hmmm, what do you mean? The maka ʻike is a gift from                    my                    father?"
    She takes a sip. "So you actually don't remember anything you write down right before you have a seizure?"

Tiki ponders for a moment, "Uh, no, not really. Before, I could. But recently, they've been getting stronger and I don't remember what I wrote until I look at the paper and see the words. Then it comes back to me. It's weird though. I remember that I'm writing real fast as the world slows down."

"Hmmm, that is interesting because you write super, super fast, And neat, neater than you write when you're awake." She giggles at him.

"So basically, your body locks up and starts twitching. And then your fingers start squirming for the pen and paper.

That's when I start hearing strange voices and strange languages coming from all directions. And then the voices seem to go inside your head and take over like one demonic possession, and it's really frickin' scary. And it should be really scary, but it somehow has a familiar feeling to it so I don't actually freak out when it goes down.

Except, this morning, I do believe it was your father that took over your hand and wrote some freaky shit down after the spirits kicked you out of your own head. And it lasted for several minutes."

"No shit." Tiki's eyes bulge, "Not sure how you was able to keep that under wraps all day. And what did he write?"

"He wrote that he was abducted, tortured, experimented on, and forced to conjure strange powers from beyond our natural heaven and earth." She munches on some pretzels while he processes the information.

"He took over my pen and wrote this shit in my book? For several minutes? While I was evicted from my own head?" Tiki grabs a pretzel, but doesn't eat it.

"Yep. Like, at least three minutes. Like I said, you were pulled out and the spirit world completely took over. So, your mind is receptive to this transference of spiritual energy and it makes your aura radiate with this ancient power, you know, the devil's reincarnated magic." She continues munching and watches him process the news.

"Are you shitting me with this right now?" Tiki almost drops the pretzel in the sand.

Alana closes the bag, "Nope. I'm not making this up. You should have read this shit yourself."

"Nah, sometimes there's hidden code in the text and buzzes my brain. That's why I like you to read it to me." He smiles up at her as he rests his head in her lap. "How much time we got left?"

58

"Don't worry about it. Just get the screwdriver and move the minute hand so we don't get shorted on the paycheck. So the one that abducted your father uses the devil's magic to make him conjure this energy. He explained you will have to use this energy or you will become his slave too. Oh, and die in battle or by your own hand." She smiles down at him.

"What the shit? That's what it said?" Tiki shrugs, "Hell, that's pretty much what I thought anyways. Except, today I realized that my mom leaped off that Ke'alohi point to be reunited with his spirit. But I always had this feeling that my father was still alive."

Alana rubs his neck, "Still alive, but who knows for how long. On the last phase of the moon, he was going to leave this earthly plane and send you his spiritual transference, as he called it. I bet that means he and your mother have been in purgatory this whole time. On the last moon phase, maybe they will both find peace. Oh shit. Remember last week when you wrote something about your 'aumakua (ancestral spirit protector) and the kupua (shapeshifter)? What if that tiger shark that offered you that fish was actually the embodiment of your father's spirit?"

"Son-of-a-bitch... and we ate that aku (skipjack tuna). That's about when I started getting nosebleeds too. What if it was actually my mother? Could have been, you know. Things really started ramping up with the maka 'ike at that time. After that 'da kine' with the tiger shark and the aku... everything really progressed, I mean, the nose bleeds, the shivers, the inter-dimensional pakalolo with the eternal buzz, the wild pig and the snake, the possession by my father's spirit, the visions of dancing demons..." Tiki stares upwards to the stars, not realizing the iris of his eyes are fluttering, vibrating around his pupils.

Alana stares down at him, resting in her lap. He appears to glow in the pale light of the building's fluorescent bulbs. "Eh, um, you wouldn't be getting the maka 'ike right now? Eh?"

"Uh, no." He's not sure if he should smile at her.

Alana shrugs, "Just checking. I mean, it would be nice to have some sort of warning if there was danger looming over, ya? Like you could see with some special sight if there were trouble. Your eyes do that, right? You know, like the hazel parts of your eyes get wavy and shit. Does your vision seem glittery and shit?"

"Ya. But, no. I can see, but not now. No more nothing, no worries. If there was something weird going down, I usually get this hazy kind illumination from the light, like when you stay in Auntie's pool for too long and you look at the street lights and they glimmer around them and shit. I can also visualize a person's electromagnetic radiation and see if they're an asshole."

Alana lets him gaze in her eyes, "Well, if you see something, you let me know. The last hours of this eventful day are ticking by as if the world just left us stranded here. It's almost midnight. And also, have you noticed that the moon was getting darker all week? What moon phase are we on right now?"

"Ya. That's a good question. Now that you bring that up, I was looking into the moon phases. The new moon is on Thursday. You like know when low tide is?" Tiki checks the shoreline for the water level.

Alana shakes her head. "Ok. You really should have read that journal entry dood. Your father wrote on the last phase of the moon, he was going leave this plane of existence."

Tiki squints at her. "So he's going to die tomorrow. Is that what you're saying?"

"Stoner." Alana brushes the crumbs off his shirt. "It's almost midnight. It's about to be tomorrow already, pretty much after lunch break. Tomorrow night, Wednesday night, when the moon comes back up, it will be the last phase. Whatever witchcraft your father was dealing with is about to be your problem."

"Well, fock." Tiki shrugs. "I think I should have read the dang journal. But I didn't want to because of that stupid report. Was totally the

60

best bullshitting I done the whole semester, I better get a focking 'A' on that thing. Maybe we should just bag 'em for home after we clean the tanks. Apparently I have some more homework."

"Ya. Well, seeing how you're extremely receptive to this spiritual energy, you should just let me read it to you. Can't have you show up to psych class tomorrow with the eternal buzz. Or buzz yourself into a seizure. Or one out-of-body possession. Or any kind of conjuring of spiritual transference. Or any poisonous snakes chasing after you. Or..."

"Oh what the shit?" Tiki blurts, "Just take it easy with all that. Ok? You're tripping me out right now. A lot of my brain power already went to that psych paper, I'll admit. But it's not like I don't have all this shit under control. Let's just make it back to Waialua. Maybe we could give Auntie Ruby a call. She's good with this kind stuff. Ya?"

"Ooooh." Alana sets her sandwich down. "She's gonna shit. Then she's gonna kill you. Then she's gonna tie you up, put you on severe cleanse and pray at you like an exorcist for twelve hours straight. You'll totally miss finals. But seriously, sometime in the next twenty-four hours, there's a chance any of that stuff could occur. Don't you think? So what kind of warning signs, or how exactly would you sense, or detect any supernatural or spiritual occurrence? Eh?"

"Well, baby..." Tiki wipes off his hands like he's supposed to before touching her. He puts both hands on her neck and cradles the back of her head. "Usually my mind starts to tickle, like I can feel an electrical charge vibrating up my spine, all the way up my neck and into the center of my brain. I can taste it, like I'm starting to cook from the inside, but it doesn't hurt. Then my eyes start to light up and quiver inside. Kind of like, reality changes form into something ... more in a liquid form, and it pours into my eyes and ears and I perceive the reality differently. There's more energy to work with instead of just empty air. I mean you feel a connection to all things, including the air, and you feel an elemental magnetism. And, magnetism is energy because it's shared with all things. Make sense?"

"Focking stoner!" Alana jams her thumbs into his ribs and forces him to flail in a laughing fit. "What the hell kind of weed are you guys

61

growing?" She continues to poke at him as he rolls deeper into the sand. "You already got the mana and the maka 'ike and the eternal buzz! You got sharks following you to the beach, you got pigs in your pakalolo orchard, you got poisonous snakes slithering at you! Not to mention the giant waves suddenly appearing, trying to pull us in the shore break. How can you possibly have any of that shit under control?"

Tiki rolls far enough where she can no longer reach. "Damn! Your claws are so angry! You think I don't have my shit under control? You think I'm losing it? Am I acting mental?"

"Well, not beating up the Chan brothers did seem a little out of character."

"What? Eh, it's the twelve boards of Christmas. I'm totally going to beat them up right after I get my four new boards. I'm going to get one longboard. Waikiki, full moon, we paddle out together, you and me. Eh?"

Alana flicks sand at his face, "You got every shark in the seven seas following your ass! You think I like get in the water with you? You got 'aumakua watching over you. That means the snake has got to be the shapeshifter? Ya?" Alana rolls forward and slithers on top of him.

He latches onto her like a boa constrictor and squeezes, "You see how much detective work I got already? Without even reading the journal today, Inspector Mano cracking the case."

"You're too stoner for detective work! Maybe if you quit smoking your pakalolo."

"Eh, Shag and Scooby Dooby were stoned every show! They spent the whole time on munchie patrol. Still yet, they were always the ones who muscled down the monsters!" He tries to pin her down and fails.

She digs the fingernails back into his ribs, "But the smart ones solved the mysteries." She squeezes onto him and never plans to let go.

"Well, that's what I got you for babe, smart and beautiful." His carefree smile melts away her tension. "This, I want to tell you..." He hovers over her and speaks softly into her ear, "I had this vision yesterday. I've had this one before, but I never told you or wrote it down. But yesterday, I had this vision and never got the quakes after. That's when everything came together and learned it is possible to control my episodes and use 'em. It's because we have a son together. The vision is about him."

"Son? Not one girl? A baby girl would be so precious." She coos.

"Babe, please. I see our son trying to survive in a violent, cruel, bloody world. Everything about nature changes. The world changes. I see him as the kupua. His whole tribe is shape shifters, and he is the shark. And they hunt him down, and they kill him, just like the sharks. I see how he dies and then bleeds into the earth. I see him die over and over again. Each time different, each time he bleeds into the earth and returns to get hunted again. Him, and the girl he loves, and his entire tribe.

But, I cannot see the killer. They, or he appears only as a dark blur, or a shadow. All I can see of this killer is his snakes. The snakes watch for him. And, the focking snakes, they never blink or look away. They never stop looking at me, I mean our son. So, whatever happens in front of the snake's eyes, the killer in the darkness always sees."

He watches her gaze up at him silently for a spell. Tiki continues, "Anyways, I saw this today riding in Bri's truck. This really scares me. But, at least it means nothing can happen to us until we have this child. These are signs for me to make a change in my life. That's when I told them I was out of the pakalolo business. Also, I was thinking, why don't we move somewhere far away? You know, someplace we can start over and not be found. Like Kaua'i with your sister or something."

"Uh..." Alana is astounded. "Uh, my sister? You're funny. This is why you're so touchy about having kids, eh? What is it about this dream that could suddenly make you change your life so much?"

"I don't know Alana. I guess my father was always trying to warn me of something that happened to him. Maybe this is it. Maybe his fate is mine too, you know, as well as our son's. I guess it's in my blood. I guess we have this connection."

Her eyes pierce, "You guess? Come on Tiki. Now, I never pressed you about your episodes. I kept myself from digging into the crazy shit in your head for four years. I suspected you didn't want me having that shit in my head too. I thank you for protecting me from this haunting, just like I protect you from mine.

And, I do feel like this is a haunting. But, we were drawn together tightly for a reason. And together, we can find our path, a safe path, especially if we are to bring a son into this twisted world of ours. You sure the hell do not want my sister digging in your shit. You know what I am capable of seeing. I think you owe me a straight-up rationalization and a plan to deal with it."

Tiki is amazed at her clarity. "Ya. You're totally right. I never wanted to bring this onto you. I have seen things that make my mind a glowing target for what ever is out there in the spirit world. The deeper I get, the more this energy shines out from me. I want your help. I need your help, but only if it doesn't affect you. Let me think."

"And what if it's already too late for that?" Alana uses his neck to pull herself up. She sits against him, still holding on.

"Nah. I would know. The maka 'ike helps me see things. Plus, if this was affecting you like it does me, you would have smacked me up-side the head already." He kisses her entire face. "I like go rinse off the sand."

Alana can already see his relief. "Babe, go for a quick swim and let me clean this up. When you come back to me, let's discuss what you see coming. I want you to tell me what you think is out there. Then, let me tell you what I see. You're not the only one with the maka 'ike you know. You know what, screw work. Let's just burn the shreds and then bag for home. Forget those stupid tanks. Just adjust the hour hand, punch the cards, then fix 'em back. " She kisses him and watches his tank top float to the ground.

He sighs, "Wow. It feels good to talk to you. I was feeling like a prisoner in my own head."

"Tiki, how do you think that poor fish feels tied up in the back window of Brian's filthy truck?"

His laughter gushes out.  Tiki dives into the still water and vanishes.

Alana peers across the surface of the lagoon.  Tiki's aura makes the dark water shimmer.  Her eyes follow him underwater all the way to the other side of the lagoon.  The unnatural perception of him radiating on the beach makes her pulse race.  Suddenly, sparkles begin dancing under her eyelids during every blink.  An abrupt panic of falling makes her flinch.

With her eyes closed, she becomes more aware of this strange perception looking inwards.  Her vision begins casting backwards into the darkness of her head.  Her mind processes the impulses with sparkles and iridescent shimmers.  Stimuli from all over her body glimmer into tiny streams, connecting and weaving their way to her spine.  The inner-workings of her body harmonize and take shape.  She quickly notices a faint light proclaiming its presence.  Her eyes trace down deep inside her womb.

This light is the very fear that Tiki just revealed to her.  She sees this sparkle as energy spawning to life.  This instant is their new pregnancy coming to fruition.  With a gasping breath, she feels the sound of violent pounding entering her ears.  Her eyes quickly regain their focus outwards.  She calls out to him, "Eh! Tiki!  Doesn't that sound like drums?"

"What?" He stares down the distant shoreline to the north.

"Drums!"  Dancing sparkles now appear to be floating along the horizon. Alana stands, "Eh! You hear drums or what?"

Tiki stands tall on the beach, mesmerized. "Drums! Ya! And you know what... it kind of sounds like chanting!  From the point way down there! Kualoa!" Tiki strolls along the gentle waves washing across the sand. He turns to look at Alana, still sitting next to the dock. "You know what, I bet that's Brian-them with the barbecued pig!  They must be coming down from the beach park!"

Alana turns and begins packing up their lunch. The pounding drums reverberate inside her head, causing her to shake and flinch. "Tiki! Your friends are too fockin' lazy to walk all the way from the beach park! And that is chanting! Your friends are definitely too stupid to chant like that!"

She peers out at the distant mass smoldering down the shoreline. Alana closes her eyes and allows them to reset. Upon opening them, she sees the light of pale white torches moving closer at an alarming speed. "Tiki?" She finds Tiki standing still against a flowing current of fog. Everything goes painfully silent just before she calls out to him again. "Tiki!"

The dense fog of volcanic ash and salty mist appear to be galloping towards them from the trees to the north. Every particle in the lush valley is drawn to the vacuum of this speeding locomotive. The pounding drums and eerie chanting resonate through the air. Alana becomes dizzy at the sight and sounds of an unnatural horde. Her senses throb from the drums marching towards her.

Her attention slowly draws to the fierce splashing in front of her. Tiki's voice brings her back to focus, "Babe! Let's go! Pack 'em up! Get inside!"

"Tiki, what the hell is that?" She is already packed, but stands frozen in place.

"It's the maka 'ike! It's going off right now." Tiki practically carries Alana and their bags up the dock to the boathouse. "I never dreamed of this shit. But I should have known!"

Alana staggers in his arms, "Known what Tiki?"
"The last moon! The twenty-seventh moon phase! The Night Marchers- Ka huaka'i o ka po! That's when the Night Marchers run through the ancient battlefields. All of Kualoa is ancient battlefields. They're headed this way." Tiki throws their bags through the doorway and clutches tightly onto Alana. "E hana make ia ia! They're chanting, 'Kill him! Kill him!' I don't know who they mean!"

Tiki slams the metal doors and helps Alana scurry past the massive saltwater tanks. "Babe, your aura is glowing. Why?" He stares into her eyes, "Your eyes babe! The iris, the pupils- they're rippling! It looks like they're on fire! What are you seeing? Where that small screwdriver stay?"

"Forget the fockin' time clock. I can see that you're glowing too! Tiki wait. If that is the Night Marchers, we just bow on the floor naked and wait for them to pass. Just don't look at them, and we'll be cool, right?" Alana points over to the laboratory lobby, "We'll just go hide in there and wait for them to run past!"

Tiki pulls her into the first office and kicks their bags against the wall, "Uh babe, they got camera's over there. They're going to think we're humping. All naked on their floor, we'll get fired for sure!" He locks the door and closes the blinds, "But, if we lay right under the cameras, then they cannot see us straight below and we might get some actual footage of the ghosts! We'll have proof that I'm not crazy!"

Alana drops to the ground under a curtain of long hair, "Mano... Tiki, they are calling your name."

Tiki flings his wet shorts against the wall with a splat and covers her, "Eh, mano means shark too. They got two tiger sharks in the tank right over there. Eh, you don't think the Night Marchers are the ones killing all the sharks, do you? No way, that cannot be right." Tiki slides over and peeks out the window blinds. "Oh damn. The sharks are thrashing. I think they want to bust out the tank. And there's something, some light illuminating behind them. Not good. I'm pretty sure ghosts can get through the doors without setting off the alarms. This doesn't make any sense though."

Alana sees the light from the tank coming through the blinds and pulls him back, "No Tiki. Listen to me. Ka po nui ho'olakolako, kea o nui ho'o hema hema. The great night that provides, the great day that neglects. Guidance is given in dreams, but we misunderstand."

Tiki slides back to cover her, "Eh? Oh, sweet. Now you're talking in riddles like the voices in my head."

"They're not chanting 'kill you, kill you!' I think they're commanding you- Kill him, kill him!"

"Ya. I think so." Tiki huddles over her and whispers, "Because something is in there. We're not alone."

"What do you mean, something's in there?" Alana peeks out through the door way and hears foot steps and something scraping across the glass of the 80,000 gallon tank. "Tiki, what is that standing next to the tank?"

"Waiho wale kahiko." Tiki crouches over her, "Ancients exposed. Old secrets revealed. That is the shapeshifter. The snake charmer."

"What are we going to do?" Alana slides over to get a better look out the cracked doorway.

"This is where I summon the mana and go to battle." Tiki holds her still.

"Bullshit. Those drums are in the building now. The night marchers are coming here. Just stay down with me and let them take care of what ever the fock that is out there." Alana clutches his arms.

The muddled sound of a hundred ghostly voices emanates through the hallway. The scraping against the glass intensifies until suddenly the tank wall shatters. Water bursts onto the floor and then gushes through the office door as if it were kicked open.

Their naked bodies wash across the grey marble floor until they collide against the back wall. Alana drowns in her hair but feels Tiki holding her tightly. She looks up at Tiki sliding across the floor. He peers out the open doorway at the two tiger sharks writhing on the floor. "What ever you do, don't look up!" He cradles her head and kisses her cheek, "Stay down from the Night Marchers, hide here until I return. E lei no au i ko aloha (I will wear your love as a wreath)." Tiki presses her hand around his heart.

"No wait." She won't let go of him.

"No babe, don't worry. I promise I will return. I've seen this battle play out in my mind a hundred times. I know exactly what to do."

"No. But I don't." She clutches his arm tightly, "No Tiki, wait. I'm already pregnant."

"What? Wait, what?" He drops back down over her.

"Right when the Night Marchers showed up on the horizon, I felt this buzz awaken in my stomach."

"What? How do you know? When? From today when we went... No way!"

"Yes Tiki. From today. I know I'm already pregnant because I can feel the life of this child inside me. And I can feel your energy growing stronger because you're connected to him, like you're connected to me. Just like I can feel the dark energy of that devil coming after us right now!"

Tiki wraps his arms around her and then pops to his feet, "Then I have to kill him before he gets to you!" Tiki turns to the doorway as all heat and sound pull out of the room like a vacuum.

The silence becomes sickening for a moment, "I'm not the one you want to kill!" A raucous growl burns into their ears from the open doorway as Tiki charges forward.

Suddenly, a massive thud strikes the wall above Alana. The limp body of the six-hundred pound young tiger shark hits the ground and rolls against her. Covering her head, she refuses to look up. The metallic smell of an electrical fire fills the air. Alana can feel Tiki running back towards her, heaving the battered shark off the ground. His body crackles and sparks like an incredible voltage is searing through him. As he charges forward, his steps sound as if he is now made of concrete. Alana catches her eyes trying to open, but she squeezes them shut. Tiki collides with the lone

69

stalker as both men howl with rage. The sounds of shattering glass and pummeling boulders rumble down the corridor.

Alana suddenly feels alone and vulnerable. A single ghostly voice whispers into her ear, "Kapapa ulua (To drive ulua fish into nets. To obtain a human victim or sacrifice)."

An explosion flexes the walls and ceiling throughout the building. The lights surge and flash before going out. She cracks her right eye slightly open. There appears to be only a single light on her from the emergency exit sign. She peers out through her hair. The demolition speeding down the corridor sounds like wrecking balls crumbling through the concrete. The building shakes from their thrashing. "Maybe you can move one hair with your pinky finger. Maybe one small breath." She whispers to herself, trying not to flinch at the crashing and roaring in the distance. "Kapapa ulua... That's what Tiki says when he gets the fish into the net..." She squeezes her eye closed before the tears escape, "A frickin' riddle? To obtain a human victim, to make the sacrifice."

Through the violent devastation, Alana hears the inhuman chanting again, "Waiho wale kahiko."

She whispers loudly enough to acknowledge she hears the voices, "Ancients exposed. Old secrets revealed. What happened to my Tiki? The mana has been revealed? Is that the ancient secret?"

The fog seeps into the room, leaving Alana shivering in the cold. One-hundred ghostly voices now surround her, "E ulu, e ulu kini o ke akua, ulu o Kane me Kanaloa!"

She thinks quickly to decipher the meaning as the voices and drumming fill the room around her. "Inspire?" She mutters, "Spirits enter and inspire... the gods Kane and Kanaloa... possessed by a god for creation. What did you do to Tiki? Is he possessed? Is Tiki the sacrifice? Or am I?"

Cold shadows pound drums over her body as the chanting swirls around the small office. She erases all thoughts from her head and tries to remain statuesquely frozen. Alana presses her hands tightly over her face as the voices blare across her skin like trumpets. The pounding of her heart causes her whole body to pulsate while she concentrates on not fainting.

Suddenly, an incredible weight pounces onto her and then rips her off the ground. Wrenched and twisted high in the air, Alana becomes overwhelmed by violent dizziness. Instantly, she is numbed of all senses except for her own faint inner voice, "Ho'oponopono, to make family right through mental cleansing. I live now under the protection of Ku, Kanaloa, and Kamohoali'i. Let the wisdom of the spirits guide me and give me strength. The mana is now living in my body as I dream. When I awaken, I shall bear, nurture and raise this gift until the wrong is made right."

Then, pure blackness drapes her mind...

# Uhane Kihei Pua
## Flower Mantle Energy

From opposite sides of the darkness, two ghostly voices echo faintly, "I learned everything I need to know about you when you kissed me."

"I never kissed you."

"Then what did you dream about my dear?"

"Dream? I haven't slept."

"Of course you haven't slept. No one can. It's a bloody revolution. Dear child, you're dreaming now."

"I know who you are. And you know I'm typing my report, which must continue without distraction."

"You have no idea who I am. You have no idea who you are. Yes, and I'm on the other side watching a masterful dance on this strange typewriter. It must be fascinating to read, but sadly, I cannot. I never learned to read that language in this life. Your words are like nothing I have ever seen."

"This daydream, it's fascinating that I'm receiving a foreign consciousness directly into my own, possibly electronic, perhaps magnetic stimuli, without affecting my ability to generate this document. I seem undistracted. You are seemingly isolated into my inner dialogue, but I cannot stress the importance of not interfering with this report. Uncanny. What do you think you know about me? I never kissed you, nor dreamt of kissing you. Only nightmares of snakes every time I try to rest."

"And this is why you type so diligently? You suppress your sexual desires while I imagine what those hands could do for my pleasure. Would it disturb you to realize those nightmares of snakes is what your mind constructed instead of seeing our sex? Things suddenly have a certain potency for you, yes?"

"I'm required to produce a tremendous amount of data for this medical research to be effective. Please explain how you are on the other side, in what form of existence, and how this conversation I am actively engaged in is a dream state."

"You are a fascinating creature. There was indeed a magnetic attraction when we met. I usually spark repressed, uncontrollable carnal lust. No? I am an exquisite African queen and definitely the most desirable woman you have ever seen, doctor. Sadly, your masters have robbed you of your natural desire for pleasure.

Fortunately, your ambition to learn and your warrior spirit have made you a rare, exotic killer. You are the last son. When you die an excruciating death at the hands of your enemies, the spiritual energy of your ancestors, down to the first father, will die with you. I'm sorry lover. Impregnating me will not carry on your pure, doomed lineage. Mestizo is something your people despise. But, you are the first conqueror to come to my island and cure my people of small pox, measles, and typhus, while inflicting your plague on my white oppressors.

My tragic savior, the sad warrior. Mon cheri, listen to me. I am sharing my gift of second sight with you and offer you a choice from your commander's vulgar betrayal. I will promise you two sons before your widowed wife bleeds to death."

"You are right about one thing. Besides my wife, you are the only other woman I have had any sort of intimacy with. My father arranged this marriage before I was born. You will need to explain further before I would be able to quantify any consequences from this choice you are presenting. Specifically, the betrayal of my commander, the insight you have on my wife, and how your second sight is enabling our conscious minds to meet without disturbing my concentration on the report I am currently composing. Please bring to light."

"Bien entendu, mi amore. I owe you this for the people you saved, for the people you killed, and the people soon to die. First, understand, to love me is eternal. I will empower your dwindling lineage, and you shall empower mine. You will then shine like a beacon in the vastness beyond this mortal prison, and entities will take notice. They will come for you. Your mind is already open and vulnerable, it always has been. However, your crumbling soul is detached and too faint to see."

"Detached?"

"Your soul is the fuel that ignites the engine of your flesh. You don't necessarily have to be inside of it to command it. But you will find yourself in purgatory, only to be collected by an entity with the sight. You will need my protection. You will be my ally, my lover. I shall nurture the soul energy of your great lineage, and I shall share with you the soul energy of thousands of great lineages.

Perhaps not dreaming of our sex has saved you from bringing unpure shame to your Satomi. You shall remain faithful to her, at least in your mind, and she will ultimately survive her pregnancy through the coexisting pregnancy you have just given me. Your delicious twin boys will survive childbirth if you return to Japan in time to save Satomi. I will show you how.

However, you may never bond with your sons after they are born. You will send them away to be educated as your father did you, in a time of great rebuilding. Only after they are as strong as you are now can you expose them to our empowered light. They must be given this choice as freely as you are to make to me now. To be my ally is powerful, no? This is what I am offering to you, survival and power. The power for revenge, revenge to make you more powerful."

"I must weigh the betrayal you speak of. Please enlighten."

"Surely, you must know already."

"My father? Is it he who diminished my family's honor?"

"You know nothing of yourself aside from what your masters have programmed. And you owe them nothing. Mi amor, Shiro Ishii killed your father when you were a child. He became your master and educated you along with a hundred other orphans in order to reshape Japan into his wicked agenda.

He terrorized and assassinated Japan's civilian government until there was no one to oppose his army of orphans. His extreme right-wing militarist faction will eventually deceive and seize complete authoritarian control of your entire nation. He will join the Axis camp and plunder the pacific rim through genocide and slavery. This treachery will ultimately end in the greatest disaster ever suffered by any nation in history.

By executing his orders, you are responsible for planting the seeds that will inevitably bring a shameful defeat and universal misery, as thousands of souls are extinguished in a fiery end. One choice, leaves these souls lost in purgatory. One choice empowers our patronage to survive into the coming world. Your father followed his commander's orders, just as you. Your fates are identical because you were programmed into blind loyalty. Where is the honor in following orders when your masters are small-minded, greedy, racist addicts? You've squandered your kills."

"What does this mean, into the coming world?"

"Maybe you should visit our neighbors, the Aztec. Their astrological calendars are magnificent. They are savage and would be ravenous to eat you. You see, we are currently in the fifth world, soon to enter the sixth. There is an absence of a fundamental element that swirls outwards from the center of this universe, thus trapping us on this earthly plane. We are blind, caged animals here. This will all change as we enter the next world where this universal energy element becomes abundant for all living creatures and connects us spiritually. Only those with a powerful lineage will thrive. The others become prey."

"What is this element?"

"That is the secret I can only share after you commit to my ceremony. This is the power I wield. I have already shared enough of my gift for you to see the world as it really is. You cannot unsee this truth nor can you walk away with knowledge of its existence. Shall we begin your ceremony? You must decide now."

"Ho'oponopono, to make right through forgiveness, prayer and mental cleansing. I now live under the protection of Ku, Kanaloa and Kamohoali'i. Let the wisdom of my ancestors' spirits guide me, inspire me and give me strength. The Mana is now living in my body as I dream. When I awaken, I shall bear, nurture and raise this gift until the wrong is made right..."

These thoughts float in the darkness around her like storm clouds. Her own faint inner voice echoes from the distance. "I... I must be a ghost... just a dream..." A single twinkling particle begins to shimmer through the black void. She becomes fixated on the delicate glow as her vision develops from nothing. When a second speck emerges and orbits, a sense of motion awakens. The growing dizziness begins to define the form caging her thoughts. Alana becomes entranced by the twinkling sparks circling in her vision. More and more, the dawn awakens.

Atrophy quickly releases its grip. A sudden blast of electrical pulses ignites her mind. Her vision begins spinning wildly within the hollow shell of her body as if her mind is not yet secured within her skull. Sparks from every direction shower against her as her shape solidifies. Lightning flashes in the silence, then the thunder rolls. "I must be a ghost. I do not feel my body. I'm not breathing. I'm dreaming. My eyes are opening... I can see light, movement... What are these shadows, pushing against me? Is that thunder?"

The shadows take form and the thunder draws closer. Alana realizes she is not dreaming anymore. An explosion of panic bursts in her throat as her sudden gasp draws in seawater. Her lungs are already flooded. A hundred sharks circle her drifting body. Every species of shark has come to represent their kingdom in this gathering. They are not frenzied and she is not drowning. Tiki has spoken of this many times and the significance of this gathering means a powerful savior shall be born.

As quickly as the fear swelled up and detonated, it subsides and soaks back into the core of her heart. Alana stares calmly into the eye of the most magnificent creature she has ever seen. A massive tiger shark glides upwards to her lifeless body. All she can do is stare. Its coarse skin begins scratching up against hers. Alana's senses are awakened by a pulsating charge of friction. Her body flails against its battle-scarred trunk. Intoxicating waves pulse through her mind. The electrical current rips down her spine and sears into the flesh of her limbs. Her body has woken. Her body is under her command. Grabbing onto the towering dorsal fin, she forces her thoughts to become focused.

78

Alana soars alongside the ancient predator, clutching the shark like family. The thunder grows louder as they near the surface. She lets go as the 'aumakua gives her a push upwards. A passing wave takes hold and whisks her towards a jagged ridge. The wave crashes across the steep bank and leaves her clutching onto a boulder. She looks down at the gathering of sharks vanishing into the dark ocean. Their electrical fields dwindle away, leaving her with only the buzzing in her womb.

The frothing water sucks off the rocks as the next wave builds. Alana scurries up the ledge like a crab. It strikes below her feet and batters her against a boulder. The impact gushes the water out from her mouth and nose. Alana holds herself against a series of waves, vomiting and gasping for air. The rocks lacerate her skin while she waits for a lull.

Alana staggers up the shore as the mountains become lit with a purple dawn. The burning red backdrop elevates from behind the vertical cliffs. Alana stands naked at the forgotten edge of the island, "How the hell did I get here? Tiki? Where are you? Tiki!" She screams knowing no one will hear her. Alana's world has been set back in time 400 years as she walks along Ka'ena Point barefoot, naked and alone.

She stops under a throng of coconut trees and gathers fallen leaves. Alana begins weaving feverishly trying to fight the tears. She holds a coconut in her hands and sadly stares at its face. She remembers the story of how the coconut came to have a face: A sad wife buries her beloved husband next their house as the husband's last wish. A tree soon grows from that spot and fruits a coconut. "With this coconut, drink when you are thirsty, eat the flesh when you are hungry. Use the emptied shell for utensils and tools. Use everything from the tree to clothe, build, and comfort yourself. When you become lonely, hold the coconut in your hands, look at it's face and remember that I will always be here to soothe you."

Alana sobs, "Naha na 'omaka wai a ka lihilihi. Broken are the water holders of the eyelashes. That's what Tiki would be telling you if he saw you broke-down, crying like this." She stands and proudly arranges her woven garments. "Waiho wale kahiko." She treks on. "Ancients exposed, old secrets revealed. E ulu, e ulu kini o ke akua, ulu o Kane me Kanaloa. Spirits enter and inspire, possessed by a god for creation. Tiki used to grumble about riddles. He hated them leaving riddles in his head. Now I'm grumbling about your riddles in my head."

Staring at the ground until a road is under her feet, Alana rambles, "It's either the riddles in my head making me sick or the baby in my belly. I should have seen this coming." She growls, "I'm not the one you want to kill! He knew Tiki would kill him and he says that shit to us. I should have looked at him. I bet he's not the only one out there. And now I don't even know what the fockin' monster looks like. What happened to you Tiki Doll? Where are you baby? What did the mana do to you?"

Alana walks cautiously up to an old car parked on the side of the road. "This car smells worse than Brian's truck!" She turns towards the footsteps from the trees.

"What, did you fall off the luau bus?"

"Tali! I need a ride home! It's an emergency!" Alana demands.

"Holy shit, Alana! Where da fock you been? We been looking for you for like two weeks already!" Tali stares as if she is a ghost.

"Wait, what? The fock you mean, two weeks? What day is... never mind! Give me a ride!" Alana shivers.

"Uh, ya, no worries. Did you make that outfit yourself?" Tali extinguishes the joint on the bottom of his rubber slipper.

"Kook, do I look like I want to hear your stupid shit right now? Clean your front seat and throw out whatever is making that smell!"

"Ok. For sure. You want a towel? Eh, where's braddah Tiki? Him and the Kau's kind of vanished you know, no one's heard from them in a while. I was just looking for surf, but it's always junk when Tiki's not around. Nobody's surfed in two weeks. That's how I know something's focked up. You look total wreck, are you alright?"

80

Alana struggles to open the window, "Tali, just stop talking. Look, Tiki disappeared last night, or two weeks ago. I need you to help me find him."

"I been trying. No surf, no pakalolo, UH lost, men's basketball and women's volleyball - the whole fockin' island's a shit-fockin'-sandwich right now. There's only so many places he can be. What are you doing up there? Nobody surfs there. Where's your car? Did it break down? You didn't try to drive it around Ka'ena Point did you?"

Alana holds her face out the window, "Tali, just stop talking. I washed up there and I couldn't find Tiki. He might be at work. Can you go look for him after you drop me at home? Tali, it stinks in here. It stay hauna (smelly), brah." Alana turns to look in the back seat, "Tali, there is a dead focking chicken in your back seat. Why?"

"Oh. Ya, there was a fire last night at my cousin's house. Was fight night. Some guys was smoking the funny stuff. You know da kine, with the super chickens. They pump their chickens with so much steroids, no can control the mob and shit go outta hand. My cousin lost his genetically enhanced chicken so I grabbed this one out da fire. We was supposed to hook up and I don't want the car to smell like weed. Wait, what do you mean you washed up? Tiki disappeared? Where you been this whole time?" Tali veers his old wagon down the road as he glares at Alana in concern.

"You've had a dead, charred chicken in yo' car for two weeks because you planned on buying weed and was afraid it would stink in here? Eh buggah, I need you to drive a little faster please." Alana tries to move the surfboard wedged between her seat, blocking her view out the side window. "And feeding your chickens gun powder does not modify them genetically, it's just mean. So stupid."

The frustrating nature of this conversation has kept her from crying. "Eh, thanks for the ride. I think Tiki is in trouble and the trouble is still out there. Please keep quiet about this until we find out what happened. Ok? Tali, you understand? We were attacked at work and I was dumped in the ocean." She watches him stomp the gas pedal as the old car growls painfully with no acceleration. "This is serious. I'm sorry to get you

81

involved. Drop me off before we get to the house and you keep quiet. Go check out Brian's place and I will call your house later. Ok?" She watches him nod with his bulging eyes scanning feverishly out the cracked windshield. "Don't act weird."

"I'm not acting weird. I'm just not stoned. Everything is fockin' weird. I don't understand Alana. It's not the cops, not the gangs, not the cartel. I mean why da fock? Who da fock? Where da fock? How da fock? This don't make any sense. I mean Tiki had really good weed, everybody knew that. Nobody would ever mess with him. The Kau brothers were fockin' lolo, nobody would ever mess with them. I don't know what's going on. Are they being dicks at work?" Tali shudders.

"It will be alright. You know I will find Tiki. Try maybe drive around Kualoa fast kine, then by the Kau's. Stay out of sight boy. I'll call your house at sunset. If you no answer, I will assume something happened to you. Can handle?" Alana jumps out of the sputtering wagon behind her block and scampers into the tall grass. She is well camouflaged to make it to the back fence undetected.

She looks through a hole in the wooden fence and sees the contents of her house broken and scattered. The burning sickness she suppressed all morning erupts into a violent burst of dry heaving. "Pull it together girl." She squints the tears from her eyes before the panic can take root. Intuition declares it obvious that she is being hunted, haunted, watched. It is not fear or paranoia making the world seem different. The sight of her house in shambles makes her nauseous. She grumbles, "I just wish one of those big fockin' sharks would bite the hell out of the bastards who trashed my pretty house."

Feeling confident no one is inside, she slithers to the lanai door. "Ok. Grab that bag quickly. Grab your essentials quickly. Search quickly." The phone lines have been pulled from the wall. Creeping into the kitchen, she sees one phone sitting smugly on the table, not where she left it.

Scrounging for a few more items is distracted by the silence of that misplaced phone. With a full bag, she peers suspiciously into the kitchen once more, frozen in her crouch. She slowly backs towards the lanai as her breathing becomes a shallow panic.

The painful silence has her entranced until a ringing screech knocks her over onto her back. Her ear scrapes along the side of Tiki's guitar amplifier. At that moment, she glances immediately at Tiki's journal wedged tightly behind the speaker in it's hidden crevice as the phone wails a second time. Before a third ring can roar, she catapults over the fence and vanishes into the grass.

From the shady blades, Alana hears the answering machine project a soulless voice towards her, "... Security Office ... Applied Eugenics Biology Research ... vandalized ... Cooperate with authorities ..." Time for her to run. The aimless chugging of her sprint eventually veers towards, "Aunty Ruby! Get your ass to Aunty Ruby's!"

Mind blank, body broken, at least she is too exhausted to cry. Four miles up the steep hill to Pupukea, Alana never slowed down to see if she was being followed. "Think fast Alana!" She pleads to herself as she knocks on the door. Where could this explanation possibly start? Nothing feels right. Nothing makes sense.

Her dear Aunt Ruby is already there, "Get your ass in here!" Alana is yanked inside before the door slams behind her. "Are you alright? Where's Tiki? Did you get in a fight?" The smothering hug makes it impossible to respond. Alana becomes weightless, momentarily free from the buzz scraping the inside of her skull. The cleansing touch sluices the frailty and doubt. "You're a mess girl, go bathe." Aunt Ruby releases Alana and swiftly sails her towards the back of the house. "Oh honey, you're spotting. Malia! Try come help your cousin!"

Malia clutches Alana's arm and slings her into the bathroom. "What, did you and Tiki fight?"

"No. Of course not. I wish I could explain, but I might be in trouble. Help me think of something to tell your mom." Alana bathes and unloads the scoops for her younger cousin. They have always been best friends and every word is believed without question. Alana has always been the smart one in the Ohana (family), even though they are not blood related.

"So why is your punani (vagina) bleeding? Were you abused, like sexually in that creepy little laboratory? By those creepy little fish scientists?"

"You're the creepy one you little witch. If they tried to touch my punani, I'd fockin' know. No human being laid a hand on me. It was something else, not human. You still have my old driver's license? I need that back. Sorry cuz, you don't want to be buying beer with my name any more. I don't want to lie to your mom."

"You cannot lie to her, no one can. You need to call your sister." Malia helps dry Alana's long hair and start a braid. "You need money too." She pulls a shoe box from under the bed. "Don't lie to mom. I have money for you."

"Where did you get this?" Alana demands.

"I dance at da kine in town on Saturday's. What? Don't look at me like that! I used your ID so they don't know I'm only seventeen. You can't tell mom!"

"How are you able to hold a secret from her but I cannot? Eh?"

"Look at these earrings - jade. Look at this necklace, rose quartz. Obsidian ring here, jasper ring here, tiger's eye ring here, amethyst, turquoise, citrine, moonstone, bloodstone, sapphire..."

"Ok. Fock. More rocks than Waimea Canyon. That shit works? Girl, you better be taking care of yourself. I mean it. You are too smart and pretty to get into sex and drugs and drinking..."

"I know. Don't worry, I never drink or anything. I just dance from ten to two on weekends and leave with a shit-ton of money. Drunk men disgust me, so I feel like it's my duty to take all the money I can from those idiots. I tell mom I stay at a friend's house for volleyball practice. I'm ahead of the game. I saved all this money, and now I know why. It's meant for you. Take your ID back and use this money to go find your sister. I can finally take off all these fockin' rocks and breathe again. No need to lie anymore. I'll feel better once you're safe and Tiki's back." They embrace for a spell and prepare to spell out the truth to Aunt Ruby.

Gathered at the table with dinner waiting, "Alana, I promised you a long time ago I would take care of you no matter what. I can handle anything. Look what Malia puts me through. Don't give me that- holehole iwi (strip the flesh off the bone) kind stuff. You won't endanger me by telling me this. What could you have possibly done? No bullshit girl."

"Holehole iwi, I'm afraid to reveal what happened because it will cause trouble for your family." Alana reasons.

"Ok girl, now you really need to tell me what is going on. Where is Tiki?" Aunt Ruby draws her painted eyebrows down to signal that a clear explanation needs to surface immediately.

"Ok, no bullshit. You know those episodes Tiki's been having? Well, they got worse."

"You never took him to see one doctor because you were afraid of what would happen to the doctor, ya?"

"Ya, well, he had a bad one last night. I mean two weeks ago. That would have been on the twenty-seventh phase of the moon. And we were attacked by something that was not exactly human. And then the night marchers came and took me away. I woke up this morning underwater in a shiver of sharks, crawled up at Ka'ena Point. I went home to find my house all trashed and a message on my answering machine saying the security company at work wants to hold me liable for vandalizing their facility. I think I'm pregnant."

Alana watches her Auntie's eyebrows jerk upwards, almost off her face. She continues, "Ya, uh… I know Tiki wanted to get married, but he didn't propose that night because he left the ring at home. He looked into the diamond and saw something terrible. I looked in his eyes and I could see this. It was the last thing I saw in his eyes before we were attacked."

"Wot!? Terrible? I helped him pick out that diamond from Phil's! I get all my diamonds from Phil! Ain't that right Malia? No, it wasn't the stone. It was the maka 'ike. Where is the ring now? Maybe I could see what Tiki saw..."

"I don't know, I couldn't find it. I don't know where Tiki hid it and I couldn't find it before I ran out the house!" Alana collapses on the table momentarily. The loss finally hit her.

Malia picks her back up and steadies Alana to continue. "Remember how I told you that the visions he was having with his seizures were leading up to something? Well, the night marchers came at the same time we got attacked. Tiki got attacked and the night marchers took me away. I blacked out.

Before I woke up underwater two weeks later, surrounded by the sharks, I dreamed I was going to have a child. I was told to protect this child. But that wasn't the strange part. There was something else... something before I dreamed of the child. Like a dream before I could dream. It's still there, but I cannot see it.

I remember the child dream because it was for me... but there is something else in my head that was not my dream, not meant for me. It's a splinter and it's been bothering me auntie, I cannot tell where it hurts, but it is in my head."

Auntie Ruby becomes considerably shaky. She motions for the two girls to go sit in the living room. A bible, several ti leaves, lava rocks, three glasses with ice and a bottle of Canadian whiskey plop down with her. "Dammit girl, damn. I never seen you cry like this. Your house, did you get your address book?"

"No, it was gone."

"Dammit girl, my address wasn't in there. No, ya?" Ruby pours drinks.

"No, of course not. I never needed to write your address or number in there."

Ruby sighs, "Well, we probably have a little time before they come looking here." She gulps the whiskey down, ice and all, "Why did the night marchers come after you and not take Tiki? What does that mean, 'I'm not the one you want to kill?' What a bizarre thing to say. What kine accent was this?"

"Well, was not fockin' pidgin (local dialect), I tell you that." Alana squints at the migraine twisting around her eye sockets. "That's the part I don't get. We was naked on the floor.."

"No Wonder Hapai! (Pregnant)" Malia blurts.

"Ah! You little mutt!" Alana counter-blurts.

"Just saying..." Malia winks at her mother trying to lighten the concern.

"Well, under normal circumstances... So stupid. Camera's everywhere. We were really strict with work because we knew someone was always watching. I mean, I wish we could get a hold of those security tapes, but they would either prove we were attacked, or we somehow tripped out and caused the damage because we clearly lost our mind, or I don't know. But that's the puzzle, ya? Tiki is pure blood warrior, I am kanaka maoli (pure blood). We bowed down, eyes closed, full respect protocol. I thought they was coming to help us with that, focking whatever the fock..."

"That's it. The only explanation." Ruby pours the whiskey and digs the ice out of Malia's glass with her long painted fingernails. "Was one foreign devil, strong enough to summon the help of the night marchers to save you, but could not save Tiki. I mean, that is a foreign company, foreign employees, doing what exactly?"

"Conservation of the reefs, sea life, biology research. I never seen the research. It's all on the computers, no printed words. Only code, no more nothing, just numbers and keypads and buttons and cameras. Just one banana asian guy from the security office that left us our paychecks every week, but he was hired from our school too. Foreign fockin' devils." Alana deflates, a little less hopeless but still helpless.

"We gotta find your sister. You need to get off this island. You got her number?" Ruby waddles over to her phone book and starts flipping pages. "This number I got is from four years ago. "Malia, try dial this number for me."

Alana reluctantly digs out Tiki's journal and sets it on the table. She closes her eyes and opens the cover. One by one, she carefully flips the pages with her face slumped over onto her palm.

"Mom, that not the number. Say it again. See, that's different than the first number. Kapakahi (all messed up)! Try start over. Hemajang (all mixed up)! Junks! Geev'Um!"

"Wot! Chee! Cannot handle you no more! Try cut your fingernails!"

"You so lompai (bother)! You went make me dial da phone because your nails stay longer than mines! Unreal. Ready for skin one fish with your da kind."

"K-den, try this one. Try wait... I get one-nother-one.... Just dial the number, that's your kuleana (responsibility)."

"And then.... And then.... And then... No huhu's (to be upset), but this one no work either." Malia glances over at Alana, slumped in the recliner, "See! Went moemoe (sleep) already waiting for you!"

"What? Nobody going nene (sleep) when you go yell like that!" Ruby barks.

"I'm not sleeping. I'm just not looking. Malia, try dial this number." Alana keeps her face covered with one hand, pointing her finger down onto the journal with the other. "I'm afraid to read this damn thing, but I think there's a number right here where I'm pointing."

Malia pulls the phone as far as the cord will reach, "Eh, there is a number. From December 24, 1984. Wow, exactly one year ago. Yep,

Ikaika, the alcoholic husband, says right here. Probably called to wish you a Merry Christmas."

"No way. We were here last Christmas and we didn't have the answering machine because you gave us the answering machine on Christmas Day and we didn't hook it up until after New Years." Alana maintains her slump. "Tiki never liked anyone to read this, I don't know how I knew it was there."

"But you were meant to find it. Here, it's ringing." Malia holds the phone up to Alana's face as they both turn away from the journal.

Alana clutches the phone into position, "Eh, Keala! Pueo (owl)? No, Alana! Not the pueo, your sister, Alana! A - La - Na! Wot-Da-Fock! Yes. Hunaka'i. Yes, I miss you too! Oh, nah! Ya, no shit... Ya, the focking airport! What, you think I was going to jump out the plane and land on your house? I don't even know where your house is! How did you know I was going call? How would you know that? Ok, fine then. I'll be there. No, I don't have a gun. Why? You better pick me up! I'm not spending Christmas at the airport. K-then, bumbye."

Alana hands the phone back to Malia, "Well, that was weird. Oh, try give 'em. I gotta call Tali. Mind if I dial?" Alana doesn't expect him to answer on the first ring, "L&L Drive In? Tali! Knock it off, it's me, Alana..."
Her eyes glare at Ruby as she listens, "Where is Lani? Ok. Look, go to to your dad's house and watch over them. Don't stay there, don't go back to the Kau's. Don't go back to my house. If you find out anything, call my Auntie Ruby. I'm sorry Tali, I know you like bus' somebody up, but you need to stay away from all this. You need to stay low for a while. I'll be ok, I'm getting off the island. You be careful too."
Alana hangs up the phone, "I gotta get off this island! He said the Kau's are gone, all of them. Their house is empty, all their plants are gone, their dogs are gone. I can't stay here. I better call one cab at the market!"

"Dammit girl, no way. Get in the truck. I'm taking you to the damn airport myself." Ruby starts waving her fingernail, "Bullshit, ain't nobody messing with this Tita (sister) in my pick-up truck!" This is something that cannot be argued with:  No one messes with a Tita in a pick-up truck, nobody.


Lihue, Kaua'i. The Garden Isle.

Alana walks out into rain and breathes in the tropical potency.  The moment she nears the curb, tires screech into a skidding stop at her feet.  The passenger door rips open as a plumeria lei lasso's her neck and yanks her in.  The gut-wrenching race towards Poipu begins, "Eh, I don't think anyone will be able to keep up with your Ferrari!  Can we slow down a little?  Keala, what the hell?"

Keala studies her face longer than a driver should not see the road, "My God I missed you.  I'm sorry, but I don't do slow.  Akila's home by himself.  There's no time.  Not enough time."

"Akila?  What happened to Ikaika?  What is wrong with your seatbelt here?  Please slow down." Alana whimpers.

"Ikaika's dead."  Keala solemnly blurts as the back road gets much more twisty and narrow.

Alana is lost at sea, dizzy, nauseous.  "What are you talking about sister.  When was this?  Who is Akila?"

"You look a little green around the gills there girl.  Don't puke in my truck."

"Dammit, I want to choke you right now, but I cannot let go of your dashboard.  Why is there no seatbelt here?  We're not being followed.  And you're making me sick so if I puke, it's your fault." Alana's head bounces off the passenger window twice from the same pothole.

"There's a harness behind the seat.  You have to pull it over your shoulders and hook it under your seat."  Keala holds Alana's hair from entangling the straps, "Remember dad had one like this in his old car for

90

the dog? It's been three years. Long years sister. You really look crappy. Where's Tiki?"

"Where's Ikaika? I asked first." Alana clutches her belly.

"Ok then. Well, right before hurricane Iwa, Ikaika returned from a fishing trip in Alaska and started to prepare the house for the storm. The day Iwa hit, I woke up and he was gone. The storm ripped the house apart and these lawyers handed me a non-disclosure agreement and a life insurance award. They said Ikaika's boat was lost in the storm in the middle of the ocean, but I knew that was bulai (untrue). So I bought a house outside of Poipu and had our son, Akila. I know we're not being followed, I always drive like we are, though. Just keep looking out the window anyways. Tiki?"

"Ok then. Well, we got attacked by something horrible at work, but the night marchers took me away and dumped me in the sea unconscious for two weeks. I woke up at Ka'ena Point looking for Tiki, but I cannot find him. They trashed our house so I came here to hide out. I think I'm hapai, so can you slow down please?" Alana reasons.

"Well, how's us? The Hunaka'i sisters singing the same song all over again. And... here we are." Not much of a warning before swerving left off the road, through a canopy of trees and skidding to a stop next to a boulder. "Akila! Come say aloha to your lolo (crazy) auntie!"

Alana sits in the truck, too dizzy to move and begins a cramping spell of dry-heaving. Helpless in the harness, her vision blurs and she feels cool flushing from her face. Keala walks around the truck, unfastens the carabiner from between her knees and flings the straps over Alana's head. Her long hair strangles her neck and binds her to the back of the seat. They both tug as the rain quickly soaks in. Alana slides down from the seat and collapses to her knees.

"Mom, is she ok?" The child runs over and reaches out to grab Alana's hand. The moment their hands touch, a static shock crackles from their fingertips.

Alana's head jerks towards the sky as her eyes roll back, into the darkness.

From opposite sides of the darkness, two ghostly voices echo faintly. "What happened to my father?"

"Does this matter for revenge or for dishonor? Why does this burden still weigh on your decision? I thought saving your wife and sons would..."

"Please excuse. Any deviation from my assignment will set off a chain of events that will be met with catastrophic consequences."

"You are communicating in code to your masters, yes?"

"Are you aware that there are details in the structure of my reporting and transmission that allows my commander to detonate my entire arsenal at his discretion? There must be synchronization."

"Of course my dear. Your father designed this weapon. Your father designed everything for Shiro Ishii. Unit 731, this was all your father's doing. More precisely, the weapons systems. Exploiting the women of your country was Ishii's doing. The applications were composed by Ishii and when he was promoted to general, he murdered you father with this very invention. Voluptuously delicious, no? You can murder millions with tactical precision and yet it is bland as the sand for you. But your lust finally erupts when I feed you a worthy betrayal to enact revenge. Yes?

I am nourishing your dream state only. We are indeed isolated here in your thoughts, as a deeply-rooted day dream. Do not worry about your report, doctor. Your father's soul is suspended in purgatory. He has many secrets to offer as buoyancy on his descent to hell. He is drawn to me, as are you. As are thousands of souls soon to be liberated from their cages. They are drawn to my light. You've already made your choice to be my lover. Going after Ishii is only for your pride. But I will not allow you to disrupt what is coming for Ishii, not even for your wife and unborn sons."

"Ishii is obligated to provide health care for my wife at our facility in Tokyo. My father's legacy was the health care reform to ensure repopulation for war. She should not be in any danger. I must know more. Please explain."

"Well, in that, he succeeded. Overpopulation is the leverage in Ishii's argument for military control. Hence, the rise of the Japanese fascist movement. Scarcity and war opened the door for Ishii to sell his wicked vision. Ishii arranged the deal to sell your father's health care and education reform to the Mitsuizaibatsu monopoly. He convinced your father to apply the proceeds towards establishing the Army Epidemic Prevention Research Laboratory.

With the infrastructure in place, your father began his work on the Togo Unit. While your father worked on water purification and epidemic prevention, Ishii began working on the political and ideological instruments for his coup d'etat on your civilian democracy. His clever propaganda promoted racial superiority, counterespionage, political sabotage, and murder. It was when Ishii brought his racist theories to your father that this ultra-japanism was born. Only they could bring the eight corners of the world under one roof. This is what you want to hear, no?

Your father was manipulated into turning his work towards chemical and biological warfare. This is perhaps the greatest weapons system the world has ever seen, or rather, will never know about. Your father designed these seeds you have been planting around the world. Die by the sword of your enemy, or by your own. Yes? Your father established Unit 1644 in Nanjing, making the 'rape of Nanking' possible. The fail-safe mechanism on your plague weaponry was developed at this facility. This, however, was the line your father refused to cross. It was one thing to plant these seeds undetected around the world, but to give the trigger to one man? Your father saw the flaw in that design and decided to create a bypass into the system. So? Did your father betray his benefactor to regain his honor? Or, is there no honor in betraying your benefactor, no matter the reason? Your warriors gain honor by serving, so serve me.

Your father was murdered with phosgene, hydrogen cyanide, bromobenzyl cyanide, chloroacetophenon, diphenyl-cyanoarsine, arsenic trichloride, sulphur mustard and lewisite. I do not know what any of these words are, but you do. You have them here. With your father out of the way, Ishii alone held all the cards and laid them down on Sadao Araki's table. The Imperial Way Faction and Tojo Hideki promoted Ishii to general. Enslaving fathers, abducting children, exploiting women began on his political opposition. Soon, Ishii will enslave your entire nation to fuel, feed and fuck his military faction. With drugs and propaganda, Ishii will conquer your entire country within a year. This is who you are serving. They are destined to suffer a magnificent defeat by the most explosive weapon in this world's history, by the white oppressors you were trained to despise.

Hmmm... you are concerned about the prevention measure your father designed, no? This I cannot see clearly. If Ishii knew of this, he had motive to betray your father. If your father was successful in deceiving Ishii with this bypass in the design, only he would know. This is impossible. Ishii is untouchable. This information is unattainable. The only way to know for sure is for you to commit to this ceremony. Then you may see for yourself."

"Ishii does not want to detonate the seed here. It is meant for New Orleans. Yet, he will certainly erase any trace of my existence if I were compromised. The only way to guarantee our safety from Ishii is to return to Tokyo with you as my property. He will be infatuated with your spiritual power and I will murder him in the isolation of my research facility."

"You would go to murder Ishii and assume control of this global plague system, at the expense of your wife and sons? Sorry child, she believes you are already dead. She is now a civilian and your family no longer has access to your hospital facility. Even if she did, they only want your sons. They would leave her to die, or worse, send her to become a comfort woman to produce more purebred sons for their army. You must assume you are sitting on a biological time bomb that will destroy my island at any moment, upon General Ishii's command. There is no going after Ishii, this fate has already been set into motion.

Don't you see? There are thousands of souls on the horizon that I am going to pull through you, but only if Ishii lives. You are worthless to me if Ishii dies. You can only go after your family, and only with my help."

"The only way to know for sure if we are safe, and my family is safe, is for me to return with you as my captive."

"Am I your slave?  Or are you mine?  Oh lover, this is not a game you want to play with me.  Well?  Fine.  I will tell you this and then you will commit to me.  I disarmed your seed on the first night my dear.  Your wife is on borrowed time.  There is no other option for you.  Whatever revenge plot you are conjuring, it will fail.  Ishii already gave the command to detonate your weapon last night.  I pulled your father into my light and used him to disarm this seed just before it went off.  Ishii expects you to die.  Ishii expects everyone on this entire island to die.  But here you are, still transmitting your codes.  He expects you to be dead and yet, you are explaining to him that my spiritual powers are extraordinary.  Powerful enough to survive this pathogen bomb?  We will both be his slaves if you continue this plotting.  Your blind loyalty plays right into his hands, just as you were trained.  Ishii lives, your countrymen die.  You commit to me, and I will grant you two strong Japanese sons, and perhaps your wife will survive.  But only if you act now.  Are you ready to make your decision?  I will survive this.  You, your people, my people are all waiting for you to choose my patronage?  What do you say, lover?"

"Mom!  Look at her eyes!"  Akila yells, "I think she found her way out.  I just saw them roll around."

Alana feels her body shiver while her eyes adjust to the sunlight.  The dark remnants of her nightmare slither around to the back of her vision until the light's haze burns away all traces.  She flees towards the light of consciousness, feeling the ghostly stare from just beyond her gaze - behind her vision.  Humid air pierces into her lungs as if she had not breathed in a while.  Still sluggish, deflated, heart barely pumping, Alana feels her sister's presence and hears her comforting voice, "What kind of shit are you on girl?  Where did you float off to?"

Alana draws in enough air to strain words, "I think I blacked out.  How did I get back in the truck?  Get this stupid harness off me.  Did I black out?"

95

"Ya, you're still in the truck. It's more like a comfy-cozy little hammock, ya? You got a nice view of the trail going maka'i (towards the ocean) over here. We left you in the truck because we thought it would be more safe. You were really spazzing out. Plus, you need a bath. We couldn't get you out of the harness, your hair was totally tangled up in one big knot. But it all worked out because you were wiggling around so much. And then you punched my face, I had a black eye for a week."

"Da fock? A week? How long was I out? Do I have bangs now?"

"Uh, Lana, you were in some kind of druggy trance for two weeks already. Are you on some freaky shit or what? Do you do this often? Yes, you were all tangled up, and you now have bangs. So cute. But you don't worry about that. We got beef stew, that will make you feel way better. No worries."

"Well, shit. I guess this is what Tiki was going through on his dream trips, but not for two weeks. Oh hi sweetie, you must be Akila. Can you get me out of the truck? Which one of you cut my hair?" Alana reaches out for Akila's hand and then pulls back, "Wait, I remember reaching for your hand and then I got zapped. That's when I freaked out, ya?"

Keala helps her slide down from the seat, "Ya, you got zapped. You actually ate your own hair. You went chewed it up and ate it. Except some you swallowed, and some came out when you was snorting, was flapping out your nose with the hanabata. So we pulled it out and we gave you a little trim to even it up. He actually cut your hair, but he cuts mine all the time. Does a better job than me. The cute, I like it."

Alana's knees get shaky and needs support. Keala signals to the rubber slippers and bearhugs the full weight of her sister while the child slides them on her feet. "Sorry you stay all wet. The storm put a tree branch through the truck and I never got 'em fixed. That's why the seat is always wet, but the rain is healing water. The rain and wind provide protection for us sometimes when we are afraid or agitated or anytime we leave the house. It can get really staticky, especially for Akila, and you too apparently. You seem to hold a bit of a charge there sister. Kaula uila (streak of lightning).

Maybe your child needed a spark or maybe you needed cleansing. Dr. Maile came by and asked if you were ever a heroin junky."

"Wait, what? A doctor? Eh, no fockin' doctors! No records, no I.D.'s, no numbers. We don't do that!" Alana tries to squirm from their grip as they help her with baby steps.

Akila holds her belly, "Lono returns from the sea. Mano kanaka, Mano hae. Shark man, fierce fighter."

Alana stares at the child upon hearing this. The words tickle her ears. "Mano, that's his father's name." Alana giggles.

Keala asks, "Akila, is that your cousin Lono in there? He's gonna love the pipi (beef) stew, the little bugger. Eh, don't you worry about Dr. Maile, she was my doctor to help me with Akila, so you can trust her, ok? If she can handle me and my pregnancy, she sure as hell can handle yours. She said there was no drugs in your blood test, but that you were really showing signs of intoxication and addiction. You was all focked up."

"What? We don't do blood tests Keala! Are you crazy?" Alana jerks loose from their grip and takes a wobbly stumble backwards. She rolls to the side, twisting her ankle and begins tumbling down into a deep, dark cave. "Aah, wot-da-fock! Why is there a frickin' crater in the middle of your yard?"

Keala and Akila hobble down after her, "Wow, look at you bounce on the boulders! Like one jellyfish. Are you alright? Just take it easy there sister. Welcome to our storm shelter. Isn't it awesome? I know it's a little muddy in here right now, and maybe a little cock-a-roach or two, but it's really coming along great don't you think?"

"Ya, great for your werewolf, you psychotic wench. Can you help me out of the mud? I think I went broke my foot." Alana's eyes cannot adjust to the dark. Wriggling in the mud, suddenly panicking at the sense of something black slithering with her. She feels a presence lurking on the outskirts of her vision. She screams out, "Koheoheo! 'A'alaioa! He po'e 'a'a hewa!"

Keala whispers to Akila, "Poisonous-natured person. Wild, demented person. People acting wickedly. Kila, hurry and grab her." Keala quickly reaches out, "Eh, don't worry, your foot will be just fine after one bambucha (big) bowl of beef stew. Eh, and don't worry about Dr. Maile. She knows privacy is really important to me and always drives out to see us. And, also, there was one incident with the receptionist so I'm not exactly allowed back at the building, so it's totally cool. She went gave me this one-kind look, and then I gave her one stink-eye back. She picked the wrong day and found out upside her head. But you don't worry about that, you'll be just fine."

Alana peers deep into the cave as they whisk her up the carved stone steps, "Chee, you could totally drive your truck right down here, it's so big. Are those fishing poles?"

"Actually, those are spears. These ones over there are fishing poles." Akila places his hand on her belly, "Don't worry auntie. You are under the protection. Nothing can harm you. Lono is just fine, he's buzzing in there, I think he likes it here. Does your big toe always stick out sideways like that?"

Keala pulls her up to the sunlight, "Oh, we'll just pull that little piggy back into place later. No worries. Let's find you some dry clothes since you never brought any kind luggage with you. When did you learn French? It sounded like you were mumbling some French shit during your little acid nap. You sure you don't remember dreaming anything?"

"No, I don't speak French. You know it's weird that the keiki just said I was under the protection. That's what I heard the last time I woke up from one of these trances. You know I'm not on drugs, but waking up from these dreams feels like I'm totally on drugs trying to sober up." Stepping out of the bunker, "This place is beautiful. How come you no more neighbors?" Alana gazes around the dense rainforest veiling the lone house."

Through patches of hazy sunlight, "It's actually one old construction office. They stopped development on the neighborhood after the storm. Everybody was broke at that time, but I got Kaik's insurance money. Lucky I bought it before they started cutting down all the trees, so we're here alone right outside Poipu. I don't know for how long though. Still yet, nobody bothers us and no one can sneak up on us either."

Keala settles Alana next to the bath tub and helps peel off the muddy clothes. She snaps her toe back into socket without warning. "Isn't that better. No, don't cry, just get in the tub and relax."

"Chee, thanks, eh. I almost puked there, but I don't feel like I've eaten anything in a while. What else did this Dr. Maile say about me?" Alana falls limp in the hot bath.

"Well, she said dealing with a drug addict is going to be quite a challenge since you're pregnant, delusional and paranoid to the max. She has plenty of experience dealing with addicts, tweakers, crackheads, junkies. So, you'll be really temperamental, and moody, and distrustful, and manic, and impulsive. Oh, and depression is going to be one issue, but not for your baby. Your baby is super healthy."

"Hmmm. I guess that's why you're trying so hard to be nice. But you just said I passed my drug test."

"Ya, well, that doesn't mean there's nothing in your system. You were showing all the signs of heavy drug use, it was one hell of a trip. Anything you'd like to tell me about?" Keala remembers how the sisters would wash each other's hair, "You haven't had bangs since you were six."

"I'm not on any drugs. I was having a vision, some kind of spiritual trance like Tiki was having. He would chant things too, but not in French. Wow, my toe feels way better than I thought it would. Ever since I crawled out the water at Ka'ena Point, everything seems different to me. My vision is really hazy, but bright, more focus. I'm getting bad headaches, like something is poking at my brain. And I'm not paranoid, I'm just trying to deal with the fact that I was attacked by a procession of ghosts and my fiancé went missing after he underwent some kind of transformation and fought one demon. Eh, screw you. Quit looking at me like that!"

Keala gazes at her with a wide smile, "I'm just saying, it's really one hell of a coincidence that you are going through exactly what I went through.

You are in the same boat I was when I lost Ikaika. Except, I wasn't a total crackhead tweaker like you, but we are going to get through this. As long as you stay calm and take it nice and easy. Nice and relaxed, mellow, mellooooow."

"Shut up, creepy witch. Tiki was growing Ikaika's weed. Captain Cannabis. So strange. What if it was this stupid pakalolo plant causing all this trouble? For real. He only had a few plants, but they were getting more buds than they could get rid of. It was helping him with the headaches, but what if it was giving them the maka 'ike? The blessing and the curse."

"You're so frickin' weird right now. You know what Akila wrote a couple of days ago?" Keala locks stares with her sister. "The Lord God has set before us a blessing and a curse. God gave man this world as a gift. Man revolted, paradise fell. The rebel leads his followers deeper into the dark caverns at the midnight hour of perverse imagination."

"He's three years old." Alana raises an eyebrow.

"Yes, akua noho - a spirit takes possession of people and speaks through them, as a medium. Sound familiar?" Keala doesn't blink.

Alana also doesn't blink, "Yes, Tiki would leave his body and something else, like an ancestor, would take control of his pen. Aren't you scared for your keiki?"

"Well, no. 'O ka pono lo'u ala hele - my course is righteousness. Anyways, this is the Omega Prophecy. History is woven from two strands. One formed in the fall of satan and one golden thread of salvation of Yahweh. The curse and the blessing."

"You're smoking the weed." Alana finally breaks the stare and blinks.

"So, we got rules. Ok? Na'au'aua hele - to wander about in grief is kapu (forbidden). Cool head main thing. So what we have here is akua noho. In your case, ho'akaku - you're seeing a vision. He po'e 'a'a hewa - people acting wickedly. Popouli 'a'aki - a night so dark, it bites with teeth. This dream you had, it was not our ancestors teaching us or warning us. Ho 'ike

100

a ka po - revelations from the gods, no, not this. What you are seeing is something different. Kona ha'i maoli 'ana i kona hewa - the true confession of his offense."

"Who's confession? What are you even talking about?" Alana's eyes bulge.

"E maka 'ino aku ia i kona hoahanau - his eye shall be evil toward his brother. That's who."

"Eh?" Alana's eyes really bulge.

"The koheoheo - the poisonous-natured person!" Keala tugs on Alana's hair.

"Eh?"

"Sister, maybe I'm looking into this all wrong, but we're all having the second sight here. Except you were attacked. What if you are somehow tuned in to your attacker? I mean, you have a definite connection that we don't have. You were in the presence of this demon. 'Imi a ho'akoakoa - to search for and gather. You have to be the one to solve this puzzle."

"Eh? Fock that shit."

"Uh, you really don't have a choice. Do you? 'O mo'o lau ke ala e - a path beset by many monsters. I know it's scary, but our enemy is revealing himself and you have to learn everything you can. You're the only one who has this connection."

"Oh, like hell I do. This doesn't make sense." She tries to submerge but her sister won't let her go under.

"It does. Your blood was spilled. Your attacker's blood was spilled." Keala tries to reason. "There is a connection, you are tuned in. Only you can see this. Puni hai - you cannot run off in fear."

"I cannot run off at all. I cannot hide from this if he is in my head already! And you're making it worse!"

"Alana, if we knew what you were seeing, or dreaming, we could learn from this and maybe figure out where all this is going. It's not like you can stop it, so you might as well find some more clues for us. Meanwhile, don't get discouraged. You are under the protection and your child will be a great warrior. Ok? So, is the crack whore ready for some stew?"

Sitting at the table with her nose over a steaming bowl, Alana giggles while Akila sings to her, "Maika'i Kaua'i, hemolele I ka malie. Beautiful Kaua'i, peaceful in the calm."

"I can just sit and listen to you sing all day little Kila. You're just the cutest thing ever." Alana coos.

He smiles across the table at her, "Oh, good. Mom said I have to sing because music calms the savage beast."

"Oh, did she now. Well, you just keep on singing. It keeps me from getting headaches. I cannot believe you caught the fish, that's amazing. You're a little fisherman, just like your father. Keala, so let me get this straight. You moved off O'ahu in 1982, and got married at a little church in Hanapepe. And Ikaika had a house in Kekaha? I wasn't invited to the wedding so I didn't know anything about that."

"No, you were invited to the wedding. Except, your fat ass wouldn't leave O'ahu
and you disapproved of me moving to Kaua'i. Have you tried the ginger and pineapple with the fish?" Keala slides the bowl over.

"Ok, fine. I promised mom that I would always watch over you but I could not leave O'ahu. You pissed me off and look how kapakahi (all mixed up) things got. Bad shit happens when we're apart. I did not disapprove, but we're stronger together. So what happened then?"

102

Keala shrugs, "In October, Ikaika and his two cousins boarded a ship set for Alaska. It was a new commercial fishing and research vessel and an overseas company. All three Pa'i boys on one ship, mana'o 'ino (bad idea). They didn't know that much about it, but they were recruiting an experienced Hawaiian crew and it paid well enough for him to leave my ass for four frickin' months.

Before he left, Ikaika passed his physical and brought a stack of waivers, insurance papers, non-disclosure agreements home to sign and notarize. Full benefits for us. He couldn't pass it up even though we knew fishing Alaska was dangerous.

On the first night after he left, the moe 'ino (nightmare) began. I was hearing owls in my sleep, talking to me, whispering in my bedroom, hovering above me in the daytime. I was having visions of Ikaika being devoured by owls, then turning into one himself. I was waking up in the morning screaming.

The visions of Ikaika covered in feathers. I saw him rising in the clouds with the masses of pueo screeching cries of battle. I dreamed of Ikaika being impaled at the top of an icy Heiau (shrine) with ancient priests and warriors all worshipping, praying for him. All covered in snow, they lowered him into the earth and graciously buried him like Ali'i (royalty). I kept telling myself it was all just a bad dream. I was so sad being alone, but no way was I going to go crying back to your couch.

Ikaika returned home in the middle of November, alone, weathered, beaten, and changed. Something happened to him in Alaska, but he would not speak of it. We slept for two days together. It felt like two days. But there was no more time to rest. Hurricane Iwa was marching right towards us. He started working on the house because he knew the storm was going to steer northeast at us, he knew it was coming for him. We braced for the storm surge. The morning it hit, I opened my eyes and he was gone. He took nothing, no trace, just gone.

The storm grazed the southern tip of Kaua'i on the twenty-third and I cried alone in my dark home. The terrible clouds and the black sky circled over me and hammered the walls, shaking the foundation. The wind began screaming through the roof and all I could do was scream back. Iwa peeled the roof up and ripped the walls away, spiraling up into the atmosphere.

I just sprawled on the floor, waiting to be washed out to sea. But, sand was getting pushed up the yard, churning with the wind. The sand started to build up, covering what was left of the walls, swirling higher and higher,

103

taller than the roof. The angry wind was blocked out. I felt the impact of the storm surge against my sandy tomb. The waves washed over the top, but the sand soaked up the foamy ocean water. I lied on my back, staring through the eye of my sand dune, into the eye of the storm as it passed to the north.

I woke up to the calmness of the storm just passed, but I was sick. All that remained was the floor and Ikaika's favorite chair. I just sat in the chair and stared out at the leveled neighborhood, dead still and quiet. The storm's energy soaked into the earth and left a static charge in the thick air.

I sat quiet all morning in that chair until this black Ford rental car rolled up. I started getting that anxiety, that panicked feeling from those bad dreams. A couple of lawyer-looking men handed me a stack of papers to sign and gave me a black suitcase. A letter from the company that owned Ikaika's boat, Paragon Research Fleet deeply regretted to inform me that their ship, the 'Ubiquitous' was lost at sea.

I had to sign papers acknowledging the loss. They ripped the bottom yellow copy and gave me the suitcase. I watched them drive away, swerving around the broken trees. I opened the case and found stacks of focking cash. I always thought opening a case full of money would be more, da kine, gratifying. But I signed that yellow paper. I accepted their lies and they legally bought my silence.

I was alone. So much of the island had been destroyed so I kind of felt lucky to have all that cash and a comfy chair. I helped people in my neighborhood with the clean up, trying to forget my troubles. You could only imagine my surprise when I found Ikaika's cousin, Kaleo wandering around in the mud.

The same fockin' Kaleo that was supposed to be on Ikaika's ship. His home was nearby and he invited me to stay with him until I figured out what to do. Something was wrong with that guy though. I did not feel comfortable around him. Something happened to him on that trip to Alaska and he was really disturbed.

He wouldn't eat, wouldn't sleep, never left his room and could not answer any questions about what the hell happened to them. He was having nightmares about the heiau like I was, so he stopped sleeping. I was getting scared every time I asked him about Alaska and Ikaika. Was guilt.

As soon as the bank opened, I paid off all the bills and then found this construction shack in Brenneckes where they were supposed to develop a new neighborhood, but stopped because of the storm. I bought it from the developers, changed back to my maiden name and never went back to Kaleo's. I hated to leave him like that, but he was rotting away, constantly smoking this repugnant chemical out of this glass pipe to keep himself awake. It was the guilt that he made it home and his brother and Kaik's didn't. He was lost and I left before he forgot I was there to help him. I promise to stop by and check on him now and then.

It was really no surprise that I discovered Paragon Research Fleet did not exist. I found no records of the company or the boats or the employers, nothing. But I was pregnant and alone and vulnerable and no one was coming after me. My dreams were telling me - child of the owl, whose father is not known. The guardian owl belongs to heaven and earth. The owl who sings of war, the owl as a protector in battle. These things you were chanting in your little acid nap."

Keala snaps her fingers, "Akila, how long has she been asleep?"

"I'm not sure. She hasn't moved since you started talking. Try check to see if her eyeballs are pointing to the front or to the back." Akila starts cleaning up the dishes.

"At least she's not convulsing and yelling spooky shit." Keala shrugs and continues eating.

He pauses, "Should I keep playing the ukulele?"

She nods, "You know what, bring the dishes to the sink and then keep playing. I like her quiet like this. Let's not take any chances."

Alana wakes on the couch. The morning sun is medicine. Her body is so sluggish. She's heavier than before she fell asleep, but with buoyancy. The ebb and flow of current to her womb feels substantially more immense. She fights herself from crying at the time lost.

The voice comes from just behind her ear, "Well, what did you see this time?"

Alana jerks, "I watched our children grow up, that's what." She latches on to her sister for startling her. "They learned to surf, like their fathers."

105

"This whole time, you dreamed of them surfing? Just like their fathers." Keala starts breakfast for them. "We noticed you weren't convulsing, snorting, growling, pissing, puking."

"Ya. Nothing to snarl about really. I felt like I was there watching them all day. Go surf, go fight each other. They would sit and fish all night. Ka ni ka pila (playing music) in the shade. Singing, playing the ukulele. The were so sweet singing songs to me, dancing hula, carving wood. I was just sitting with them all day, all night, watching them learn and grow right here at this house. We were together, but they were older already. I feel like I was older too, like I am older. I was hibernating like one bear. Except, I felt I had power, power to manifest this dream into our reality and I never wanted to wake up."

"Oh, awesome. Akila will be happy to know. He's been playing the ukulele for a month straight, keeping you calm this whole time. His fingers get sore, or he has to go shi-shi, and then I would take over. Then, you start snarling at me, and you piss me off and hurt my feelings and I give the thing back to Akila for go play for you." Keala glares.

"I don't know. Maybe I just like his song better." Alana tries to smile.

Keala crosses her arm, "It's the same damn song. I teach him new songs because he gets tired of playing the same shit all day."

"I don't know, you sing so pretty even though you talk like drunk Popeye. Maybe there's sadness in your voice."

Keala shrugs and has the Spam and eggs over the rice ready, "What ever. I got plenty other shit to do anyways. You can change your own damn diaper."

"I'm wearing a frickin' diaper?" Alana pulls up her mu'u mu'u (slip-on dress).

Keala sticks a fork into the rice and slides the plate over, "Ya, you're wearing a frickin' diaper or you're hibernating in the sand down at the beach."

Alana digs in, "You know what, that actually sounds more better than wearing a frickin' diaper."

Akila yells through the window, "See! I told you she likes the beach mo' better!"

Alana glares back at her sister, "Do you leave me out in the sand? For how long? Wait, did you say a whole month already? A fockin' month?"

"Yes, one month already. Get over it. We made a sled and would take you fishing. And usually only for as long as it takes to catch one fish. Hard to say. Sometimes the fish bite, sometimes the fish no bite. But, this whole month, you never saw clues to this attacker, this villain?"

"A month? That's why my belly is so much bigger. No. Not really. Nothing. I was so immersed in the learning, the farming, the songs. I was happy to be spending so much time, even if it was only a dream. I felt like we were really teaching them, real living reality. Not just wasted time unconscious." Alana becomes saddened again.

Keala reasons, "You know what, I always wondered what made Akila such a fast learner. What I think is that your wacky little brain is really one open channel and the guidance of our ancestors is flowing through you, into our sons. This is the same channel that is allowing you to peek into the guilty mind of our demon. Causing you to be a strung-out junky, crapping on my futon. But still yet, there's a good reason for me to have to scrub your pilau okole (filthy butt) every week."

Alana is confused, "Wait. You actually leave me in one dirty diaper for a whole week?"

"Sister, you only go kukae (eliminate waste) but once a week! I don't feed you. No need. It's amazing you stay momona (large) like that."

Alana growls, "I'm the same size as you, you heifer!"

"Just so you know, I leave you in the bath for days. Just salt and lipoa (seaweed). Sometimes you go underwater for hours and don't drown. It's impossible, but you seem to be alright. You're so weird." Keala pours coffee but doesn't share.

"Is that why I smell like seaweed, and tuberose? Well shit, that's why I still feel like I'm underwater. Seriously, I'm still sloshing around like I'm underwater, or drunk. Probably just a full diaper. You know how the sunlight looks hazy and streaky when you swim for too long? There is a residual high I'm trying to cope with. But at least I don't feel suicidal this morning. I feel my baby is happy, he's already learning." Alana reaches for the guava nectar, "You know what makes our boys happy? Fighting. I've already seen it, a lot. Fighting and fishing. There's some other 'F' words I hope I don't have to watch, but fighting and fishing mostly.
You know I watch them fight when they surf. Not like local mokes being bullies to haole's in the line up. But using their surfboards like clubs, flying up, over the wave and kicking their boards into people's face. I watch them do this and I feel proud. But, I try to look at the people they fight with - and I cannot see their faces. In fact, all the people I see them pummeling, I can never see their faces. Only the faces of our sons. They're so handsome, and they're so good at everything. Especially the fighting. There is a name for every fighting stroke, even their fight-surfing."

Keala wipes tears from her sister's eyes, "You mean you cannot see these faces like you cannot see the face of Tiki's attacker? Just blank, just black? Ya?"

Alana nearly drops her juice, "Hooo, you're right! This is a clue. I can see this, but I cannot see this." Her hands are so clumsy, "I am getting better. One of these times, I need to convulse into a bad trip again. I need to take another snarl nap and get more clues. Why don't you sing me a song?"

"Oh, you think you're really funny. Ya? Try wait and find out where you wake up next. But for reals, we are going to avoid the acid naps until after the baby is born. When you get high, your baby gets high. I guess I got seven more months of diaper duty still yet. Unless, you can stay awake and wipe your own okole (bottom)."

Alana sympathizes, "I'll stay awake as long as I can. But if I go moe moe (sleep), I promise to keep teaching our future sons all the good kind stuff. Don't worry. I got it under control."

"Well..." Keala gently pats the top of her sister's head, "You really don't have it under control." Alana slaps her hand away and glares up at her. Keala explains in a soft voice, "Now, just take is easy there sister. You did this with your own fingernail..." Keala unravels the cloth and bandages around Alana's wrists, "You don't remember this do you? See, we thought you were wide awake, acting all normal and shit. And then, out of nowhere, in the middle of the grocery store parking lot, you went totally banana's on these two haole ladies. Your damn eyes rolled in the back of your head, you starting screaming 'Bosol! Bosol!' And then you went grabbed one lady, bent her the fock over, and acted like you was pounding her up her scrawny white ass. It was really embarrassing. Then you stabbed your wrist and dug your damn nails all the way up to your elbow. Luckily those two old ladies ran off because you was spurting blood out all over the groceries. So embarrassing taking you anywhere."

Alana gapes at the sutures in her forearm. "Are you telling me I did this to myself? With my own damn fingernails? I don't even remember going shopping."

Akila walks past with clean folded towels, "We sand them down every couple of days so we don't go through that again." He reaches over and touches the tip of Alana's thumb with his finger. The arcing flash suddenly rips up her spine. A bright flash of light blinds Alana for a spell before it fades to red, then to black.

From opposite sides of the darkness, "You must tell me now that you accept my hand in marriage and you choose to love me eternally. Your ancestors will flow through me. My ancestors will flow through you. The souls you collect will enflame passion in my soul. And my eternal strength will strengthen you."

"Yes. I choose to love you and accept this bond. I will comply with your initiation ritual. There is however, only one way to proceed. I must state my intention to die by my own hand. It is necessary to regain my honor in this manner. Ishii will not take this away from me. He is still bound by this tradition. I need more time."

"This you call, Seppuku?"

"Yes, I believe he will give me the opportunity to die by my own sword, for his cause. He will allow this to play out and not interfere."

"You are willing to risk this? Why? You are still plotting to murder him. Are you not? He wants you dead, just as he killed your father. The reports he makes you type, your research data - are already sold to the Americans. They are sold to grant him amnesty, not you. The Americans want to study your war crimes and have already promised him asylum. All your treachery, your human experimentation and torture, your plague weapons, are going to earn him a fortune and a new life of freedom under the white oppressors after the war - that is his contingency plan. But, only if you are dead. I will not risk what I have built on him honoring your traditions. You must commit to me and forget this lust for revenge."

"Please, listen. He thinks he detonated it already. The device I am typing on is the weapon. He must already be suspicious of this contradiction. He surely has a unit on the way here. He needs to know if there has been a malfunction with this device, if I discovered a way to override it, or if I somehow found a way to survive the pathogens. There have been only two cases of survival after a detonation. It is a puzzle we have yet to understand. I will report this discovery. What is that smoke seeping down from that vent? There is some psychoactive compound in it. I felt it since I arrived. I smell that in my dreams."

"You believe your commander will be interested in something like that? You know cannabis, yes?"

"That is not cannabis. I have cannabis."

"That is the mother of all herb. The only reason you are still alive is because they are all smoking this herb in the dancehall and it is seeping down here. They wanted to kill you and steal all your equipment, so I gave them the herb stalk. When they run out, then they will come to kill you and steal all your equipment. This herb is what opened up your mind for me to visit. It's a portal to dreams."

"This herb enabled a portal to my dreams? This subject is of great interest. Discovering a psychoactive agent of this potency will pique a notable tangent to my agenda. This will buy us time. I need more time before I leave to New Orleans."

"This herb, you want me to share with the general who wants to murder you and all my people? Few throughout history have ever smoked this original strain. It can only be grown correctly under a rare, exotic permaculture environment. I would sacrifice my entire island before I share this herb stalk with him. But you think he would not kill you for this?"

"Yes, I already reported my interest in the cannabis on the first day, and they responded urgently. This is a significant dream-state catalyst. This is the element you spoke of earlier? Yes?"

"Not exactly, mon cheri. It merely makes you more receptive. And in this receptive mode, you can manifest a great many things. It will take five days to teach you this. Your ceremony will take five days and then I will take you to New Orleans myself. This will keep them from coming after you? This will keep your family alive. And you will have the honor of serving your mission. But you must commit to me. And no more talk of seppuku. There is no honor in squandering your soul. Shall we have a go?"

"Wait. I'm not following this timeline of events. There appears to be contradictions in the chain of actions you just described."

"Tout a fait, l' amoureux. I am not necessarily bound to your physical reality. That is not how I work with your dimension. I have transference across several planes of existence and manifest spiritual energy throughout different realms simultaneously."

"Do I exist in different realms?"

"You are not ready to learn this."

"Am I to learn of this after my ceremony?"

"I think you already know more than you know. That is why I chose you. And you chose me. Would it surprise you to learn we already have children in another existence? It is but fate that we become lovers here and now. I only need you to acknowledge this union."

"We have twins. Yes?"

"Exactement. You already know this to be true. Your racist purebred ideology is but a weakness. Our creole twins blend across dimensions with spiritual transference and dominate the crossbred DNA with native species. Ancient beasts like the serpent have dominant DNA and exist in other dimensions, like sharks, turtles, cats, eagles. Our twins can merge with them, use them. Our creole twins can merge with your unborn Japanese twins and become gods in other worlds.

Do you see how primitive your masters are to me? What do I care of their mortal schemes to dominate this earthly prison? While their savagery ends in every other existence, ours will flourish. If I speak in riddles and contradictions, it is only because I already know how this all played out in other realms. It is all the same, it is fate. But you are mine. And I am yours. You only have to commit."

"When do we begin?"

"Sweet child, my hounsi are already on their way."

# Ka Lele ‘O Ka Pueo

## The Flight of the Owl

"Oh, you and Kaleo, eh? I always knew you had a thing for him. Was just a matter of time." Keala chuckles. "So nasty."

"Wait, what? Oh fock no. Please don't wake me up like that sister." Alana struggles to open her eyes and sit up. "What was it you always said to me? Eh? I would drive Tiki away and Kaleo was the only person dumb enough to put up with me. Always trying to get me to move to Kaua'i with you so you wouldn't go alone. And you went used the lolo-est one as bait? What's wrong with my eyes?"

"And yet, here you are. He's still available you know." Keala stuffs pillows behind Alana's head, "No seriously, went dodged the bullet there. He's a total fockin' tweaker. You would murder him - he's that stupid. Him and his big brother. But they were good on a ship and the boys watched over each other. And you helped us with another clue!"

"I what? Ya?" Alana wiggles gingerly, squirming off the atrophy.

"Ya. Unfortunately, Kaleo's my only link to finding Ikaika. Usually, he's really scary and disgusting. But we went found one pattern on his calendar. The nights you snarl his name the worst was on the 27th moon phase. That's when every frickin' owl on da island perches on my gutters and shits all over my lanai (porch) furniture. And you know, I cannot get mad at them because they're just trying to get my attention. So cute, like lovebirds. But in some other parts of the world maybe a parrot could just say some words. But here, oh- we got so much bird shit I gotta put saw dust on the ground so you don't slip on your way to get the water hose. But, that's actually when crackhead lolo-boy scores his crank. Ya, just before the New Moon and the tide swings level out. But just right before that, you know, he really mellows out. I mean, he usually goes steal shit from the neighborhood, he tweaks it all up, and then sells the stolen shit back to his neighbors. They all seem to like him."

Alana has trouble focusing her eyes, "So what, how did you find this out? You went spied on him? I know it already!"

"Ya. I went broke in his house and saw his maritime calendar."

Alana tries to glare her crossed eyes in her sister's direction, "I thought you said don't go there!"

"Nah, nah, nah. I said YOU don't got there. Not until Lono is born. Then he's all yours. Skanky tramp." Keala pets the top of Alana's head.

She spots the calendar on the wall and sees the picture of lehua flowers is different. "So what, that's it? I lost a whole month of my life for what? Your big clue, hmm? The crackhead went scored some crack?"

Keala signals for Akila to fetch the ukulele, "Ok then. Getting a little crabby there. Now don't worry about that so much. You're safe and healthy. The keiki is safe and healthy. Time goes by for all of us sister. It was actually two months this time. Aw, please don't cry. Please don't..." She snaps her fingers for Akila to skip the tuning and just start playing a song. "Listen sweetie, what you're doing is very important. It's very important to me, to all of us. You've been chanting about Ikaika, the pueo, Lika, Kaleo. It's all we've got. It's all I've got. Right before dawn everyday, we see a flash of light behind your eyelids. You're just so much easier to deal with when you're asleep."

"Wait, what?" Alana's eyes are not quite synchronized yet.

"Ya. I mean, I never told you that my last night with Ikaika was like one out-of-body kind experience. Because, when I say it was like a dream... or like one dream come true... I mean I was in a dream state when he walked through that door. And I don't mean like he's got one big bambucha, or like the way he makes me feel and I missed him so much... but like, I was blinded by the intensity of that moment. Like falling in a dream. Then I woke up with my house destroyed and I knew he was gone."

"The flash of light. What is going on?" Alana requires a slow, deep breath.

"Oh. Ya, just like the green flash when the sun sets on the ocean. But, like, coming out of your skull. That's the magic hour. We think it's a flash of a different image each time. Like one old cartoon animation. You know the kind, when you went draw on the corner of your notebook and

116

then flip the pages and the shit moves. Ya? But we kept seeing your eyelids light up and wondered what was going on in there."

"Oh. Ya. For sure. That seems a little strange don't you think? What kind of light comes from someone's head? Like, from inside my head? Ya? That's disturbing to me. Where are you leading me with this? How freakin' bizarre is this conversation going to get?" Alana peers around the room with the eyes of a clumsy chameleon.

"Well, your slow ass was taking so long. Could not tell there was a pattern with all the weird stuff that goes on with you. We were just drinking coffee and kind of noticed the flash and glow. No telling how long it was happening before we investigated. So, we had to stare at you every morning until we saw the pattern." Keala peers into her sister's eyes, "We really want to try and speed you up. But since you're so hapai (pregnant), no can. No can, so we're going to slow me down. Ya?" Keala and Akila nod and smile at each other. They have waited a while for this pitch.

"I knew it!" Alana blurts. "You went hang out with cousin crackhead one time and your manini (tiny) little brain stay lolo (crazy) already! Only took once, I told you! I seriously don't know what you're telling me right now. It sounds like bad news. And really stupid."

Keala chuckles, "Ah, you bugger. So funny. Just shut your furry clam and listen. Ya? First, he hasn't even seen us yet. He don't know nothing! The 27th moon phase and the New Moon ain't until next week. So, he's the most normal this week."

"You're less normal this week." Alana closes her eyes to rest and reset.

"Right before he scores his shit, he makes some kind of ritual. Coincidently, that's when the owls gather. He drinks the kava kava and then he goes lays in the tide pool for days. I really think he's drowning himself." Keala explains and wipes the tears from Alana's face.

"And this is important because why? What the fock you need me to do?" Alana looks up when Akila stops playing and swivels a Shaka to his mom. Her eyes close and she sinks back into the pillow. "Oh, the both of you's, eh? Akila, I need you to tell your mom that whatever this is - is stupid. And stop trying to be so nice and calm at me. It only makes it worse."

"It's ok sister. Just chill." Keala uses her soothing voice, "You just have to stand by the road and feed the chickens. Ok? That's all you gotta do. I thought you wanted to get out the house."

Alana bobbles her head up towards the morning sun, "You like me to go feed Kaleo's chickens? Why?"

Keala wrings out the warm soapy towel she uses only for Alana's face. "Ya. He's uh, got a perimeter of chickens around his yard. They will make noise and alert Kaleo. So feed them and make friends. So they stay quiet."

Akila reasons, "He tries to train stray dogs, but they always run away. He has security chickens."

Alana rubs the soap out of her eyes. "You two have been at this for a while. After two months? And your little brain came up with a real clunker."

"Ya. Since the first night." Keala massages her sister's neck.

"Since the first night what?" She pushes her hands away.

"Since the first night you came here. Sister, if all I was getting out of you was just your snarling acid naps and humping old haole ladies in the parking lots, your pilau okole (dirty butt) would be sleeping in the cave. But the hour right before dawn, you calm down and get really still. That's usually when we clean you up and give you soup. And then we hold your eyelids open and point you at the ceiling above the bathtub. Then we wait for your eyes to roll around and flash an image, like one slide show projector. Except it's just one flash of one image, once a day and it's really frickin' slow. That's why we need to go steal some weed tomorrow."

"WOT?!" Alana pushes her sister away. "Wait. What?"

"And some kava." Keala high-fives Akila and smiles.

"And that's why you want me to go feed the fockin' chickens while Kaleo drowns himself? You like break into his frickin' crack house? And steal his shit? So stupid!" Alana slouches her face down into her hands, "Is that why my eyes are all wacko? You're sticking your filthy fockin' paws in my eyeballs everyday? Eh, remember how I said I felt like my home was bugged? You think they're not watching him? Let me tell you this - the night before Tiki vanished, two guys tried to steal Tiki's weed that he was growing in the Kau brother's yard. They were attacked by a wild pig. That's when all the shitty things started happening. Tiki vanished! The Kau brothers vanished! The night marchers went threw me in the ocean for two weeks. I'm telling you, what if it's this fockin' weed that's causing all these problems? It's the same weed that Ikaika was growing here and then gave to Tiki to grow on O'ahu. You don't think I know about that?" Alana finds an angle where she can give dirty looks to her sister and nephew simultaneously.

"And what if it's this same weed that's going to help us see how to solve these problems? You gotta admit, those boys were all very, the kind, *receptive*." Keala tries to reason.

"Ya. Ok. We got the thieving loner pot-head single mom and her epileptic suicidal sister with Tourettes syndrome! This is getting so much worse. This whole time I was struggling to find answers locked away in the back of my head. It itches inside my head! Like an old radio with loose screws blaring static. You have no idea how frustrating it is to rip through a seizure for a whole month straight and come out with nothing. Worse than nothing- complete moronic bullshit. Why am I doing this to myself? I thought having the baby would help keep this all straight for me." Alana starts crying again. "How come I have to go through all this, and your ideas just keep getting worse?"

"Honey, I did the exact same thing. Alone. I didn't realize it wasn't just a dream until this one came along." She pulls her son in close. "At least you have us watching over you." Keala hugs them both.

119

Akila starts chanting in his sweet voice, "Aia i ka opua ke ola. Aia i ka opua ke ola. Aia i ka opua ke ola."

Alana is soothed. She gazes at the keiki, glowing in the morning sun. The static attenuates and she tunes in. Her eyes finally focus, "Life is in the clouds. Tiki used to chant that to me. We used to lay in the shade, watch the keiki's swim and play. He'd wait for the sun to almost go down. And he'd sit at the shore break and wait to see if there'd be a green flash for him when the sun hit the horizon. That's when he would paddle out for go surf. He'd tell me he knew all the ways to make me happy by how the colors ran across the clouds at sunset. Of course, he would also light up a doobie and try to make important decisions based on how the smog flew out while he was hacking his lungs up. Whatevers, I think it's a bad idea. And what, you going to get high and then what exactly? You going to jump in the bathtub with me and poke me in the eye with your grubby fingers?"

"Don't be silly. We all cannot fit in the bathtub. We're going down the beach to the salt ponds."

"Ok. And then?"

"And then we honihoni (kiss, greeting, press foreheads together and sniff) until our minds connect and then we see what we can see. Don't look at me like that, because I'm going to be more, you know the kind, *receptive*. We read all about this in Tiki's journal already. He wrote about it and never tried it with you because you never like smoke the pakalolo. We think it's worth a try. It's your boyfriend's idea, why wouldn't you give it a shot?" Keala adjusts the tuning pegs while Akila strums softly.

"You been reading his journal? Ok. Fine then. But what if we both start having seizures and don't wake up for a month or two? Who's going to take care of Akila? And why does he have a knife? Who let's their keiki cruise around with a knife?"

"It's my carving knife. Good for wood, fish, I use it in the garden. I made you one nice cane auntie. I carved the plumeria on the handle, your favorite. We use the sawdust for the bird shit." Akila is so proud to show off his work.

"That seems strange. Akila? Is that fish you're cooking in there? Did you catch, clean and cook that fish by yourself? Do you do all your mommy's chores around here? What did I frickin' miss? What *is* the date today? I'm awake one day out of the frickin' month and everything seems really lolo around here. You know, I knew I was tumbling down a mad rabbit hole coming here with you, but wow. Maybe I should go stay with Auntie Rubie for a while."

"No can. Only we are meant to see this. No one else can be a part of this. This dark cloud is for us alone." Keala leans back on the futon and pulls her sister to a tight snuggle in the warming morning sun. "Who else could survive this? This is our path. And what if the owls follow you and shit on auntie's truck?"

Riding in Keala's truck through a light mist, Alana peers out towards the drenched, luscious foothills. Each droplet sparkles like a diamond in the moonlight through the darkness. This is what she remembers of her mother. She recalls riding in the car at night, little girls trying to stop their mother from crying. "Maikaʻi Kauaʻi, hemolele i ka malie. (Beautiful Kauaʻi, peaceful in the calm)." Alana witnesses the mist thicken into a dull fog around them. "Except for when the Hunakaʻi sisters drive into town. Then it's 'Hana mao ʻole ka ua o Hilo'. (Endlessly pours the rain of Hilo)." She feels everything pretty evaporate around them. "Ka hale koʻekoʻe o ka po. (the cold house of darkness, death). So what, we're just passing showers everywhere we go? Just dark clouds all the time. Depressing sometimes to be out here, nobody talks to us, we don't talk to nobody. I mean they wave, but we're invisible. Why we always gotta get up and go before dawn?"

"Less people out before dawn. Dawn Patrol. It's a small island. Misty dawns are like normal, so we fit in better. Dood, you growled at the minister in front of the Korean church and was yelling 'dirty focking shit fock' at him for no reason. He was trying to pull you inside the church for an exorcism. That's why we dawn patrol. Where did you even get that?

That's some stupid shit the Pa'i brothers say when they fock shit up, except their eyes don't roll in the back of their head.

Anyways. Everybody knows I stay sad for Ikaika. We were all hurting after hurricane Iwa. But, they give me my space, it's better this way. I don't like to answer questions, so people don't ask. But it's rainbows and sunshine at our little Hale Koa (House of the Warrior). Try watch, Hanapepe is going to get real foggy. Any kind of tragedy makes the place foggy, especially for us. Especially fishing village kind. Fog follows sad spirits. Like the kind, San Francisco. Ya? The boys always talked story about the Dungeness crab there. And that's what Kaleo's house smells like, by the way. But more like Chinatown because he likes to burn the incense."

"And I bet his house has one dark cloud too. Because that's what we do to people. Out spreading the madness." Alana turns towards the window.

"Oh. Ok then. Kila, surf wax in the ears please." Akila motions as if he is really stuffing a wad into his ear canal. "I thought we agreed we were sharing my perspective on this. Why don't you snack on some cereal and keep that stupid clam of yours busy. Eh?" Keala turns up the radio.

"Oh, well. For sure. You think this dark cloud is to protect us from them? It's to protect them from us." Alana whispers.

Keala keeps her eyes on the road and whispers back, "Mom had to protect us from him after he lost it. Dad saw, heard, or felt something that made him snap. She was fiercely loyal to him and chose to drive over the cliff with him so he wouldn't go alone. Everyone has a limit. He freaked out and we were not safe."

"Bulia. (You lie.)" Alana straightens in the seat harness. "We drove him mad and mom felt guilty because she passed this maka 'ike on to us. She left us. In such a bizarre manner, just like Tiki and Ikaika-them."

"You know, that's why I don't let you drive. You think we would rid the world of our dark cloud if we drove over the cliff? We are going to ride this thing out and use the maka 'ike to see. I mean really see some shit. You just don't want to help us. You think we're attracting all the bad things in our lives. Except, we're revealing things no one else can see." Keala turns the radio down.

"Go ahead. I just don't want to have a baby in your twisted little crack house. If you're gonna be the next addict, you go stay with the lolo cousin and leave me and Akila to have the baby without you. You're gonna be his crack ho." Alana mumbles.

"You serious? It's weed and kava root. I know you think I have addictive tendencies, but I can handle this. This is something we have to do. It's worth the risk. Wrestling with you every morning is gonna take us forever. Now flip your fur muncher into a smile because here we are."

Before Alana can unfasten the seat harness, Akila is already out through the hole in the roof. She watches him disappear into the mist. "Where's he going? I gotta go shi-shi too."

"Really? Then you gotta go by the back of the truck. He's hiking maka'i (ocean), we're hiking mauka (mountain)." Keala grabs the bag and shuts the door quietly.

"Wait. He was supposed to stay with me. Right, ya?" Alana takes her new wooden cane and continues looking behind her where Akila vanished.

"Nah. He's going along the shore and he's going to climb a tree. We're going up the trail behind Kaleo's house. We just gotta make sure he's not at home still yet. I want Akila up in the tree so he can make sure he's still drowning himself in his little pool while we go spock the house. If Kaleo's not there, then Akila will come by and get you back to the truck. Now, you can handle this, right? Ya? Fast kind. In and out. I promise, nothing weird is going to happen. Trust me."

"Hold on. Why do you want the keiki climbing up a tree?" Alana holds onto her sister's arm, checking behind and up front.

123

"Well, Kaleo sometimes crawls through the grass like a, like a, like one cat. Don't worry about Kila. He's done this before. I'm worried about you. Ok? What do we do if something comes slithering up in the grass like one cat? Ya? We go the other way fast kine. Got it? Ok sister, you have an important job. Now, just keep walking down this trail until there's no more fence. He's the last house. Just stay on the trail and when you get to the last kukui tree, you will see a chicken. Feed the chicken. More chickens will come. Just toss the Cheerios until you run out, and then quietly walk back to the truck. No worries. Stay quiet. No weird shit, I promise. In and out." Keala pats the top of Alana's head and veers off the path of eucalyptus trees. "Just keep waddling that ways."

Alana tugs at Keala's ponytail, "Wait. Cats stalk and pounce. They don't slither. You know what slithers? A focking snake."

Keala tries to slither away, "Snakes? Nobody said snakes. I didn't say anything about fockin' snakes."

Alana has her long hair twisted around her wrist, "You didn't have to. I already knew you were about to fess up and tell me there are fockin' snakes around here."

"Eh! I wasn't about to fess up nothing. You da one that said snakes. I'm telling you, eh? I have never seen a fockin' snake around here on this island. We got the chickens. We got the mongoose." Keala unravels herself. "Go ahead and let me know when you see a fockin' snake around here, ok? But if you see something slithering at you, just go the other fockin' way. Ya? Alright?"

"Oh, bulia out your fricken' poi-hole! Are there snakes or not? You know I often dream of snakes right?" Alana tries to swing her new cane at her sister's feet.

"I'm telling you - I never actually seen a snake here before. I suspect the shit out of those slithering fockah's. Maybe they're around, hiding out, but I haven't seen one yet. And that's the truth. Bye bye." Keala backs quickly away from the trail.

"Why are you going that ways? I can't believe you're all leaving me. This is a stupid idea. Never been here before." Alana finds herself alone as the first trace of sunlight pours its purple colors over the horizon. "I can already hear the stupid chickens. And these Cheerios are stale."

Alana stops at the last kukui tree and smells the small white flowers. The first curious chicken arrives, followed by another. "Hello you little feathery friend. No worries. Just on a little walk with a bag of cereal, surrounded by a bunch of clucking chickens, and a peacock. No weird shit happening at all. We're the frickin' weirdo's around here." She cannot see up into the yard or down towards the beach through the mist. "I cannot believe she let Akila walk to the beach by himself. I hope you're safe in your tree little man."

Akila scurries along the shore towards the salt ponds before making his way into the dense palms. He moves silently up the ridge and right up into a leaning coconut tree. Akila slowly pulls the fanning leaves to cover his position. He watches his uncle, already writhing in a shallow rocky pool between the beach and the grass. Kaleo slithers out of one and slips right into another tide pool along the shoreline. The water goes still. Akila scours for movement, but nothing stirs. He holds his breath to measure the time his uncle has spent underwater. Akila quietly begins to gasp inwards after slowly expelling the last bit of air he can hold in with still no movement in the waters.

Suddenly, a rough hand swiftly moves over his mouth as he hears a raspy whisper into his ear, "Child of the owl, you're coming with me." Akila is plucked clean from his perch before he can recognize he is now pinned under Kaleo's arm. Running down the steep tree, sprinting across the sand, diving into the same tide pool he last saw his uncle dive into and disappear. Akila looks up into Kaleo's eyes just before they submerge.

Akila does not struggle. He is held still underwater for longer than he has ever been comfortable with, but now without panic. Kaleo stares into to the child's eyes and presses his forehead against Akila's. He rolls them over so only their faces surface and he whispers, "You look just like your father boy. I can't believe it. Listen up grommet. Your father keeps you a secret. You need to keep this a secret from your mom. Ok? He battles everyday, like one gladiator. They force him to sail around the world because if he doesn't, they will come after your mom. Don't tell her I know anything about your father or she will come after me. That's the deal. Lika, your father, me, we are his slaves. They will come for me and you can't be around. Don't tell your mom this stuff.

This is something you need to prepare for in case they take notice of you. You need to learn to hunt the snakes now. They're trained to watch you. And they never blink. The snakes cannot see us underwater, it's the only place you can hide from them. But you can see them clearly underwater if you fill your eyes with tears. Tears through ocean water - you can see anything evil. The sad warrior sees the real world through his own tears. Get yourself some chickens, and one good mongoose. After your cousin is born, the snakes will be watching the wahine.

Your cousin is the mano-child (shark). Shark and pueo (owl) are good hunters. You're the only one I can talk to. You're doing a good job taking care of the sisters. But don't come back here. I set traps. Your mom and your auntie should be fine. I've already deployed the peacocks. Snakes won't go near the peacock.

You need a better knife. Take this one. Your dad has one just like it. So does your uncle Lika. When a snake dies, you stick your blade down it's throat and snap off it's fangs. Snakes are nothing without the fangs. Look into the reflection of it's eyes, with venom on the blade, and you can see what the other snakes are watching before it dies - they're all connected to their owner. Snake blood and snake venom on a shiny blade make a bridge that you can see, look into the blade like a mirror into the eyes. That's why they slither on your bloody weapons. That's some weird shit, ya? I cannot even tell you about how weird the shit actually is.

That sounds strange as fock and people think I'm fockin' lolo for saying things like that. Sometimes, when I'm, you know the kind, *receptive*, I can see the image of my cousin, your father, and my brother, your uncle, as the snakes are watching them, even now, still yet. And if they are, da kine, *receptive* too, we can watch each other through the eyes of these cursed snakes. That's how I know they are alive. Like a fockin' walkie-talkie CB radio and shit. They need us to stay alive. They're not done studying us yet. But if you're looking into these windows, they're gonna be looking back through at you too.

126

Listen to me, don't come back here. I hunt snakes by your house all the time. Don't tell your mom. They won't go near your auntie's baby. Don't worry. The baby gives them this, da kine, static, the keiki has a strong charge. The snakes lose their vision, their connection, their venom, if they stay in the static like, for too long. You have the strong static too. But, da kine, that's when they are easy to kill, but useless. So strike quickly. No can see nothing in the eyes of a dead snake if they get too much, da kine, static before they die. Poisonous snakes, more potent, stronger vision. I don't know why or how we all started staring into the eyes of dead shakes... curious...

But don't forget, eh? Strike fast. And burn the snakes. Leave no trace. They don't belong on the Island. They come crawling out the guts of fockin' zombies, nasty buggers. Burn the dead bodies because they might get snakes hiding inside. Eh, you get all that?" Kaleo whispers with only his mouth and nose above the water.

Akila tries to whisper without disturbing the water's surface, "Uncle, how did you know who I was?"

Kaleo dips under and scans around the beach from under water before raising his mouth back up to the air, "I seen you before, through the eyes of the 'aumakua, the pueo that watched over us in battle. That was almost four years ago. I guess that's why we look in the eyes of the animals. Hmmm..."

"You saw me before I was born? I'm only three." Akila raises three fingers for his uncle to count.

"No, I saw you just as you are now in the eyes of our protector, the great owl, but was four years ago. You haven't seen it yet, but you will see it soon, very soon. And after you see through the eyes of the 'aumakua, you will have to be ready for the snakes to come watch you too. If you can see them, they can see you too. That's what we was afraid of all this time. We all kept you a secret but they already knew. But we fought, and battled, and thought we could die. But they won't let us die.

But let me tell you this: Watch out for the yellow eyes. You don't want them looking your way. Got it? It hunts from the darkness, but you can see it's yellow eyes reflecting, watching you. Always watching you.

Glowing through the eyes of these snakes, always watching you from far away. Let the snakes get close, when they raise their heads off the ground, swing the blade. Remember, all zombi are mesmerized by dance. Hula is the same as fighting strokes.

I'm sorry to tell you this, but you will need to fight to survive. They will only respect you if you can fight. Good fighters become their prize, prestigious and shit. I wish I could tell you more, but there are things I cannot remember. They can make you not remember. Once they take notice of you, they start making you forget. That's how they hide. Now go. Run along the shore. Don't come back here, especially on a new moon. Never on a new moon. Go little warrior."

"Uncle. Are you saying I can see my father in the eyes of a dead poisonous snake?"

"You got the mana, keiki. You got the maka 'ike, you will learn to see. Like the sisters, they got the maka 'ike so bad, they get really scary. They don't like for you to start seeing into the mana, because like I said, you never know who's looking back at you."

"Eh, one last thing. Are you trying to drown yourself, or are you hiding from snakes?" Akila is not ready to let go.

"That's how I learned how to hide from snakes. This life makes me want to drown myself. I don't want to be an addict. Don't want to be their slave. Don't want to be their trophy. That's how I learned to see past this world, through my own tears. Crying underwater, trying not to live like this anymore. Just, angry, I want revenge. Guilty for not saving my brother, not saving your father.

I cannot find a way out of this twisted, violent shit. Dying would only complicate their experiments, but I don't want to let them gain anything from my mana. I know I'm an addict. And I know they make me forget things. But being a drug addict keeps them from taking my true power, my pure mana."

Kaleo tugs the child underwater and presses their foreheads together for a sad, still moment. The feeling of electric charge buzzes into their heads. They are indeed *receptive* to each other. Akila watches his uncle's eyes fill with tears, and then the ocean water between them

128

suddenly becomes clear. Akila stares deep into the pupils of his uncle. His iris quiver as if on fire, burning from the inside. Then as quickly as they leaped into the pool, Kaleo leaps out, slithers up the sand and vanishes into the palms.

Akila climbs from the shallow pool and hops across the rocks to the sand. He doesn't stop running until he reaches the trail towards the road. He sneaks quietly through the grass towards the truck, listening to his mother arguing.

"See, he's right there. Right on time. I don't know what you were so worried about. Crapping in your diaper for nothing. Like I said, completely undetected. In and out. No weird shit, right? Now get in the truck, let's go." Keala holds the door open and waits for her sister to shake the sand off her slippers.

"That peacock was so pretty. I almost brought him with me." Alana stretches the harness into position. "Akila, where did you get that knife?"

"Kaleo gave it to me."

Alana is alarmed, "What? I thought we weren't supposed to... Oh- this was a bad idea! He wasn't supposed to see us! Did he talk to you? He talked to you didn't he?"

Akila smiles up at her, "It's ok. We were safe. He is really sad, and lonely. He said dad has a knife just like this. This time, he taught me how to kill the snakes." Akila stares at the battered six-inch blade, seeing the world reflecting off the blade.

"Oh. You mean cats. Your mother said it was cats that was slithering around in the grass. No more snakes on the island, ya? Slithering around in your own lies, you slimy skank. Wait. This time, what? How many times are we talking about here?" Alana scans the streets at the people just waking. Cars going to surf, trucks going to market, no cars following them. "Can you just slow down a little? I can't believe you talked to him. Have you ever talked to him before? And he just gave that to you?

129

Am I the only one who doesn't want to give the keiki a blade? Crap. I freegin' knew you guys was hanging out with that crackhead. That's why you're so lolo all the time."

"Eh! This is news to me! Not really." Keala reaches around and pulls the knife over to inspect it. "I had a feeling he knew we were snooping around, but thankfully, he was not ready to make contact. He doesn't want to talk to us. Hmmm, Ikaika had a knife just like this. That was sweet. Ya, no - I don't want none of his crazy mixing with my crazy."

"It's ok auntie. We never talked before. One other time, he didn't know I was there, but he showed me how to carve the wood, but without talking or looking at me. And one other, other time, he was tying fishing knots real slow, like teaching me but pretending not to see me hiding. That's all. This is the first time he said anything."

Akila tries to calm her down. "He said I look just like my father. He said he could see things when he was more, the kind, *receptive*, just like mom said. I think this is going to work. And the tide pool, he said the tide pool is the safe place. See auntie, this plan is going to work just fine."

Akila leans over and presses his forehead to Alana's. "Honihoni, that's the trick. Just like Tiki wrote in the journal. Just relax, we got it all under control. Nothing weird, I mean he's a little weird. But cannot make things any more weird. Ya?"

Alana floats in the shallow rock tide pool, surrounded by sand. The small waves of high tide barely make it over the ledge to give her ripples. She splashes at her sister's back and laughs at almost extinguishing the doobie, "You're not even coughing. That's what the boys always say - if you don't cough, you don't get off."

"Boys are stupid. I smoked this whole chonger and never coughed once. They just like laughing at each other's misery. I'm sorry I cut you off yesterday. I know you miss people, on O'ahu. Things are more potent on Kaua'i, the highs, the lows. I see you cry when Akila sings to you. And then you stare at the floor with the weight of the mountain against your heart. I know you want to talk to Auntie Ruby and your friends, but you cannot. You cannot have our dark cloud over them. One day, we go visit. Show

Auntie-them our boys. But we have to contain this horror show, not share it. They all know when this is over, we will come back to them. They will wait for us."

"You're not high at all. I think the kava is working against the pakalolo. You smell like a muddy bong. And I don't even feel a trance coming on. Can we just go make breakfast?" Alana rubs her belly, feeling the static charge pulsating within, radiating.

"I think you're right. I don't feel a thing. I mean, I feel a little buzz from the kava, but this weed ain't shit. I'm gonna light up the other one before Akila makes it down." Keala sparks up, "Maybe it should be the kava or the ganja, but not both. It don't matter, it's going to be a beautiful sunrise. We should catch some fish for lunch, maybe go get groceries later. I was going to take Akila to the library and let him look up poisonous snakes, he's been asking so many questions."

Alana rolls over, "Here comes the keiki. Let's just swim and watch the sunrise. I would like to go to the library too. Maybe we could talk to some people, real people, normal people." Alana floats over to her sister, "Eh, try feel this. The baby is really squirming around in here."

Keala flicks the end of the spliff to the sand and sinks next to her sister. She huddles over Alana's belly like a crystal ball, "He likes it here, so early in the morning. Eh, is that you buzzing or him? Little Mano, sharky baby's so happy in there." Keala kisses the baby just as Akila walks to the edge and plops in next to Alana.

The instant the water splashes, a spark unleashes a bright surge of electrical power. Time screeches to a halt. Crackling voltage flashes in an instant, light without heat. Streaks of cold lightning rip into their limbs with violent pressure and bore into the base of their skulls. Their muscles lock up from the sudden burst. Then, the seizure turns into an icy shiver, stretching their souls out through their flesh. Their bodies go limp, floating together in a shallow pool on the rocky shore. The brilliant surge splits their conscious minds from their eye sockets like an explosive flash in the distance. The white light and the electrical current fade from piercing red to numbing black blurry streaks. They drift deeper into the darkness until they lose all feeling, as if floating away from their material bodies, away from the present reality of time.

White light suddenly returns with a sensation of soaring. Their consciousness snaps into place directly behind the eyes of large, white snowy owl. The nerves intersecting into the brain of this winged creature sputter with an electrical fizz. Until, the wild waves of impulses tune sharply into a steady, focused stream. All the living stimuli from the majestic ʻaumakua begins pouring into their souls, feeding them, trapping them together into its life force. They see, feel and hear from within the owl, but have no control. The sixty-inch wingspan draws thrust and propels them with force as if an involuntary movement is guiding them. Other birds quickly converge. Soon, surrounded by hundreds of other owls, screeching, circling counter-clockwise, they form a massive gathering in the cold night sky.

The Pueo (owl), occupied by the Hunakaʻi family, begins drawing into a tighter circle. They quickly enter what would be the eye of a living storm, far above the white powdered coastal rainforest of Alaska. They drift downwards, still spiraling, fluttering towards a large clam-shelled grotto on the side of a steep mountain. Once below the gyrating ceiling of birds, their Pueo floats calmly and perches on the rocky roof of the cave. They look directly below at three men lying on the icy floor. In the center of the frozen mote is a massive stalagmite of black lava rock. The sharpened column nearly reaches the top of the clam-shelled cave, thirty-feet above. The Pueo peers below at the men sprawled out with their heads at the base of the stalagmite. Looking straight upwards along the pillar, through the eye of the storm of owls, one of their voices rings clear, "He ʻelele ka moe na ke kanaka- A dream is a bearer of messages." Keala instantly recognizes her Ikaika. "And we all had the same dream. Ya? The same but different. Ya?"

The other two men respond in unison, "Roger that." Lika rolls a can towards his left and right simultaneously before opening his own beer.

Ikaika continues, "We all had dreams of that little pink gecko sneaking onto the Ubiquitous, ya? And then crawling along the plumbing under our room and into the wall of the lua (toilet). Ya?"

132

Each man takes a turn suppressing an abrupt giggle, followed by coughing. "Get it together boys." Silence passes while they flinch from withholding their coughs and snorts.

Crumpled beer cans sail into a large wooden canoe at the edge of the circular ice mote, "Roger that." The other two respond as they gaze to the sky. The beer mostly pours into their mouths held up from arm's length.

"And then it crawled across our faces as we slept, crawled back down under the lua, out the building, and then right up to the top of this stack of rocks. Ya?" Ikaika points upwards along his line of sight while tilting the can just enough to let a small stream of beer trickle down. It quickly foams up and bubbles into his nostrils and ears. "How long before them damn birds swoop down and eat the little bugger?"

Kaleo suggests, "I don't think they seen him yet." Kaleo barks out a boisterous laugh before catching his composure.

"No way brah, owls see everything. They, uh... they uh, seem to be busy doing something else. Otherwise, they would have crapped on us by now." Lika reasons before he has to pinch his nose from a snorting giggle.

Kaleo assures, "I'm telling you brah, this is the best spot. They're flying circles so fast, all the shit is flying outwards. Like when you da kind, spin the umbrella. Don't step in the white snow out there, brah."

"Brah." Kaleo quakes from a deeply rooted laugh. "The focking snow stay white already brah!"

"Brah! There's snow white and then there's bird shit white! Snow white stay blue from the moon shine and bird shit stay white white because it just flew from the bird's ass. Shit don't reflect moon shine so more blue white, only white white. Ok?" Ikaika claims.

"Oh. Ok." Kaleo lays back down flat, "This snowy shit's all new to me. Brah."

Ikaika signals for another beer. "This is new to all of us. But. This is right where you want to be. Right in the center at this big ass rock pile. Right where we were meant to be. Who knew brah? Who knew?" Ikaika reasons, "This is where they want us to be. The ʻaumakua (deified ancestors, occasionally in the form of animals). The gecko. The pueo. The ancestors. You know what... I'll be damned if I don't see one turtle flying around up there. And one big focking fish, like one barracuda. Way up there. Flying around. Ya?"

Lika confirms, "Ya brah. How many focking owls would you say it takes to snatch one sea turtle out of the water like that? Hmmm. Assuming the turtle is not flying around on its own and shit. I mean, this has been one strange month. Full of lolo (crazy) surprises. Unreal. Was there a point where we could've avoided all this madness? Or, was this meant for us, our ʻohana (family), na kupuna (ancestors) has led us down this path?" He squeezes his empty can into a disk and hurls it into the canoe with the others. He reaches into the cooler and grabs three more. "They said we was gonna catch some focking fish up here, but I've never seen anything like that. Some of the most bizarre shit I ever seen. Went broke the nets we was hauling in so much catch! Unreal. Was like hoisting a school of piranha. Every fish in the sea, just coming at us - Brah, I felt like the worm on a giant fockin' hook. How did we become the bait? Why was the fish so angry and shit?"

Ikaika unravels some humor and strains to not laugh, "I guess that was the trick the whole time. Eh? Score amazing shrooms at the port. Get all focked up, get sick, puke over the side, be the first to puke over the side of one brand new luxury yatch, and then what? Eh? Get attacked by giant focking halibut? I mean, those fish seemed like they seriously focking hated us. Huhu's (upset) brah, mean kind like that, to the max, eh?"

Kaleo is clearly spooked from that, "Fock ya, unreal. I heard the cold waters was rough and shit. But was unnatural. That was a frenzy. That was a gathering, just like this. Except the fish wanted to kill us, and now the birds want to give us swirlies. Eh, we should get a bigger boat. You see the kind, the fockin' commodore rolled up with? Fockin' had one hot tub! Styling brah."

Ikaika counters, "Nah. The Ubiquitous is the best, and the fastest. No telling how many cursed-ass fish are out there waiting for us, but I don't trust any other boat. You know the locals here, brah. That one orca show, the killer whale and shit, went capsized the boat and got revenge for his Ohana. Brah, we need a bigger harpoon! We're gonna jack that fockah, and sail straight back to Kaua'i. Hawaiian! We're going to load it full of beer and spam and get the fock outta here. Ya?" Ikaika begins choking and rubbing the tears from his eyes. "Hold it.... Hold it together."

Kaleo and Lika respond in unison, "Roger that."

Lika asks, "I'm thinking about blowing up all that benzene in the basement. How come you didn't see the underground laboratory like me? And the benzene?"

Kaleo clarifies, "I was shown the mess hall. That's why, I'm getting the beer and the spam. Ikaika was shown the control room. He's opening the bay doors, unlocking the doors to the barracks, and cutting the power so we can kill the computers and jack the boat. We each saw what we was supposed to see. Why, you think you can haul more beer than me? Your fat ass is going to eat, drink and smoke half of it before you even get to the boat!" He covers his mouth and squints his bulging eyes, as one would appear while holding down a powerful sneeze.

Lika opens another beer. "Nah. I just want to blow up them fish tanks. This fish farm is cursed. Those lolo halibut are cursed. This focking meth lab is cursed. All those focking tweakers working here are slaves. Bunch of addicts butchering up their cursed fish. This whole operation goes up in flames tonight. But, try get those Frito's, and plenty cans of that chili. Ya? Not going to make it home without that."

"I'm getting plenty more of these shrooms. These have been like, the best part of this whole focking trip. If it weren't for the shrooms, none of this shit would be making any sense right now." Ikaika pours beer over the track marks on his forearm. "We should never have let them start doing blood tests on us. I swear, they're pumping more shit in than they are drawing out. Ain't fooling nobody. They want to make addicts out of us like everybody else around here. Even the fockin' fish are lolo (crazy) crackheads. It's the shrooms pushing that crank out of my arms. Gotta be. Shrooms have natural cleansing elements. Or, they re-wired my brain to expel the unnatural substances from my blood, out through my pores. Or, like the same holes they came in on. I think I rewired my brain to repel negative shit!"

"Gotta be the shrooms." Kaleo agrees. "When I found them in the back fridge, I focking knew these were the kind, brah. The same kind that haole gave us when he handed over the vessel. Ho, they're not too strong, but they really open the mind. It really tickles brah. These people have an honorable respect for all-natural purity in their horticulture. The villains always have the best shit. Except I didn't see it then, but I realize it now. There's definitely something strange about our employer. Ya? I mean who goes 'Don't wreck the boat. Oh, by the way, there's a shitload of magic mushrooms in the fridge. Don't die.' But he seemed cool, ya? Brah, we gonna die smuggling drugs in dead fish for these cartel fockah's."

"But would we have seen through the bullshit without the shrooms?" Lika delves. "Ok, now I don't really recommend operating a commercial fishing vessel on shrooms anymore, but I don't think we would have realized the sinister plot going on here and then found a means to escape. When I saw that little gecko on the wall, was like deja vu. Weak kind visually, but mentally was solid. But it was definitely the shrooms that brought all this together. And the pakalolo's not bad either. Not like home. I feel really good about this. Eh? What else they got back in there?"

"Bunch of shit. Bambucha (big) shit, brah. Fockin' baggies, fockin' bottles, fockin' vials, needles, pipes, sheets of acid, every color of pill you can imagine - basically no excuse to not be an addict. I just grabbed the shrooms and the weed." Kaleo opens a fresh beer. "They got fockin' poison. This place is cursed. That's why they're out here all by themselves in the middle of nowhere. They got plenty to hide. Not supposed to be out here, no wonder the fish hate us. Locals here are mean, no more aloha. This is some kind of mafia underworld kind shit, brah. They want us dead, no, no.... they want us alive! But they're not going to let us out of here alive. This is playing out like one Bruce Lee movie. Guaranteed they bugged the Ubiq." Kaleo cuts off two involuntary snorts before beer foams out of his nostrils.

136

"Guarans-ball-bearins brah. But I definitely don't trust any other vessel. We will just have to route the ignition wires again. Take power from the computer system, no more bugs, trackers, kill switch, anything that can sabotage our get-away. I know every wire on that boat. Hot-wire the fockah, in no time, wikiwiki (fast) kine. We can check all that on the ride home. We can stash this boat on Kaua'i. No worries. They won't find us. I promise." Ikaika throws another can in the canoe. "Kill the power to the building, blow that fockin' crack lab up. Everybody going scatter like cock-a-roaches. They won't even notice we're gone. It'll be focking mayhem. Chaos brah."

"Chaos like the boss, brah." Lika and Kaleo chime. They look to each other, holding their breath until they seize their restraint. Suppressing spasms of laughter makes their eyes bulge.

Ikaika squeezes his can, "Maka 'ike (second sight), brah. We got the sight tonight. We have the plan. We have enough weed to live off of until all this blows over." Ikaika slaps his leg several times, "That was focking laughing right there you dumbass! You owe me some push-ups. Both of you's!"

Lika gathers more cans from the cooler, "No, you owe us push-ups. I'm not doing shit until you flip the fock over and give me another twenty! And what'choo going to tell Keala? Eh? We stole drugs and a fishing vessel from the mafia? She's going to find out you snuck back home early. Focking hiding out until all this blows over? There's no fockin' hiding from her brah! If you go back to Kaua'i, she will focking know! She will know and then stab me in the neck for not keeping you out of trouble. I say we sail to O'ahu."

"No can brah." Ikaika reasons, "Cannot hide a boat on O'ahu. Gotta be Kaua'i. As long as I don't touch foot on the Island, Keala won't even know I'm there. Promise. I'll just stay on the boat for a couple of weeks until all this blows over. When the coast is clear, I'll go home and explain the situation to Keala and how we had to get out of here. We're so far off the grid anyways. She will totally understand. We'll be fine. Guarans brah. I feel really good about this."

137

"Oh, but you cannot go surf either. You touch that reef and this shit's over with." Kaleo points out.

"No, fock you." Ikaika disagrees.

Kaleo slaps his leg, "Nope. No surf either. You stay on the boat. If we go home and you don't stay on the boat, she's going to find you. You gonna swim back to the mafia to get away from her. Brah, she's going to string your balls!" Kaleo blurts, "She's going to stab him in the neck. She's going to cut off my ear. She's going to string you up by the balls and then stuff all these shrooms down your throat until your head explodes! Brah! She fockin' ran my Yota off the road when you got that DUI! Remember that kook?"

"Eh, your Toyota was one piece of shit! That's why the cop pulled me over in the first place." Ikaika defends, "She barely side-swiped you. You're the one that hit the damn tree. What are you crying for? I'm the one that flew out the window. Let me worry about Keala. We got paid already. You can buy yourself a new car when all this blows over."

"Ya. You know, you're right. That car smelled so bad. Fockin' hauna (stinky) to the max. Gas mileage was good, still yet... and the stereo. Stereo was righteous. Ho, look out brah. But, eh, I feel really good about this. Ya? We're definitely high enough to pull this one off."

Kaleo reaches over to a beer can rolling his way. "At least it's not the cops we gotta worry about. No way these people want to get the cops involved. That's one thing for sure about dealing with the kind, underground mobsters. Once we get back on the Island, they can't touch us. Kaua'i boys!"

"Kaua'i boys!" Ikaika reassures. "This heiau (temple) proves we were meant to be here. One ancient Hawaiian heiau, all the way in Alaska giving us the mana we need. The gecko who gave us the visions in our dreams. This tornado of owls, all the fish that attacked us, and this stack of lava rocks - this was all meant for us. Except, I'm kind of worried about what was carved inside that canoe. Eh Lika, try read it again."

138

Lika belches so he can lean over the side of the canoe filled with war clubs, helmets and feathered cloaks, "Hele aku ʻoe maʻaneʻi, he waʻa kanaka; hoʻi mai ʻoe maʻo he waʻa akua."

"It says: when you go from here... the canoe will contain many men... when you return, it will be a ghostly canoe. Hawaiians sailed these three canoes all the way here. This is the path that was revealed to us. From the looks of all these bones, they died here before they could sail home. They left them here for us. Except, I'd like to jack the Ubiq'. No need disturb the sacred ground, eh? I'm not going to let us die here tonight boys. We're going home. Is uh, is it getting warmer?" Ikaika slowly sits up and notices the snow melting away inside the cave. Did I just piss in my pants?"

Kaleo stands and places his hand on the lava rock formation, "Well... I'm pissing in my pants right now. It's so warm, there's no stopping it. Boys, I'll be damned if this stack of rocks isn't vibrating. It is vibrating, and it's definitely getting warmer. And you know what... what are these lava rocks even doing here? No more pissing! I bet they carried them inside the canoes from the island. I mean, that's really bad luck and might explain why all the kanaka's never made it back home. Could it have been intentional? To carry this much rock away from Hawaiʻi? It's sacrilegious... no wait, desecration.

We're desecrating the heiau by taking a leak right here. I can't stop peeing. But there's crumbled rock on the bottom of the canoes and the insides is all scratched up. Interesting... I wonder what they were up to? What if they could manifest that bad luck into something equally powerful, but useful? Eh?" Kaleo peers into the porous black stone as it becomes too warm for his hand. He slowly backs away as the heat radiates and begins pulsating in waves.

Ikaika crouches and stares down into the mother-of-pearl mote of ice beneath them. "Brah, I think we are experiencing an earthquake right under our feet. There's cracks in the ice." The dim blue glow of the crescent moon illuminates to a deep purple. Streaks of crimson light refract from underneath the ice. "Holy shit brah. You know why it's getting warmer? That's lava below us. Ya?"

The host owl looms over the edge of the clamshell cave. The family watches the ice shatter from deep below. Thick red steam engulfs the three drunken sailors. Pores in the rock hiss out steam, up and down the great stalagmite. The hissing squeals louder until it becomes screams of banshees. Out from the core through interwoven vessels, molten lava pulsates and weaves together webs of black smoke into the building fog.

The owl watches all three men crawl to the mote's outer edge. They help each other stand and stare upwards towards the sharpened tip of the porous black rock structure. The gyrating storm of owls flash and glow like an atomic mushroom cloud from a lightning storm forming just overhead. A crackling white shard of lightning strobes directly down the center eye of the storm, striking the tip of the stalagmite. The bolt of energy is pulled into the stone shaft like heroin drawn into the syringe. The lava splatters outwards and showers the boys as they lean back away from the structure.

Kaleo sputters because he was caught with his mouth open, "Did that shit just happen?"

Ikaika rubs his face, "I don't feel like laughing now. Brah, that tasted different than what I expected. I thought it would be, like, hotter... or like more spicy and shit."

"Roger dat." They calmly concur, unmoving, saturated, dripping.

"Maybe the Hawaiians never brought the lava rocks in the canoes. The lava was already here. Still yet, I don't think this was just regular lava. Maybe there's something else in it. It's not all rock." Ikaika rolls his eyes in big circles, peering through the thick layers.

With smoldering red tar caked and oozing down his entire head, "This shit is totally in my eyes. It's seeping into my eyes. Brah. I think the shrooms is finally kicking in." He soon finds himself flat on his back staring upwards into the vortex. The magnetism of the pillar pulls at him like a vacuum. His jellied eyes swirl with the ceiling of birds. He abruptly slides feet-first back towards the base of the molten tower. The rotation above accelerates so rapidly, his eyes feel like they're spinning in their sockets. Until, his vision slowly synchronizes with the vortex. As they lock on to the

140

frequency of the storm, the portal of owls halts before them and then it becomes the incendiary lava tower that spins wildly under their feet.

Ikaika's body feels no motion, only the cold breeze from the fluttering wings of the white owl gathering. The arctic wilderness pours silently through the dome of birds, causing the black smoke to eloquently dance with the red steam. The muffled rumble of the spinning stalagmite reminds him of the boulders tumbling under a heavy wave at the Ranch, on the Makaha side of O'ahu. The barrel is loud on the inside, but it becomes a silent rumble that is felt deeply when one tries to dive through the back of the wave. The vacuum of the churning wave pulls you along as the sound of bubbling water deadens.

Ikaika imagines himself reaching out to a rolling boulder in hopes that the wave will eventually slip its grip. His attention eventually drifts to realize he is lying still with Lika to his left and Kaleo to his right. "Ok braddahs, I'd like to discuss that music I was hearing when the manini (small) gecko was showing me my dream. I cannot explain it, but I have a theory I'd like to introduce to this situation in particular. It all seems to fit. It sounded like some punk rock shit, but I think the lyrics somehow apply to what is unfolding before us at this time."

"Affirmative captain. Sea Weedie Martini, that's what I heard him call himself before he started playing the punk rock shit." Lika confirms. "I was just reminded that I experienced some kind of deep understanding in my gecko dream too. I think we heard the same shit, but within our unique dreams. My song was curiously similar in the fact that I was having deja vu, just before you mentioned the music just now. Go on Kaik's. Sorry to interrupt."

Ikaika catches himself just before he laughs aloud, "I remember liking the music because it was all about surfing and shit. But it caused a thought process to unfold as I heard it. You know da kine? It was the key to interpreting the trance. Ya?"

"I got it cuz." Kaleo rationalizes, "You know how you play the Ozzy record backwards and you try to listen for da kind hidden messages from the devil? Except the frequency isn't revealing some satanic bullshit, it's revealing some realization this Sea Weedie guy had, presumably while he was tripping on some shrooms. Tripping in the same frequency situation as we find unfolding before us right now. Ya? We are not alone on this wavelength. That's what that means. We achieved a special frequency, a much higher frequency, if you will."

"Roger that, lieutenant commander." Lika chimes. "The way I imagined the music I was hearing was he was playing the music at a live concert. And, I imagine he was on shrooms too. Like... like, Woodstock. I also think he was tripping on the same exact frequency that we are experiencing at this moment... but you know what... I cannot tell if that music was the past, present, or the future. If we were hearing music from a concert that hasn't happened yet. Wow, that's really going to bake my noodle in the morning."

Ikaika chuckles, "Focking guy. Oh, that's going to scramble your shit? What if it is music that hasn't happened yet? The meaning is there, the realization is there, and that this frequency occurs in the past, present, and future... or simultaneously all at once. Lightning without heat, lava without burning... I think it's because we have achieved this special frequency, same as the music and the lava and the lightning. And I don't know why there's a big ole' focking turtle flying around up there, maybe he's on the same frequency as us too. Ya?"

"Ya, but still yet..." Kaleo adds, trying so hard not to laugh, "It's not just achieving, or da kine, tuning into the same frequency, as the lava and the lightning, and the same music, but also having consumed the same elements within our bodies. It's a part of us now and we are a part of it. It could be something in the lava, the shrooms, the weed, the fish, the lightning, or the smack they shot us up with. But this Martini bugger is truly focking wacky. I think he's totally tripping on shrooms, and when the music stops, he starts focking laughing. I hear him laughing at shit that voices are telling him. And I think all those voices are from dead focking ghosts. I think he cannot hear them when he plays the music, but when he stops the music, the ghosts tell him shit that he thinks is funny. And he repeats shit the fockin' ghosts tell him and he seems like a crazy mothafockah. I think they are driving him crazy and I feel bad for laughing at him."

Kaleo momentarily looses control of his chuckle, "That's it. That's totally it. It's the focking farting that's killing me. You know what else is going to bake my noodle, the fact that there's some farting focking ghost from the future that made its way in my gecko dream. What if that ghost starts haunting us and we have to listen to non-stop farting until we go insane? Poor bastard. We cannot let this interfere with the plan."

Ikaika pulls all his wits to suppress his giggling, "No, admiral, you seriously have to block out the focking farting ghost. You still owe me some push-ups. Ok? Let that crazy Martini fockah deal with the ghost comedy. We have just tuned into one of the greatest wonders we always knew existed. We talked about something missing from our world. We just found it. Whatever is in this lava, is now in us. I feel like we are finally complete. This is the mana. We tapped in, tuned in, fueled up, we have a good plan and we know what we have to do. Roger?"

"Roger." After a brief, convulsive struggle, the boys lie still in the red fog.

"I know what it is called." Kaleo pauses through a deep smooth inhalation. "Etera."

"Etera?" Lika pauses, "What da fock is etera?"

"Etera." Kaleo repeats slowly, "Ancient Hawaiian, the word is etera."

"Ya, but..." Lika repeats slowly, "What da fock is this, etera?"

"I don't know what it is." Kaleo reasons, "I just know it is what has been missing in our world until now."

Ikaika ponders, "I think etera is what gives us the mana. Or etera is in the mana... or *is* the mana. We have the maka 'ike because we now have etera in us somehow. That's what the world has been missing. It's the missing element and our bloodline is incomplete without it. Until now. This is all unfolding before us because we now have the missing elements

143

and we are finally tuned in... Wow. Brah, these shrooms are definitely the shit."

Lika points to the sky, "You know what... I wasn't fockin' wit-choo guys when I said there was one giant turtle flying around up there... I get what you're saying. There are nutrients our world is missing, or, being kept from us. Or the world used it all up already, extinct. Or so we thought..."

The turtle in the sky suddenly hurtles through the tunnel of gyrating owls and impales onto the drilling tip of the lava pike with a dense explosion. A large owl then strikes the pike's tip next, immediately followed by a barracuda. The momentum of the massive fish shatters the bodies into to pieces, slinging down a chunky rain of blood to splash onto the mote of ice crystal shards.

Lika looks to the bones rattling loose from the spinning cave walls and tumbling across the ground. The bones sink into the silence of the mote's red fog. Black ashes flutter out and swirl into the red glow. He grabs hold of Ikaika, who grabs hold of Kaleo. "I think maybe the ice is mixing with lava rock and turning this into some kind of kanaka (man, intended of Hawaiian ancestry) magnet. Should we fight it or let it have our bones?"

Ikaika finds the brothers both staring at him, "One kanaka magnet... brah, how do we know if those bones are from the Hawaiians... or the enemies they killed? I think it's pulling us in. It wants us in there where, da kine, bloody cold meets the magnetized lava. That's where the flow goes. I think we were meant to go. What choice do we have? Try to handle this trip, or embrace the life of a drug smuggler? What do you say boys?"

Kaleo floats with his back suspended in the chilly fog. The cave spins wildly around the lava rock shaft, alternating the bloody red glow from the roof of the cave to the blue ice of the Alaskan forrest outside. "I know what this is. I can hear the song. We sing - Cast off at midnight!"

"Holy shit brah. This is a portal. We heard this music in the gecko dream. But it's now coming from this cave. I think this cave is like one giant satellite and it is opening up a portal for us. One portal into the future." Ikaika blurts out unbridled laughter for just a moment.

Lika tries to sit up against the pull of the red fog. The spherical nature of his body causes a waddling affect. He gets no grip on the ice and clutches onto Kaleo's knee. His face bounces off the ice's blue reflection of Ikaika on his back, staring straight up the shaft. In an elliptical roll, Lika clamps down on Ikaika's knee and still cannot stop himself from hitting the other side of his face. He tries to keep hold of both kneecaps while focusing on the red reflection of Kaleo on his back, staring straight forward as well. The momentum swings him back around, "Ikaika's blue..." He sits up, "Kaleo's red..."

"Nah brah, Ikaika's red. You're blue." Kaleo declares.

"Not even brah. Lika's red. You been blue all fockin' night." Ikaika has no idea where his beer went.

"Ya, but still yet, I'm either blue or red depending on positioning and perspective. According to my individual interpretation of the gecko dream, I'm not blue or red. But white, white as the snow, white as Santa's focking ass in a bowl of rice." Lika finally sits up. In a dizzy circular motion, he finds his own reflection while looking down towards his crotch. "But here, right now... I'm looking at myself totally blue with my right eye... and totally red with my... other eye. But, at the same time... I'm both... and it's not purple. But I'm not white at all. But that's what the reflection says. So weird."

"I never saw you white in my dream. Like a polar bear tea-bagging his nuts on a mountain of Colombian coke, white. I'm having all this in deja vu kine right now, and you stay blue. Not white brah." Kaleo hasn't blinked in an hour.

Ikaika continues his unflinching glare, "He's totally right, except you're totally red. And you stay red until... until I don't know when. Brah, what happens after this? I remembered my version of the gecko dream perfectly until... until I actually don't know what happens after this."

145

Kaleo snaps, "Why is that important right now?"

Lika explains, "It's a puzzle piece that needs to fit correctly in order to transition. That's why."

Kaleo agrees, "Brah, you know what. We just experienced everything exactly as the little gecko revealed to us. Wait a minute... What do you think happened to that little bugger? Anyways, I don't think we're fully tuned in this frequency just yet. There's something that we haven't got yet. Something's missing. Eh, you think that owl focking ate him?" Kaleo points up to the grand pueo hosting the Hunaka'i's dreamworld.

Lika finds the reflection of the pueo perched on the roof looking down upon them. Staring down at the floor, "Eh, wait a minute... Try look into the eyes of that owl and tell me you don't find something familiar." He tries to bend forward and peer down into the reflection but his belly won't let him. Pulling on his own knees is the only way he can get his face closer to the ice between his legs.

Ikaika pinches his middle finger and thumb together and snaps his first finger against them several times, "Fock brah. Holy focking shit fock. That focking owl right there... right focking there... That's Keala's eyes inside that owl's focking eyes!"

"I focking knew it!" Kaleo blurts as he wipes red spooge from his eyes and slings it to the side. "I focking knew Keala was going to find out about this shit somehow and cut off my focking ear! There's no way I'm going to have two focking ears after this. It's all over cuz!"

"Just calm down. Alright?" Lika tries to settle them, "Just listen to yourselves. That's focking lolo. That's the lolo-est shit I ever heard."

"Nope. Nope. She's gonna stab you in the neck and she's gonna cut off my ear and she's gonna string him up by the focking balls." Kaleo continues to stare through the eye of the owl storm as his voice trembles in uncertainty. "That's it. We're focking done for. It's a fockin' royal fockin' shit fock!"

146

"Ho braddah, just hold on a second." Lika reassures, "I know she go spark the second sight and all. I mean, she's *really intuitive* and shit, but it just doesn't make sense. I mean, we ate some shrooms. Ya?" Lika peers deeper at the reflection of the owl. "Ya?"

"Roger that." The other two confirm.

"We smoked quite a few fat focking doobies already. Ya?" He gazes into the eyes of the great white owl from the reflection. "Are you high?" Pointing at one, then the other, "Are you high?"

"Roger that." They concur.

"Went pounded a case of beer already. Ya?" He squints intently, "I mean we're *totally* shit-faced right now. We're tripping focking balls, high as fock, drunker than shit. No way, no way Keala could be spying on us right now through that focking bird because she don't get high. And that focking bird didn't get high. Eh? Did anybody ever pass the focking doobie over to that focking bird over there? Eh?"

"Negative." The other two chime. But not loud enough so they have to confirm more robustly, "Negative."

"Well I sure the hell didn't share any kind shit with that bird. It took a whole hell of a lot of shit to become this, da kine, *receptive*. We are tuned into a very special frequency here. I'd say it's a rather exclusive frequency to tap into. It's something we had to achieve. Ok? We find ourselves in a very special place. And we're on the verge of turning a very bad situation around for ourselves. The three of us... and that bird. That 'aumakua. Eh, did she ever get freaky with one bird before? - I didn't think so. Eh? She's never been focked up at this level and she never will. Fockin' no chance brah. Right? So there's no way she could be spying on us. Ya? So you just stop it with that shit. Just stop it."

Lika continues to stare down at the ice, not willing to miss the sign he's been waiting for. He argues at the color-distorted reflections, "Even that Martini bugger singing from the future had to eat some shrooms to tap into this frequency. Focking, you know that. Clearly it's reserved for only the highest of highnesses. We're totally cool here. That shit's just your own mind focking with you. Don't let it bring you down. Not right now. You're going way off course. Adjust your rudder moddah-fockah's. You fockin' fockah's need to stay focused on our path. Ya? Follow the focking ghost farts. And stop fockin' laughing! Just stop it. Ok? Ok."

Kaleo has doubts, "She sent that gecko to spy on us."

"Nope. Nah. No way." Lika instantly refutes, "That little gecko would never have shown us, or you to be precise, any of that weed and shit if he was in cahoots with Keala. You're the last moddahfockah she woulda shown that to. You kooks are just projecting your fears and self-doubt into the eyes of that bird. It's just the reflection of your own doubt. Now focus on the plan. You want some more shrooms? Shrooms will fockin' fix that shit right the fock up. We got a good plan and we're all buzzed up enough to pull this off. The path has been laid. Roger?"

"Roger that." They find their way back on track.

"I mean... that bird does have a familiar kind of sense and all, but it has nothing to do with Keala. It's our 'aumakua. That's the mana of our ancestors you're feeling, not Keala. Is she our ancestor? No. Right? So forget about that and try to focus on this transition point we find ourselves at right now. I'm looking for the sign and you kooks are stressing me out. I mean, I'm looking at myself and I am still red and blue. That is what got us to the present. The gecko dream is about to transition and we need to stick to the plan. Otherwise, we're lost down the rabbit hole."

Ikaika ponders, "Wait, how do you know the gecko dream hasn't ended already and we're now transitioning into the next phase? Are you seeing into the future?"

Lika feels the vibration of his body rattling the bottom of his feet against the column of rocks, "Nah. Something is missing still. I see the dream ending when I turn white. Then it all turns red and then fades to black. That's when we transition to the next phase of our plan. That's when we execute. That's when we transition from the dream to the future. The future becomes the present at that moment. When everything turns white, that's the key to all this.  Got it?  Until then, I guess we keep drinking more beer."

"Roger.... Wait... What?  You think this is a portal to the future?  Ok."  Kaleo's head wobbles with the gyration of the kaleidoscope of owls.  "Is this the way into the rabbit hole... or out of the rabbit hole.  You know what, doesn't matter.   Anything's better than being a drug smuggling donkey for the mafia."

"Ah, no worries brother."  Ikaika reaffirms the positivity, "We're here to protect our bloodline.  I doubt our ancestors care about drug smuggling.  We're the only ones who didn't turn into drug addicts around here. This is about something else."

"Hoo, now that's kind of funny."  Lika chuckles, "We're tripping balls so hard right now, but we're the only ones that aren't addicts!  Talk about pick-your-poison.  Eh?  Somehow, the hallucinogens actually made us see more clearly.  How's the irony?  As in, eye-ball-rony!  Come on, fock you. That was actually funny.  But true ya?"

"Roger that."  This makes them smile but they refuse to laugh.

Kaleo agrees, "The dream goes red, then black.  That's the end, or the transition.  Wait... Catch me up, fast kine.  The white... whiteness... it goes white because... the portal opens... but we don't go through the portal... something comes through to us... the transition is the mana... coming through to us.  It's not from the fockin' future... it's the mana from our ancestors... from the fockin' past.  That's what transitions us into future."

"Hmmm."  Ikaika evaluates, "Dood, you totally lost me.  If this is indeed a portal, it seems like it's bringing it all together:  past, present and future.  Things will never be the same after this sailor boys.  Wait... you hear that?"

"Brah."  Lika closes his eyes.  "The farting stopped.  The voices stopped. The laughing..."  It goes silent.

A burst of laughter erupts from the three sailors along with a hundred ghostly wailers as one last squeal rips through the silence. The bolstering continues. Eventually subsiding to muffled chuckles, the silence soon prevails. Only the flutter of wings from above stirs the thickening fog.

"Brah." Lika continues with his eyes closed, "It's time. This is where the dream world ends and the spirit world begins."

It remains quiet for a spell. "Brah, that's Keala up there in that owl." Ikaika relaxes and takes in the possibility of sensing her presence at such a wild occasion. "I'm telling you."

Kaleo gazes back to the reflection of the owl perched above. His eyes drift to the black space next to the owl, in the center of the swirling cloud of birds. The red glow fades from the owls. Blue ripples darken the mass of birds, drawing in a cold vastness from the black sky like cold liquid pouring in. All light fades when the fog rises within the cave. His attention churns with the storm for a spell before he swings his vision back to the perched owl staring down at him, "We're totally getting fired tonight. How are you going to explain how we all lost our jobs? There's no explaining this shit. This shit's unexplainable. I hate hearing- *I told you so.*"

Lika finally opens his eyes with a deep inhalation. He watches the final glow of red and blue subside from the reflection of owls above. One small crack in the ice pierces the silence. The next two cracks ring out with a bright reverberation. Lika reaches out to clutch the kneecaps of the others in order to halt the wobbles. Before he can make contact, the wild storm of owls and the spinning column cease to an immediate stop. The wild spinning motion transfers to the center of their heads.

Lika stares at the ice as a single streak of lightning chitters down from the sky. The flash catches thousands of white owls in a single strobe, freezing the image in time. The reflection ignites the ice in a blinding vision. The lightning develops a path from a web, spanning across the black sky above the side of the mountain. Lika is caught between heartbeats, as the world has been frozen. It strikes down, too fast to see, but slow enough for his mind to comprehend the energy transferring down through the rock formation to the frozen pool of lava below.

150

"No!" Keala screams from behind the eyes of their great white owl. The sisters stare down at the fiery explosion rumbling the entire mountain. They feel the saturation of heat energy from the arc flash, but without immense pressure or pain. In the blinding flash, they feel the physical form of their host owl transforming under the rupture of the explosion. It is not a deformation, but a new way of exchanging the flow of elemental charge. It is not a change of structure, but a heightened interaction with magnetic fields and electron flow from the surroundings. The physical properties of their matter are behaving differently with the presence of something that has been missing from this world.

Keala welcomes the introduction as she would the spirit of a lost relative. Every element in the universe now contributes to their spiritual energy. Suddenly sharing and harmonizing with the vast universe, electrical energy and magnetic charge bind their life force to every other atom that has ever existed. Their time-space reality is now an open channel. The vibrational interaction harmonizes and magnifies their power. Mana is the concept she welcomes in this moment of intense stimulation. This connectivity turns every inanimate matter into a living extension of their glowing souls.

She acquires a subconscious realization that they have been introduced to an element that reacts as a great catalyst between the physical world and the spirit world. This missing element has enhanced her existence in a way she won't be able to define or quantify. But now, Keala's spiritual energy has suddenly become nourished by it. This owl's natural body has fused with the molten minerals of the lava. Every universal element, every configuration of neutrons, protons and electrons are now present in their spiritual illumination. All in a fiery instant.

The orange glare slowly fades. The pulsating earthquake diminishes. It becomes silent for a moment before the mountain above begins rumbling. A rolling wave of snow avalanches upon them. A low boom rumbles the valley until a powdery blanket extinguishes the red glow under the cave. Hissing steam instantly squelches the heat from the lava.

The Hunaka'i's host owl shakes off the coat of snow. Their vision slowly returns to reveal their great white owl is now comprised of sleek black obsidian. Everything they see below emits a radiance and gives definition as if fiery light were present. They now perceives images in terms of magnetism, radiation, along with what light energy reveals. They feel intoxicated by the magnetism, as if it had always tickled them but their minds were never capable of interpreting it before now.

The heiau becomes as silent and frozen like it had been for three hundred years. The blanket of snow from the avalanche dwindles away, evaporating to ash as if it was never meant to exist. The fog eventually clears as the Hunaka'i 'aumakua stretches its black marbled wings. It fans the ice mote clean from the dusty fallout. They find it frozen back over. The owl can see its own reflection from the edge of the overhanging dome directly above. They notice the swarm of owls has vanished. The cave has completely returned to its state before they found it.

The owl does not take its eyes from the mote. They stare in silence until a single crack reaches the surface from deep below. Several more cracks follow until the sound of shattering glass reverberates within the cave. The mote begins to shift around like creatures stirring in a pit of a thousand diamonds. Keala sees the glow of a glossy blackened arm reaching up through the shards. It has a familiar glow, a shimmer that she has always loved. She watches a black marbled version of her Ikaika crawl up the rocky sides of the mote below.

He holds the ledge with one hand and reaches back down with the other. He pulls up a large fish's tail fin of black steel and yanks it to the surface. The fin resembles that of the sleek barracuda that was impaled on the tip of the stalagmite. Yet, with human legs protruding from its sides as two creatures fused into one. Its head pops up for a second to reveal the face of Kaleo before it sinks below again. Ikaika heaves up a leg sticking out the side of a boulder. The obsidian barracuda slithers up the side of the mote and crawls to the other side of Ikaika. Its head and arms submerge and get underneath the boulder. They hear Kaleo's voice, "Your fat ass needs to help us you focking mutt!"

Ikaika sinks into the dark pit of broken glass for a moment and then bursts upwards. He stretches out his great wings, like a demon emerging from a tar pit. His wingspan anchors across the sides of the mote as he thrusts his arms upwards with a monstrous cannonball in the form of Lika. "Fat fockah, you!"

All three tumble over the ledge and clank across the stone floor of the cave. The Hunaka'i sisters gasp with shocking fascination of what the men have become. To their eyes, the living souls of each man shimmer from within the opaque obsidian creatures. Each one has the features and aura of the men, but incased in the frame of the three 'aumakua that were sacrificed upon the point of the lava rock pike. The owl, sea turtle and barracuda have given their structures to shell around each kanaka's soul. From a distance, they appear as glossy gargoyles.

The great owl swoops in closer and they can recognize each man's glowing soul within the monstrous forms. It circles the black stalagmite just above the kanaka's heads as they look up confused and dazed. Keala tries to scream out to Ikaika but her voice cannot breach the owl's obsidian shell. Only the light from her soul's illumination can gleam out to him. The black crystalized owl perches back on the high ledge of the cave and peers down at the shapeshifters below. The Hunaka'i family tries to listen, but the men have lowered their voices dramatically.

"You hear that?" Lika squirms on his back looking over to Kaleo for assistance, "Did you hear him? Right before the lightening, I heard him singing some shit about the etera again." Lika doesn't get the help and flails just like a turtle on its back.

"I heard that. That's what I heard just before everything went white, just like you said." Kaleo stands over his brother, staring down without extending a helpful limb. He whispers, "He was singing a line from a song... something the Aztecs would chant. Something about the forth world was ending and the fifth world was beginning. The fifth world is our time period without etera."

Lika looks up, disappointed he was not getting the help he needed, "What, you understand Aztec now?"

"No, stupid." Kaleo swats Lika's hands away, "I don't understand the language. I understand the meaning. You know what... brah, I understand meaning all of a sudden. This got deep brah."

"So stupid." Lika clutches on to Kaleo's arm, "Help me up you fockin' mullet." Lika grabs his leg and rolls Kaleo underneath him as he flips over. "Brah, those shrooms are really kicking in now. I mean... I see you standing right there, but I see one giant black barracuda around you. It's kind of like a shadow. You're like, living in some fish's shadow."

Kaleo squirms underneath his brother's mutated mass, "Why couldn't you have crossed up with that little gecko you frickin' bowling ball. Get off me. You look like a turtle in an oil spill."

Ikaika stands and stretches his newly transformed wings. Barely audible, "Braddah's, we have been blessed. Mea ho'ololi kino (shape shifter) is what the lava gave us. There was something in the lava. Like the song said, I think the etera was in the lava from the previous world. Now it's in us. Then we got the magnetism, the lightning, the blood of the 'aumakua, the ice- and then you add all that shit mixed with the shrooms and we tapped right into the spirit world. Ya? Etera is the mana, from the spirit world? Ya? I'm having understanding too now that it's gone so quiet."

"I don't know. Let's back up to the sequence of events." Lika whispers, "It was the weed and shrooms we got at the Nawiliwili Port. That guy was cool. Haole, but still yet, for someone associated with this mafia shit, he had a cool vibe. Not like anyone else we met since we been here. Then they gave us the blood test and pumped us full of that white shit. I'm assuming that was heroin like they got everyone else hooked on. Those guys totally did not have a cool vibe and we should have skipped their little physical exam. But they gave us a brand new ship to deliver to this place. But it was when the fish attacked us in that frenzy that I think we first tapped in to the mana. The fish definitely did not have a cool vibe."

Kaleo interjects, "They were also trying to feed us the cursed halibut. That's when the static was hitting the brain, ya? The injections and the cursed fish was clashing with the vibe of the weed and shrooms. Ya?"

Lika agrees, "Good point. The headaches hit after they tried to feed us the cursed halibut. We was clashing big time, like... like the stereo in your piece of shit Toyota playing two radio stations at the same time. And somewhere in that static, we tapped into the little gecko. Brah, I swear, you actually look like you're wearing one giant focking bird suit. You think we really went shape shifter? Or, the shrooms are just having us believe that we went mea ho'ololi kino (shapeshifter). Because, you really look like your flying around in a giant focking bird suit."

Ikaika chuckles, "Brah, seriously. Just ride with it. I mean, you look like one fat focking turtle to me, but that's just the shrooms focking with you. You definitely don't want to be tripping so hard that you jump off the roof, thinking you can fly like superman. Ya? We gotta play it safe out here. Ok?"

Lika has doubts, "I don't know. This fockah really does look like one slimy black barracuda."

Ikaika never likes to argue quietly but maintains his whisper. "Remember when we ate those shrooms after the football game and thought we was still wearing our helmets? And we thought we could put our heads through the back window of your truck?"

"Well, actually..." Lika chuckles, "We did put our heads through the back window of my truck."

Ikaika starts to chuckle along, but snuffs it. "And when Keala found us stuck in the sand the next morning, all bloody and covered with glass, what did she tell you?"

Lika stops chuckling, "Right before she kicked my tooth out?"

"Ya." Ikaika responds. "Right before that."

"Well... she asked if I was the one that scored the shrooms. I said yes. And then she said never eat shrooms on a new moon. Then she asked if I wrecked the truck and we flew through the window again. I don't know why I said yes, but that's when she kicked me in the face. I didn't want to admit we was shrooming the first time we crashed through the glass, but she knew already somehow. As soon as I did say yes, I remembered she said she was gonna kick me in the face if we ever flew through the glass again on shrooms, but it was too fockin' late. I didn't get to hear why we're not supposed to eat shrooms on a new moon because I went face-plant in the sand. But I was always curious." Lika recalls.

Kaleo chimes, "She kicked me in the gut. I fell over and was choking on sand. Went puked several times. I didn't hear why either. I just remembered not to focking do it. She was serious, I don't think she was in the mood to take questions at that time. It happened really fast."

"Ya." Ikaika huddles in a little closer, "I got slapped upside the head and my ears were ringing for long time. I didn't hear why either. Could not hear for three days. But, I never shroomed on a new moon after that incident. Curiously, we never went crashed the glass again either." Ikaika leans in a bit further, "Until tonight."

"What?" Lika and Kaleo look to the sky and then to each other. Kaleo starts to raise his voice but catches himself, "Fock no. It might be a new moon, but we're not going to fly through any glass, period. A third time would be suicide. I think we can all agree on this."

"Yes. Well, the night is just getting started. We break no glass tonight boys. Ok? Lesson learned." Ikaika looks to the ground and sighs.

Lika tries to peer through the snow capped trees, "It opens us up to lost spirits. We glow in the moonless night on shrooms and attract lost spirits in the dark. That's why. It just came to me, just now. Suddenly, I am having understanding too. Fock. Actually, some focking lost spirit just whispered that shit in my ear just now. But you still look like one big focking bird."

Ikaika shakes his head, "Ok, fine. Maybe we're all seeing some deep shit right now. I mean, if you really want to think you're one giant black steel turtle on shrooms, just go with it. It's been pretty fun so far. Ya? But all I'm saying is pretending that you really are one giant focking sea turtle made of out of rock while shrooming on a new moon is a lot like thinking you are wearing a football helmet and bashing your head through a focking window. I say we play it safe and just agree to be our regular selves while we execute this plan and get the fock outta here. It's a good plan and we're probably peaking on the shrooms right now. Right focking now. Ok?"

"But you were focking flying. Is that the shrooms, or are you really flying around like you're wearing a giant focking bird suit? Eh?" Lika reasons. "It's all so confusing."

Kaleo responds quietly, "It's the shadows. Black tracers in the dark. New moon or not, let's keep our shit together. I'm just saying let's try to tone it down a bit. It's a good thing all we gotta do is just what the manini (small) gecko told us. The odds are starting to stack against us, but we just gotta stay on course here. I totally get what you're saying, brother. Roger?"

Lika reassures, "No, Roger that. I'm with you. It's just been a rollercoaster for me. It's just the farthest we've ever been away from the Island and I was surprised to see this heiau in the middle of nowhere. I got homesick, that's all. Of course I don't really believe I'm a giant turtle. I'm not that focked-up. I mean, I'm totally focked up, but I'm not that focked up."

Kaleo supports, "So many ups and downs. This has been one hell of a trip brothers. Kaik's is right. You do look like one fat focking wrecking ball of a turtle, but that's just the shrooms on a new moon. Playing tricks with our heads. Ya? And ya, it's spooky as shit when ghosts sneak up and whisper in your ear. But let's try not to get carried away like we did after the football game. Strike three on the crash-da-glass-on-shrooms thing is not gonna happen. I pissed in my pants that morning. But for reals, though. You cannot get lost in the high. No turtles, no barracuda, no owls. Well, except for that black focking owl up there. We're just a couple of sailors trying get home, just like the little gecko showed us."

Ikaika stares up to the ledge of the cave for a while and takes a leap. One compression of his bat-like wingspan and he is thrust over the cave's ceiling. Ikaika perches next to the black pueo and slowly reaches out to it. He gently puts his hand around its neck and brings his eyes closer. He whispers silently to himself, "They *are* here. They're *in* here. They are all in here. I see her... I see them... all of them." On the outside, Ikaika appears as black stone. On the inside, his glimmering soul fills the shell with his unique glowing life energy. In that moment, a single drop of condensation forms on his eye, collects and drips from his cheek. At the same time, Keala cries within their crystallized owl. Tears emerge from the owl eyes as they stare into the glow of each other's soul.

"Alright boys." Lika commands. "We're on the clock now. Guarantee they heard the explosion at the compound. We gotta move."

"Guarans-ball-bearings brah." Kaleo flips over the ancient canoe and finds a pair of clubs coated with the black obsidian crystal, "Mean eh, the pahoa (war club). Brah, these bad boys are sharp as broken glass. These one's are mine. Cuz, you like some? Eh, Ikaika? You trying to make out with that bird or what?"

"Eh, fock you you fockin' flounder." Ikaika mutters as he swoops down from the ledge. He walks up next to Kaleo and whispers, "I swear, Keala-them are totally inside that focking bird. You were right." Ikaika sneaks a look over his shoulder up to the ledge. "You better watch your shit, brah. Alana's in there too."

Kaleo panics, spins and glares desperately up to the owl. He stares for a moment, "Dammit. She's the one I'm scared of. Well fock a muddy duck... where's braddah Tiki? That's not Tiki... Tiki no stay in the bird... That's not him, but there is another version of Tiki in there. There's another version of you in there. You got one focking kid up in that bird, brother Ikaika."

Ikaika launches thirty feet straight up, snatches the black owl and plummets back to the ground. He puts his eyeball right up against the bird's eye, "No way! Keala's not hapai! No way she went get hapai like that!"

Lika snatches the statuesque bird from Ikaika's grip and peers into it for a spell. "Hmmm. Yeppers. That's your keiki in there. You've got one keiki brah."

Ikaika takes another look in disbelief, "How in the fock? Who-and the what-and the why in the fock? If I had a fockin' kid, I would know if I had a fockin' kid and we ain't never had a fockin' kid without me knowing about it!"

Kaleo laughs, "I told you! I told you kooks- this bird was from the fockin' future!"

"Eh fock you." Lika hands the bird over to Ikaika, "You said the portal was from the future."

"Eh, fock you, you fockin' fockah! How can the portal be from the future? The portal was right in the present, but it linked us to the fockin' future on the other side!"

Ikaika holds the feet and points the bird's beak at Kaleo, "What are you talking about kook? The bird was with us before the portal opened up. Keala-them was in this bird, watching us the whole time already."

"Whatevers, I was still right! The future Keala is in there! Keala-them are in that focking bird right focking now, but from the future! They will watch this in the future, which makes right now the fockin' past for them. If they was in the past, or even the present, we'd all be focking dead. She'd already have cut off my focking ear, stabbed him in the neck, and strung you up by your focking balls already!"

"Wait... what?" Lika needs a moment.

"Hold on. Just hold on you fockin' mutt." Ikaika tries to look into the bird's eye for confirmation. "Either way, we're fockin' focked. It's a shit-focking sandwich Leo."

"Wait, just hold on a second boys." Lika reasons, "This is a good thing."

"Eh?" Ikaika and Kaleo in unison.

"This is a good thing." Lika retorts, "Did you knock her up before you left?"

"Eh?" Ikaika hides the bird behind his back.

Lika calmly smiles, "Did you went da kine her before we left on this focking trip brah?"

"Uh..." Ikaika shifts his weight to his other leg. "Uh, no actually. She was pissed at me. She thought this whole thing was a bad idea and that we were gonna fock it all up and get fired."

Lika chuckles, "Well there you go. How she gonna get hapai (pregnant) if you never went da kine her yet? That is your boy, captain. See? That means we stick to the plan, which is a good plan. These shrooms are really tripping me out right now. I say we go for it. Make our dreams come true, right now. We go charge 'em. We gonna make it back home, just like the manini gecko went showed us how.

We lay low for a while and when all this blows over, you go back home and explain all this to her. She's gonna understand we had no other choice, she's gonna forgive you so you can go da kine her later and make the hapai. See? Just like the manini 'aumakua instructed you.

Now, I never suspected I was going to turn the big body into one giant-ass sea turtle, but you're right. This is a blessing. This is the 'aumakua watching over us to make sure we make it home so you can go da kine her and make the fockin' keiki already. It's the only way any of this makes any sense. Ya?"

Kaleo concurs, "Ya. Ok. I got-choo brah. See Kaik's, just like I was trying to tell you. The only way the future Keala can be in that focking bird with your keiki right now is because we perceived this plan, interpreted it. But I'm with you though. Alice had a guide in Wonderland.

I like the idea of being a lava demon barracuda. It's a really cool way to experience this hallucinogenic episode. It's like I manifested an entire world from my imagination and shared it with my true brothers. I'm really freakin' trippin here boys! We're the only ones who can pull this off! We bust in, load up the Ubiq, and sail back to Kaua'i. Somehow, you are

160

going to find a way to make her forgive you for all this shit. No more strike three. We're counting on you. I'm not losing an ear for this one brah. Ok?"

Ikaika looks at him for a moment, "Brah. You really don't have ears right now. I don't know why you're so worried."

Kaleo grunts, "Eh?"

"Your ears, they're gone." Ikaika looks him up and down, "You stay one fish now. You're one barracuda, that's why no more ear. When was the last time you saw one fish with ears? Or one boto (penis)?"

Kaleo looks down, "No, the wanker's right here. The black barracuda is just a visual projection of the mana. It's just because of the shrooms. I'm packing the mean hammer right here. Ya? I thought that's what we just agreed on. Just ride the trip, don't let the trip ride you. Eh? Ain't nobody shooting my ass tonight!"

Ikaika looks away, "And your ala-ala's brah, when was the last time you saw some nuts on a fish?"

"Eh, fock you!" Kaleo shoves at Ikaika, "Ain't no boto on your fockin' bird suit either!"

"Eh, calm down. Dumb-asses. You're gonna get your dicks back when the shrooms wear off. Otherwise, how you gonna go da kine and get all hapai with the keiki? We need to hurry up and get moving down the mountain. Now, lets go get the Ubiq loaded up. And just be cool about the shapeshifter visual shit." Lika huddles them in close and whispers, "And cool it with the shroom talk and shit. Keep the incriminating shit to a minimum. Keep talking stupid shit and Keala's going to snap. She's gonna get that focking owl to claw *your* ear off and clamp that beak around *your* fockin' nuts."

Ikaika sets the Hunaka'i Pueo down softly as it becomes restless in his hand. It immediately soars out of the cave and perches on a branch down the trail. It hops to another branch, trying to lead the way for them.

Ikaika walks over to the canoe, "Come on, grab some clubs let's get down there. What happened to the beer?"

Lika flips the other canoe over, "Aw. All the beer blew up. But here's the box of shrooms." He scrapes at the inside of the canoe, "Check this out brah. All those doobies you went rolled up, they're all cindering inside this canoe from that explosion. They're all lit up already. Gotta smoke 'em on the way down."

He gets them between his fingers and starts to pass them out. "Brah, my fingers feel like they're made out of rocks. Not easy to handle a joint, but it's going to be fun busting open those tanks and blowing that meth lab up. Are you sure I'm not really one giant stone turtle? Because I actually feel like one giant stone turtle. I'm going in as one giant stone turtle. Cannot help it."

"Fockin' lava demons." Kaleo chuckles, "Brah, I bet they never imagined they'd see some shit like this coming at 'em. I actually feel like I'm wearing a giant fish suit. Is the stoney turtle super stoned?"

"I don't know brah." Lika walks while concentrating on each joint between his fingers and the battle clubs clutched under his arms, "They got so much drugs down there, I imagine they imagine a whole lot of weird shit. Wait. I'm so stoned that they are going to see me as one giant turtle too. Like, I'm so stoned it's going to make them stoned. Can you project intoxication if you're in the spirit world? Do you think we're contagious?"

"It's possible. Anything is possible in this state. I imagine everybody is on something. That's why I'm particularly worried about some people having guns. What if they're tripping too and actually think we're monsters and shit? Give a crackhead a gun and some moddah-fockah's getting shot. Hopefully they're on heroin and just like, fall asleep." Ikaika considers.

As they catch up to the guardian owl, it flutters to another tree further down the trail. The owl tries to quicken their pace, but the clumsy stone creatures maintain their attention on puffing away at the cannabis while it lasts. Dropping a joint in the snow would be unacceptable because they live by a code.

162

"Eh, you think all those addicts are going to run out of there all screaming to be free or try to stay for the drugs? I don't think there's enough supervision. They could totally overthrow that place. We cannot be the only mutineers in this operation." Lika ponders.

Kaleo reasons, "Once an addict, always an addiction to fight. I was talking story with some guy washing fish guts from a barrel last week and you know what, brah. He said he was actually better off stinking like dead fish all day, slaving away in the warehouse than living on the streets, cold hungry, stealing for food. Always searching for the next high. But here, he's getting high all day long, thanks to the mob. Gutting cursed fish for the drug cartel. Living it up, brah." Kaleo plucks a single joint from the many lined up, and extinguishes it on the side of his head. "Brah, I'd rather fockin' kill myself than live like that. I mean if there's no way out of the addiction, what else can you do? Fockin' poor bastard. I mean, I feel sorry for them, even if it's not their fault. Fighting everyday of your life. I hope they don't attack us when we blow up their crack factory. What if they got drugged involuntarily by the fockin' area managers and their creepy technicians? Eh? Unwilling addicts? Gonna be one revolution."

"Well, they tried to drug us. Blood test, my ass. They wanted us to be their junkies too, but it never worked. I wonder why. Don't you? I really want to find out why they couldn't smack us out on that heroin shit. Everyone else got hooked, fast kine. Everybody was getting off on that shit but us. Ya?"

Lika has fallen behind. He stopped walking after his last joint burned away. "Gotta be the shrooms. Everything good happened as soon as we got hold of those suckers. We went from failing the drug test to here's a fishing vessel full of drugs. Turned the bad vibes all good. Now, watch the big body shoulder roll." Lika leaps over onto his round, shelled backside. The thud and roll sounds like a boulder snapping across tree branches. He picks up speed and tumbles past Ikaika down the trail.

Ikaika hurls himself above the tree tops with a few deep thrusts of his wings. Kaleo finds himself alone. He begins trotting through the shallow snow, dodging spruce trees. He runs right past Lika before

163

slithering around and sneaking up behind him, "Eh, brah. What the fock? Are you dropping nuggets?"

"Eh?" Lika continues walking quietly.

"Did you just take a dump right in front of me? Kook. I almost stepped on it." Kaleo hops to the side quickly.

"Take a dump? I didn't take a dump. I don't think I just took a dump. I may have farted once or twice." Lika defends.

"You nasty fock. Brah. When you gotta go, you gotta go. I guess." Kaleo chuckles.

Lika chuckles too, "I don't think so. If I was to let loose, we'd be dealing with another focking avalanche over here."

Ikaika swoops in through the trees and perches just overhead, "He's right. You're dropping nuggets. They're glowing red inside. I think you just shitted lava out your okole (butt). Nasty fock."

"What?" Lika doesn't like being embarrassed, "You guys don't want to be focking with me right now. I'm ready to go down there and bust through some walls and shit."

Kaleo hunches over, "He's right. They're totally glowing. You just shitted some hot lava nuggets out your pilau (dirty) okole! Just think of the crazy magical shrooms that's gonna grow out from your mutated turtle shit! You know, like da kine, cow shit. We should totally take them with us!"

Lika's had it, "What was that kook? You like me bust up your teeth? You'd be eating turtle shit mushroom soup, if you keep focking around like that because you no more teeth. I'm about to give you both some custom dental work. Now how about you shut the fock up? Supposed to be quiet. We're almost there."

Ikaika shushes them from high up on the branches, "How about you both shut your fockin' clams? Someone's coming." Ikaika launches

164

past the tree tops and vanishes in the cloudless sky. Kaleo and Lika instantly freeze their postures awkwardly as they look towards each other. Ikaika suddenly lands between them and compares the grotesque absurdity of their altered forms for a moment, "Eh, uh. We got two people walking up the trail. I don't think they know we are here. They probably cannot see us because we're in the spirit world."

Kaleo ponders, "Hmmm. Do you think they will see us or the black lava rock demon shadow versions of us? This will be the test to see how hard we're actually tripping here."

"Wait. What kind of people? Like security people with guns and shit, or some focking tweakers, or some dopey hippies and shit?" Lika inquires.

"Couple of tweakers. This one focking hippie dood, and some strung-out chick with a bag." Ikaika reports. "They're walking pretty slow. Probably all focked up already, just like us. Probably grabbed a sack full of drugs like we did and snuck the fock out of there."

"I'd like to check out that bag. I totally want to bring these nuggets." Kaleo points to the baseball-sized rocks, glowing red in the snow.

"I was totally going to smack your stupid head wide open just now, but I don't want to scare off the hippies. Here they come. What should we do?" Lika remains frozen in the same suspicious position.

Ikaika whispers, "Just be still. Don't want them to freak out."

Kaleo whispers back, "Ok. We'll just stand right here like statues. If they freak out, then that's because we actually are lava demons and this twisted hallucination is now our reality. If they don't freak out, then they see us in our human fisherman form and we truly are tripping balls right now. Roger?"

Lika agrees, "Maybe they won't see us at all. Because we're actually in the spirit world."

Ikaika, "Well, they'll sure the hell hear you if you two don't shut the fock up."

The dazed couple stumble slowly in the dark. They stop at a clearing to light up cigarettes, appearing to shiver in the cold. As the girl sinks to her knees, the young man tries to pull her back up. "We gotta keep going. Come on Wendy. They said we have to walk around for another hour."

"Screw those pigs. My feet hurt already." She's had enough. "My stomach hurts. I just want to go to sleep for a while. Why are we even listening to them for? They're not the fucking boss of shit."

"I know. I know. Just one more hour. We promised the little pigs we'd fuggin' do it. Let's keep going before they come check on us." He pulls her up and both stumble for a bit.

"They're not going to check on us up here. They never go outside. They probably got camera's out here and shit though." The girl turns around and looks directly at Kaleo. "Why don't you go ask that guy if they seen any fishermen out here." She points and stumbles their direction. The girl hunches over and starts heaving.

The hippie steps behind the girl and pulls her long, stringy hair to the side. "Hey, you guys seen some fishermen out here walking around?"

Lika looks over to him and then whispers back to his shipmates, "Wot-da-fock? I don't think they see lava demons. Hold on..." He turns back around, "You talking to us?"

The hippie snorts and rips a series of dry coughs. "Ya. Buddy. Talking to you. I wanted to know if you seen some fishermen out here. Walking around and shit."

Kaleo replies, "Fishermen? What do they look like?"

The hippie coughs up and spits out some sticky goo. "Ya. Fishermen, they wear the orange suits with the big 'ole fuggin' boots. And

166

the brown gloves and shit. You seen any fuggin' fishermen? Walking around up here?"

The mutated fishermen huddle back up and giggle to each other. Ikaika politely asks, "Definitely didn't see any fishermen like that. Why are you out here looking for fishermen? Why don't you go check the docks?"

"The dickhead security guards are checking the docks. They told us to check up here. Aren't you out here looking for them too?" The girl stands up straight as she can and spits, "What are you guys doing out here?"

Kaleo clears his throat and replies, "We're just partying."

"Oh. Hell yes." She drops her bag and several hypodermic needles roll out. "Oops. We're partying too." She laughs at first, until it once again turns into a heaving cough.

The hippie haunches over for some boisterous coughing and spitting. He nearly falls over and catches his balance, "They said the fishermen got all fucked up and wandered off with a shit load of crank. They said there wasn't anymore left. Except for this here. We got the last of it. Why? You got some crank?" He lets go of the girl and takes a several clumsy steps towards Lika. He suddenly starts coughing uncontrollably and falls to his hands and knees.

The gangly young girl hobbles after him and collapses at his side. She starts heaving and snorting. "You got some crank? We're looking for some crank. What are you partying with?" She looks up for a moment and then locks up in a heaving muscle spasm.

"Uh... No. We don't have any crank. I got a couple of doobies left." Kaleo watches the frail girl wretch into the snow for a moment. She looks up and tries to crawl closer to him. She stretches a desperate smile across her sparsely located teeth until the heaving resumes. Kaleo turns his head towards Ikaika, "Wow. Oof." He tries to erase the cringe from his face before turning back to her, "Sorry, eh. Just some weed. Is that what you got there? Some crank? In those needles inside the bag?"

167

She crawls a bit closer and looks at the steam hissing out of her bag. "Nah, weed sucks. Smoking weed doesn't even get me high anymore. After I got on this crank, nothing else seems to work. What the... This shit's bubbling out. I never seen it do that before." The hippie stumbles and drops to his knees beside her. She opens the bag to show him, "What's going on with these? What the hell? The shit's bubbling and seeping out of the needles. It's all ruined! What are we going to do?"

The hippie accuses, "What did you fugging do? That's all we got left! Give it to me!" He tries to snatch the bag from her. They wrestle violently on the ground, coughing, snorting and spitting onto each other. It only takes a few seconds before they exhaust their energy and quietly go limp.

Lika chuckles for a bit, "Eh, you two ever seen anything like my friend here?" He points to Ikaika before getting his hand slapped away.

"Uh... ya." The hippie moans.

Ikaika is startled, "Wait. You mean you've seen a person like me before? Don't I look a little strange to you?"

"Uh... strange? Sorry, they told us not to mess around with the natives. I didn't mean to call you strange." The hippie defends.

Lika steps forward a bit, "Mess around with what natives?"

The girl looks up and stares at the three Hawaiians for a moment, "The Aleut. The Indians. They said don't mess around with the Native Americans that live near here. They said you creep around and perform rituals to cleanse the land because you don't like the fishing boats. They said to stay away or you'll kidnap us and sacrifice us in some kind of ritual. Maybe even eat us."

The Hawaiians huddle and chuckle to each other for a moment. Lika turns and hunches over to get a little closer, "We're definitely not going to eat you. Are you saying my friend here looks like an Aleut Indian to you?"

She spits to the side, "Ya. He looks like an Aleut Indian in a big fuggin' bird suit." Lika bursts into a hefty laugh. She points to Lika, "And you look like a fat fuggin' turtle. And he looks like he's wearing a dragon suit. Are you sure you're not going to eat us and shit?"

All three men laugh in wonder. Kaleo steps forward, "I'm not a dragon. I'm wearing a barracuda suit." He gets closer and bends down to her as she looks up and nods in agreement. "Is this what you guys are hitting? Did you get this from the back of the barracks?"

Kaleo slowly reaches for the bag of hissing needles. The girl nods her head briefly before putting her face back down to the snow. He picks up the bag and carefully pulls out a hypodermic needle. He slowly lifts it as he stands back straight, watching the white fluid inside bubble and fizzle out the tip of the needle. Lika and Ikaika step closer and look over his shoulder. Kaleo slowly brings it closer to eye-level as it begins to boil more rapidly. "Well that's strange. I don't think this shit likes me very much."

He leans in to study the volatile reaction increasing within the syringe. The Hawaiians lean in, mesmerized by the affect their proximity is having on the fluid. A small pop shatters the syringe as the white percolating chemical splatters across their faces. "Ah! What the Fock!" The fluid bubbles violently for a second before evaporating clean off their marbled faces. The chemical sizzles to steam and vanishes, much like dripping water onto a hot cast iron pan.

"Hey!" The hippie declares, "Hey, don't waste our shit! That's all we got left!"

"Oh, sorry. Eh?" Kaleo wipes his eyes and realizes it has evaporated cleanly. He shakes the bag upside down and drops the remaining needles in front of the girl. "Eh, sorry about that. I never seen shit like that blow up in my face before. You mind if I use this baggie? Can I keep this?"

"Uh... sure. Go for it. All yours." She says while scrambling to collect the the syringes out of the snow.

Kaleo smiles and turns to show off his new bag. He looks behind at the couple flicking off the caps and feverishly stabbing needles into their arms. "Scored. Let's go back and get some of those lava turds. I'm gonna chunk 'em at the fockin' guard shack." They turn and start walking away, back up the trail.

Ikaika looks back and sees the wretched couple ease down into the snow. They appear to deflate into a spell of bliss and serenity, unfazed by the cold. "Eh, brah. I don't think we can just leave them there. They're gonna freeze to death out here." They all stop and turn around. "I mean, I'm glad they finally calmed down. They were really grossing me out. Thought they was gonna puke on me and shit."

Lika confirms, "Ya. We probably cannot leave them like that in the snow. Let's go back and grab the nuggets and we'll scoop them up on the way back." Lika turns and finds Kaleo has already slithered away. He and Ikaika stand and watch the couple cuddle into each other's warmth as the itchy spasms dissipate. "At least they have each other." Lika looks to Ikaika, "Brah. So what, does that mean we really are shape-shifter lava rock demons or did she say we look like natives, but wearing costumes?"

Ikaika continues his stare, "Well, if you want to take the word of those junkies, I guess I look like an Indian in a big 'ole bird suit."

Lika confirms, "You were focking flying braddah. And I was smashing through trees. And Kaleo was running at like, 40 miles per hour. I know we're tripping balls right now and shit, but we really are something else right now too. Look, Kaleo's already back with his sack of turtle shit lava."

"Wait... you see that?" Ikaika continues his stare at the junkies, "That didn't last long. They're spazzing out again."

Lika peers over at them, "Maybe their shivering from the cold."

"They're convulsing." Ikaika takes a step towards them, "Maybe they O.D.'d on that shit. That's the same shit they tried to shoot us up with, and it didn't take. We expelled that shit right out the holes in our arms when we got to the heiau. And after we went fused with the lava, that shit went fizzed out when we got close and it blew up in our face. What if the lava causes a chemical reaction with that shit? Or, a magnetic reaction. It went bad when we got close and then they went shot it up. It turned into poison because of us. What if they fockin' die out here?"

"What are we supposed to do?" Lika follows, "We can't babysit the junkies right now. I feel bad for them, but we cannot risk our escape dragging these two around all night."

Ikaika stops before he gets too close, "This shit's all focked up. This is totally gonna bring me down." He watches the convulsions regain their intensity.

The girl's eyes suddenly open and she gives Ikaika a look of despair. She lets out a painful whimper as her pinned eyes go solid black in their sockets. They both begin heaving violently, coughing and spitting as they squirm to their hands and knees. Kaleo walks up from behind and stops in between Lika and Ikaika, "Holy-hell! Somehow they look worse."

The junkies look to the Hawaiians with one last plea for help before their back muscles haunch their spines. Their black eyes widen as if the pressure in their skulls is cracking the bones from the inside. Their jaws have locked open and every muscle in their bodies have strained to the point of snapping. Kaleo cannot look away, "Eh, uh... I think we should get the fock out of here."

Lika agrees but cannot break his stare, "Affirmative corporal. Let's leave these two lovebirds at it." Before they can make a move, they hear the jaw bones snap and unhinge. Lika tries to grab his brother's arm to push them into motion, but freezes at the sight of blood spurting from the hippies' necks. "Definitely time to hele (go) on braddahs!"

With blood spewing from their mouths, both junkies give one last powerful heave from deep in their bowels. Their mouths fill up and stretch with a large black object, cutting off the circulation and stopping the blood flow. The object continues to work its way out until the tip opens up. A red forked-tongue slithers out and begins stretching its way towards the

171

Hawaiians. The snout gains momentum when a pair of yellow eyes slides free of the junkies' jagged teeth. Once the heads of the black pythons emerge from the couple's mouths, the two massive snakes slither freely to the ground. Both the girl and boy collapse lifelessly to the snow, allowing the snakes to gain speed towards the Hawaiians.

Lika screams first, "FOCK THAT SHIT!" He squats lower, preparing to take a powerful leap up into the nearest tree.

Ikaika screams right after, "Ah! Hell no! I focking hate snakes!" He stretches out his marble wings and readies for launch.

Kaleo reaches into the bag and pulls out a pair of glowing red, baseball-sized lava rocks. As the snakes quickly slither straight towards them, Kaleo hurls each stone. Both Lika and Ikaika spring airborne as the stones connect with the top of each snake's head. The stones shatter upon contact. Red lava splatters across the snow. The snakes instantly stop their forward assault and begin writhing violently. The lava melts away the heads of the snakes, leaving twelve-feet of their bodies squirming painfully in the snow. "Wow. The shit fockin' worked. We need more fockin' shit!"

Ikaika finds himself perched on the same branch as their guardian owl, "Now there's focking snakes? This place is totally cursed!" He looks over to the owl for guidance, "This is getting complicated."

Lika is impressed, "Hell ya the shit focking worked! You fockin' nailed 'em! Good shot brah!" He scours the ground for more snakes, "I left you a couple more flaming shits down there. Let me know if it's not enough. I'm gonna fill up that whole focking bag in case all the junkies got snakes in their bellies."

Kaleo walks around the writhing serpents and kicks over the two shriveled corpses the snakes left behind. "So, that's probably the weirdest shit we seen all night. I was afraid they was gonna puke, but like some green beens and shit. Not some twenty-foot boa constrictor. Can we get the fock outta here now?"

"Roger that!" Both Lika and Ikaika drop to the ground and choose to walk into the thicket of trees to avoid the bloody clearing.

Kaleo walks back to inspect the snakes and sees them both barely twitching. He finds three separate piles of glowing lava nuggets on the ground and chuckles aloud, amused at how badly they all hate snakes. He scoops them into his new bag and gives one last look at the carnage the two junkies brought up the mountain.

Kaleo squats down near the puddles of cooling lava. With a small stick, he sifts through the dissolving snake flesh. He finds part of an eye socket and flicks it away from the steaming lava puddle. "Eh, you guys should check this out...". Flipping it over, he finds the snake's eye still intact, still unblinking, still watching him. "Eh, you guys should really take a look at this."

"Nope. We can see you from here." Lika shouts from down the trail.

"No, you should really check this out. I found an eyeball. I think it's still looking at me." Kaleo explains.

"Negative. I'm keeping an eye out for more tweakers. Get it? Keeping an eye out. Eh, fock you, that was funny." Lika says from the trail surrounded by trees. "Captain Kaik's and the bird went to check out the trail below so keep it quiet. Also, here's some more lava shit nuggets."

Kaleo peers deeply into the eyeball, "Brah, you know how you can see the Hunaka'i chicks in the pueo's eyes? I can see someone looking through this focking snake's eyeball too. Come check it out before it melts away."

"Nope." Lika declares. "Not while those dead fockah's are still squirming. And how the fock do you impregnate a couple of tweakers with giant snakes anyways? Eh? Did they swallow the snakes, like when they were babies? And then they grew inside? Don't snakes hatch from eggs? Swallow some eggs? Ya? Stick the eggs up their butts? Like during their physicals? I'm concerned. Wait... They're coming back."

173

Ikaika swoops down and lands next to Lika, "Holy-focking-shit brah. Everybody's out in the yard. I can see them from the ledge over there. We're at the bottom of the trail already. There's tweakers everywhere."

Lika questions, "What do you mean there's tweakers everywhere?"

"I mean there's junkie fockin' tweakers all over the yard. Right inside the fence, all over the yard, all spread out everywhere." Ikaika holds his arm out for the great black owl to land. "What's Kaleo doing over there? Digging through the snake guts?"

"Ya. He uh... he says there's someone looking at us through the dead snake's eyeball and shit." Lika explains. "This shit's starting to get really weird. If everyone's out in the yard, why don't we just cruise down to the shore and bust into the bay doors from the water?"

"Well, I thought about that." Ikaika reasons, "Except the guards are all lined up at the docks. I think we should stick to the plan and go through the yard with the tweakers. They are all just standing around, just sitting around. Get Kaleo over here." Ikaika whistles.

Kaleo stabs the stick through what remains of the eyeball and flings it to the snow. Walking over, "What's this I hear about people out in the yard? Are we going down to the docks or going straight through the yard?"

Lika catches him up, "The braddah says all the guards stay at the docks already. He wants to stroll through the yard with the tweakers. Whatchoo think?"

Kaleo ponders the choices, "Guards got guns and shit. But what if all the tweakers start yacking up snakes at us?"

"Talk about a shit-focking-sandwich." Ikaika debates, "I got it. How's about I go back to the heiau and grab the red feather cloaks from inside the canoe? Those two tweakers thought we was Aleut Indians, so what if we wore the feather cloaks and disguised ourselves as Indians? Eh?"

Kaleo is on board, "Oh, I get it. And not just stroll through the yard, but we go dance through the yard. Fockin' hula our way through the crowd all the way to the front door, ya? They don't want to mess with the natives."

"Hmmm. That's not the stupidest thing I heard tonight. Ok. Let's do it. Get the cloaks while we fill the sack up with more nuggets. I like the way the lava splattered. Had some impact. It really sends a message." Lika approves. He watches Ikaika sail over the trees. "You think this is a good idea?"

Kaleo grabs hold of his brother's shoulders and looks him over, "I was joking about the hula, but fock, I actually read somewhere that dancing hypnotizes snakes. If the tweakers start puking snakes at us, I really think the hula will help."

Lika ponders, "It wasn't until those junkies went shot up that crank that made them puke up the snakes. And they did say that there was no more crank left. Maybe we got a chance here."

"That's true." Kaleo thinks back, "But they were gagging and choking the whole time. You saw the shit fizzing up inside the needles. I think we have that affect on the shit because of the lava, like we're radiating some kind of energy. Like our magnetic field, our radiation clashes with the chemicals in that heroin. And if those tweakers are pumped full of that crank, our presence will make their blood boil. And what if that's what makes the snakes want to bust out their guts? Does that make sense? There lies the conflict. It's possible, ya?"

Lika nods, "That does make sense. Those snakes did not like us, like the fish did not like us. But I don't want to get shot and realize we're not bullet proof. The security guards are total dickheads. Snakes and bullets are the exact shit we need to avoid here."

Ikaika returns, "I got the helmets too! Oh, wait. Kaleo, I don't think you can wear one helmet on top of that mullet head. What? You guys think this is a bad idea now or what?"

Kaleo reassures, "Nah, nah, nah. That was the plan from the beginning. Just was not expecting a yard full of junkies with giant snakes sloshing around their guts. But with the feather cloaks, and the helmets, and the hula... it's just ridiculous enough to work and I'm plenty, plenty super buzzed right now. Let's do it. Let's do it super fast kind. Stick to the plan."

"Wait." Lika ponders just before they distribute the red and yellow feathered cloaks, "What if they put the snake eggs into the heroin and they incubate inside the junkies? Ya?" They all seem stunned, frozen at more thinking. "Ya. Are they running a fish farm or a snake farm?"

Ikaika digs deeper, "Oh nah. The fish farm is how they run the drugs. But a snake farm? That's one step beyond."

Kaleo adds, "You know how much smack you can hide in a god-damned boa constrictor? That fockin' snake went on fo' days. And nobody's gonna look inside a dead snake for drugs. That's the fockin' play here boys. Drug smuggling. Ya?"

"We're about to blow up some serious cartel shit here boys." Ikaika agrees. "We gotta blow up the other boats so they think the whole fleet sank and maybe they won't come looking for the Ubiquitous. As long as we make it back to Kaua'i, the cartel won't come looking. And even if they did, it's our island. We'd be doing our people righteous for keeping this curse off our 'aina (land). " He holds out the cloaks for them to take, "Pono (necessary, righteous)-up brothers. This is what the gecko showed us. The mana has been given to us. Our guardian owl watches over us." He looks up at the black stone owl perched above, "This is our kuleana (responsibility) now. If we no take care of this curse, I'm afraid our 'ohana (family) will have to deal with this later."

The three Hawaiians, energized from the spirit world and transformed into creatures from the past, gaze upwards into the eyes of their 'aumakua. The Hunaka'i family receive the stimulation from their host owl as a gift. But, Alana knows this transfer of energy into their minds also comes as a curse. Keala and Akila cried for answers. Alana knows this

176

is precious to them, yet she already fears the price they will have to pay when this energy ceases to pour into their souls. When they are left alone in the darkness, traces of this energy will lead this curse straight to them. Inside the owl, their thoughts, feelings, worries are shared without words.

Alana focuses back through their owl's eyes and watches the Hawaiians prepare for battle. The men fasten the cloaks to each other, still trying to suppress their laughter. They strike each other and argue the possibility of actually being fused with crystallized lava. They each select a pair of obsidian war clubs from the assortment Ikaika brought back from the heiau.

"Fockah! I'm telling you." Lika asserts, "If hitting me with that pahoa doesn't hurt me, then we might be bullet-proof!"

Kaleo confirms, "Fat fockah's got a point captain. I'm really pounding his gut over here. You sure you don't want to run down to the shore and sneak in from the docks? You heard the hippies. Your bird suit is real."

"Kook! I know you're pounding his gut plenty hard. So focking loud- you!" Ikaika shushes them, "Them fockah's with the guns is probably wondering what all that noise is. Cheez. If you mutts is so tough, then why are you so afraid of the snakes for? Eh?"

They rub their chins and think for a moment. Lika admits, "Well, because we don't fockin' like snakes. That's why."

"Of course you don't like snakes. Nobody likes snakes." Ikaika tries to calm them, "But it's just a bunch of tweakers in the yard. We don't know if they actually are full of snakes. And even if they were, by the time they puke 'em all up and shit, we'll already have hula'd our way through the front door. That's just another reason we no break-da-glass. I ain't never seen a snake chew its way through a glass door."

"Well, that was a big fockin' snake." Kaleo reasons, "And it was coming straight for me."

177

"True." Ikaika agrees, "You're clearly the ugliest. Maybe they thought you was their daddy in a turtle shell. But we stay with the gecko's plan. If all the tweakers are out in the yard, and all the guards are out by the docks, then there won't be anyone to stop us once we are inside the building. Get the shit, fast kind, and then get on the ship and go. The whole place will be burning down. If there is anyone inside, I'm betting that they aren't junkies with snakes in the gut. Honor the plan."

Kaleo nods, "Ya. True. Well let's go. Let's do it. Fast kind."

Lika agrees, "Stick to the plan."

The Hunaka'i Pueo propels into the treetops after the Hawaiians swiftly turn and jog onto the trail. The family watches the red cloaks reach the edge of the forest and become illuminated by the fluorescent lights on top of the fence line. Their owl is imperceptible hovering in the black open sky above. Even though the men have transformed into bizarre monstrous creatures, they retain the clumsy, childish motions of their original selves trying to dance through a crowd. Ikaika tries to lead them from the trail's opening along the side of the fence, but Lika pushes him to the side at the clearing. Kaleo slithers to the front of the line as they climb from the gully up to the road.

As they near the open gate, they begin dancing hula in unison, as they have practiced hundreds of times since childhood. Upon entering, they look through the crowd of workers, all spread out across the yard. No one pays them attention. No one bothers to look. The Hawaiians continue dancing but with better form, more relaxed, more confident. Lika turns and skips directly in front of a young couple. Their dizzy eyes glaze over his form and movement for a moment before they look to each other and chuckle softly. They smile and look back to Lika, laughing, trying to mimic his dance. Lika spreads his cloak and spins several times as if imitating a ballerina. The young couple attempt to spin and collapse to the snow covered ground. Still giggling, they reach out to him and smile in a chemically-induced ecstasy.

He gets back in line as the other two wait for him to catch up. He whispers, "Fockin' La-La Land brah. They're definitely high on something.

But we got a clean shot to the front door." He nudges them to proceed as they continue scanning over the people as they pass. "You think someone got hold of the shrooms after we busted out? They all look high as shit and none of them's wearing coats or boots or nothing."

"Maybe brah." Kaleo agrees quietly, still dancing along the sidewalk leading to the large glass doors. "At least nobody's coughing and puking."

Ikaika remains skeptical, "This might be the weirdest thing all night. This doesn't seem right. They never let anyone out of the building like this."

Kaleo suggests, "Well, you know what, that other couple said they were out looking for the fishermen. If there's no more heroin, maybe these people got hold of the shrooms and couldn't even make it out of the fockin' yard. They're all tripping and forgot all about the fishermen. That's what we'd do. Except, they're not highly-functioning stoners like us."

Lika agrees, "He's got a good point. Look, we're about half-way to the door. The plan's working. Keep dancing. Keep quiet. Keep moving boys."

The Pueo circles high above the yard. They watch the Hawaiians in red feather cloaks dance and weave through the throng of people. Their dance is having a hypnotic affect on the people as some take notice and slowly sway towards the sidewalk in the middle of the yard. The keen eyes of the great owl suddenly catches sight of a burst of light from the docks. It only takes a moment for the crack of a gunshot to be heard. They see another muzzle flare from the docks quickly followed by several more. The sound of sporadic gunfire erupts as the Hawaiians freeze in their tracks.

"I knew it! They're focking shooting at us!" Kaleo gasps.

Ikaika leaps over the crowd for a quick look and drops down, "From the docks, the dickhead's with the guns opened fire on us!"

Lika hunches down, pops his head up and ducks back, "But they're not hitting us, they're hitting them!"

Kaleo hunches down, "Fock! This is not the crowd I want to be in right now! The gecko said stay on the path, but the buggah never warned us about this. Let's get to the door!"

The boys stay low and push their way through the crowd. Ikaika notices, "They're not even shooting at us. They're executing all these hippies! This is some hard core mafia shit, killing off all the witnesses!"

Kaleo steps over several corpses as he holds onto Lika's shoulder behind him. Lika reaches back and clutches on to Ikaika. Fresh bodies hit the sidewalk just in front and begin bleeding out in the snow. The blood appears to gush out red but quickly fades to black as it cools in the moonless night. Kaleo motions for them to step around the lifeless corpse. It appears motionless except for slight twitching within the bowels. He stares into the open wound, split open and stretched from intestines pouring through the gash. "Uh... boys." Kaleo notices a writhing behind the spilling innards. "I don't think they are exterminating the witnesses."

Lika and Ikaika tug on Kaleo's shoulder for him to back away. "They're releasing the snakes on us!" Kaleo takes a step and sees the tip of a forked-tongue slither through the rupturing tissue. "It's a dirty focking shit-fock now you pirates! Listen to me. Get to the door!" He turns to see Lika's expression of horror turn into a smirk.

"What did I focking tell you mutts! Eh? We're not the only thing that manifested here tonight." Lika grabs hold of his brother and begins charging towards the doors with rumbling speed. "It's a fockin' royal fockin' shit-fock boys!" Lika jerks Kaleo off the ground and heaves him up and over several more corpses lying in their path. "Get the door opened brah! And watch the glass!" He realizes he threw his brother much harder than he meant. Sagging electrical cables snap out of their boxes above. Lika laughs when he hears his brother call him a dumbass.

As the bullets continue to fly, Lika leaps shoulder-first into the crew of six forklift operators he once saw playing cards. He remembers they wouldn't let him join in. He recalls one of them looking over his shoulder growling, "Locals, they're all cheats." Lika sat across the picnic yard, tied knots with two short ropes, and watched them lose money to each other. At least two of them never took their distrustful eyes off Lika at any time. Lika sat and listened for just the right insult before he triggered the urge to pick a proper fight. But he remembers them explaining to each other superstitions about witchcraft. They had mistaken the Hawaiian for the real local tribe of this shoreline.

Lika questioned himself as the haole, not local at this Alaskan fishing village. Lika did not pick a fight that night. He felt homesick. He also felt guilt for not picking a fight on behalf of all the other indigenous. He remembered they all appeared pale, sick and addicted. They all coughed and snorted. Lika felt disgust. He became distinctly repelled from them as he observed them all to be clawing at their stomachs and throats. He watched one stab himself below the ribcage and appear to have relieved an itch. He walked away from that fight as he did not want to contribute to the misery of their existence. Releasing them from this curse now seems like mercy.

Lika is unfazed at the impact, shattering their bodies with the blunt force of his mighty bouldered shell. Steaming blood showers the frigid air, quickly turning to fluttering snowflakes of red. The fluorescent lights overhead flicker a kaleidoscope of living tissue- spraying apart and freezing into crystalized prisms. Lika plows through the blood cloud like a greased umbrella. He faces downwards but can sense the life force extinguishing into the cold.

In contrast to this charge of life, there suddenly exists a vacuum where a pinpoint of black void has developed. The glowing charge from the living blood vanishes and appears to create a dull cloud from within the shimmering light of electrical cellular impulses. The cloud condenses and darkens into a mist of shadows. The dull gray smoke solidifies once it becomes pure black. Lika witnesses the manifestation of a dark electric charge into physical matter that exists in total contrast to his own ether-infused form. The static sparks black as a photographic negative would appear. The dark sparks collect and take shape into the birth of a cobra. It takes a moment to register the dark entity manifesting from the driver's life force.

181

The black cobra wriggles out of the dying torso of the forklift driver. After shedding its skin from dormancy, the full grown reptile slithers free for the first time. The eyes take only seconds to acclimate to air and it immediately takes notice of Lika. Several more snakes writhe free from the throats of the other convulsing bodies. The colorful vipers molt and hiss upwards at him. They fight to wriggle loose, fangs dripping with potent venom. The life-force of the dying men sucks into the snakes and flips to its contrasting, opposite existence.

Lika visualizes the dark electrical stimulation controlling the physical matter of the snakes for only a second. Staring into the electrical transformation affects his vision like staring into a camera flash. He is instantly repelled. If the flashing of bright light had an opposite, it would appear as light being sucked into a void and compressing it until the vacuum occupies physical space as dark matter. Lika runs past the clusters of snakes before they can even slither after him. Dark shapes linger and float in his vision, tracing the sight of the snakes as he ran past. He focuses on the doorway ahead. He widens his eyes to counter the streaks left behind as if looking away from a welder's flash.

Ikaika rips off his cloak. He whips it back and forth across the sidewalk to clear away several snakes gliding straight towards him. He flings them across the snow only to see them waggle and twist their way back his direction. "Aw-Fock-Aw-Fock-Aw-Fock! Fockin' snakes everywhere! It's a focking trap! I ain't going down like that!"

Ikaika leaps from the ground and thrusts his wings to catapult him towards the vestibule. He continues to swing his heavy cloak wildly to clear the foyer as he lands. He skids to a stop at the double glass doors and pushes against the steel handles. The doors rattle against the frame without opening. He quickly turns and whips the cloak in circles like a propeller with one arm. He shoves on the door handles with the other hand, "Fock this shit! Fock these stupid doors!" He turns back around to see Kaleo and Lika sprinting full-speed with several clusters of snakes following close behind.

"*Pull* the focking door open, lolo!" Kaleo hollers.

"*Pull* it?" Ikaika panics.

"Pull the focking door kook!" They both holler.

Ikaika continues to whip the cloak like a weed-whacker but hooks onto the handles and gives them both a quick yank. They open only a little before steel chains snap against the inside handles. "They chained the fockah shut!"

Lika grabs hold of Kaleo again and hurls him onto the foyer. Kaleo raises his pahoa, "To the side brah!"

Ikaika steps to the side and holds one handle steady as far as the chains will allow. The obsidian club slashes cleanly through the chains. Sparks shower to the ground before the chains can fall away. Ikaika and Kaleo open the doors wide as Lika tromps onto the foyer and leaps head-first through the opening, followed by the Hunaka'i Pueo. Ikaika pulls the doors to the latches while Kaleo wraps the chains into knots around the handles.

Lika slides across the concrete floor and shatters a desk against the wall. He stands up holding a phone book and walks up next to Kaleo, admiring the sturdy knot of the chains. Lika stuffs the phonebook into the mail slot to prevent access. Dozens of snakes crawl against the double glass doors and dozens more slither up the vestibule steps. Kaleo points to the doors, "See? That's why we no break-da-glass. Eh? I bet you was wondering why I brought all that shit up earlier. The glass is the only thing keeping those slimy fockahs out. That was a valuable lesson we learned. Ya?"

"Well dammit." Ikaika agrees, "I guess that makes sense. What doesn't make sense is why the snakes hate us."

Lika offers light, "Just like the fish. The cursed halibut hate us too. You know how we was talking about how we were on this certain frequency? Tuned in? These snakes is on the contrasting, opposite frequency as us. They manifested dark electrical energy from light energy, it's all relative."

Kaleo chuckles, "Oh, you one smart bugger all of a sudden. Akamai (smart), you. When did you come up with this? Eh? I already figured this out from the two snakes the hippies puked up on the trail."

"Oh ya?" Lika challenges, "Well why didn't we go down to the shore and jump the fockah's with the guns?"

Ikaika offers, "Brah, I don't know how I know, but I know I don't want to get bit by a fockin' snake right now. Eh? And if I know I don't want to get bit by a fockin' snake, then I also know I don't want to get shot by a focking gun either. Roger?"

Lika checks the effectiveness of the phone book in the mail slot, "Roger. You make a good point. I know I don't want to get bit by some snake right now. I mean, I feel like one mean wrecking ball. But I can sense that venom, for real kind. They manifested some dark energy and poisoned all those tweakers. And murdered them. This is the most cursed shit I ever heard of. This kind shit should not exist in our world."

Kaleo interjects, "Well, neither should we. But we had our gathering of owls. I guess the mafia is having a gathering of snakes. Ya? Equal opposites. Yin Yang."

Ikaika breaks his stare out the window, "They're still shooting tweakers out there. What if they start shooting the glass? Eh?"

Lika blurts, "We better get our plan fockin' rolling then. Ya? Here's where my gecko dream ended. I cannot see the dream anymore because I still see the flash of the dark energy in my head. You know, like staring at a camera flash."

Kaleo agrees, "That's why we cannot see the gecko dream anymore. It's been blocked out by the contrasting energy. This shit's gettin' twisted. Now listen... it sounds like this place is empty. Let's try not to kill anybody inside. You never know who's gonna barf up a snake. And remember, no break-da-glass. We all know the plan. Roger?"

All in unison, "Roger that." They each look to one another pointing and confirming which direction each one goes. Then they all point in the direction of the Ubiquitous and hold their Shaka's for everyone to confirm and admire. They stand and salute each other for a spell before nodding and turning away.

Kaleo zips down the hall to the right, mumbling away, "Spam, chili, shrooms, beer, pakalolo, rice, rolling papers, batteries, propane tanks..." He turns the corner and vanishes.

Lika pounces down the hall to the left without saying a word. Ikaika watches him around the corner and then looks straight up to the second floor of the foyer. He sees the Hunaka'i Pueo looking down at him from the railing. Launching upwards and perching on the rail next to the black owl, Ikaika scans the hallway. He can hear footsteps and metal clattering along the hallway. It's the sound of two large men walking cautiously in unison. Their long, slow strides indicates they crouched low. Faint circles of light swirl around the adjacent hallway, indicating vigorous scanning motions from a flashlight.

Ikaika wraps himself tightly with the large wings protruding from his shoulder blades. He marvels at the feathers scraping against each other as if each one were a steel sword. Yet, from within, the wings give the sensation of his own flesh and bone. Ikaika waits silently as two guards step into the light at the far corner of the hallway and peer his direction. They begin scanning the glass doorways.
Ikaika remains frozen as if they don't clearly see the marbled gargoyle perched on the ledge at the end. Both guards use their feet to push open doors and peek inside. The flashlight and barrel tap around the doorway during the search inside. They rest the forestock of their rifles in their bent elbows as they report their findings over the radio. Ikaika cannot make out what they mutter to each other, but they don't seem roused or frantic at the sporadic sound of gunfire continuing to sputter just outside. They seem indifferent, apathetic to the murder of every last worker in the compound.

Ikaika stares into their eyes for signs of darkness. He searches his senses for the presence of static or contrast opposing his own magnetic field. He feels nothing except the urge to enact the thrill of vengeance. He is piqued at the chance to deliver justice. In a feverish motion, Ikaika lunges forward. His wings spread and hurl him towards the two guards. Ikaika reaches up and claws the long fluorescent bulbs with his hands. They pop with a flash before the zone goes dark. Ikaika flies past the next array of ceiling lights and shatters the glass. A shower of sparks hit the floor as the next section goes dark. The two guards gawk at the sight of the demon gargoyle riding the surge of darkness straight towards them.

They reel in their rifles and fumble the mechanisms to ready their shots. Ikaika swings his legs forwards and sprawls his talons to clamp his prey. The muzzle flares burst the rounds into flight. Ikaika sees the spiral trajectory zipping through the air. He raises his head and lets the lead alloy ricochet off his stone shoulders, leaving only a small chip and a slight crack in his crystallized lava armor. His talons wrap completely around the guards' heads and detach them from their necks with little effort. He slings them back and then skids to the floor and turns. Ikaika glares at the decapitated bodies. They fall clumsily to the floor as the heads roll past. He extends his obsidian war clubs for any sign of snakes emerging from the corpses. He holds his position, ready to pounce. Blood spurts out with each remaining pump of their hearts. But, nothing stirs as the twitching diminishes.

Ikaika listens to the footsteps approaching, summoned by the pair of gunshots. He turns the corner again scanning for an awareness of negative energy and contrast. He finds a dozen armed guards stunned at the sight of a winged creature standing over their dead comrades. They raise their guns. Ikaika launches at them with fury. Several shots are fired, but the sharp edges of Ikaika's war clubs rip through their bodies with great speed. Their limbs are flung through the air. Their guns prattle across the floor.

Ikaika studies the bodies and the blood spurting into the air. He finds no snakes or signs of addiction. He observes closely and chooses which ones require additional hacks from his clubs. On the other side of the building, Ikaika can hear Lika pounding away in the basement level. The foundation jolts and rumbles from Lika's demolition. Ikaika is amused at the destruction below but is curious why these guards did not respond to the scene. He backs away from the pile of motionless bodies and stalks the hallway towards the control room.

Ikaika nears the metal doors where he first reported to the fleet commander. He hesitates. Even through the double doors, he can feel a vacuum of energy on the other side. He should have known the mafia boss would be waiting for him here. He considers backing away silently and darting straight for Lika, but something is pulling at him. Something invites him, oppositely attracting without aggression. Then, a sense of duty comes over him, he is the captain. Curiosity and invincibility arouse his ambition.

Ikaika places his hand on the door without allowing his club to tap against it. His other hand tightens around the handle with a pause. He takes a calming breath before giving a pull. Opening the door slowly, he peers across the floor and sees no one. Ikaika stands in the open doorway and can feel a presence through the dimly lit room. Although he senses a calmness, he spins both clubs around his grip and then clutches them in a ready position. He does this with style.

Still, nothing stirs. Ikaika blinks his eyes to reset the image of the room. Only the lights of the camera monitoring screens and a few control panels keep it from being totally dark. Ikaika raises his club against the wall to flick a light switch. Before he can make contact, a pair of yellow eyes gleam out from the far corner of the room. This freezes Ikaika. He then taps the switch upwards but only one ceiling light ignites a faint glow in the center of the room.

The yellow eyes whisper, "Amphetamines. It's an addiction we assign to the desperate-natured aggressors. The souls are dim, but the short lives are useful." Ikaika remains still and calm in the presence of a dark vacuum of a vibe. The whisper continues, "Your uniqueness, your singularity brings honor to my house. I have never witnessed such a large window of vibrational transference. Your lineage will make me a god in the next world. I am honored to have you as my guest within this compound."

Ikaika becomes focused on the voice and emerges free from all sensation within his body, "Am I your guest *out* of this compound?"

The yellow eyes with vertical black slits replies as a whisper, "Oh, please stay as my guest. Once the vipers are out, there's no getting them back in."

"I'm your guest? That's why you're going to tell me what you're actually doing here?" Ikaika stands frozen. His consciousness suddenly exists on the outside of the crystalized form, no longer within it. Instead of experiencing the world from behind his open eyes, he now perceives all electromagnetic connections from all over his entire form. He deeply reads the room, feeling the presence coiled up in the top corner.

"It would be rude not to. If I gave you an explanation, would you consider investing in our venture? A vested partnership if you will."

Ikaika whispers, "You brought the snakes."

"And you brought the owls." The eyes glare unblinking.

"You just murdered a village out there." Ikaika searches the distance for a connection with his guardian owl. "I cannot partner with that. I cannot murder people like this. I cannot have that on my soul." He finds the pueo's vibrational source and beacons a prayer from the top of his mind like a lighthouse.

"The addicts will be lost at sea. Unfortunately, deep sea fishing is hazardous. I gave them a great purpose. And they served that purpose by turning a wasted life into an eternal force. A force that I can harness. The same eternal force we are sharing now, but in a more magnificent splendor. I offer you a partnership, as you deserve. It would bring honor to my house."

"As long as I stay in your house?" Ikaika listens to the rumbling destruction of Lika's vengeance far below. "I don't belong here."

The eyes never blink, always piercing, "It was amazing to discover your ancestral artifacts in this wilderness. So many treasures came together here to make this night possible. See? You, in fact, do belong here. You are already latched in my fangs. I will always be in your dreams, erasing all traces and you will never see me coming. Leaving here will bring venom into the lives of everyone you know. And I will be right there, drinking their souls dry.

Besides, I'm not the one you want to kill. And, killing you will allow my brother to gain favor. Therefore, I offer you guest or prisoner? Listen, I know you must be experiencing the incredible hallucinogenic affects of those mushrooms right now. And the cannabis? They are my favorite too, but I've never ingested them in such amounts. It's astounding the three of you are not in a coma, much less enjoying this experience. But I beg you, please ride this episode out peacefully with your companions and we will discuss terms later with more coherent minds."

Ikaika pauses and becomes fascinated at the images of his own mind working from within. He visualizes luminescent metallic gears, much like the decorative inner-workings of a fine watch, coated sleek black with oil. Reflections of blue and red refract off the intertwining parts, churning, weaving in complex patterns. The mechanical movements gyrate and emit grey steam outwards filling his head and pressurizing his eyes and ears. He definitely confirms the potency of the intoxicants with a tickling giggle. "You've been poisoning us all since we got here. Even the fish are cursed."

"Yet, you rejected everything synthetic we gave you. Our manufactured substances won the addiction of everyone you saw at this facility. But the natural substances awoke your vision in a manner we rarely observe. We've got so much more to share with you. Peyote is the best, you will surely agree." The eyes continue to whisper.

Ikaika questions, "So you did not spike the weed? Or the shrooms?"

"Of course not." The whisper declares, "Synthetics can never achieve this success. We harvest our natural substances with great respect. Only in their natural potency can we entice this spiritual transference. That is why I would rather have your compliance than your submission. Please accept my peaceful invitation. Successful cultivation is a high honor."

"After I consult my crew. The all-natural craft is right up our alley. But I can already tell you what they're gonna say about the synthetic stuff." Ikaika requests.

The eyes continue to glare, "Of course. May I request that the big one ceases the demolition immediately? Your hallucinatory episode will take a dark turn if the vipers get into the facility. You're current composition is causing them distress. They will never cease to hunt you and we will never be able to rid this facility of them once they're inside."

"Oh? You want me to go get him to stop?" Ikaika asks politely.

"Yes. Please. He is causing a great deal of damage." The eyes urge.

"Sometimes he doesn't listen to me. He's tripping pretty hard. He thinks he's a giant turtle. They had me convinced earlier that I was a giant owl. Made out of stone, flying around and shit." Ikaika shares.

"Curious." The eyes scoff and chuckle slightly. "Are you implying that you no longer think you're a giant owl?"

"Nah." Ikaika assures, "I kind of sobered up when you started shooting everybody. Totally lost it."

"Fascinating." The eyes stare hungrily, "I usually prefer MDMA and cocaine in this situation, but I would enjoy experiencing psilocybin with you and your crew. So, you are really not perceiving yourself as an owl any longer?"

"Nah." Ikaika explains. "I stay completely sober right now. I was royally buzzed until the bullets started flying. You totally snuffed all the fun out the room already. Strange vibe there, cousin."

"Yes. Indeed." They yellow eyes glow and pierce. "You could say we have contrasting vibes. Especially in your current composition, your source energy is completely out-of-phase with mine. Remarkable. I told you you're unique in that manner. I appreciate your civility. I'll make a deal with you, Mr. Owl. In order to lighten the experience, I will order my

190

entire security force to shoot themselves and it will only be us left. And of course, the cleaning crew and a small fleet crew needed for the mass sea burial. They will, in fact, go down with the ship. Now, will you please advise them to stop damaging the building?"

"Ya. Sure. Give me a minute." Ikaika immediately backs to the door. Each step away from the dark entity brightens the pulsating intensity of his intoxication to its previous level. He quickly feels submerged into his own body again. Once he descends the stairs, he regains the full thickness of his hallucinatory state. He leaps down to the foyer floor and begins soaring towards the docks. Ikaika skids onto the Ubiquitous and finds Kaleo stuffing the cupboards below deck with everything he promised.

"Brah, no more room. I told you. Nobody can haul more beer than me." Kaleo ties down the beer cases against the floorboards.

"No time for that brah. We gotta go get Lika." Ikaika explains.

Kaleo continues to pull his half-hitch loop snug, "Already tried brah. He's having too much fun down there."

Ikaika reasons, "He keeps wrecking the place, the snakes are going to get in."

"No worries brah." Kaleo organizes the cans of chili label-outwards, and then secures the latch on the door, "He said he no break-da-glass. Plus, there's nobody in the building and all the guards are sitting in the yard with the dead hippies. Try listen brah. No more shooting." All goes silent for a moment until they hear dozens of shots fire off simultaneously.

"Ok, now there's no more shooting. But not nobody brah." Ikaika explains, "Somebody went talked to me upstairs."

"What? Who somebody went talked to you upstairs?" Kaleo halts the organizing.

191

"Fockin' da boss went talked to me brah. We gotta go get Lika." Ikaika grabs Kaleo's arm and runs up to the deck.

"Wait, da fockin' boss went talked to you when you went to the control room?" Kaleo inquires.

"Da fockin' boss was waiting for me in control room, brah." Ikaika reveals.

"What? So everything stay powered up, still yet? Oh shit brah. What about the plan, coz (cousin)?" Kaleo becomes worried and holds onto Ikaika's shoulder as they walk swiftly to the stairwell.

"Ya brah. Everything stay powered up still yet. Was weird brah. I had these two guards with guns coming at me and I just snapped. Fockin' went lolo-kind on 'em, laid them out flat. And I was checking 'em out for da snakes when I went felt some strange vibe in da control room.

Brah, I tell you this: I could feel the bad vibe hanging up from the ceiling. But I could not see him. Except the yellow eyes. I could see the yellow eyes but nothing else. Went thought he was one snake. He totally killed my buzz, that's how I knew he was da boss. Dat's why." Ikaika scurries to the bottom of the stairs. The rumble of crumbling concrete drowns his voice. "Lika! Eh! Brah!"

Ikaika and Kaleo approach a large pair of glass doors as a bright flash detonates down the hall. The explosion drowns out the sirens and the emergency strobe lights struggle to shine through the dust and ash. Kaleo reaches for the door handle and stops as a wave of bloodied water washes across the floor and splashes against the glass.

They watch Lika tumble and skid towards them. He manages to halt his momentum just on the other side of the glass door in front of them. "Eh, try wait." Lika chuckles, "The alarms automatically lock all the doors." Ikaika and Kaleo look at each other and then watch Lika toggle at the locking mechanism on top of the door frame. He tugs on the casing and yanks on the door handle. Kaleo and Ikaika cringe at the sound of the glass doors rattling and scraping against the steel frame. "Ha! There we go."

Lika carefully pulls the door open in front of Ikaika as he notices the lock housing drop down and dangle from a single red wire. They watch as the wire's slack takes up and the latch begins to spin around next to the door directly in front of Kaleo. The dangling latch taps against the unopened door, causing a tiny chip. It instantly grows to a tiny crack. The entire glass door screeches into a web of cracks from top to bottom and then suddenly crumbles as a thousand shards drop to the floor. "Eh! I didn't focking do that." Lika declares holding the other door wide open.

"Brah! What the fock!" Kaleo is alarmed.

"Eh! Don't focking worry about it. Just go through this one." Lika growls and steps to the side to let them pass. "Eh, brah. I thought you was gonna cut the power."

"I was intercepted in the control room brah." Ikaika confesses without stepping through the doorway. "The boss wants us to stay here as his guest. He wants us to stop wrecking the place before the snakes get in."

"Eh?" Lika is caught off guard, "What boss? You stopped by the office and talked to the boss? You mean human resources or the fleet commander?"

"No, no. Da big boss." Ikaika tries to explain. "He talked to me upstairs after I scrapped a pile of guards. He said if we don't stop wrecking the building, then the snakes will get in and come after us."

"What boss is this? What'd he look like? Fockin' haole or what?" Lika inquires.

Ikaika shrugs, "Never actually saw him. Just his yellow eyes in the dark. I was afraid the fockah actually was one big snake himself. He said we could either be his guest or his prisoners here, but not to let the snakes inside the building."

Kaleo interjects, "If he was so worried about the snakes, why did he have the guards murder all the tweakers? Eh?"

Ikaika reasons, "The trap was laid brah. I guess we're both guests and prisoners. But he told me he ordered all the guards to kill themselves to make this a more pleasant experience."

"So what brah?" Kaleo examines, "It's just us and him left here now? Everybody's gone?"

Lika ponders, "Us, him and a thousand poisonous snakes? Fock it brah. Let's get our shit on the Ubiq and get the fock out of here."

"Roger that." Kaleo concurs.

"Roger that." Ikaika turns back towards the stairwell. "Brah, I don't see the boss letting us leave without a fight. He had the look of a hunter."

Lika questions, "I thought you said you couldn't see him."

"I could not see him." Ikaika explains, "Only his eyes. His yellow eyes glowing in the dark corner of the ceiling. Looked like one giant snake coiled up, ready to strike. He's a killer. Was staring at me, never blinked, one stone-cold hunter. If I'm the owl, and you're the turtle, and you're the barracuda, then he's definitely one mean poisonous snake."

Lika replies, "You know how you kill a snake? Eh? You swing the pahoa when he raises his head."

Kaleo refutes, "Fock that. Let's jump on the Ubiq, blow up the bay doors and sail the fock out of here. She's already ready to go already."

Ikaika agrees, "I like that idea. I've had enough snakes today. There's no one left to stop us from jacking the ship."

Lika disagrees, "Except the boss. Doesn't sound like he wants us to leave. Not without a fight. Kaleo, you take the controls, me and Ikaika will post up portside in case we have to fight our way out."

"Nah, fock that." Kaleo expresses, "I'm so much faster than you, you fockin' lug-butt."

Lika shakes his head, "Fockin' mutt. Listen, you got the most important job: Protect the ship or we're stuck here. There's too many things that can go wrong if we lose the Ubiq. If we get in trouble, only you are fast enough to save us and the ship. I really want to scrap the boss, but I also want to get the fock outta here. If we can sail away clean, we go. If we gotta fight, I'm ready to pound the fockah! Right?"

Ikaika buys in. "I like that." They start walking together towards the stairwell. Lika releases the door and passes his brother. The lone door creaks shut and taps against the metal housing dangling from the red wire. All goes silent just before the glass shatters and splashes to the ground behind them.

"Eh! I didn't focking do that either." Lika declares. "Technically, the door was intact when I passed through it." They walk calmly to the stairwell, shaking their heads to the sound of broken glass hitting the floor. The quietly sprint up to the dock level and peer out across the enclosed docks in the hangar.

"No signs of people, no signs of snakes." Kaleo continues to scan.

"Try look for the yellow eyes. In the shadows, they was glowing. And they never blink. Creepy as fock." Ikaika warns. "And the bad vibe. He said we achieved a spiritual transference, that's why he wants our cooperation. He also said something about our current composition and our source energy. That's what the bad vibe was about, we must be contrasting with his composition and his source energy. He knew about the heiau. See? It must be something in the lava. That's what he's after. He said the hippies served their purpose, which was growing the snakes. He murdered all them, but not us. Which sprung the trap. But he wants us to be his guest, probably to get into the mana we tapped into at the cave. This is stressing me out. I need a beer."

"Well, we got plenty beer on the ship." Kaleo smirks as he unties the knots on the dock cleats. "So, the boss wants the lava, eh? He's after the mana. Except, he's not Hawaiian, no way. Guarantee. So he's gonna vampire the mana out of us. He couldn't tap the mana from the heiau, so that's why he won't let us leave. Spiritual transference, my okole (butt). Focking vampire. I say we take him out, pound the fockah."

"That's what I'm saying- pound the fockah!" Lika agrees.

"Eh, keep it down kook. Let's just check the ship and sail out quietly." Ikaika reasons.

"He's not going to let us leave without a fight brah. That's how the mafia cartel do." Lika stresses. "Can you feel the bad vibe right now? In here?"

"Negative." Ikaika scans his senses, "Not in here. But who knows what's waiting for us when we bust through the bay doors. But don't worry boys. I went summoned our guardian owl."

"Eh?" Both Lika and Kaleo are intrigued.

"I chanted a prayer to our 'aumakua when I was upstairs. Our pueo should be circling the yard outside. If we have to fight, we will have the protection of our owl."

"Eh, what about the rest of all those focking birds?" Kaleo wonders, "What happened to the fockin' flock? Is our Pueo gonna bring all her buddies?"

"I don't know." Ikaika begins scanning the ship for unwanted stowaways, "I don't know where all those focking birds went. But I know owls hunt snakes. And I can feel the mana of our 'aumakua watching out for us from above." Ikaika heads below deck, "Let's make sure the ship is clean before we crank her up."

They scan and scour the hatches before energizing the controls. Once they confirm the integrity of the vessel and crack open three beer cans, Kaleo powers up the engines. Lika crouches on the bow, waiting for Ikaika to fly to the top of the hangar and pry the bay doors from the magnetic locks. Once free, Ikaika drops down to the deck of the slow-moving vessel. Lika somersaults up from the bow and plows the bay doors wide open with a loud metallic crash.  Lika ricochets into the channel and immediately swims to the starboard side of the Ubiquitous.  He climbs up to the bow and snags his war clubs.  He gives a hoot to Kaleo and the engines suddenly let out a boisterous roar.

As the bow of the vessel raises from the powerful thrust of the engines, Ikaika and Lika stand poised for battle.  Kaleo races to the harbor entrance.  Ikaika searches the black sky and finds the silhouette of their guardian owl directly above.  The Hunaka'i Pueo hovers high in the sky, just below a gyrating grey cloud.  "There's our pueo!  The owl storm is back!"  Ikaika points up.

Lika scans the yard as they pass in the channel, gaining speed with every second.  "Nothing but corpses in the yard!"  He continues to search, "Where the fock did all those snakes go?  Eh?"

Kaleo becomes anxious as they near the harbor entrance, "Smooth sailing boys!"  Just then, he notices two small vessels on the outside of the rocky harbor entrance jetty drifting slowly towards the opening.  "Holy fock!  Hang on boys, we got company up there!"

Ikaika spots the two boats crossing the channel and launches himself airborne.  Lika sees the obstacles in their path, but quickly turns his focus back towards the yard.  "There's that fockah!"  Lika zeroes in on a single figure standing amongst the piles of shredded corpses in the yard.  "I found da boss!  Looks like he wants to scrap after all!"

Kaleo hollers, "No!  We can make it!"  He sets course through the narrowing gap between the two vessels.  He watches Ikaika dive towards the small boat on their starboard side from high above.  Ikaika tucks his wings behind and extends the razor-sharp talons out in front.  He speeds through the single man at the ship's controls like a torpedo, splattering the flesh into an explosion of blood.  The unmanned boat spins out to sea as Ikaika gracefully spreads his great wings and soars upwards.  Kaleo confirms, "We can make it boys!"

Lika locks stares with the yellow eyes glaring back from across the yard. "Ho, this fockah like beef, brah. I don't think we're getting out of here without a fight!" He says as he clanks his obsidian clubs together.

"We're sailing the fock outta here brah!" Kaleo hollers as he swerves past the lone boat at the harbor's opening. Just as they clear the other vessel, Kaleo spots a flash of light from the jetty at the shoreline. Then, the sound of cannon fire catches up to them. He can only watch as a glimmering silver harpoon crashes against the portside hull and jolts the entire vessel. Kaleo instantly feels tension against the controls. The chain connecting the massive harpoon to the jetty snaps tight. All forward momentum diverts hard left and the engine's thrust swings their vessel around violently towards the shore. The Ubiquitous nearly capsizes in the shallow waters as they slam against the shoreline. Lika is flung to the rocks.

Ikaika turns and watches in horror as their ship flounders uncontrollably into the shallow rocks below. He sees Kaleo crash through the forward glass of the bridge, bounce off the bow and disappear in the rocks. He hovers, scanning the waters for Kaleo and finds him clinging to the shoreline rocks, gaping at the damage to their escape vessel. Ikaika quickly focuses on Lika, standing on the jetty with his clubs. "Lika!" Ikaika shouts, but he already knows the fight can not be avoided. He lets out a wail to signal the battle is imminent.

Lika lets out a roar and begins his charge across the field of corpses. Ikaika thrusts his flight directly towards the lone black figure standing tall in the red snow. The flickering wall lights illuminate the red mist floating just over the ground. Steam from the spilt blood has nearly quelled completely in the cold. The entire yard appears dead still, blood-soaked, and silent. Lika stomps across the yard, sloshing over the piles of ripped flesh.

From above, Ikaika spots movement in the blood-drenched wake of Lika's charge. "The snakes!" He quickly identifies the snakes have retreated back inside the warm bodies they emerged from. Like disturbing an ant hill, serpents all across the yard begin writhing out free from the dead. This does nothing to slow Lika's charge. Ikaika sets his focus back on their target and anticipates to swoop down on his prey just before Lika makes his strike.

As the red snow stirs from the slithering vipers, Ikaika hears a monstrous screech from above. Without taking his eyes from his target, he senses his guardian owl sailing just over his shoulder. Lightning flashes in the black sky directly above the battlefield. In the strobing lights of the sudden lightning storm, hundreds of white owls shoot down from the sky around Ikaika. The owls dive with great speed and dart at the snakes chasing closely behind Lika. Ikaika sees the owls ambush the snakes from his peripheral vision, but his sight is locked onto the top of the black creature emitting a dark field of energy. The owls pick off snakes in their talons as they roll across the red snow and thrash them apart with their beaks. The bloody owls begin clearing a path for Lika's charge.

Ikaika readies his talons to strike, just before Lika makes his frontal attack. The black creature has remained completely still during their swift approach. Until, it calmly leans over and pulls a chunk of flesh from the dead body at his feet, flinging it towards Lika. The fleshy mound unravels in mid-air, revealing a copperhead snake lengthening from its coil.

Lika charges right into the snake as he takes his swing. The blade of his obsidian club pierces the extended arm of the black creature, severing it completely and launching it in the air. Lika lowers his shoulder and collides with the ominous human-formed creature. They both spin away from each other from the impact. Lika hits the ground in a splash of orange, convulsing violently with the snake latched to his neck.

Ikaika diverts his assault towards the creature spinning off to the side. It's remaining hand tosses another mound of flesh into the airspace of Ikaika's trajectory. Ikaika can no longer stop his momentum. He prepares to gouge his talons into the creature's torso despite the lump of flesh suspended in his path. Suddenly, a clean white owl swoops in and snags the fangs of another viper springing from the flesh. Ikaika pummels the creature into the snow and rolls away. He quickly looks to Lika and finds him convulsing in a puddle of lava and crumbled obsidian.

Ikaika fixates his stare back to the glowing yellow eyes of the dark entity. He gets between the creature and his wounded companion, carefully reaching down for one of Lika's clubs. He watches the creature walk slowly towards the severed limb and reach for it without breaking the stare. It holds its arm in place and squeezes the wound, shaping it together as if were made of clay.

"That was remarkable." It growls. "I would like to continue this battle. You are very impressive, a worthy opponent. It would be a great honor. But your friend will not survive that venom unless you surrender to me immediately. I can neutralize that venom if you will allow me to inject him with this syringe."

Ikaika holds his stare and tightens his grip on the club. He can see Kaleo streaking silently across the yard, behind the dark creature. Owls continue to drop from the sky, snatching the slithering serpents and maintaining a perimeter around Ikaika. "Why? To be your slave? He doesn't want that. This is a fight to the death."

"You're no use to me dead. You're going to enjoy fighting like this everyday. I know I will." The creature slowly backs away from Ikaika and plunges his re-attached arm into the flesh of several bodies piled upon each other. It suddenly spins away from Ikaika and yanks its arm free. A chain of large snakes form in its grip, each one biting into the tail of another. It snaps the writhing chain of serpents like a whip, popping the blood and flesh into the air.

Ikaika takes a step back and plucks the copperhead off Lika's neck. The creature takes another step back from Ikaika and swings the chain of snakes around in a large circle. Ikaika squeezes the copperhead's neck and runs its head along the edge of his club, slicing it off. Ikaika drops the snake and prepares to take his swing.

The black creature suddenly spins away and lashes out towards Kaleo as he reaches striking distance. Kaleo heaves one of his clubs into the creature's chest just before the snake at the end of the whip rips free and latches onto Kaleo's thigh. Kaleo lets out a scream and scrapes the snake clear with his other club. The creature snaps his serpent whip again while dislodging the club buried in his chest. Ikaika is already airborne.

From above, Ikaika hurls his pahoa and severs the arm a second time. He takes a dive and clamps onto the creature's skull, thrashing it from side to side. The creature quickly plucks the whip of serpents from his severed arm and cracks the end at Kaleo. Ikaika jerks the creature off the ground and slings it towards the brick wall. He drops down over Kaleo and finds the snake's venom has already taken affect. The obsidian case that housed his soul has melted away, leaving his bare natural flesh. Kaleo struggles in the puddle of cooling lava and shards of volcanic glass. "Just get home brother!" He gargles, vomiting smoldering orange lava from his mouth and nose. "My gecko dream takes me down a different path."

"Eh?" Ikaika pops the skull of the black mamba attached to Kaleo's throat with his thumb and flings the smoldering serpent to the side. The venom has already reacted with the obsidian flesh and melted away a portion of Kaleo's jaw and neck.

"My gecko dream takes me right over there. I'm going grab that pahoa and then go pound that fockah in da dirt. Your dream takes you home."

"What?" Ikaika grabs a dead owl from the snow and wipes the molten area of Kaleo's wound with clean feathers.

"I know your dream takes you home. My dream takes me over to my brother and we're gonna go beat the fock out of that focking fockah over there. He won't kill us. But only you can save us." Kaleo pulls the snake from his glowing red arm. The obsidian flesh smolders around the bite and starts to melt away. His tattooed skin begins to liquify as it rips from the fangs and oozes away.

Ikaika pinches the head of the snake in Kaleo's grip. He yanks another one off and forces his thumb through its skull. "I'm gonna go focking kill that thing! There is no way home brah!" Ikaika looks across the yard and finds the creature standing up slowly next to the wall. It clumsily unsheathes a silver katana with only one arm by clenching it in the armpit stump of its severed arm.

Kaleo hocks up a lump of molten lava from his throat and spits it towards the wall with great distance, "Not this time brother. Things are about to get weird. Well, me and Lika are gonna go bust that fockah up first. And then things are gonna get weird. Psychedelic weird. You ever tried peyote?"

"Peyote? What da fock? No. I never tried peyote. What-choo-ma-focking saying weird psychedelic shit for? He told me about the peyote, that yellow-eyed fockah over there. Are you gonna kick his ass or go score some peyote from the drug dealing fockah?" Ikaika tosses the smoldering bird in the snow and grabs a fresh one.

"We can't leave, kook! Boat's wrecked. We can go pound the fockah, but we cannot kill him. We are prisoners here and they're gonna drug us up and shit's gonna get weird. Eh! Lika!"

Lika climbs to his knees and vomits a chunky stream of steaming lava from his mouth and nose. "What!"

"We go pound da fockah! One proper scrap, brah. But we cannot leave. Lika!" Kaleo yells.

"We go! Give me a minute. Eh?" Lika leans back, hocking and snorting.

"Wait. What?" Ikaika gets angry when left out.

"Brah, he wants to fight. We're gonna go beat his shit wide open. But there's no way home for us. Only you. But you will come back for us brother. No matter how much drugs they pump us full of, I know it brah. You will come back for me. That's what the gecko showed me already." Kaleo explains.

"What? Fock that! I'm not bailing on this scrap, brah." Ikaika declares.

"It's not up to you brah." Kaleo points straight up to the sky. "Nani ho'i ua ki'i 'ia maile e make, he aha la ho'i (Since I am indeed summoned by

202

death, what of it). Tell Lono, remember Kanani. Eh! Child of the owl, keep your damn shorts on!"

"Brah. Wait. What?" Ikaika keeps his vision locked on to the yellow eyes and realizes that the severed arm lies next to Lika. "Eh? You talking to me or the bird?" The presence of the bird intensifies like a magnet drawing near.

"From here on out, this turns into me and Lika cultivating psychedelic plants and fighting for our freedom. This mean fockah likes the challenge. We're gonna fight everyday. That's what da boss wants." Kaleo squeezes Ikaika's arms to his waist and raises him into position."

Ikaika closely watches the yellow eyes darting around for its lost limb. "Ho, brah. Is that what the gecko dream showed you?"

"Yep." Kaleo explains and tilts his statuesque friend to the left a bit. "You know, I thinks it's the snake venom eating away at my lava composition. The shit's sobering me up. I've already seen what he wants. But if we beat him in a fight, he will award us free-time from this gladiator drug farm prison. We are the family trophies. Maybe if you become, you know, da-kine, *receptive*, you can tune in with us. Aloha brother, time to go."

Before Ikaika can look up, the large black talons of his guardian owl strike against his back and clamp around, into his chest. The claws pierce into his ribs like daggers through styrofoam. He is instantly plucked from the ground and launches upwards with incredible speed. "Kaleo!" He screams and sees Lika and Kaleo helping each other stand. He suddenly realizes that this is what he prayed for and exactly what he dreamed would happen. He was on his way home just as Keala dreamed and prayed for.

Inside the great Pueo, The Hunaka'i family's vision begins spiraling wildly to the sky, ascending in the darkness. The absence of moonlight over the dark ocean leaves them with the sensation of spinning blindly. Their guardian owl grows more powerful as if resonating in harmony with Ikaika's energy. Their senses suddenly begin pumping in the intoxication from bloody contact with his core. A rush of heat consumes their Pueo.

203

The black sky around them ignites in a bright yellow burst as they gain speed and altitude. The sky stretches out and then they pierce through the black veil of the Alaskan physical realm. They enter into a plane of existence that resonates with every other source of vibrational energy, in all parts of the universe. They spiral wildly, emitting their radiation into other realms. They leave behind a bubbling wake, like the churning propulsion trailing a massive sea vessel.

Burning through the vast layers of intertwined physical realms becomes so intense that they lose the distinction of movement. They burn in the sky like the Phoenix across the pacific. The white glow of heat dims to yellow in mere seconds. As the glow deepens to orange and then darker red, the Hunaka'i family is cast into the striking physical sensation of spiraling wildly once again. The need to gasp for air suddenly becomes urgent. Their owl quickly regains its mettle. The lava in their composition has vanished, yet they have not completely formed their original physical matter. The owl ducks down into the beach's shore break and clamps onto Ikaika's battered mortal body submerged in shallow water. Their energies transpose from the spirit world to the earthly domain, solidifying their matter deeper with each passing second.

Their pueo furiously churns its wings until the ocean water gives way to air. As the owl rises into the dawning sky, Alana and Akila realize Keala is no longer with them inside the guardian owl. They do however, feel the magnetic pull between Ikaika's bedraggled soul and their little house where Keala's soul is waiting. This was her wish all along. Keala has created an ephemeral window into her past self, once again living out the enigmatic morning she thought was only a dream.

By the time Ikaika and their guardian owl restore their full composition, the magnetic pull of the lost lovers becomes too much for the owl to control. Ikaika's weight rips him free and he hurls through the canopy trees in front of their home. Ikaika strikes the ground and tumbles to the front door, nearly breaking it off the hinges. In a swift movement, he brushes off the mud, grass and blood and disappears into the house with no explanation prepared for Keala. She no longer needs one.

Alana and Akila remain within the Pueo. Dense static in the atmosphere reveals the volatile consequences of their voyage home. The owl quickly burrows deep into the twisted branches of a majestic banyan tree near the house as the brilliant colors of dawn fade to grey. The trans-dimensional energy they consumed to return home spawned an equally powerful force. Alana suddenly realizes the exact date and what is bearing down on Kaua'i. This part of their vision is from November 23, 1982, and they are about to experience the rage of Hurricane Iwa inside an owl, wedged in the banyan tree of Keala's front yard. "Is this the price we gotta pay?"

Alana calls out to Keala, not knowing if she can be heard over the intensifying wind. "Is this our fault? Hurricane Iwa? Did we cause this to happen?" Alana wants the vision to be over but she knows Keala has prayed for this moment. "We brought the mana across the pacific. We manifested this. Iwa was drawn by the maka 'ike, the mana, and is meeting us here. This is not coincidence. I hope you're enjoying yourself in there! We're stuck inside a fockin' bird, stuck in a fockin' tree, in the fockin' rain!"

"Auntie. Maybe we're out here for a reason." Akila's voice rings through the storm. "My father vanishes during the storm. Maybe we can see who took him."

"Maybe you're right." Alana agrees. "We survived a massacre in Alaska. I'd rather be home in a hurricane than stuck there in the ice. You're right. I bet they're out there right now, watching the house... waiting for Ikaika to return."

Alana tries to peer through the darkness as the rain squalls. The pressure of the 120 mph gusts thrash the owl within the weaving branches. Their senses are overloaded with the force of the storm's surge. But within the natural chaos, Alana somehow feels something silent nearby. Even with the keen eyes of their owl, the wrath of the storm prevents any visualization from becoming distinct.

Yet, Alana can feel an absence of turbulence in the darkness, moving calmly towards them. As the storm continues to rage, Alana realizes they are not alone. A dark entity has taken notice of her vision, her maka 'ike. Alana panics and forces out a shriek. She screams so hard, with so much force, that she breaks the mental link she shared with their guardian owl. Alana is cast through the numbed, silent void and is thrust

205

back into the center of her own mortal mind. The Source Energy ignites the spark of vision behind her eyes as she continues to scream. The pain incinerates her throbbing cage of flesh. She is thrust into the eleventh morning of September 1986. It has been nine months since she woke in the ocean with the sharks, without her Tiki. Nahu kuakoko (travail of childbirth), the contractions have already begun.

# Pu'uwai Hao Kila

## Heart of Steel

"March 11, 1936

Kanzo Semp

It is possible that this date is incorrect. I have been hiding in the basement of this building for what feels like a week- no food, no water, shaven and painted black with some sort of urine-smelling tar. I completely abandoned my orders the day the revolt began and agreed to remain hidden, as their captive. My entire unit has vanished and I am alone with several cases of rum. The only provisions I managed to salvage are the biological agents I released onto this wretched island of slaves. I believe the priestess suspects my deception. Nonetheless, she has agreed to initiate me into a ritual ceremony that will establish Patronage with my true ancestors, an event that will help deliberate my purpose from this point onward. If this is a path to death that I am taking, then I pray for the fortitude to document my undertaking and retain my honor. The spiritual transference I have experienced here is unlike anything else I have encountered. I always knew it was possible.

On the eve of my first of three ceremonies, the Kanzo Semp, this vodou priestess, Manbo Margaret Lysius, promises to open the gates of the spirit world and I will learn of my ancestors. That is comforting to me and is all the hope I have left. I can no longer deny the effect that these dark circumstances have taken on my mind. From the moment I arrived on this forsaken island, I felt consumed by fear and deceit. I

208

am a lone militant xenophobe abandoned in the wasteland of my nation's enemy. The priestess stated that fear is the first enemy a man must overcome on his path of knowledge. I do not know why I trust her, except that she seems as interested in harboring the guidance and wisdom of my ancestors as I. My mind is wandering on horrible tangents. I find the infinite echoes of gunshots intensely distracting.

As I was recently advised, it is in the steps a man has taken where he finds his strength. I will now make an effort to document the steps that has resulted in my confinement here. This will not be an easy task as I suspect that I have inadvertently been exposed to the tools of my own abominable deception. Since ingesting my third bottle of rum, I cannot help but laugh at the irony of being incarcerated with my own weaponized vials of plagues and poisons. I removed the labels of what she called my Pwen, or power objects. Though she speaks French and English, she claims to have no ability to read. I am not willing to take that chance. I believe she possesses the means to manipulate the knowledge of others, alive or dead. I do in fact know that I still possess a catastrophic supply of heroin, morphine, phosgene, hydrogen cyanide, bromobenzyl cyanide, chloroacetophenon, diphenyl-cyanoarsine, diphenyl-chloroarsine, arsenic trichloride, sulphur mustard, lewisite, anthrax, and bubonic plague. If this priestess kills me and meddles with my devices, she will certainly destroy this entire island, including the U.S. Marines occupying the ports to the north. However, in this particular situation, I felt a profound attraction to the symphony of serotonergic entheogens at my disposal. I always found mind-manifesting phantastica psychodelics to be useful, especially when challenged to utilize new perspectives for survival.

I will attempt to document my findings beneath what sounds like a raging civil war. I must confess, even in my earlier more sober state, I have witnessed nonsensical occurrences and unimaginable events. I overheard someone explain that if a person feels like they are being 'called' by the spirits of Haiti, the first thing they should do is serve their ancestors. When I first made contact with the village healer, Manbo Lysius, by shaking her hand, I was utterly stunned by a profound sensation of a thousand voices screaming into my ears at once. I watched her fall to here knees as well. It struck like the discharge of static shock. I became debilitated for several hours with vile and unfocused images flashing throughout my vision. It does not seem possible to document these images as I have no words to describe such depravity. I sense that these images remain on the outskirts of my peripheral vision. The images appear to be manipulated, likely by the Manbo. Yet, it sickens me to deeply stretch my eyesight beyond my normal range. It feels as an infection penetrating into the sclera deep inside my orbits, itching its way into my neuronal axons. This is a phenomenon I am intensely curious of.

Over the next several days, other bizarre episodes became unbearably distressful and draining. I have observed the most disturbing behavior from these natives. There are times when they seem capable of showing etiquette and politesse of gracious hosts. Yet, the modus operandi of this race is grotesquely vulgar and obscene. As I write in my log of these particular circumstances, my eyes feel to be heating up as I focus on specific words. My memories have become painfully animate in this way. I am becoming aware that certain aspects of my consciousness are experiencing intense delusions and altered states. As I concentrate, I feel the threshold of my perception expanding beyond normal, abstemious experiences. This began to occur even before we opened the container sealing the biological agents.

I dismissed them at first, then, tried to conceal my turmoil. We were, after all, under the guise of humanitarian efforts. The priestess approached me and without asking of my condition, explained that she was aware of the fact that the energy I was experiencing was god's will becoming available from my ancestors. I could see her becoming intoxicated with my contact, as I am undoubtedly the first Japanese she has ever met. I questioned what this strange African priestess could possibly know of my ancestors. She responded by explaining that the will of God could be channeled through her and into me. She smiled, touched my hand and stated, 'You don't pray to the gods, you become gods.' Doing so made her shake and laugh mockingly as if touching my hand was inebriating her and draining me.

I would never have considered her words to be possible. Except the mysterious priestess then asked me to clarify the words, Takamagahara and Yomi. She then pointed to my bayonet and asked if it was the Kusanagi no Tsurugi. I could not speak. I tried to empty my head of all thoughts regarding my humble perception of the High Heaven, the Underworld and the legendary sword. I retreated to my barracks and began journalizing my data as to protocol. Documentation is how scientists justify and absorb findings. Unfortunately, I do not know the English words, or Japanese words for that matter, to describe the fear I was experiencing.

After executing my orders, as I watched the encryption spill out across the pages, it became apparent that the path of deception I had taken was burning a trail for me to the Underworld. The treachery I have inflicted upon this deplorable nation has made me question the ideology of my nation's militarist policy. The words I chose to express my concern began to affect my senses in the most peculiar manner. The letters formed by my typing keyboard began creating a profound tickling sensation that altered my focus. The words began coming to life before my eyes. Mastering code within text is a skill necessary for my survival. Yet here, I began to wonder if Amaterasu, the Sun Goddess herself was summoning me to the plane of High Heaven, or more fitting, Susanoo to the Underworld. I quickly learned that the spiritual belief system I had been taught was a mere construct to veil any deeper perceptions. As I analyzed the code within my encrypted transmissions, I discovered these exact entries haunted my consciousness in this inebriated state. I heard the priestess laugh and claim that I do not know myself. This bothered me, or rather haunts me. I simply outlined the steps that have led me here and found a spiritual transference in a most potent form:

In the autumn of 1920, I received correspondence from my estranged father to transfer from Tokyo University to Kyoto Imperial University. He commanded that I advance my medical studies in a more militant direction. I believed I had honored my family with academic excellence and after eighteen years, my father could not help but take notice. The Imperial Rescript on Education instituted neo-Confucian virtues, loyalty and self-sacrifice to the Emperor; which contrasted with the egoism of Western democracy. I hoped to acquire a wider view of the world since he was said to have been stationed overseas and to have created the educational reforms. I dared not vocalize my insubordinations and remained completely obedient to my father's commands. Since I never knew him, I never realized I was born into the house of a true warrior.

212

I had proven myself academically, now my father demanded that I study the art of war. I was to commit my mind and body to the Bushido.

In the spring of 1930, under my father's sponsorship, I became inducted into the Amur River Association and became a member of the Kokuryu-kai, the Black Dragon Society. Though I did not completely understand the functions of this membership, it was regarded as an extremely high honor. No one so young has ever been granted this opportunity and I felt gracious of my father's influence. Two years later, I became the living property of the Kempeitai, again under my father's orders. I could not know the power and influence of my father's favor. I yearned for the day I would finally meet him. As my paramilitary unit perambulated behind enemy lines, I discovered that the weapon system I was planting across Siberia, Manchuria and Korea were in fact my father's design.

In 1934, I learned that my father authorized me to command the Epidemic Prevention Research Laboratory. I was quickly promoted to commander of a covert special duties squad to be known as Tokumu han- of the secret research group, Unit 731, the Togo Unit. I never questioned his intentions and accepted the high honor of this promotion to benefit my house. This was a time of great discovery as we collected immense data on the affects of pathogens on the human body as well as to the ecosystem. Our experiments on live subjects lead us to develop advanced weapons of war this world has never experienced. The precision and vast effectiveness of our manufactured agents enabled us to carve out swaths of territories completely unchecked by our enemies. Our early successes granted us unlimited funding towards our explorations of weaponized 'spiritual transference'. This was a secret directive, mandated personally from my father, to explore the

213

outer states of consciousness triggered by measures of extreme stimuli to the senses. This would be the closest form of contact I have had with my father.

On January 1, 1936, I was summoned to a meeting with the Genyosha, the Dark Ocean Society. These men divulged my father's secret agenda for foreign expansion, and I was a key element. They summoned my Togo Unit to infiltrate the U.S. Marine occupation of Haiti. This was my opportunity to prove to my father that I was worthy of his benefaction. While in Tokyo, I was notified of my marriage arrangement and was granted three weeks leave while my benefactors prepared for my new assignment. I understood joining two houses benefited my father in some manner of prestige or equity, but the bond between my dear Satomi and I proved immeasurable. All the yearning for family I had been denied was finally quenched through this union and I did not believe it would be possible to abandon her for this mission.

In Ville des Anglais, I was ordered to establish a water purification system for the people of that village. I knew nothing of the Genyosha, except that they were privileged to be independent of the military. I was led to believe that these men were under the direct command of my father. They would not confirm or deny my inquiries. The primary stipulation of this mission was that the U.S. forces occupying the country were not to discover our presence. It was my objective to then infiltrate New Orleans and plant my weapons of biological warfare up the Mississippi River. If I could manage to plant these seeds and return to Tokyo, I would be entitled to a full retirement arrangement from the Genyosha. This became my obsession.

My team departed with great ambition. We travelled undetected out of Barranquilla, Colombia on a fishing

214

vessel to a small port on the south side of Haiti. The village healer, an African priestess, Manbo Margaret Lysius, first greeted us. She agreed that it was wise to remain hidden from the Americans. There was an obvious resentment. As I absorbed the alien surroundings, I suddenly realized I was being overwhelmed by an emotion I was trained to abandon at an early age. My arrival had marked the first time I felt a fear of loss from my first and only gift of joy in this lifetime. My men were crippled with fear the moment we set foot in the mud. This was the first display of emotion I have ever observed from them, yet they managed to maneuver unnoticed by anyone of significance.

Sometime during the twilight hours of the next day, one of my men vanished. The priestess declared that people often vanish without a trace, mostly from anacondas. I was not able to believe that at first. Within three days, I was suffering from extreme mental fatigue and delusions. I was in fact witnessing the most unbelievable display of lawlessness, revolt and grotesque debauchery of any people I have ever observed. It appeared as though I landed in the midst of a civil war. I spent my time observing the healing powers of this Manbo Lysius. I learned of ancient practices that cannot be explained by my medical studies. I must admit that I was amazed by her methods. I felt compelled to share with her my modern techniques. This did not suppress the tumultuous nightmares and daydreams I was experiencing, it only passed the time. Her interest in me gave some hope that her entourage would not murder us.

On February 26, 1936, I learned of the failed coup d'etat by the Imperial Way Faction to overthrow the ruling elite of the Control Faction. This assassination caused me to question whom I was actually taking orders from for the first time. Being so far away, I did not understand which faction held the favor of the Emperor. It was on this date that I received orders, signed by my father, to release a biological agent into the clean water supply that I established here. I could not restrain the qualms I had with this new order. My avulsion was noticeably apparent, but my men proceeded as ordered. The natives suspected nothing of our ploy. The sudden illness was blamed on a plague at first, and then it quickly progressed into a curse.

Within five days, most of the villagers were infected and dying. In the chaos, three more of my men vanished. I began to feel the guilt of my terrorism when I observed the healing power of Manbo Lysius. I witnessed an incredible turnaround in her people, as no one suspected the water supply or its contaminants. I walked into a hall where 50 children laid dying, crying for their mother. The priestess kissed each one before they ran out past me laughing. I cannot explain why, but I felt it necessary to begin administering immunizations that were intended for my own personnel. Manbo Lysius revealed that she was also impressed with my Pwen, or power objects. She stated that she knew I was a Bokor, a sorcerer, when we first met.

After a drastic decline in the mortally ill, a vicious revolt
began. Lysius then confided to me of a secret society, the Makaya. They warned her that news of a plague was consuming the village and the U.S. Marines intended to 'contain the infected population'. Two more of my unit vanished in the violence. The last three of us were advised to paint ourselves black and hide from the American military. We could not attempt to fake composure. Nothing could have ever prepared us for these conditions.

216

After several days of violence and ritualistic orgies, I found myself alone with no means of escape. At this point, my logic had been consumed by fear. I clearly recognized many men and women, who I witnessed lying dead in the trenches, were now running the streets naked with machetes. They had the appearance of being dead for several days, but were indeed wildly animate.

Manbo Lysius implored me to retreat into her secret Djevo, the inner sanctum of her vodou temple. She led me to a sinister looking crypt and pointed to an elaborate sarcophagus. Here, she stated that she should induct me into a ritual ceremony to contact my ancestors, my Zanset Yo. I had no choice but to agree to this Bat Guerre, battle of the spirits. I do not know what to expect, except for some ritualistic infliction of torture. I am tempted to ingest a lethal dose of heroin before they arrive, but the words of suicide do not glow in the manner as the other blinding words I wrote of my path. This is the path that has led me here. This is the path that glows with the will of my ancestors. The Bat Guerre is clearly the path illuminated before my eyes.

They have just begun to sing outside so I must assume that night has come. I can still hear the violence and madness in the streets. This will soon stop and everyone will join in singing their Roman Catholic hymns as if falling under a mass trance. It won't be long before the pounding of the drums become as deafening as mortar explosions. At which point, most of the savages will have become belligerently drunk. Like wild animals, many will be vigorously dancing with machetes and fornicating in the yards. Then, they will come for me.

217

It is necessary to document that I have just consumed the fourth bottle of rum, and will open the fifth. Unexpectedly, I feel nothing of the liquor's effect, nor am I hungry or weakened. In fact, in this numbed state, I have found a curiously alien clarity and focus that would seem impossible to achieve without ingesting some amount of heroin or other psychoactive mu-opiod substance. I have checked the vials for tampering several times and found them all sealed. I did notice signs of deliberate tampering on my encoder. Yet, the sequencing remains calibrated and no pathogen vials were detonated. I believe it is the stress or inadvertent exposure to the water that is causing this intense delirium.

I can now hear the heavy chains unraveling against the wooden doors. Only the Manbo's assistants, the hounsi, would have keys for those locks. It is almost time. A large crowd of hounsi has entered the temple above me. Even with the exploding drums, I am able to hear them paying homage to their ancestors. Next will be homage to the nations of Lwa, or angels- aspects of God's will/energy. It was explained to me that these Lwa are available to man through bodily possession. This is why Manbo Lysius stated that you don't pray to the gods, you become them.

The Lwa are said to 'mount the cherval', or horse. This was said to me with great enthusiasm by the hounsi. I have learned that this vodou is an ecstatic rather than fertility type of religion. Homosexuality is not discouraged; in fact, I have witnessed the lewd vulgarity of drunken male intercourse openly displayed by many of the Manbo's hounsi. When they are ready to begin my initiation, I heard them say they will come to 'bosal' me. It sickens me that my imagination has already assigned the most grotesque definition for the word bosal. I have never experienced the effects of heroin on my own body. Yet, according to the findings of the human experimentation studies of my division, I can presume that a small dose will relieve the agonizing repulsion of being sodomized by these ferocious savages.

It just occurred to me that I have no means to precisely measure this dose. If I am the horse they intend to mount, then the hallucinogenic interpretation my mind will perceive under too large a dose may prove fatal. It would magnify the perverted torture beyond my threshold of endurance. Yet, I cannot imagine a more fitting punishment for what I have inflicted upon these people.

As the screaming crowd burrows deeper into the chasm under the building, my senses have begun to feel electrified with some sort of unnatural stimulation. I can hardly stare at the words I am writing, as they seem to be spreading the illumination onto the walls and ceiling of this cavern. I may no longer need this small lantern to measure my heroin. The time has finally come for me to prepare myself mentally. I would like to live past this ceremony only to document my initiation into this demonic religion, while under the influence of a powerful hallucinogenic agent. If I shall die as the result of this carnal ritual, then these savages will ultimately have their justice. That is, until my commander detonates my weapon remotely five days from now."

"Untie her hands, fast kind! No, leave the gloves on honey bird. They match the baby's. Did you drop the mango in the sand again? Not so fast little weasel. You give me yours. Because, you bugger! You went throw da pooper-scooper right there, that's why. Cheez. Ooh, ya. Peel me one new one. That's the kind, keiki. Nice. And peel auntie one new one.

219

She's already moved past the twitching. She's just wiggling now. Yes, good idea. Throw the mango peel in the same spot as you throw the pooper-scooper. Ya. So you know where the poop stay from now on. Roger that. Wait. But you just went dropped the mango right there again. Same spot. That's how hard you're slinging the poopies, that whole general area.

No. I don't want to move to the other tide pool. I like this tide pool. Because the other one - no more sand and it hurts my okole (bottom). If it hurts my okole, then it hurts her okole. Ya, I know she's not flinching anymore. That's why we need the tuberose. She's gonna wake up soon. I know she cannot smell underwater. She's gonna pop up soon, monkey nugget, and you better have some lei's ready. Unless you want to deal with her cranky ass.

Nah, she stopped twitching hours ago so make me some lei's now and go fish later. What do you mean the sharks never left yet? Did they bring you another aku (skipjack tuna)? Nothing? Well, I guess if all the sharks are here, all the fish would be somewhere else then. Roger that keiki, but I don't know how to get rid of sharks. Right, I bet baby Lono would know. Ya? Try wait...

No, her eyes opened. No. That's not how you tell what phase she's experiencing. What are you some kind of fart reader now? Eh? What, you can tell by the bubbles? The tiny bubbles? Ya, sometimes the big ones move the sand around and then it's just rocks underneath. That's why hard, hurts the okole. What do you mean, flavor? That's because of the lipoa (seaweed). No, that's because of the poi. What, you're some kind of connoisseur of farts now? Wait. How did this turn into me all of a sudden?

Quit feeding the baby and go make the lei. Try wait... Alana? Eh, there you are. Alana? Ah, screw it. She went back to sleep again. No, don't tie her back up. No, keep them handy, there's always a chance she's gonna freak out. Alright then, ten bucks. Ya, just like last time. No, no you little monkey turd, and you wash the dishes too. It's his nap time. Eh? Then go make the lei's over there. Ah, you Bugger."

Alana whispers, "Keala, pull me up. I can't breathe underwater."

"Well actually, you can." Keala sits up and slides Alana up close with her legs. Continuing to hug her and her baby softly, "There you are. Just sit up slow and be still. Your baby was about to take a nap. We was waiting for you for a while. How are you feeling, sister?"

Alana deepens her breath enough to reply, "Oh, ok. Is my baby ok? Am I ok? How long have we been underwater?"

"Uh... like three weeks already." Keala gently places the tuberose lei across her sister's chest. "Nice and easy there. Cool head, main thing. Good girl."

Alana whispers gingerly, "Keala. I'm too weak to move. Lono was born three weeks ago? I cannot remember. Are we ok?"

"Are we ok? Well, you lost a bit of blood." Keala whispers in her ear, hoping her sister doesn't have an emotional response.

"From the child birth? That's actually the only area that isn't hurting right now." Alana's eyes are not able to adjust to the sunlight. She scoops Lono up and presses his face against hers.

"Oh, would you look at that..." Keala wipes the baby's nose and mouth with the clean towel.

"Eh. You been sticking your fingers in my eyes or what? Cannot see." Alana sniffs deeply as the baby breathes out, her mouth feeling the contours of his face. "What are we looking at?"

"Well I imagine that was placenta that just squirted out Lono's nose and mouth. Hard to tell because he's been underwater this whole time. But it was like a jelly, but not like snot. In fact, he was like jelly. Easy childbirth because the bones were not hard at all, like jelly. So it's good to see you both not underwater today." Keala gently rolls Lono over and wipes the other side of his face clean.

"Eh? What are you talking about? Is something happening?" Alana tries not to let her sister distract from the joy of feeling newborn hands caressing her face.

Keala rinses her sister's eyes and dabs her face dry, "Nothing's happening now. It's a pretty quiet afternoon. Try wait. Kila, can go get some hot soup for auntie? Ya?"

She waits for Akila to get out of range, "Ok. I like give it to you straight. Ok? Was all kinds of bloody hell when I woke up from our vision in Alaska. I went from waking up during hurricane Iwa, 20 Mar 2024, 10:23 to really for real waking up with Lono at the end of an umbilical cord. Just swimming around in the tide pool. I thought you was dead at first, or still dreaming, deep trance kind. But you and him were underwater, just chillin'.

When I pulled you up, you went blasted my face with water and then was suffocating like you couldn't breathe in the air and shit. Little Lono was a little fish out of water so Akila dipped him back under. He seemed to like it better, so I plopped you back under and the two of you's went and snuggled up. So you've been under water snuggling together for over three weeks already."

"What are you even talking about? So stupid. I would like some soup." Alana is drained, famished, but sustained in loving contact with her newborn.

"Eh. You listening to me? You got the hanabata (nasal discharge) in your ears or what? I'm not joking. It was the umbilical cord that was so fascinating. I figured we were supposed to cut it, you know, like you're supposed to. Right? Akila said it was a bad idea, but what does the manini (small) menehune (mischievous elf) know about childbirth anyways? Ya? He thought it was like, making the ocean water like the placenta for you two to survive in. You know?

And then I was thinking about being in that vision, inside the owl, ya? And there was a lot of drugs involved, ya? And here I got this little four-year-old keiki (child) all exposed into some weird-ass wicked shit. And I was worried he was having some residual kind side affects and it was making me paranoid.

But after a couple of days of you not breathing or eating or drinking, I was starting to get kind of worried. I mean, you two looked very happy and peaceful and sweet. Your hearts were beating, but you just weren't breathing air like I expected was necessary. And I was worried that the umbilical cord was going to go bad and cause an infection or something really nasty. But it wasn't. It was perfectly fine. You were perfectly fine together, squirming around the tide pool, holding each other. It was a beautiful time for all of us together. Bonding time is so sweet.

But after a week, I was getting hungry. My pickled ass hurt. So as soon as we went cut the cord, a flash of lightning came out your ass and totally fried our shit. Like, blurry kind, burning, smokey shit. Just a blast of lightning and all hell broke loose. That's when you started spraying out blood like you was being eaten by piranha's.

We jumped out and took the baby with us. You was cussing away like a French pirate and your keiki was suffocating out of the water, but we didn't want him in there with you in the middle of your crazy ass episode. Oh, also, we noticed there was an incredible shiver of sharks right there at the shore, all frenzied up, thrashing around in the little shore break right next to us and our bloody asses."

"Eh? What do you mean an incredible shiver?" Alana interrupts.

"That's what you call a gathering of sharks. Like a school, or a flock, or a herd. I thought you would have already known that. But that's not important right now. The tide was coming up and we had to move out from the bloody tide pool to a clean one up the beach. We quickly noticed little Lono here wasn't quite ready to breathe air yet. He likes to come up and nibble on the mango, but it didn't really seem like he wanted to leave the water.

Anyways, you went ten days growling some wack shit in French and spurting out blood like you was in the middle of one knife fight. Then you started to calm down, underwater this whole time. What was really amazing though, is that you don't even have any scars on your body. Maybe like one or two. But your skin was just rupturing open and blood kept squirting out of new gashes all over. And then they would close right up. That's probably what your feeling right now. You need soup."

"Cheez, you're so full of shit right now." Alana has kissed her baby boy over one hundred times by now, causing him to get sleepy. "You and your stupid shit is not going to mess up my baby time. I cannot see. Is he beautiful?"

"He's absolutely gorgeous. He looks just like Tiki. But you're eyes just need time to adjust. They're totally pickled from the water all this time, but I'm telling you, our entire beach looks like a chum bucket. I'm surprised the shiver of sharks ain't frenzied all up.... Wait a minute..." Keala sits up and looks out. "What in the shit..."

Akila walks up with lunch, "Eh, mom. What happened to all the sharks?"

"Ha, what do you know... I guess the gathering's all pau (finished). Eh, keiki, go see if they left us another fish. I really liked that aku. You never know." Keala slouches back down in the sand, pulling her sister on top of her again.

She waits until Akila gets out of range. "I focking saw him. Sister, I focking saw him. I had to jump back in the water and hold you down. You were hitting your head on the rocks. So I got on top of you and pinned you to the bottom. I could see flashes behind your eyes so I went honi honi (kiss, sniff, press foreheads together) you and could feel heat from inside your head. Had to get Akila to tie your hands and feet. Could not hold you still and hold little Lono. I did not want him to see what your were seeing. I got two black eyes and you went busted out your front teeth from my chin... but it seems like you grew them back already. You know, like sharks do and shit. You're so weird."

"Ho, talk about the side affects of drugs. That was the stupidest story ever. My eyes are burning." Alana giggles.

"Are you even listening to me? Do remember our vision in Alaska?" Keala tries not to get impatient.

"Oh ya. All the way up until you left my ass outside in the tree. I was inside an owl in the middle of a hurricane watching your keiki, while you and the birdman was busy making your keiki, and I was out here giving birth to my keiki." Alana speaks in her cute baby voice, enjoying the beating heart of a napping newborn.

"Ok, now that is something I didn't want the keiki to see." Keala keeps it soft, "That, and his father getting wasted with his stupid uncles... and the

224

crack whore with the cobra busting out of her gut... oh, and decapitating those army guys, that was a bit much..."

"Eh, how much of that madness does he remember?" Alana feels guilty about participating in that scheme, "I told you it was a stupid idea. Just one time. That's what I told you, it only takes one time you skanky tweaker chick. Gateway to addiction."

"Oh, ya. He remembers everything. Except only the yellow eyes, not a clear image of who that monster was. And after he saw the yellow eyes, Akila said he saw the yellow eyes reflecting in the eyes of the snakes. Ya, so he goes out hunting snakes with his new knife. He likes to bring them back and burn them. I saw him feeding snakes to the sharks. Your little shark friends went totally bananas on the snakes." Keala looks out at Akila scouring the sandbar for fish. "But anyways, what exactly do you remember of that monster?"

"I uh... well... actually.... Da fock... I don't think I uh... I see Ikaika, I can see Lika, I can still see Kaleo, even though I don't want to, but... it's blank. It went blank on me. What am I missing?" Alana is slightly more interested without giving away any focus on her child's sleep.

"When I touch you, I cannot see him. When I let go, I can visualize an image of him. When Akila touches us, I can see a black hand trying to reach in and cover your eyes from seeing things clearly. Strange, ya?"

"Wait, reaching in from where?" Alana is curious.

"Well, it's like a window opening in your mind and one black creepy claw reaches in and claws at your eyeballs, playing tricks with our vision. Make sense?" Keala realizes it sounds suspicious.

"Sure. Manipulating my memory? Is that what you're saying? Or my actual eyeballs? Because they kind of hurt right now." Alana is not going to let the pain keep her from enjoying a quiet moment with her child.

Keala blurts, "That's what I'm saying." She looks over for Akila's location, "I'm saying, you have a connection with him."

Alana becomes triggered, "This feels different. The pain behind my eyes. It was always there, itching at me, burning. But now, Lono is born, and that vision left my window wide open. I knew it was a bad idea. Now how do we protect them from this?"

"Just take it easy there. Ok? Now, we needed to see him. He's hunting us." Keala refutes.

"He's grooming our children, he's stalking us." Alana exhales her anxiety. "You're right. We needed to see him. Even though we cannot actually see him. And now we get snakes? Like the kind that went bust out of the crack ho?"

"Oh, we get all kinds." Keala is proud of her child. "Akila has some chickens, one good mongoose, probably a whole family but they all look the same, ya? And a couple of stray cats. They make a good team. I wish I knew where to get one peacock. I know how much you liked him, but I'm not willing to go ask lolo Kaleo how to get a hold of one peacock."

"Wait. Is he clawing at your eyes too?" Alana releases the anxiety and melts Lono into her chest, breastfeeding in his light sleep.

"He claws at me through you. Your window is wide open. Oh, let me tell you this." Keala raises a Shaka to Akila, heaving a fully-grown aku to the shore. "So we went tied you up and covered you up in the sand. Now, this was possible because it was coming in waves. You would spaz out for a spell and then you would quiet down. That's when we would let Lono breast feed until you started back up.
And we buried your legs in the sand because you went kicked Akila in the 'ala'ala's (small stones) so hard he flew out the pool. And when you was really getting worked by the big waves, we'd see the flashes behind your eyes. The flash was coming through the window in your mind. You know, the same window you get the claw from. Your windows are aligned and these flashes are coming out his window and into yours and into ours. Makes sense, ya?"

Alana feels an optimism as Lono feels timeless in their connection. "Well. I can totally follow that perspective of all this. I'm actually having some clarity right now. And, I don't know how you managed to pull this off, but thank you. 'O wau no me ka mahalo (I am yours respectfully) my sister. My world can only be shared with you."

Keala melts for a moment. "Well, instead of you making me focking cry, I need you to answer me some questions before the next set hits us on the focking head."

"Eh, take it easy. Oh, let me have a little nap first. Just because I just woke up doesn't mean I was sleeping." Alana pleas.

"Oh, ya, I know. I don't know how you can survive this. I don't know how long we can survive this. You was literally kicking our asses. You were fighting for your life. And I was holding on to you so tight like riding a wild... I wasn't going to say pig or hog or boar, or heifer or anything like that, I swear.
But there I was with the snorkel and shit. And Akila cut out a white piece of paper and put it in the goggles. Then you would get real still for a spell, and you would shiver a little bit. Even the focking sharks would get real still and stare at you. And then the flash would come. I would open your eyes and you would flash out onto the white paper in my goggles. I could peak into the window of this monster and see what was flashing in his world. Again with the projector and shit."

Alana realizes her nap is over. "Are you telling me this slide show shit coming out of my head is real?"

"What?" Keala is stunned, "I told you this shit months ago. This has been a very important part of everything I have told you for the last ten months. What?"

"Oh." Alana is a bit unclear, "I just wasn't sure how much was actual reality, and what are you putting in this soup?"

Keala explains, "Sister, I don't know how much time we have. We broiled the aku before we threw it in the soup. More ono (delicious) that way. This is a dangerous window shining terrible things through your window. I don't know if we can stop this, but we cannot hide if the connection exists. What are we doing here?"

"What do you mean, what are we doing? What can I do? Can an exorcist close my window? I don't know. But I have a little time and I want to spend it loving my child. So, what is it that I need to know? Can you find Tiki?" Alana cuddles back down and pulls her sister's arm around her belly. She covers Lono with the tuberose floating on the surface.

"Hmph... Can I find Tiki... I've been so wrapped up in finding Ikaika... I don't know how to look for Tiki. I hope to God he's not involved in what ever you seem to be fighting your way out of. But I'm convinced this monster is connected to Tiki somehow. That makes four of our men he has taken. And now he's after our sons with his snakes. And if his snakes are here, then he's here." Keala scans the beach.

"Then, what you're telling me is that we have to find out who this creature is so we can find the kanaka's." Alana already knows she is several steps behind her sister. "So I believe there is one pivotal event in this creature's life, and that is the opening of his window. This light is cycling its way across existence and aligning itself with my window of perception, and this is what you are interpreting to me. Ya? After you snuck in Kaleo's house, stole some of his pakalolo, and cast some lolo images out to the universe from our windows too? Ya? So this creature is getting into my window, eh? Why can't you get into his? And maybe see something useful about Tiki?"

Keala has been hesitant to reveal the details, "Because I think there is someone else that got into his window, another creature that opened his window up. And I don't want that creature getting into ours."

Alana feels a splash of anxiety, "Shut your clam for a minute..." She lowers her voice, "I'm not the one you want to kill. You remember that? I heard that with Tiki. I heard that in the Pueo with Ikaika-them. We have to get into his window to see who this other creature is. Ya?"

228

"Roger that." Keala responds hesitantly, "Like the master vampire. What if we're dealing with a family of vampires? Butt pumping, sword wielding vampires."

"Wait. So, you were saying that my skin was rupturing and I was spraying out blood?" Alana hesitates, thinking she may not want to hear the answer. "What was going on with my butt?"

Keala sneaks a peak to Akila, making sure he's still piling up fish on the beach. "Well, I was trying to think of different ways to tell you, or not tell you, that they were totally humping this guys okole and stabbing him with swords. I was watching this vision of him through your window. Your body reacted like it was happening to you. That's what was flashing out your eyes. Pivotal moment indeed. Ya? What ever this guy got involved in opened a window for sure."

"Opened a window in his okole." Alana squirms, "But why does it hurt my okole?"

"This is passing through your body, and your body is experiencing the pain of it. Not just that, I'm feeling the effects of some serious heavy drugs. You were saying about gateway drugs? You were feeling the pain of it and I was experiencing the perception of it. And Akila was just a conduit, it passed right through him, to ground. Out of focus for him maybe, but he tuned us into it." Keala assures herself.

"How do you know? How is this not affecting our keiki's?" Alana feels the guilt creeping back.

"Cheez, just look at him. Look how happy he is with his big pile of fish. He's happy taking care of us. He's happy surfing. He's happy to have a little brother. I actually hate you for making me clean your ass all day. I was not prepared for the chore of handling an epileptic vegetable. It's driving me banana's. There's no one I can call for help. I can't feed you, I can't stop you from hurting yourself. I have to keep you tied up in a tide pool or you'll spurt blood all over the furniture. You're beating us up because your body thinks it's fighting off demons. And that's what they look like by the way.

229

But no worries, the keiki's all good." Keala hugs her tighter instead of saying sorry.

"Eh?" Alana wants to ignore her sister.

"The ones I see from your window, the ones humping his ass and stabbing him with swords. They are glowing snake demons. And by that, I mean glowing green demons with snakes for dicks, humping this guy in the pooper. Do you not see that?" Keala demands.

Alana is puzzled, "Well, not really. I guess I feel like I've been in a knife fight. But it just looks like a wild hallucinogenic nightmare to me. I cannot visualize what is going on. I think it's the drugs you were talking about. I mean, I was all focked up. Can't remember shit. Frickin' hung over. Are you sure we don't test positive for any substances?"

"Nah." Keala cannot piece this together. "They aren't transferring substances into us, just the mental shit. This is a spiritual transference, only energy. Light energy connecting our maka 'ike to their second sight. We're manifesting mental energy from different realms of universal existence. Holy shit is this totally scrambling my noodles."

Alana agrees, "Is there anything else you want to ruin my lullaby-lull with? You wanted to go down this rabbit hole. You're riding me like da kind, he'e holua (sled). I suggest maybe you try to look into his window a different way. Maybe try to look at something else besides the anaconda gang bang. Try to look for clues of Tiki instead. Can? Eh?"

"I mean, I guess I could try to explore the source of the connection. I really wanted to stay away from the pakalolo and the kava. But I swear, I could really use some. I want that feeling of jumping off the waterfall and landing in the bubbly pool." Keala is happy to find a peaceful moment with the mother and her newborn.

"I feel this lull balancing things. The potency of Kaua'i. This is the extreme high in the cycle. Mahalo for having some joy with me. I can fully appreciate this moment at the peak of the high tide and the lull it holds. For however long it may last. I'm grateful for the healing powers we share on this island together. Please be quiet for a while. Just give me some precious time." Alana coos in her sister's arms, holding her newborn.

Keala reaches the pinnacle of her high. As with the ebb and flow of the tide, Keala avoids thinking of the slow inevitability of their cycle. Before any thought of the next wave disturbs her mind, she slides out from under the mother and child and crawls quietly out of the rocky pool. Akila waves for her to help clean fish. Keala monitors her sister's stillness for a moment and then collapses in the sand next to her son. "You smell like fish. Let me take a nap in the sun for a while and I promise I will help with the fish. Please keep an eye on auntie. She's breathing air now so make sure they don't go back under water."

Akila giggles, "What if she starts cussing again? She cussed a lot less under the water. Mom?"

"Mom?" Akila walks past without disturbing her. "Auntie, I like take Lono outside."

"Go ahead. Did you check on your mother?" Alana sits on the couch and wipes her sister's face with a damp towel. "K? Keala, are you ready to get up?"

"No. Trying to take a nap here."

Alana is tickled to give her the news, "Nap time is over. It's been two weeks already."

"What?" Keala sits up and checks the picture on the calendar. "How is that possible? Was I in some kind of trance?"

"No. Just a nap." Alana gets up and opens the curtains to let the morning sun illuminate the sofa.

"No growling? No skull flashes? Did you at least change my diaper?" Keala is disappointed.

"Nothing but snoring. I was really looking forward to tying you up and fingering your eyeball, but mahalo's for letting me have some precious time with the boys." Alana sits next to her sister and watches the keiki's play in the yard. "I thought about what you said. And I'm totally ready for you to get high and peak through my window to search for Tiki."

"Uh, excuse me. What?" Keala feels ambushed. "I'm not sure it works like that."

"Look. 27th moon phase is tonight. You got a hundred owls watching over the house. There's a shiver of sharks down at the bloody beach, and no snakes anywhere, and there won't be with a flock of owls crapping on the lanai furniture. Kaleo's vanished, there's no sign of him. Now how about you drink some of this special tea I made just for you."

"You're so stupid right now. No way I'm drinking that. I just woke up." Keala stands and waddles to the window. She looks out at Lono clinging tightly to her son. "Ok, I get it. Was a stupid idea. I never should have made you into my science experiment. But I got things to do. Bills to pay. I got..." Keala walks back and plops down next to her sister. "Are you ok? You went through a lot. Why do you want to go through that pain again so soon? You lost a lot of blood. Don't you want to take some time and just be a mom for a while?"

"I've been a mom for a while." Alana wraps her arms around her sister, "I found out why this doesn't bother the keiki's. When we connect with the spirit world and open portals in the dream state, we are connecting with him because he has a connection with me. But not the keiki's. When they connect, they are protected by our ancestors. He cannot see them- like how he's blocking himself from us. Our ancestors are teaching our boys and hiding them from these creatures. And tonight, when we open this portal, our children will be watching over us with the protection of our ancestors."

"And how did you find all this out?" Keala feels helpless.

"Akila figured this out. He is very *receptive* to spiritual energy. He takes care of everything around here. I've enjoyed precious baby time while you were knocked out. But I cannot really enjoy it knowing that Lono's

232

father was abducted by this monster... or monsters. The pain I went through is nothing compared to what Tiki might be going through... what Ikaika-them are going through. We found the link to Ikaika, now let's find a link to Tiki."

"Ok, I get it. Beach or the bathtub?" Keala looks around and notices how clean the house is. She suddenly feels a tremor from her sister. "How much time we got?"

"I've been getting small waves all morning. I think a big set is on the way already." Alana stands up and reaches to pull her sister's hand. "Akila, it's time. Get the wagon."

Keala looks at the tea pot, "Oh, I noticed two cups here. Are you doing some kava with me?"

"That's a kava-cannabis confection in that pot. We're doing this one together. I better not be the only one waking up with a wrecked okole this time." Alana pours the tea.

"Hold on. How is this going to work. Who's going to take care of the keiki's if we get stuck in the dream state for a month?" Keala hesitates.

"I got our ancestors to babysit." Alana holds her cup, "Kampai (Japanese for cheers)."

"You're joking. Seriously though, the kids are joining us on this one?" Keala is not amused.

"No, they're not. Akila is going to take care of Lono. I got breast milk in the fridge, the sharks are delivering the fish, the owls and chickens are watching for snakes. I have no idea what the mongoose are doing, they do whatever they want. You cannot train them for shit. If there's any trouble, Akila can pull you out of the pool. No worries, in and out. Fast kind. No weird stuff." Alana waits for her sister to pick up her cup.

"This is highly irregular. What do you mean, Kaleo vanished?" Keala moves the teacup into position. "Did you go spy on him while I was knocked out?"

"Yes. Yes we did. His house is totally empty. Even the smell is gone. There's no other way to go about this. Now is the time to get some answers." Alana rattles her cup against the saucer.

"Ok, ok. We're on our own here, I hope you know what you're doing. The last time, I was watching over you. I don't know if the kids will be able to save us if something goes wrong." Keala taps her cup against her sister's, "Cheers."

Alana chugs hers and immediately pours a second cup. "Let's finish this pot and jump in the wagon."

Akila walks through the door with Lono in a sling around his shoulder, "You ready mom? You want to walk or ride in the wagon? You can get in the wagon, Lono likes the sling."

Alana drops her cup and begins quaking in her seat. "Keala, get me to the wagon. It's starting already."

"Oh shit! You weren't kidding. Kila, help me with auntie." Keala stands and reaches to pull her sister off the sofa. Time freezes the instant she makes contact with Alana. The white light chitters into her skull and blinds her in a flash.

"March 1936

Si Pwen

234

There is no way to know how long I have been unconscious, but that word does not define the state of my mind and body. I never completely lost my awareness during the unnatural occurrences that transpired. Yet the experience remains distorted and almost indefinable. The heroin I ingested immediately affected my perception and cognitive ability. I was barely able to hide my supplies behind the cases of rum before I succumbed to an altered state. By the time the hounsi reached the inner sanctum of the temple directly above me, my distorted vision was truly the only sense I had left to perceive these events.

Through the total darkness, my surroundings became defined by some sort of illumination coming from my mind. Everything suddenly appeared reflective like glass or a silver liquid, perhaps mercury. The textures of the cave took shape from a flickering light source, imaginably as a lantern through a tank of water. I tried to rationalize how the drug was affecting my cognitive processes, but words had completely lost all function and value at that time, English and Japanese. The degree of numbness my body was experiencing made it seem separate or detached from the origin of my vision. While I was consumed in this thought, I saw the hatch open and the hounsi crawled down to get me.

With the red light of the torches above, the entire floor I was kneeling on appeared to be writhing and slithering from hundreds of large snakes. I could only stare at the ground while the hounsi carried me and lifted me through the trap door. They pulled me out to a large painted room where I can roughly estimate forty to fifty people dancing, singing, laughing, crying and screaming. The roar of this enclosed crowd sounded distant to me. I realized that I was physically immersed in this ceremony, but in my realm of existence, I was completely isolated from the pain.

The walls and ceiling appeared a dark crimson color. The fiery torches made the colors so vivid, the stone appeared to be made of living tissue. The wild hounsi were no longer human. Their black skin had turned to translucent cobalt, as if they were now demons made of sapphire. Many appeared to have additional limbs waving frantically in the air. Some appeared to have no limbs at all and were dancing on top of a large pit of snakes. The bodies of these snakes appeared as only glowing green skeletons. The flesh around their skeletons was comprised of mist or smoke. This gave off a brilliant degree of contrast between the red walls and the blue hounsi, almost too distorted to perceive.

The moment I was dropped onto the sarcophagus in the center of the snake pit, the movement and chanting of the entire cave blended into a synchronized and harmonized mass, circling around my body. A green fog began to rise from the serpents. I stared at the hounsi crawling into the pit. Their limbs seemed to melt away, and then their flesh. The blue glow of their skeletal bodies changed to green, as it appeared the hounsi were actually transforming into snakes. And also, the snakes were transforming into the hounsi.

By the time I realized that Manbo Lysius was standing over me, I was covered with serpents. I never felt when the fangs of these vipers began to puncture every part of my body. I did however, feel their venom inflating my body with a highly reactive pulsating liquid. It was more of a living current of electricity than venom. It was not a burning shock, but rather charging me with a powerful euphoria. I could feel this euphoria convecting outwards from me and into the priestess.  This energy began radiating from her and into her people.  I was completely bewildered and lost of any coherence to my situation at this point.

It was then that she opened another window directly into my dream state of subconsciousness.  She arrived from behind a vacuum of sound.  I could feel a loss of body heat being pulled out of me and into the dark realm surrounding the vision from my gaping eyes.  This is where her voice entered my thoughts.  She asked me if I enjoyed the feeling of invincibility I was granted.  It was in her laughter that I sensed betrayal.  The more her hounsi tortured me, the more powerful the connection to my ancestor's spiritual energy grew.  This is the energy she extracted from me.  My body became her conduit, pulling energy from another realm of existence.  She explained I belong to her now.  I would be hers to drain.  I would become addicted to this draining.

The brilliant colors of red, blue and green became too intense and clashed with each other.  The transfer of this energy set the crowd into a circling rampage.  The silver shimmer of their machetes was becoming more prevalent in the vortex of blinding colors.  They were drunk with my blood, snarling 'we own you, we own your family, we own your ancestors, we own your souls!'  I asked her what did I own, and she replied, 'eternal love'.

I have the greatest difficulties accurately documenting what occurred beyond this.  My vision became overwhelmed by the swirling blur of colors.  Yet, sporadic flashes of silver halted the cyclone momentarily.  For only an instance, I clearly and accurately and soberly focused on each blade hacking into my flesh.  I was being stabbed over and over again without blood shed.  They gouged the machetes into my

237

flesh and each time they removed the steel, I became immersed back into the blinding cyclone of dementia.

The silver flashes were occurring too rapidly to distinguish how long this went on. Occasionally, I could perceive someone pulling the snakes off from my flesh and the fangs ripping out through my skin. As I dreaded before the ritual, these hounsi did indeed mount my anus. Each one of them appeared to crawl into the snake pit, lose their blue flesh and transform into the green serpent skeletons. The serpents then slithered up onto the sarcophagus where they became the blue glowing hounsi again. I was aware that these demons were brutally penetrating my anus, one after another. I was able to sense their erections writhing inside my body as if they were sadistically inserting the agitated snakes. Yet, it was so enjoyable for them that the skeletal serpents were actually conjoined as their own appendages. They clawed my face and throat. They screamed into my ears and chewed into my neck and shoulders like cannibals. 'We own you!', they screamed.

No human being could survive this crucifixion without god's protection. None of this pain registered in my mind. I can assign a certain degree of numbness to the heroin and a massive amount of endorphins. But at that point of the ritual, I had no concern for the physical cruelty. My entire consciousness had been completely removed and I was no longer attached to the inside of my body. Some form of energy had replaced me; and the hounsi seemed able to tap into this source by vigorously penetrating me with their serpentine erections. I don't believe they were fornicating me, but rather the energy of the entity that had taken possession of my body They would then slither down into the snake pit, transform into the blue hounsi again, and fornicate others in the room. I observed the

238

females radiating brilliant shades of green and blue during the orgy as if they were able to store the spiritual energy as it transferred through me and into the males.

In the dark realm outside of my body, I was exposed to brilliant waves of radiation that could in no way be interpreted. I assumed that this force was the Patronage of my ancestors, just as Manbo Lysius had promised. I eventually became accustomed to this and the images it revealed. I found myself focusing my eyes beyond the physical earth. This required a cognitive effort that seemed natural under the state of consciousness I had achieved. I intend to replicate this newly found focus without the Bat Guerre and the Manbo. Coupled with the sort of invincibility of the Patronage, my dire circumstances will definitely change in my favor.

I realized that since my body was granted invulnerability by a temporary possession, I would eventually return to my frail capacity. I can only estimate that this experience lasted as long as it would take for everyone involved in the ceremony to ravage my body. The agony of the ritual is now setting in, but mildly compared to the actual trauma I endured. My body's endorphin production is virtually non-existent. I fear I will soon feel the full effects of the debauchery. The residual images and the complete rectal failure are too repulsive to decipher. I was able to tolerate the reaction of the first dose of the heroin / rum elixir. Therefore I can assess that a slightly larger dose will achieve the results I will need to suffer the waiting period and the second ceremony.

In an effort to maintain the visual focus until well after I am returned to this dungeon, I will measure out a total of eight lines of heroin to mix with slightly less rum. I will prepare only one line with a small vile full of rum and store it next to my gear. Before I experience the decline in that mental state, I hope to extend the quality of my enhanced vision.

While the hounsi continued to violate me, I began to take notice of a small black dot expanding in the center of my vision. Once this dot grew large enough, I realized that a dark red color of blood was swirling around with the green glow of the snakes. It appeared as the colors one would see when pressing on his closed eyelids, or from entering a dark room after gazing at the bright sky. The direction of the swirling blackness was also in the opposite direction of the circling mass of hounsi. I was eventually overcome with a feeling of nausea as the black dot consumed my entire vision. At that time I did indeed realize the ceremony was completed and I was back in the dungeon of my own body. I convulsed on the ground for what seemed like hours. This had a sobering effect and the swirling colors eventually shrank and faded to black. I felt substantially more depleted as the Manbo drained me to near death. I do feel the terrible craving to allow her to possess me again. I fear this will be the new normal.

If I am to survive this Si Pwen, I must defer the consuming power of that swirling black dot. By extending the period of my altered focus, I hope to be able to achieve contact with Kaname Ijyui, my father. As intensely mortifying and grotesque as the ceremony proved to be, the incredible reaction it evoked was equally and oppositely magnificent. By condemning my body to hell, I was granted a taste of heaven, or rather a view. It now makes sense to me why my eyes burned and my vision became distorted before I even ingested the first dose of the heroin elixir.

240

In a blinding moment of clarity, I suddenly understood the reasons for a lifetime of repressed questions, doubts and suspicions. Through this ritual, I discovered that it was never my family that I honored with my obedience and loyalty. On some level of consciousness, I believe I always knew. This may account for why I was confident to subject myself to their crucifixion.

Interpreting the success of this ritual leaves my fate in a terrible position. I believe the purpose of my father's spiritual contact was to prove that the steps I have taken to arrive here were not the steps my family guided me to take. However, if that Militarist Empire would have never deceived me, then I might never have known the true fate of my father. I recognized him immediately by the comfort in the connection. It was as though his spirit materialized into me when I was mentally detached from my physical body. I focused on his eyes as he became part of me. Finally, when his eyes were a direct part of mine, it seemed that I was looking through his vision, through his mind, and then out through a separate plane of universal reality. At first I thought this was something that could never be interpreted. But then, the intensity of guilt and regret became clear and piercing. This was a view through an incredible scope of knowledge that I do intend to document and reproduce.

The problem I found was that I became consumed by the horrible spectacle of myself. For the first time, I looked upon myself clearly- deceived, betrayed, abandoned, tortured, and manipulated to commit terrorism and murder. I therefore have no choice but to abandon the servitude of that doomed empire. Everything I see of Japan burns with a fiery destruction. It will certainly become a conquered

241

nation by the greed and ignorance of a wicked minority faction. This is precisely the value Manbo Lysius has foreseen in me. This is the reason she lusted to initiate me into these ceremonies. She intends to harness the energy of thousands of Japanese souls lost in purgatory after a fiery end to this war. I shall therefore become Ronin. I refuse to serve her. I refuse to serve Ishii. By the wisdom of my ancestors, I will change the fate of my people. By taking the power of this demonic religion, I will become an emperor of lost souls. From a slave, to Ronin, to Emperor, my race will regain honor.

I knew the silence would not last. The hounto drums from the street are becoming incredibly painful in my head. I can now feel the full trauma from the first ritual setting in. I will not be able to resist another dose of my elixir much longer. The objective of the second Kanzo Rite, the Si Pwen, is to establish a connection with the Lwa. After experiencing the clarity of my ancestors, my Zanset Yo, I can now associate the power of the Lwa to be the angels of the earth that govern the forces of nature. Here, I hope my Zanset Yo will show me the way for balance. With a balance of these unnatural forces, I hope to transpose this knowledge into physical reality so that I can evoke the power on my own.

This depends on my ability to precisely adapt my focus on both levels of consciousness. The sadistic abuse of the next ceremony will certainly prove to be more horrendous than the first. My concentration must not be thwarted by this evil distraction. My objective for the Si Pwen is therefore to achieve an altered state of awareness early- before the monstrous acts consume my attention. If this can be done, I will then call upon the Patronage of my ancestors without the Manbo's interference.

This came to me in an explosive force, as though millions of voices screamed to me at once. I was overwhelmed the first time. This force seemed volatile and unstable, unlike what I perceived from my father. I knew at once that my father has indeed been dead for many years. All of the knowledge, emotional content and intentions conveyed a feeling of a life already expired- nothing was to feel new again. This degree of regret can only come from the dead, betrayed and murdered. I distinctly sensed it to be of the past and that a painful murder had undoubtedly occurred. In comparison, the exploding surge of screams lacked the sensation that time had already ceased to grow, or progress further. It has not come to pass at this time. It is necessary then to discover how the spiritual energy of my ancestors can already exist in purgatory if they are in fact still alive. Is this the mystery of fate? Is the destructive path I have already set in motion doomed my nation to a fiery end? I assume this is why the Manbo referred to me as a rare, exotic killer on my first night here. She senses the thousands of souls I murdered on my path here, as well as the countless souls that will inevitably be murdered before this war ends.

I can now hear their singing of hymns. The tickling euphoria behind my vision is already returning. I can no longer fight the urge for the heroin, as if this urge is being summoned by the spirits themselves. The drums and chanting are magnifying the cravings. I must now prepare myself for the Si Pwen. If I cannot achieve Patronage before they take me, then I hope the Manbo burns my supplies with my dead body and destroys this cursed island."

"Alana? Wake your ass up and get in the truck." Keala taps the bottom of Alana's foot. "You like go or what? I'm not waiting around for you to put on your mascara and shit. Move it!"

"Hold on. Wait." Alana reaches out for help sitting up, "My eyes need time to adjust."

"You can adjust them in the truck. Here's your slippers. Don't tell me you got to go shi-shi because you already went." Keala pulls Alana to her feet and spins her around, "What? What are you waiting for? Eh? I already dressed you, went brushed your teeth, got your hair in a bun. Start taking steps already."

Alana cooperates with being pulled out the door. "Wait, where's the kids?" She gains her balance and walks around the truck on her own.

"We're gonna go get 'em. Right now. Strap in girl." Keala starts the truck and watches her sister fumble with the harness.

Alana finds it difficult to maneuver the end of the strap into the clip with her sister impatiently glaring at her every move. "Wait. Where are they?"

"At the Salt Ponds." Keala reverses the truck around the house and slings gravel as she revs up first gear.

"The Salt Ponds? What are they doing at the Salt Ponds? How the hell did they get there?" Alana starts to get dizzy staring out the window. "You let Akila take the baby out like that? What the hell's wrong with you?"

Keala is driving too fast to take her eyes off the road, but glares at her sister anyway. "Are you all strapped in there, chief? All righty. First off, I didn't let them do jack shit. They run off on their own."

"Whatchoo mean they run off on their own? Wait, are you saying the baby is walking already?" Alana is stunned.

"Ok, second..." Keala keeps her eyes on the road, "You're not going to like second. Your baby is four years old. Those two keiki's are driving me nuts! They run off and do shit like this all the time. What?"

"Whatchoo mean, what? Are you telling me I lost four years of my life?" Alana suddenly feels nauseous.

"What? Bother you? Eh? Four years is a long time. You slept through double diaper duty. I was taking care of both of you the whole time." Keala runs through several stop signs in a row. "Look. Sorry, eh? Don't get sad on me now. I know you think you missed out on your baby's life, but you were right there the whole time. You were actually half-awake most of the time. You're fully awake now, but maybe you can remember it like it was a dream or something. I don't know. Are you gonna puke or something? Like me pull over?"

"No. I'm ok. Just take me to Lono. Four focking years? You couldn't wake me up? What the hell is happening?" Alana suddenly feels angry.

"Eh, don't look at me like that. Remember, it was your idea to go exploring. Akila brought us down to the tide pools right when you started hitting hard. That lasted one whole month. Next thing I know, I wake up and find out Akila let Lono swim with you underwater again. He stayed with you when you were calm, then I would hold you down when you were hitting. This has been our lives for the past four years. What?" Keala reaches for Alana's hand.

"Where's Tiki?" Alana starts sobbing immediately.

"Tiki is alive. He's locked up somewhere I cannot find. It's hard to find him because he's not entirely in this realm with us. Don't look at me like that. He's mostly in the spirit world. He is detached from his body and his body is locked up and we cannot find him. Oh, how the hell do I know this? I'm glad you asked."

Keala gives her a quick smirk before careening off the main road. "Remember how we left our bodies and got put inside the big owl? Ya? Well, as soon as we went into your little acid nap, the black hand reached into your window and was trying to pull us out through your head. I spent the whole month pulling you back in, like getting sucked over the falls and trying to swim back to the surface. I fought that until I thought we were gonna drown. And I mean drowning in some psychedelic crucifixion that I don't want to explain right now. But Akila reached in and pulled us back into place."

Alana wipes her eyes. "Did we at least learn anything? Was it worth it? What did I just trade four years of my life for?"

"Aw, come on. It was totally worth it. Believe me. Before Akila pulled me, or rather propelled us back into your window, I found a connection with Tiki. That's how I learned he was crying out in the spirit world. I also found a connection to Ikaika and the Pa'i brothers. Before I entered your window, while I was still in the spirit world... try nod if you're following this... ok, I shared my connection with all the kanaka's so they can connect with each other. Eh? Did I do good or what?" Keala smiles like this was going to cheer her sister up. "What?"

"Wait." Alana stops sobbing and sighs, "How did you do this? How do you know even know this?"

"Because I rule." Keala slows the truck and approaches dozens of vehicles parked in a field. "So the boys were right about being da kind, *receptive*. They received my presence and I was able to learn a few things. Ok? Ikaika, Lika and Kaleo are their slaves. Tiki is their prisoner. There is more than one. I think Tiki is being experimented on by one brother. I think Ikaika-them are sailing fish drugs for the other brother. I think it is their father who is haunting your window. I think there is another creature controlling them all. And, here we are. Let me help you with the straps." Keala skids the truck in the dirt and kills the engine.

Alana collects her wits before she reaches for the door handle. "What are all these people doing here? Where's the kids?"

"It's Aloha Friday night. Pau hana (after work). These people are all out here getting focked up. Remember that, grandma? We used to go out drinking too you know." Keala slams the door and grabs her sister's arm. "Come on, we're not that old. You said you wanted to get out the house, right? This is like date night. Let's go chug a beer, you're my date. And then as soon as we find the keiki's, we gonna whoop their ass. Roger?" Keala weaves them through several rows of cars.

"What kind of experiments are they doing to him?" Alana realizes they are tromping down a hill and the people around them are yelling and clapping along with someone's car stereo.

"They have Tiki's spirit out in limbo while they are experimenting different drugs on his body. This is also what they are doing to crazy-ass Kaleo. Lika is working on a farm somewhere. And Ikaika is sailing a ship across the ocean. They all tried to keep this shit a secret from me, but I already told those boys- there ain't no way to keep shit from me. I focking find everything out, one way or another."

Alana stumbles on some rocks because Keala is pulling her too fast. She keeps her eyes on the ground to be safe with the sun going down, "But why would they try to keep this a secret. I thought they were trying to call us for help. To help rescue them."

Keala halts and pulls her sister directly in front, staring into her eyes, "They were trying to hide the keiki's from him. And we focked that all up. They agreed to remain as slaves, as experiments, they made a deal and it seems they are honoring that."

"How do we know these creatures have any honor?" Alana feels like crying again. "We already have snakes and shit. They're gonna come for us. What if I'm in a coma and shit? How am I supposed to protect my child?" Alana feels more anger than sadness, "I'm gonna get a submarine and hide underwater with all my sharks. My guard sharks. I'd like to see them come after us. Seriously. What are we gonna do?"

"They're not after the children. Not yet. They will honor this deal. They make wagers. They make the kanaka fight them. They're like gladiators, and they make wagers. Lika is the most *receptive* since he works on a drug farm and shit. I think that was actually his dream job anyway. He told me he bet that if he won some big fight, that they would stop spying on us and keep their distance. We haven't seen any snakes in over a year, so

247

it seems Lika actually won that fight and they are actually honoring that deal. So, let's get a beer." Keala makes a blaring whistle and gives a hand gesture to a group of guys.

"Was that the signal for beer or a hand job? Stupid, they're coming over here!" Alana turns to walk away but Keala snags her hair and unravels it. "Holy shit, you couldn't cut my hair this whole time? It's dragging the ground already!"

"Just don't focken' worry about it and grab the beer." Keala pulls her back in, "Now chug it and behave yourself." Keala smiles at two guys walking up, "Eh, howzit. You boys have a beer for me and my sister or what? Wow. That's very nice of you. Mahalo's for sharing."

One of them turns and waves a Shaka back to his other buddies, "Oh hey, I'm Ferdinand. Ferdy. Ferdy-bird. That's what they call me..."

Keala interjects, "Eh, dirty-terd, could you give me and my sister a minute. We were just discussing something very important." Keala is relieved one of them walks back to their friends.

"Oh, uh, ya. No worries. Wow, you chicks are sisters? What's your name?" He reaches over and opens Alana's beer for her.

"Mahalo's there Ferd. My name's Alana. This is my sister, Keala. Excuse me, but could you give us a second please?" Alana turns and gives her sister a smirk.

"Oh, ya. For sure. You want a smoke?" He pulls the cigarette out from behind his ear.

Keala steps in, "No thanks. We actually have something important to talk about..."

"Oh. Ok. Eh, you want to smoke a doobie? I was just about to roll one up in my car." Ferd insists.

"Ya. You know what, why don't you go over there and roll us up a doobie and give us a minute to discuss... wow... that bugger already took off... anyways." Keala puts her arm around Alana's shoulder, "Drink your beer and don't freak out." She points to the bottom of the hill.

Alana looks down the hill to the cars lined up, pointing their headlights at the center. This is where the music is coming from. She watches the crowd yelling, clapping, dancing. She mimics how drunk men make each strike of the drum their hardest hit possible and makes her sister laugh. She takes a sip and looks at two boys putting on a choreographed fight sequence with clubs. She notices everyone cheering them on. The moment Alana recognizes the two boys, she spurts out her beer just as Ferdinand walks up with his newly-rolled doobie. "What the fock? Is that our kids?"

Ferdinand is frozen and bewildered, "Uh... I'll be back..." He turns and walks back towards his parked car, staring at the soggy spliff dripping in half.

Keala pulls her sister back in and wipes the front of her shirt, "Yes. That's our kids. So much for drink the beer and not freak out."

"What da fock you mean, don't freak out?" Alana is lost, "That's my four-year old kid spinning clubs in front of a mob!"

"Ya. Well. Look at 'em go. I mean, they're pretty good. I think the crowd is loving it." She takes another drink, "I mean, I'm still gonna whoop their ass and shit. Oh, here comes your boyfriend." Keala shakes her empty can, "Hey Ferd, my sister accidentally spilled her beer. Could we get two more?"

He walks up, "Oh, ya, of course. Hang on a minute." Then, turns back to his car.

Keala helps her sister tilt her beer can for a bigger drink, "You know how they can do that? Because they learned that through you. You may have been asleep, but the knowledge of our ancestors flowed through you and into them. They are incredible. So smart... well, it was pretty stupid to sneak off after I told them you would probably wake up this afternoon and

249

all. But please don't think that the time was wasted. Or that you missed out. Or that you're a bad mother."

Alana squints across the distance, "Wait, are you letting them go into a trance with me?"

"Nah." Keala wipes beer from her chin, "More like a little daydream when you're calm. It comes in waves and shit. You know, snarling acid trips of bloody ass-pumping violence, and then lulls of peaceful nappy-nap time where you heal yourself up. That's when we clean you up and hold you in a dreamy state of serene learning and loving and caring. You actually seem half-awake and shit. You don't remember any of that?"

"What the fock? No. I don't think I remember anything like that." Alana watches the boys drop the clubs and grab a pair of large woven baskets. The boys walk quickly through the crowd, collecting money and snacks in their baskets. She loses sight of them when the cars turn off their headlights. "Eh. Are you pimping out our kids?"

"What?"

"Is this how you're paying the bills? Pimping out our kids on this little sideshow you got here?" Alana notices Ferdinand approaching with a fresh round of beer. "Eh, Ferd. Is that a doobie behind your ear? Ya? Pass it over."

"Oh ya! Now were partying!" He breaks into a little dance, "You two are definitely the hottest chicks here. Eh, get chance or what?"

Keala chuckles, "Whoa, easy tiger."

Ferd continues dancing, but closer. "Nah, for reals. You two are totally smoking hotties."

Alana laughs for the first time in years, "You better light that thing up and pass it over before I change my mind."

Keala opens a fresh beer, "You know what, I am actually married. But this one here is totally not married. But she's been in a coma for four years. Maybe you could show her how to do your little dance there."

"Oh, ya. For sure. It's all in the hips... gyrate. See how I'm gyrating." Ferdinand dances until Alana hands the doobie back. "You was in one coma, like from a car accident or something? Wow. You look super hot for someone who's been in a coma. I would bring you flowers every damn day if you was in the hospital. I would read you books and shit, and hold your hand, every damn day. I would kiss you and make you wake up like Snow White."

"Wow. That's real sweet of you there Ferdy. Wait, are they lighting a fire down there?" Alana slithers to the other side of her sister.

Ferdinand turns and looks over his shoulder, "Oh, ya. That's so crazy, ya? Siva asi. Watch, they do a mean fire knife dance every weekend. The crowd goes nuts."

Alana is alarmed, "Wait, what? Whatchoo mean, every weekend?"

"Oh, ya. Every week, we all come down to Pau Hana (after work) party and watch the show. But watch out for the Menehune's (mischievous elves). Shit gets all focked up around here if you're not careful." Ferdinand chuckles deviously.

Alana turns to her sister, "You let the kids come down here every weekend? Bad mommy!"

Ferdinand interjects, "Wait a minute. Those are your kids? No way. Those are Menehune's from the mountain. Those aren't kids."

Keala defends, "I don't let them do shit. You know what, sometimes I'm too busy keeping you alive, I can't keep them from sneaking off. They're never gone for long, I don't get how this is even possible." They stare at the ring of fire from the spinning clubs. The red glow quickly illuminates the crowd into a mass trance. Everyone goes quiet, mesmerized by the graceful

251

movements. "Wow, look at them go." Keala sips and stares, "Oh, I'm spanking their little asses, but damn, our kids are really good."

Alana replies sarcastically, "Oh ya, our kids rock." All the headlights from the ring of cars have gone out. The burning clubs are the only lights left after the sun went down. The drums reverberate in her ears. Everyone eventually goes silent, all staring at the dancing fire. She feels the heat in waves as the clubs spin through the air, back and forth from one child to the other. The drunk drummers eventually reach a synchronized beat, controlling everyones heartbeats like a pacemaker.

Alana catches her body flinching with the rhythm. "Eh, listen to me. Can you see what the fire is doing to these people? I think I'm having the maka 'ike right now. I think the fire is putting everyone in some kind of trance."

Keala chuckles, "You sure it's not the beer goggles? You went suck 'em up pretty fast, eh? For real? What exactly are you looking at?"

"I'm looking at the red glare from the boys' fire. They're really working the mana down there. Don't you think that's a little strange?" Alana says without blinking.

Ferdinand interjects, "Ho, the kids get the mean show tonight, eh? The best one yet! The fire makes all the chicks look so pretty! You like one-nother beer? Hoo, I stay pretty bus up right now, but guarantee you two are the hottest chicks around here."

Alana and Keala look at each other and laugh, "Ok, easy there flirty-bird. Thanks for the beer."

Ferdinand gives a wink, "No worries. You can have as many beers as you need. Just keep on drinking until I get chance."

Keala blurts, "You sure you have enough beer?"

Ferd replies with a little more dancing, "Eh, I got four cases in the trunk! It's only a matter of time before I get handsome enough for you!"

The sisters spurt out a mouthful of beer. Keala pats her sister's back, "Oh braddah, you funny! At least you have that going for you. Ok, Ferd, you're making my sister choke."

They watch Ferdinand turn proudly and give a confident Shaka to his crew. Alana slaps her sister's hand away, "Keala! Now he's not going to leave us alone!"

"Don't worry, he's harmless. Eh, you're not about start growling some lolo shit, ya? Uh, you about to have an acid vision or are you in a trance? What? Eh? What do you see?" Keala continues watching the show.

"It must be the boys' fire. It's burning with the mana because I can see people's aura lit up from the red glare. Some people are blurry... and some people shine out clearly. Some people like the younger boys and girls in the front have a bright red glow just like the fire, but some others... like the mean looking guys across the way, they have a darker, cloudy red- like it clashes with the fire. So weird... Nah, I'm not about to get growly on you. I actually feel pretty good. It's a good vibe. Thanks for getting me out of the pool. I forgot what it was like to be dry. And I don't just mean the cottonmouth."

Ferdinand is enthralled, "No shit. Hey, what's my aura say?"

"You don't want to know." The girls say in unison.

"No really, can you see my future?" Ferdinand steps in front and blocks the show.

Alana explains, "Uh, no. I can see your fate from your aura and it's seriously some shit you don't want to know."

A fresh cloud of cigarette interrupts, "Eh, you one fortune teller or what? What, my cigarette bother you? I got another mean doobie, eh? You like that?"

"No thanks. You go right ahead there Ferdy." Keala puts her arm around her sister and pulls her back another step, "Believe me Alana, the only thing about my fate that will surprise me is one happy ending after all this."

Alana's eyes stare widely without blinking, "Well, that's the difference between us and them. I can see it clearly right now."

"What?" Keala and Ferdinand reply in curious unison.

"Free will." Alana states.

"Eh?" Keala and their new friend give each other a confused glance.

Alana explains, "None of these people have the mana living inside them. They can go through their lives, doing whatever they choose to do, and never really know of its existence. But, the mana lives in us. Our fate is already chosen. Look at our boys. You think they are controlling that fire? That fire is controlling them! Our ancestors put them on this path and there's nothing we can do about it. The mana is using them. Using us. Tiki talked about this. One dark, violent world, no choice. No different than slavery."

Ferdinand is confused, "Wait, wait, wait, wait, wait. Those are your boys?"

"Yep." Keala blurts, "Where you been nerdy-bird? We already covered this."

"Nah!" He's in disbelief.

"Yepper. One's mine and one's my sister's." Keala assures.

"Oh wow! We all thought they were the Menehune from the mountains." He reasons.

"Menehune? How's your pakalolo Ferd?" Keala teases.

"Oh, I get da mean kind. Everybody knows that. But every week after the show, some kind freaky shit happens that only the Menehune can make happen." Ferdinand entices them by suspending his spliff under his nose with his upper lip.

"What do you mean every week? How many times have you seen these kids?" Alana demands.

"Oh ya. Me and my boys come here every Friday for the Pau Hana beers! Ho, they've been having shows here for at least tree monts."

"Did you say three months?" The sisters reply in harmony.

"Ya, at least tree monts. Hoo, and every time weird shit happens to people. It's hilarious, but no can explain. So it's just funny." Ferdinand uses his cigarette to light up his doobie. "That's why they Menehune."

"What do you mean weird shit, like mean stuff, like pranks?" Alana winces to her sister.

Ferdinand tries to share the joint but gets rejected. "Like last week, every beer went explode after the show when we opened them; like somebody went shake 'em up, every single beer. Lucky thing we never get pulled over by the cops! Hooo, was beer all over! We thought it was just us, but was plenty people. Like everybody was spewing beer. And for some reason, we all had to check every beer for the shake up. Like, we all knew it was going to explode in our face, but we all had to check anyways to see if it really was every damn beer. Every. Damn. Beer."

"For real?" The sisters are embarrassed.

"For real kine. Oh, and before that, we watched some trucks drive away and their coolers went fly right out the back! Like, ten trucks in a row. Fockin' beers flying everywhere! I thought I was the smart one because I checked my cooler and found one heavy fishing line tied to the handle. I cut that sucker and stayed for laugh at every body else. But when I went to leave, I discovered that the Menehunes went tied the other handle up to the tree too. Ho, I don't know why I never checked both handles... stupid, ya? I also never knew little wooden spikes would pop a tire, everybody had to bust out their spares in the dark one night. That one wasn't so funny. But the ti leaves in the tailpipe- oh, that was actually funny."

"Unbelievable! Oh, those kids are in trouble. That's just mean." Keala is over the magical moment.

"The kids? I cannot see how those kids could do that. We all watch those kids during the show and then we leave when they finish. No time for shake the beers, I mean every person's beer at the same time? No way. Menehunes, I telling you. Would be totally impossible for two keiki's to pull that off."

"So what Alana, sabotaging everyone's beer drinking? Sounds like some free will to me. Popping tires is definitely some free-will shit. I don't really see ancestors flipping beer buckets, so their souls cannot be tied just to this one path. And being blind to this is not an option if we're being hunted." Keala is steamed.

Ferdinand contributes, "Eh girls, didn't the angels rebel against heaven because God gave man a soul and free will? War in heaven and shit."

Keala laughs, "Hooooo, that's deep stuff for the Pau Hana beer drinking Ferdinand."

"Oh ya, trying to impress the hot chicks! Ready for another beer? I'm getting more handsome by the drop." He straightens the gold chains around his neck.

Alana looks over and studies his face for a moment while he raises his chin like a supermodel. "Hey Ferdy... don't you already have two girlfriends?"

"Wot? No way!" He refutes.

"You mean you already have two girls Ferd? You think you can handle more?" This does not surprise Keala.

Alana clarifies, "No, he has one girlfriend and one fiancé!"

256

He's bewildered, "Holy shit! You are one fortune teller!"

Alana glares him up and down, "No Ferdinand, I can only see your aura. And if you do not stop lying to them, and commit all your love to one of these girls, the fate you choose will be to go crazy and die sad and alone at a young age."

"Oh. Are you for real?" He's not convinced.

"You're damn right she's for real. The mana is shining on you right now Ferdinand. Eh. Listen to me- you are in the presence of something very powerful, ok? Powerful enough to drive people insane. I'd advise you to listen to my sister and commit your love to only one girl. And you cherish that and work hard, ok?" The drumming and swirling red lights drill the words deep into his mortal mind. "And be honest with her."

He gets dizzy and wobbles a bit, but shakes it off, "Ok. Eh, you're really tripping me out. You know what. Ok. Look, I only proposed for the money. Her father's the boss. No way I could say no."

Alana points right at his nose, "But you don't love her! That's why you cannot break it off with your other girlfriend. Ferdinand, you don't know how lucky you are to be able to make this choice right now, before it all blows up in your face and drives you mad. You really think you're a player? Keep playing and find out."

"Ho wow... you're right. I should go tell her the truth. Ya." He flicks his cigarette under someone's car and pinches the doobie out.

Alana is proud of her work, "There you go Ferdy. And quit smoking those cigarettes!" She waves bye until he turns and takes a step back.

"Ya. Ok. Eh, uh..." He stutters as he slowly turns back to them.

"What is it Ferd?" Alana and Keala thought he was ready to leave.

He looks deep in Alana's eyes, "I uh... uh... I think I love you."

257

"Ho. Focking guy. You know what, get the fock out of here!" Alana growls. She waits until he turns and walks back to his car. "Cheez. Unreal. I was about to kick that boy in the face." She yells out, "Eh! You don't deserve either one of them player!" Alana starts to giggle. "You should have seen your face when I growled at him. I was so frustrated, I could imagine blood spurting out my eyes all over him. He would've crapped in his pants."

"Oh, I was waiting for you to snap on that guy. Except I wasn't willing to spill my beer holding you back." Keala smiles for a moment. "But I don't like that talk about free will. I know what you're saying, but we all have to choose right and wrong. I know you don't want to see them enduring a life of violence, the pain, the suffering. The only choice is survival. It's not even right or wrong. It's life and death. That creature took away our choices when he started hunting our family. What? You got your ass all worked up, am I gonna have to strap you in the harness? You ok?"

Alana looks to the sky for a spell in silence, "There's something else here..."

"Uhhh..." Keala looks around at the moon and then tries to look into her sister's eyes, "The fock you mean, something else? Something dark? Snakes? Eh, what-choo-ma-fockin'-saying? You spazzing out or what?"

"Hold on... something natural... powerful... not dark or light, aspects of both." Alana looks urgently into her sister's eyes, "How about we get the keiki's and get the fock out of here."

Keala nods in agreement, "Ya. Date night's been fun, but I think it's time to..." She suddenly notices the fire is out. The music has stopped. Everyone stands frozen, still in the trance. Keala panics and grabs her sister's arm, "I smell the smoke, follow the smoke. Find the burnt clubs, we find the keiki's." She takes a step down the hill and pulls Alana, but is held back.

"Mom! Sorry mom!" Akila and Lono wrap their arms around their mothers.

Alana feels the electrical connection of her son. She looks down and sees Lono's face looking up, "Oh my god! Look at you. My little baby, you look just like your papa!" Alana starts to sob, "Where did my life go?" She strains to lift him, "Oh, I love you every day of my life. I love you forever my baby boy." She kisses his face as he wraps his arms around her neck.

Keala spins them up the hill and yanks them along, "We need to move. Can you put him down? No? Ok, I'll just carry you both then." She puts Lono's weight on her back and reaches behind around to pull Alana close. "The wind changed. Get your ass moving. You're right, there's definitely something out here." Keala keeps a tight hold on her sister and points the way for Akila to lead, "I cannot believe you two monkey nuggets did this. Of all the nights, you had to sneak off, after I told you she was waking up today."

Akila tries to explain, "You said to go buy one new mu'u mu'u for auntie so she would have something nice to wear for her birthday."

"Zip it!" Keala weaves through the rows of vehicles, "Someone's going to take notice of you, throwing flaming clubs at each other. What if they start asking questions like, why are there two little keiki's running around without their parents? Where do you live? Eh? Why aren't you in school? We cannot have that kind of attention because there's so many questions we just cannot answer."

Lono clutches Alana's neck peering at the darkness behind them, "Mom, someone's following us."

Akila tries to calm his mother, "Mom, you said she was waking up tomorrow night, not today."

"Zip it!" Keala points to their truck parked next to the last row of cars, "Wait, that's a lot more money than last time."

Akila gives her a wink, "You were right, the fire knife dance is how you end a show."

"Zip it!" Keala blurts.

Lono hangs from his mother's neck, sandwiched between the sisters, "Mom, someone's following us."

Alana gasps, "Hoo! You were in on this the whole time! I knew it!"

"What?" Keala points and snaps her fingers in the direction of the truck. "You know what, just take it easy there sis. This is all news to me. I'm sure there's a reasonable explanation…"

"Bull Shit!" Alana is alarmed, "We're being hunted and you're pimping our kids out for a hula show on the other side of the Island! What's wrong with you? Bad mommy!"

Lono is bounced around as his mother stumbles across the rocks, "Mom, someone's following us."

Keala nudges Akila to run ahead and open the doors for them, "Eh, cool head main thing."

Alana flicks her sister's ear, "That's why you got a new stereo in the truck. Eh? You're pimping out the keiki's for the whole Island to gawk at. I cannot believe you. So stupid! Is this what you call hiding out, keeping our kids safe?"

Keala refutes, "Kaleo vanished. There's no snakes. The only scary thing left around here is you. Now get in the damn truck."

Alana halts, "Oooh. You know what…"

Lono interrupts, "Mom, someone's following us."

"That's some special keiki's you have there." A raspy voice surprises Alana as a cool breeze chills her back.

Keala spins them around, "Ya, and why are you following us, sneaking up on us like that? Now's not the time mister." She glares at him but all she can see is a hooded sweatshirt and faded jeans in the dark.

"I'm a friend. I know who you are. I know your mother." The voice explains hidden under the hood.

Keala snaps, "No way. Sorry, it's time to go."

"Please, I can help. You will need my help when they return. You are right, it is safe on the Island right now. But they will come back for you when they see how powerful your children have become." The breeze picks up, deepening the chill.

Alana wants answers, "How could you know our mother? She didn't live on this Island."

"She was a conduit, just like you two, a medium between worlds. When your father opened up a portal, your mother had to blaze a path open for you. She didn't live on this Island, but all the veins of the Islands lead to the same source. Your parents gave you a link to that source so that you and your children could survive. You understand what I'm saying?" The cold wind from the north quickly brings in clouds and fog.

Keala replies, "Our mother blazed a path right over a cliff. What kind of link was that? How did that help us?"

"She created a bridge. She intended to cross that bridge, and to return, but your father got lost and she searches for him still. I can help you find your way across that bridge when the time comes."

Alana holds Lono tightly, "How will we know when it's time? How can we save our children from this?"

"You are a powerful conduit. Ancestral knowledge flows through you into them. Trust in their guidance and teach them everything you can. Don't cry for the time you have lost, cherish the time you are granted to teach. It is the most precious. Your mother blazed a path for you to survive. You will know when the time has come when you are forced to take the path she laid out for you."

Keala demands, "Are you telling us the only way to survive this is to drive off a cliff?"

"I'm telling you, when the time comes, you will know that you do not have a choice. Trust the path. I will be there to help." The cold wind begins to gust, causing the sweatshirt and pants to flutter. "I'm out of time. There were extraordinary circumstances when your mother created that bridge under a full moon. There will be extraordinary circumstances under a full moon when they come for you. I will be at my most powerful state at that time and you will need to trust me." The fluttering clothes suddenly whisk away to the sky, empty, shapeless.

Keala and Alana stand silently for a moment, feeling the wind move the tears from their crying eyes across their cheeks. "Uh... Keala... where did all those bonfires come from?"

"Uh... you know what..." Keala blinks a few times, returning from a daze, "Ya. I coulda sworn it was totally dark out here a while ago. I guess they went out and the wind sparked them back up." She shrugs it off. "I suppose we should get the hell out of here now. In the truck."

Alana notices the keiki's giggling as she buckles the harness. She looks up at the commotion and yelling around the field. "Uh, kids? What's going on out there?"

"Menehune Time." They giggle in unison.

"What the..." Alana gasps, watching the bonfires burst with steam and the bystanders jumping and screaming. She looks across the field and notices havoc wrecking across every bonfire, "What do you mean Menehune Time?"

Akila chuckles, "This is the one where the Menehune's throw beer into the bonfires."

Alana peers across the field and the people panicking and fleeing, "And then?"

Akila continues, "Well, the beer eventually gets hot and explodes." As they drive over the hill, both sisters glare down at the kids. Akila refutes, "Eh, don't look at us. Those fires were out a minute ago. Like I said, Menehune Time." He swiftly turns on the new stereo and slides the paper sack of money under the seat. He gives his auntie a hug and wriggles his eyebrows up at her. "So what, you like the show? Me and the grommet are pretty good, eh?"

"You and the grommet?" Alana laughs, "The both of you little buggers are grommets. Menehune Time, you gotta be kidding me." She cannot take her eyes off her son. The loud music helps keep her from crying. She slips out a little sob.

Lono keeps a tight hold of her, "It's ok mom. Don't be sad. This is precious time, just like the wind said."

Alana turns the radio down a little, "Keala, could you slow down a little?"

"I ain't gonna drive off a damn cliff." Keala snaps. "What? You got questions? What do you want to know? I just told you everything already." She notices her sister staring at Lono, trying not to cry. "Look sis, you haven't missed a thing. You've been with us the whole time. It's nice to see you wide awake for a change. Night on the town, making new friends. Enjoy this time of peace. Apparently, it won't last forever. What?"

"Aren't you guys hungry?" Alana tries to snuggle as far as the harness will let her.

"Uh, ya. You know what, we're gonna take you out for one nice plate lunch and the keiki's wanted to get you one new mu'u mu'u for your birthday. How's that sound?" Keala smiles over and notices her sister's twitching. "Maybe we stop and get one take-out and have a nice picnic on the beach, just us."
She notices her sister trying to hide her shivering hand in her pocket. "We can make a bonfire of our own and see if the Menehune's come try to mess with us, ya?" Keala speeds up a little without them noticing. She won't allow her sister to see her cry too. "Oh, and in the morning, we can

263

watch the kids go surf. You haven't seen them surf on their new boards yet. Yep, I been pimping out our kids so we could get them some new surfboards. You'd be so proud, they totally rip, just like their papa's."

Keala doesn't need to glance over to see her sister's head cocked to the side, locked up, teeth grinding, eyes rolled in the back of her head already. She feels her sister's pain like lightning grinding up and down her own spine. "Eh, kids. Why don't you sing auntie happy birthday?"

"March 1936

Asogwe

I have to assume today is March 15, 1936, and my seed device will detonate remotely at midnight if I do not enter my encoded data in time. The night I have spent in isolation after the Si Pwen has proven to me that these savages want me to suffer an excruciating death. I achieved an extremely receptive state of consciousness before the hounsi came for me. Their Ghede, or spirits of the dead seemed to be communicating to them that it was I who released the plague into the water supply. This was confirmed as soon as Manbo Lysius began the ceremony.

The purpose of the Si Pwen was to establish contact with the nations of Lwa, the angel aspects that control god's will and natural forces. It did not take long for me to realize I was not meant to survive much longer. It is my belief that if they are able to kill me in the final night of the Bat Guerre, then Manbo Lysius can take the Patronage of my ancestors. As of

264

now, I alone maintain the focus of my ancestor's incredible energy. And also, the Manbo cannot evoke this energy onto her people without me.

During these past few nights, my body has been burning with an unbearable pain and fever. I believe one particular Lwa, called Petwo, is seeking vengeance for the weaponized plagues I recently used to kill so many Haitians. After the isolation with this fiery Petwo, I am expected to surrender myself to their mercy. Manbo Lysius demonstrated her command of this incredible phenomenon. The Manbo revealed that she is able to evoke a surging energy of her own. She then manipulated it and inflicted it upon my physical being. She called this affliction a Wanga. It seemed that this vehement Petwo possesses aspects of vengeance and rage. This Lwa projected such vicious torment that the hounsi immediately stopped brutalizing my body and fled to the perimeter of the djevo. The powerful Wanga enabled Petwo to strike down as lightening. It has yet to cease.

By the enhanced clarity I was able to maintain throughout the Si Pwen, I proved able to recognize, transpose, and nullify the harmful affect of this Wanga. I kept my focus away from the demonic acts of the hounsi. Their repugnant and vile perversions on my body were clearly motivated by Petwo. Forgetting it's sinister laughter is something that will never be possible. Yet, by detaching my mind early, the Patronage was established and I did not succumb to the spectacle of the ritual or agony of the abusive Lwa. I could see that my body was under the most extreme and malicious tortures, by the hounsi at first, and then by the nations of spirits under this Manbo's spell. More importantly, the bubbling flesh and severe muscle spasms had them convinced that I was indeed suffering under the Wanga.

On this final night of the Bat Guerre, I intend to make it a true battle of the spirits. The Manbo considers me a Bokor. As a scientist, I can identify her strategy to defeat a sorcerer with sorcery. The Manbo is clearly dominant in that aspect of the battle. Her pregnancy does not seem to hinder her abilities to manipulate the incredible marvels of her spells. I have doubts the fetus is even human.

The weakness I will exploit is their pathetic aptitude for combat. Their proficiency in battle is at best primitive and savage. I understand Vodou as the power of will to overcome oppression, but they completely lack any ability to free themselves from their white oppressors. I grant them the motivation and rage of their demonic Petwo. The spirit of warriors they call Ogoun, offers them little more than pride and masculinity. I find it satirical that this word sounds so much like Shogun.

Tonight, I will evoke the patronage of my lineage, the Tokugawa. I am a descendent of the family of Shogun who ruled Japan hereditarily as agents of the reigning Emperor. The modern Emperor system has failed. I am Ronin because the Ultra-Militarist Factions currently do not shine under the light of His Majesty in the High Heavenly Plain of Takamagahara. They do not shine as I do. I now see the Gumbatsu as conspirators who shall unwisely, uncontrollably, and inevitably destroy the Japanese race. Yet, I also see that this wicked deception will lead to the annihilation of thousands- and it is in that fate of destruction that I shall rely upon tonight.

I understand this phenomena to be Fate's Power, or rather the supernatural energy created in the spirit world from the inevitably dead. I am not able to

266

comprehend or foresee this incredible destruction, only that I see two separate catastrophic events occurring in Japan in the near future. It is in this wicked betrayal of my people that will ultimately enable my victory. It is also this free energy through me that inebriates the Manbo and her people, feeding off the misery of others.

I stated before that it was Amaterasu herself shining her light down upon me from the high heaven. I no longer believe that to be true. Amaterasu feared her brother Susanoo returned from the underworld jaded and changed. She was fearful because of his use of power, lighting and storms to manipulate the earth. From what I have experienced, this earthly realm, the underworld, the high heavens- are merely separate planes of existence sharing the same atoms across simultaneous realities. These planes can be broken, elements shared, energies transferred and physical laws altered. Organized religions of the mortal realm are merely diluted interpretations from simple minds. It is the equity of soul energy that transfers across these realms.

As the hounsi have begun to prepare for the Asogwe, I can already visualize them like sonar, with each strike of the drum. They are gathering their torches, machetes, and have lit a fire under a large vat of oil. They will expect to find me broken mentally and physically from the torments of Petwo. With my patronage diminished, my body will be vulnerable. They intend to submerge me in this boiling vat and I will suffer a slow and excruciation death. As my body melts away, Manbo Lysius will be able to absorb the free energy they evoke from this ceremony. But I will not allow this to happen.

267

Before the Kanzo Semp on the first night, I felt it justifiable for the Haitians to claim justice for the massacre I was responsible for. After witnessing the wicked and demonic belief system of these savages, I no longer believe they deserve that justice. This wretched nation is the underworld. Their cursed rituals have left me jaded and changed. I see this as fate. I shall use the power they have evoked and manipulate it against them. They only seem able to use this power for violence and sexual deviancy. I will not surrender the Patronage of my divine ancestry to these despicable people.

I have just consumed my second vile of the heroin-rum elixir. I added a robust amount of amphetamines that would have an entire squadron of bold kamikaze pilots diving gloriously into a fiery assault. I have already extracted my consciousness from my body. The Patronage of the honorable Tokugawa is surging into the void I have created. My body continues to write as my puppet. I will need to encode an encrypted message and transmit it to my commanding officer before the ceremony begins. The supernatural occurrences I shall divulge to them is exactly what the Nazi Ahnenerbe have been lusting after with their eugenics. Soon, I will have to prepare for war under the guidance of my magnificent lineage of warriors. By the light of Susanoo and the underworld, I shall destroy Manbo Lysius, her hounsi, and this entire island.

To confirm my hypothesis, I have just driven broken glass through my cheeks with no pain, blood or damage. I trust my body will prove to be tolerant of the chemical and biological weapons I secretly possess. I will ingest the agents just before they come to take me. I predict they will sodomize me before throwing me into the boiling oil. I can think of no better punishment for those who will indulge in this vile act.

268

I will induce vomiting. I will enjoy them tearing and biting into my poisoned flesh. And if every one of them cannot devour my poison, I will ultimately burst open after they submerge me in the oil. The contents of my carcass will explode with a cloud of toxic retribution. For the abominable sacrilege they commit on humanity, I must strike them down with perverse vengeance. Haiti will become extinct from the physical earth and the underworld. It is now time for my third vile of the elixir as they have begun chanting.

My body is heaving with the power and rage of Petwo. Yet, I possess the fortitude to compose this manifesto and encode my data transmission simultaneously. I have just drenched myself with rum and mud that resulted in a cloud of steam from my burning flesh. The black tar they paint me with is melting off. I have seen what happens to the human body after ingesting these agents. I watched prisoners rupture and dissolve from certain agents during my tenure in Manchukuo. Yet, I remain invulnerable in my enhanced state. I have changed my mind about allowing the sodomy. As much as I would enjoy seeing them afflicted during their abominable acts, my pride will not allow my body's surrender to the savages.

I can hear hysterical laughter and screaming from hundreds of people. Perhaps the entire village has come to participate in my crucifixion. I will take great pleasure in destroying the first group of hounsi with my bare hands. After I collect a pair of machetes, I will demonstrate to these savages what steel can do to the human body. I will not be satisfied until I have slaughtered every last one of them. I shall leave a few alive to sodomize with my blade covered in sulfur mustard and arsenic trichloride.

In the event that I am overpowered by their numbers, or by some Wanga of Manbo Lysius, then I will preserve my honor by slicing into my own stomach. If I am not able to secure an honorable death, then I shall be murdered with the assurance that my stomach will rupture in the boiling oil and the volatile agents will annihilate the entire island.

I believe this to be fate. For the treachery, the deception, the power, knowledge, truth and tortures that I have endured, I still do not know if fate is an ally or an enemy. As a scientist and a warrior, I shall exterminate the wretched from the earth. By serving my ancestors, I am no longer Ronin.

Hideoki Ijyui."


"Oh, hi baby boy. Good morning. What are you doing there?" Alana notices she is restrained on a cot. "Where are we exactly?"

"Good morning mommy. I'm filing your fingernails." Lono gives a quick hug and then resumes where he left off.

"Well, that's sweet. Where are we? Is this the cave?" She waits for her eyes to adjust. "Can you take off the straps please?"

"For sure." Lono rips the velcro apart and adjusts the lamp. "Storm shelter. Last month this was a cave, but we had to turn it into a storm shelter. I was sharpening my spears and remembered I was supposed to cut your nails before the full moon."

Alana rests her head back on the pillow for a moment, then pops back up, "Full moon? What's up with the full moon? What do you mean you had to turn this into a storm shelter? Where's my sister?"

"Don't worry mom. The full moon's not until tomorrow, that's when the storm's gonna hit. Auntie went to uncle Kaleo's house." Lono tries to hold her still.

"Wait, what? There's a storm?" Alana sits up and sets Lono on her lap.

He tries to finish her last finger as it moves. "Hurricane Iniki. It's gonna be here tomorrow. Huakani o ka Hunaka'i."

She keeps squirming around, "What does that mean? Journey of the Hunaka'i? Why did they go to Kaleo's house? Her and Akila, ya?"

He looks up calmly and holds her hand still, "They went to see if Kaleo came back home. We think he might show up there tonight. It's definitely a trap, but me and Akila are calling this battle Huakani o ka Hunaka'i. You look worried. Remember the wind a couple of months ago? He told us about this."

"No. Hold on mister. You're still six years-old, ya? And your cousin's still what, nine? And your auntie's still a total idiot? Why do you think we're going to battle in a storm? We've got a storm shelter? There's no journey... What am I missing here?" Alana squeezes him, knowing the plan has already been cooked up without her.

"Well..." Lono holds onto her for a spell, knowing that's all she really wants. "Well, they're coming for us. They know where to find us, there's nowhere to hide. There's a chance we can attack them tomorrow when the wind is at it's most powerful, you know, the storm, during the full moon. This is how we survive. This is the trial me and Akila have been training for."

"This cannot be the way. You're little kids. There's no trial, no journey. Just madness. Is that the soup over there?" Alana sniffles.

"The soup is good. Waiting on the rice to finish. The sharks brought us another aku yesterday. They knew you were going to wake up and brought the fish. You're worried about what happened to your mom, aren't you." Lono knows she's not ready to let go of him.

271

"You know..." Alana sits up and stretches her back, noticing she recently got a haircut by the four-feet-long braid hanging on the corner of the bed. "For a long time, I thought they went crazy and couldn't understand why they would leave us. Now the wind comes and tells us they did it to protect us. I was angry for so long and now I don't know how to feel about it because I don't understand it anymore. Being angry was easy. It's hard being confused all the time and even worse, relying on my lolo sister to interpret all this for me."

"I know what you mean. Akila is older than me and already knows how to do everything. It drives me nuts because he likes to watch me struggle. It makes him happy. Your sister is older than you too, ya?" Lono hears the rice cooker switch click and points to it.

"She's not even one-minute older. In fact, they said I cried first, then she did after so I took the first breath in this world. Soup time? What can you tell me about this journey?" Alana finds the bowls and spoons.

"Well, if there's a bridge to the spirit world, and we can go and come back, and we have the wind to guide us... then taking this journey seems better than being hunted by what we saw in Alaska. Right?" Lono pulls out the chairs at the table.

"Shoots..." Alana ponders on that for a moment. "You definitely have a point there."

Lono makes her a hot tea, "While we're on this bridge, wouldn't it be possible to find my dad?"

She almost drops her spoon, "Wow. If we knew how, I guess it would be our chance. Is this what my crazy sister is up to?"

"You bet your okole!" Keala slams the doors shut behind her. "Is the soup ready? Hurry up and eat. Grab the bags, check the guns, let's get this shit going already."

"Guns?" Alana drops her spoon, "What guns?"

"Your boyfriend, Ferdinand's boss has a gun range on the west side. I told him you were gonna call him up after you woke up from your coma. He sold me two guns for super cheap." Keala smiles as Lono grabs two more bowls and spoons for them.

"You gotta be shittin' me. You went back to the Salt Ponds, pimping our kids again after that?" Alana tries to kick the chair away from her sister.

"Nah, nah, nah. Well, ya." Keala gives a wink to the kids, "Actually, I took the kids to a surf contest. They won the Menehune division. You never saw the trophy?" Both kids point to the shelf with two trophies displayed. Keala continues after getting a round of high-fives, "Anyways, turns out old Ferdy-bird has three keiki's of his own, from three different chicks. Lucky thing you was in one coma because he seemed really determined to have another. He mentioned the Snow White thing again, but I told him you were kapu (forbidden) until you woke up."

"Ugh." Alana is having a hard time enjoying her favorite soup. "The guns. You sure this is a good idea? I never shot a gun before. You?"

"Oh ya." Keala hovers just above her bowl, "Bought the guns, the ammo, took a class, turns out me and the keiki's are really good at shooting shit. Can't wait. We're gonna fock shit up."

"Wait. Hold on." Alana pushes her bowl forward, "You let the kids shoot the guns? You serious?"

"Hell ya." Keala gets up for a refill, "They got a kid's class at the gun range. You never saw the graduation picture?" Both kids point to the picture next to the trophy shelf. Keala sits down after getting a round of high-fives from the kids, "They're gonna teach you how to shoot the gun to make sure you won't shoot one of us by accident. Ok? So hurry up and finish your soup. We leave at midnight. Your nails look pretty. You like your haircut?"

"What the fock?" Alana pushes her tea forward. "You gotta be shittin' me all over the place. Where are we going at midnight? Kaleo's? We're

273

gonna go shoot up Kaleo's house in the middle of a storm? What's wrong with you? Every time I wake up, you manage to become more psychotic than before!"

"Look, I didn't want to cut it too short because it's probably gonna be really windy and you might want to put it in a pony tail so it doesn't blow all over and cause you to shoot me in the ass by mistake." Keala is almost finished with her second bowl. "Lono wouldn't let me shave your head. I think it looks pretty good."

"If I shoot you in the ass, it won't be a mistake." Alana pulls her soup and tea closer. She observes the children bundle up several spears and carry them outside.

"I'm sorry. Ok? This is the best I can do under the extraordinary circumstances we currently find ourselves in." Keala sits up, reaches for her sister's hand and looks into her eyes, "We don't have a choice. The snakes are back. The chickens are gone. The mongoose died this morning from a snake bite, several snake bites. We poured salt everywhere, they don't seem to like that shit. There's a black rental car in front of Kaleo's house.

We're going to the house across the street, everybody evacuated for the storm already. We wait and watch during the storm to see who or what is in there. If they have Kaleo, then we bust in, guns blazing, and ambush them. We cannot wait here for them to attack us. I cannot leave you here alone. This cave could be a snake pit by then. It's a shit-focking-sandwich either way.

But if you're like me, and you are my twin sister, then you'd rather take a chance with guns-a-blazing than wait for a snake to slither up and bite you hiding in the dark. We have the wind, the full moon, a trail blazed for us through the spirit world, and two Menehune champion surfers who are excellent with clubs. I got the truck loaded up and salted with a full focking tank. Oh, and got one mean flare gun too. This is the extraordinary circumstances we now find ourselves in, so please tell me I'm not totally crazy before I lose my shit and start crying."

Alana squeezes her sister's hand, "Ok. I never said you were totally crazy. But you are way more psychotic than me." Alana leans forward and presses her forehead against her sister's. "Then again, maybe not. I need a beer. And I need you to show me how to use that gun. How did you know salt would work?"

Keala wraps her arms around her sister's neck, "Akila's idea. Salt works with slugs. And it works against witchcraft. Either way, seemed legit. Look, I think your acid naps are all pau (finished) already. We had this vision of that black hand being pulled away. The windows shifted. It had a hold on you for a long time and I think it was causing your spells. But without that connection, I think that's why they are coming for us now."

Alana looks up at her, "Then why don't we just run? Take the keiki's and run?"

"Run where? How?" Keala checks her watch, "We only have power on the 'Aina (Royal Kingdom of Hawai'i), we cannot leave the Islands or we are powerless. If we are to survive this night, we attack, and then we run. But let me tell you this: I'm gonna blow a big focking hole in any sons-a-bitches that tries to take my keiki. I've lost too many kanaka's already and I'm tired of hiding, waiting for them to attack us. I don't care if this is a trap. This is the showdown. I like shooting that gun and I'd like to point it right at the focking fockah that stole my Ikaika. Are you with me?"

Alana wraps her arms around her sister, "Ok. I'm with you sister. I want to shoot one big focking puka (hole) in these sons-a-bitches too. I need a beer."

Keala drives the truck slowly between two houses, one street over from Kaleo's street. She quietly parks the truck in the backyard of the house across the street from Kaleo's and sends Akila inside to scout it out. He quickly returns and grabs a giant sack of rock salt while Lono helps the sister's shuffle the bags into the back lanai (porch) door. Keala carefully opens the window next to the front door and notices the wind just beginning to gust. "I guess the calm before the storm is over." Akila brings her a drill from the garage and she starts drilling peep holes in the plywood covering the window glass. She moves to another window and drills more peep holes, "Alana, I need you to post up here and keep watch. That frickin' black car hasn't moved. Kila, get in the attic and see if you can get a better view from up there. Ya?"

"Roger that." Akila grabs Lono and they scurry off quietly.

Alana carefully spreads the rock salt over the window sills and doorways. "I didn't realize how much I would enjoy shooting this gun."

Keala concurs, "Well, that's because we got some sinister sons-a-bitches to shoot at. Please get every room, every door, every window, every vent. One snake and this is all over. Such a pretty house, but could you imagine living across the street from lolo Kaleo? Uh... Alana? Did you just close the hatch to the attic?"

"Maybe." Alana situates herself on a stool in front of her boarded-up window and peers out across the street.

"Why?" Keala takes her eyes away from her peep holes and opens the case to her new flare gun.

"Maybe the keiki's can just hide out in the attic and let us do the ambush by ourselves." Alana rummages through the bag of snacks without taking her eyes away from the window.

"Seriously. You have to believe me when I tell you this. The keiki's can handle. You haven't talked to the wind yet. Eh, look at my holster for the flare gun." Keala gets up and walks towards Alana to rummage for snacks.

Alana keeps the nori maki arare (rice crackers with seaweed) and passes the rest, "They're kids. Ok? It's too dangerous. It's a trap. I'm about to go murder some kidnappers and I don't want them to witness some violent shit like that. No, I have not talked to the wind yet."

"Oh." Keala gets comfortable back at her window. "You're the one I'm worried about. We've actually been preparing for this for months. Those kids have been preparing for this since they were born."

"They're children." Alana continues to scan the darkness. She flicks a cracker at her sister.

"They're not just children. They are souls of warriors, connected to generations of warrior spirits. I'm worried you're gonna see what they can do and your ass is gonna freak-the-fock out." Keala opens a thermos with hot soup.

"Eh. Get snacks?" Lono asks from above.

Alana turns and looks up to find Lono's head sticking out of a ceiling vent in the middle of the room. "Eh grommet, don't mess up these people's air conditioning."

"Uh, ok. But this is a category-four hurricane and their entire roof is probably going to blow off by morning." Lono smiles down and gives a wink to his mother.

Keala slings a bag of wasabi peas without taking her eyes from the peep holes. Lono catches it and fixes the vent grill back in place before disappearing in the attic. Keala looks around the room, "Nice house but, I imagine they had to install central cooling so they could keep the windows closed. Think of what the trade winds would blow in if you lived next to Kaleo. Eh, sis, did I tell you that I believe Tiki is on some kind of ship? Out at sea?"

"No." Alana turns and glares at her sister, "No, you didn't tell me Jack Shit."

"Ya." Keala keeps her eyes fixed out the window, "Big 'ole focking vessel of some kind. Research vessel, out at sea all the time. I believe Ikaika is sailing a fishing vessel and meets up with this ship sometimes. I told you I found a link to Ikaika, ya? It would seem Ikaika is collecting fish."

Alana scoffs, "Well, if he's on a fishing vessel, that's what they focking do."

"Ya." Keala pours more soup in the thermos cap, "Ya, but no. They don't fish for the fish. They collect the fish. I believe they are cloning the fish. Remember from the Alaska vision how the fish really bothered them and shit? That's probably because the fish are not natural and the kanaka's were having bad reactions to them."

"Hmmm..." Alana ponders, "So Tiki is on a vessel out at sea, and they keep his spirit out of his body so they can experiment on him. Ikaika is forced to sail a fishing vessel and collects cloned fish. Lika is forced to cultivate drugs. Kaleo is... what, their focking junkie? What the fock are they doing with Kaleo in there anyways? And all this time, they force them to fight like gladiators? And who are they actually fighting all this time? These creatures? What does the wind say about this?"

"Not much, our wind pretty much stays around here with us, but outside." Keala screws the cap back on the thermos and rolls it to her sister. "Ya, that about sums it up though. And you add that to the bloody French crucifixion that the creature with the black hand went through... and the shit still just doesn't make any sense. But we're going to find out something when we bust through that door across the street. Who ever is driving that black car there, I'm gonna stick this gun down his focking throat until he makes all this shit make some damn sense."

"What do the keiki's think about all this?" Alana sets the thermos down next to her as she continues to monitor the darkness.

"Well, they don't really sit around and have discussions like this with me. They made a chart for me once, but if they're not surfing, they're wrestling in the front yard, or they're fishing, or they're carving wood, working the garden, or practicing hula, mostly fighting though. We spent so much time caring for you, so much of what they understand, what they know, is unspoken. I've been waiting for your ass to wake up so we could talk story. I need some fresh ears, I'm tired of listening to myself."

"So, what else am I missing here?" Alana watches her sister gaze out the peep holes. "This seemed like a short spell I was under, ya?"

278

"Ya. It was." Keala scans the room when she hears the vent grill scrape the ceiling.

"Eh, can get some apple juice?" Lono's head dips from the square hole.

Keala tosses one up, right into his hand, followed by another. "Eh, how's the view up there?"

"Really good. The wind is really howling out there. But it's chill it the attic. No lights on at Kaleo's, still seems empty. Can see down the street. No more nothing from mauka (mountain) side." Lono vanishes and slides the grill back into place.

Keala continues, "Ya, so it seems like your open windows only had a small spell of alignment. And it seemed to have passed."

"Six years is not necessarily one manini (small) window." Alana watches her sister gaze outside, "Six years of violent seizures, raising my son in a daydream. Mao 'ole ke kai o Mokupaoa (Endlessly rough is the island of Mokupaoa- *the island of misfortune*.)

Keala gives her a quick glance, "Ya, and look how buff you stay. Oh, and I stay so sexy too, wrestling with your hihiu (wild) ass for so long. That's why we're gonna bust up whoever stay in Kaleo's house. They did this to us." Keala turns back to the peep holes. "Look, I know you're angry. We need angry right now. But six years is nothing in the spirit world. Just a blink of an eye. The way you were getting ravaged in your little acid naps, makes me afraid of what they are going to do us if they capture us. You understand? Tu nous appartiens, ya? That's French for *we own you*."

"Wait..." Alana gives a confused look to her sister, "So this creature is French?"

"No, I don't necessarily think so." Keala continues staring outside, "The ones who crucified this creature spoke French. Apparently people seem to speak French all over the world, but it helps us narrow it down a bit. The kids made a chart. What I'm telling you is..." Keala glances around the room, slides over next to her sister and then whispers, "What I'm telling

279

you is, we're going to kill every last moddah-focking one of them. Ok? And if we cannot..." She looks up to the vent and then positions her sister's face right in front of hers, "And if we cannot, we're gonna have to shoot each other."

Alana stares into her sister's eyes, realizing how serious she is at this moment, "Uh, excuse me?"

"Did you hear what I just said? Nod yes so I don't have to say it again. Ok. I'm not going to let them take us for slaves. Do you now understand how angry we need to be? You have to totally trust me when I tell you this, we don't have a choice. Not with this." Keala has not cried since Hurricane Iwa, until now.

"Ok. I understand." Alana wipes her cheeks. "You already knew it was going to go down like this, didn't you? I guess I did too. We don't do cages. Alright, so be it. You don't have to convince me how pissed off I am. We're gonna fock some shit up. Blaze o' glory." Alana presses her face against her sister's for a moment, then pushes her back to her own window, "Now that we got that straight, let's go over this stinky turd of a plan one more time. I don't think you've fully caught me up here. There's some shit you ain't told me yet."

"Alright." Keala gets situated back at her peep hole, "You and Lono take the front door. Me and Kila take the back and you wait for us to bust in first. You and Lono bust in after and get 'em in the back because we're going to draw their fire. At which point, I'm going to launch the flare and light the place up. You pop off a few rounds and then run straight to the truck and pull it up in the front yard. Get your full magazine in your gun and be ready to cover us for the getaway.

Now, you can either shoot out their tires or stab them with your knife, but make sure no one can follow us. If we can save Kaleo, great. If no can, no can. Everyone gets a bullet first, then we get answers after we get them under control. But we have to assume Kaleo's going to be there, otherwise I don't know why they would be hanging out in his stinky-ass house. Ok? Makani ku Honua (wind arriving suddenly, gust). Cheez, the wind is really lashing out there. And the sun's coming up already."

They watch until the grey skies turn black and spill over the dawning mountains. Iniki finally whips its thunderous surge across the Islands, all at once. Keala can only sense the full rampage pummeling the land as it remains eerily mild inside their hideaway. The peep holes begin whistling in towards their faces and dries their eyes. The girls back away from the boarded up windows and suddenly hear a whisper come through clearly, "They are coming. I will protect you. It's time to take the koa back. Their trials begin now."

"Mom." The ceiling vent drops to the floor and both kids jump to the ground, "Mom, I can see headlights coming down from the highway."

Alana reaches for Lono, "Save the koa? Wait... You mean Kaleo?"

Lono wraps his arms around his mother's neck, "We have to save uncle Kaleo. That's the trial."

"Wait a minute." Alana glares at her sister, "I thought you said if can, can, if no can, no can? Are we doing all this just to save Kaleo or what? That was the plan the whole time, eh?"

"Well, it's time to get him back. The only one who can help us find the kanaka's happens to be Kaleo. Ok?" Keala doesn't like the smirk she's receiving. "Don't look at me like that because you know it's true."

Alana sits on her stool so she can hug Lono and look out the window. "Well, he's riding in the back. And why do you want me to drive? I never drove your truck before. I never drove around here before."

Keala scoffs, "Nah, nah, nah. I don't want you to drive. Just drive the truck across the street for us. Any more than that's just asking for trouble today."

"Keala?" Alana turns to her, "What does that mean, their trials begin now?"

"Oh." Keala hands the snack bag to Akila and the kids scurry out the lanai (patio) door. "Their mana is going to be tested and when they pass, they will be granted more power from the lineage of warriors."

"Eh?" Alana watches the kids run in, grab the bag of drinks and run out the back door.

Keala walks to her sister and grabs hold of her arms, "Sis, they have to prove themselves by saving Kaleo."

"Prove themselves to who?" Alana feels a chill enter the room.

"I imagine the ghosts of all the Hawaiian warriors before them. They don't share their mana with just anyone. Not everyone deserves it. Not everyone can handle it. I know you know what I'm talking about. The night Tiki was attacked. You were already hapai (pregnant), ya? How did you end up at Ka'ena Point? What, two weeks later? You were blessed. It's in our bloodline. We've been tested our whole life. Our keiki's have to earn this blessing. You're with us on this, ya? You got a job to do."

"Ya, of course. Yes. Blessed, cursed, I suppose all this was to prepare them. I was hoping me and you could go kill them and then we take the kids and run. Go hide somewhere. But..." Alana allows her eyes to stare off without focusing on anything but thoughts.

"But there is nowhere to hide. Not from the spirit world. Not from what is out there stalking us. This is an incredible power. Think about it... the reason for this sacred mana, the reason for this trial... This is all to create balance for something that measures up as incredibly evil. You experienced that evil, first hand, right into your soul's window. Now, let's take this journey as a blessing. Our mother's bridge is a gift." Keala waits for her sister's acceptance. "Eh? You ok with this?"

Alana stands frozen as she was, staring off into nothing. Keala gets in front of her vision and notices the iris of her eyes fluttering as if the wind is stirring inside her head. "Keala..." Alana whispers. "There's something wicked coming right towards us..."

"Holy shit mom!" Akila busts in from the lanai door as Lono jumps for the ceiling hatch. "There's a van coming down the street. I want to see it from up there." Akila follows Lono to the ceiling look-out.

The sisters slide to their windows and watch a black van drive into Kaleo's front yard and reverse up to the door. One man exits the driver's side and fights against the wind towards the back of the van. One man exits the passenger side and kicks the door shut. Keala chuckles anxiously, "Oh, look at this fockah, wearing a suit in a hurricane. His damn tie is whipping his face. You got to be kidding me... he's gonna try to light up a smoke?"

"I cannot see what they're unloading from the van..." Alana peers through the rain, blasting sideways in dense waves. "But I don't like it. What else are you supposed to tell me about this situation? Eh? It feels dark. There's dread, there's death"

"It feels like it shouldn't exist. We have one chance to rid the world of this creature. All we have to do is not miss." Keala scours for movement across the street. "Cannot believe that kook was able to light that cigarette. You know what, I can sense Kaleo. All his sadness, regret, guilt... I guess I expected to feel more fear from him, especially with the presence of such a dark entity. But I can read Kaleo, plain as day, and it's not fear I'm getting from him. It's avulsion."

Alana chimes in, "Yellow eyes! That's what the flare gun is for! Ya?"

"Ya. That's what the flare gun is for. And then I'm gonna put the lead in that fockah's head." Keala stares out the peep hole with her hands on her guns. "What if he's here to make a deal? What if that's why Kaleo's relatively calm... like, he knows it's a trap, or he doesn't want us to make a bargain with this cartel?"

"What if he offers to take us to our men?" Alana glares over to her sister.

"In exchange for what? Not even. I'm gonna take the focking shot. I need this thing to be dead." Keala caresses her Glock 19 and flare gun simultaneously. "I'm not the one you want to kill. I dare him to say that shit to me."

"Wait... Where's this guy going?" Alana becomes alarmed as the van rolls slowly onto the road against the brutal wind. "What are the chances they came in from the boat harbor? What if he's going to get another van load of fockahs and bring them back here?"

"Guarantee they came in from the boat harbor. I bet there's a whole boat load of suit-wearing fockahs. But I only sense one Kaleo and the dark entity. We should go now. I'll leave the engine running. Just jump in, put it in gear and floor it. Ok? Just bust in with Lono, blast a few rounds, and then go get the get-away truck. Ok?" Keala walks under the ceiling vent and gives a whistle, "Kila. We go."

Both kids drop from the hatch with their heavy, carved wooden clubs in hand. "We ready? Let's get it on." Akila walks over and hugs his mother.

Lono runs over and wraps his arms around his mother's neck. "I'm so grateful for everything you did for us. You don't have to go inside the house if you don't want to. You can just run and get the truck."

"No honey. I have to make sure you're safe. And if they have guns, I have to take them out." Alana kisses his face. "If there's a chance I can kill the one with yellow eyes, I gotta take it. I wish we had more time, just talk story, you and me. But don't worry about me, this is about you, proving yourself."

"It's ok mom. Just follow the wind. The wind will guide you." Lono squeezes so tightly.

"What are you doing? We have to go now. Iniki's really bearing down." Keala pushes everyone out the lanai door.

Alana steps out into the storm, completely enclosed in a bubble of calm air. Shrouded from the torrential wind and rain, Lono takes her hand and leads her around their truck. They walk slowly around the flexing fence and can hear the wind beginning to roar through their hideout. Alana looks

284

over the bushes whipping in the wind. Several roof tiles vanish before the entire structure lifts from the walls and sails away overhead. The roof twists around and crashes into the side of the neighbor's house. Lono smirks to his mom, "I told you that roof was a goner."

They crouch down at the edge of the flailing shrubs. Keala motions for Alana to wait  for them to run across the street. She points to Alana's fire arm and taps the safety to remind her to be prepared. Alana gapes at them running off with the wind pushing them along with incredible speed. Lono lets go of her hand and grasps both of his sharpened pahoa (clubs). He looks into her eyes for a moment while Keala and Akila run to the fence in the back yard.

Lono watches and waits for their signal. He helps Alana to her feet then taps his clubs together several times. Alana pops open the snap on her holster and readies her grip on the pistol. She pulls it free and looks down to ready it for the first shot. She looks back up to see Lono taking two big steps and then effortlessly hopping through an agile front flip. He takes a couple more steps and then hops into a double front flip, holding his clubs tightly across his chest.

He stalls and motions for her to catch up, "Are you ready mom? Ka leo o haukani (the voice in the wind), listen for the wind, it will guide you." Lono turns and grins to her. "Don't be afraid of what you see in there."

"You know what I see?  Ho'akua noho'i kana hana (his deeds are marvelous)." Alana runs after him, gliding with the force of the wind. Her bubble feels weightless in the storm's fury, like riding a kayak through the rapids. "There goes Akila, get ready to charge 'em son." Alana is ready to go around the bushes and rush the door, realizing the wind is already in control.

"Now." Alana hears a calm voice ring through despite the ferocity of the storm surge. She stands and looks over the flailing branches to see the flash of Keala's first shot. Lono takes off in a burst of three steps and then curls up tightly and somersaults with enough momentum to catapult over the wooden porch. Alana rides in her protective bubble right behind Lono as he extends his legs and shatters the front door into splinters. He extends his clubs, causing the entire door frame to burst free into the house as the wind and rain pour through like a waterfall.

Alana stops just into the gaping doorway and gasps at the sight of her child sliding past two men wearing black suits. Lono pulls his extended clubs forward as they slice cleanly through their abdomens. Everything packed into their torsos, from their ribs to their hips, empties and sprays out simultaneously against the wall.

Lono quickly turns back towards Alana and hurls his club. The wind blasts it from behind, creating a sharp whistle. It spins and sails just past Alana's right shoulder. Alana snaps her head around as it strikes into the wall next to her. She finds another black-suited man standing at the wall. His extended arms, still clutching a pistol aimed at the side of her head, sever from his elbows and bounce across the floor towards the kitchen.

Alana quickly extends her arms and fires a round directly between his eyes at close range. As his head is flung out and away, she finds her aim already at a second man standing along the wall. His firearm is already in position for the shot, but his face gets splattered with brain matter and blood from the first man. Alana recovers from the recoil and squeezes the trigger in alignment to send another round into the center of his face. From the corner of her eye, Alana watches Keala's red flare chitter across the ceiling, igniting an instant blaze. The red cloud bursting out the back of the man's skull glows in the fiery glare before it jets off and vaporizes across the room.

Alana turns from the wall towards the kitchen. She finds Lono crouched, spinning across the floor on his knee. With both hands, he swings his club around his body and splits a man's legs apart at the knees. As Lono spins across towards another man with the same attack, Akila stomps across the kitchen counter with a club extended in each hand.

Akila springs from the counter and decapitates both men in a single pass. Simultaneously, Lono slices through the second man's knees. Lono skids to a stop and crouches facing his mother. He motions her out the door as he turns and faces into the adjacent bedroom. He turns back towards her and again points for Alana to run for the truck. Alana feels the wind nudging her bubble backwards out the front door. She watches Keala's muzzle flare flashing in the darkness like a strobe light, revealing several more men in black suits continuing the firefight in the dining room.

Alana turns and sees both Lono and Akila squaring off cautiously in front of the bedroom doorway. She uses the leverage from her shoulder and lifts the club stuck in the wall. Once she pries it free, Lono extends his arm towards her without looking away from the bedroom. Alana flings it softly with an underhand pitch and the wind sails it directly into his grip. Alana tries to turn and run, but she hears several wild growls from inside the room and stop her in her tracks. She needs to see what sort of creatures could howl with such hostility, but the wind forces her out the front door.

Alana holsters her pistol as the wind carries her bubble across the yard and into the street. She turns to spot anyone chasing behind but can only see the muzzle flashes through the black rain. Alana arrives at the truck and lets the wind fling the door open. She jumps to the seat as the door slams behind her and reaches for the wiper switch. Revving the engine several times, she notices no rain or wind is hitting the truck. Dropping it into drive, Alana speeds just past a section of wooden fence skipping by like a centipede. She pulls through the driveway and skids to a stop in the middle of the front yard.

Alana follows the sequence as planned: Gearshift in Park. Switch out new clip. Grab the knife. She lets the door swing open as she jumps from the seat. Extending the gun and then supporting it with the arm gripping the knife, Alana scurries towards the car in front of the garage. As she crouches down to hammer the blade into the tire, the door opens and slams against her hip. Alana bounces to the grass and loses grip on the gun. She watches it tumble towards the street but quickly catches her balance and crouches to her feet.

Another man steps out the car and jerks the slide back on his gun. Alana instinctively pinches the blade and slings it. The wind lets out a fierce whistle and drives the tip of the blade into the knuckles of the fist holding the gun. Alana spins and lunges for her gun in the grass. By the time she grabs hold of it, the man has already pried the knife free and is trying to run against the wind towards her. Alana ducks and rolls to his side and manages to squeeze one shot into his ribs and one into the side of his head.

Suddenly, a great force rams into her from the side. A second man ran from the car and tackled her to the ground. Alana strains to wrestle her pistol from his grip, when a gust of rain strikes from the ground-up and lifts him to his feet. She squirms away on her back and quickly gets to her feet. She raises her pistol and rushes towards him as he flails, suspended from the ground. Alana is stunned as a shot explodes through the plywood from a window next to her head. The 9mm round screams past her and detonates a red cloud of vaporized flesh out from the man's face. His body spins off and tumbles across the mud. The shattered plywood whisks away. Alana gapes through the shattered glass and sees Akila standing in the middle of the living room, "Stop shooting, mom!"

Alana runs to the doorway and enters a stand-off. Lono and Akila stand poised in the middle of the living room, ready to pounce the corner. Keala stands in the kitchen aiming her gun across to the living room. Alana turns to see Kaleo in the corner with four nooses tied to his neck. Tied to the other ends of ropes, Alana stands in shock to see four children the same age as Lono. Kaleo struggles to clench the ropes around his arm to relieve tension around his throat. He manages to growl, "Just shoot the little bastards!"

Alana steps to the side and aims a shot to the head of the nearest feral boy. She squeezes the shot off as the snarling boy turns to her and jumps. The bullet rips into the side of his neck and tears through the rope restraining him. He spins wildly to the floor and immediately scrambles towards the bedroom. "He's going for the machetes!" Kaleo barks.

Lono intercepts the raving boy and pummels his chest with an upwards stroke of his club. Lono turns and makes a downward hack and severs the upper arm from his shoulder. The boy slides into the bedroom as Akila slices off a hand of a boy screaming to his face.

Alana feels an instant repulsion to the presence of these children. They are emanating the aura of dread, pain, hatred that she thought was the creature stalking her visions. They snarl and hiss at her family with sharpened black teeth, painfully filed down. They wear only black shorts and they have been painted with a thick tar, except for their hands and bare feet. She raises her pistol to the boy writhing to attack Akila, "Why don't I just shoot 'em in the chest?"

"Shoot 'em in the gut!" Kaleo screams.

Alana takes her shot. The boy hunches over and attempts to catch the bullet in the rope around his neck. The bullet rips through his chest and then strikes Kaleo in the thigh. "Shoot him again!" Kaleo yells.

The boy grabs and climbs up Kaleo's shirt. He gnashes at the rope around Kaleo's neck with his jagged teeth. The one-armed boy hurtles out of the bedroom and slams against the hallway wall. Lono lunges right after him and buries his club into its jaw and neck with one swift hack. The snap of a rope propels another child free from Kaleo's neck.

The savage boy lunges at Akila, but gets pummeled into the kitchen counter from a leveraged arm-bar. The boy hits the floor, flips over and then fiendishly runs past Lono into the bedroom. Lono peels his club out from the convulsing boy pinned to the wall. Lono spins around, but Akila already has his club swinging to block a machete striking down at Lono's head. The machete digs into the club as Akila hooks his leg around the boy's leg.

Akila wraps his arm around the boy's neck and launches him over his hip into the bedroom door frame. Lono strikes his club into the back of the boy's head and then turns to Kaleo as another rope snaps. Alana runs over and fires another shot into the chest of the last boy tied to Kaleo's neck. The boy continues grinding the rope in his teeth as Alana stands over him and sets off another round into the back of his head. "Are these kids yours?"

Kaleo needs help loosening the nooses from his neck, "Just focking kill them!"

Alana stands to take aim at the boy being intercepted by Lono when she hears her sister scream, "Behind you!" Alana turns to see Keala leaping from the kitchen past Lono and the wild boy. Alana turns and raises her aim at a man just entering the front door. He and Keala fire their shots at the same time. Alana adjusts her aim lower as Keala's shot strikes him in the chest and he hunches forward. Alana fires her shot directly into his head. A curtain of blood sprays from the man's jaw and sails past Keala.

Alana looks over and sees Keala grabbing at her left hip. She runs over and catches her before she collapses to the floor. Alana looks over to Lono in combat with a savage boy while Akila pounds his club repeatedly at another boy kicking on the ground. Keala coughs, and pleads, "Get me to the truck!'

Alana gets cooperation from the wind to lift her sister to her feet. She pulls her arm over her shoulder and heaves them to the door. Alana hobbles her sister to the truck's open door and helps lift her up. She has her eyes on the doorway and rushes to return. She hears her sister yell from the truck, "Get Kaleo in the truck!"

Alana rushes into the house ready to take aim and finds Kaleo face down on the floor. Lono has one of the savage boys pinned with his knee locked around his neck. Akila continues to land strikes with his club. He kicks the rabid boy away and lands a heavy strike into the boy's neck and shoulder as he charges again. The blade of the club digs into his chest, but the boy continues to scratch and claw away at Akila.

"Get Kaleo to the truck!" Akila shouts.

Alana aims her pistol at Lono's attacker, but cannot find a clean shot. She backs away with the gun ready, but cannot hold her aim and pull on Kaleo's arm at the same time. She flips him over and finds him foaming out his nose and mouth. Alana crouches and attempts to aim again but has to pull her shot away.

The wind bounces Lono's second club across the floor. Lono reaches out and snags it. Lono quickly stands and swings his club full-strength into the boy's abdomen. The club rips in clean and spews the bowels into the wind. Lono immediately launches upwards and comes down in front of Akila, hammering down on the other boy's backbone. Akila twists his club and flings the boy to the floor. Akila swiftly drops to his knees and severs the boy's head against the ground. Akila stands and watches the body continuing to writhe across the floor.

Alana pulls Kaleo to the porch and rolls him down the step. She turns to run back in the house when she hears her sister yell, "Get him in the damn truck!" Alana grabs Kaleo's arm and tugs him through the mud. The wind helps her get him to his feet and over the tailgate. Alana turns back to the door when she hears the burning roof creak and collapse into the house. She runs to the door as Lono and Akila come running out.

They yell in unison, "Get in the truck!"

Alana runs to the open door and finds Keala sliding away from the driver's seat. "Eh! I thought you said I wasn't driving!"

Keala coughs in pain, "You're driving now! Get in!" Keala gets tangled up in the harness, "Look up the hill! The van is coming back! Get us out of here!"

Alana looks behind at the boys pulling Kaleo in the back of the truck. Akila knocks on the window, "They're coming back!"

The tires spin in the mud for a moment before they skid onto the road. Alana steers the truck through their hideaway yard to get off of Kaleo's street. "Oh my god Keala, you're really bleeding a lot! We need to take you to the hospital. I don't even know where I'm going!"

Keala coughs and winces, "Go right on Aliomanu road and take it around to Kuhio."

"Ok." Alana turns out the back window, "Akila, your mom got shot! Come up and put pressure on her leg!"

Akila slides right through the window and pulls out a towel from under the seat. "This is not so bad mom. We need to use your belt to squeeze down on the towel." Akila looks out the back and reads the hand signals from Lono. "Auntie, you should go faster. The van and the car are behind us."

"What the shit, sis?" Keala sits up and tries to see out the back, "You never popped the tires or what?"

"Could not!" Alana weaves through Kaleo's neighborhood searching for Aliomanu road, "There was fockah's in that car. I had to stab one and then shoot him, twice. You shot the other one through the window. You almost shot me you know. Damn, you look really pale. You lost a lot of blood. Fockin' shit fock! I focking wish I knew where I was focking going. And does somebody want to tell me what the fock was up with those kids? Were they even human? Kaleo! Kaleo, why the hell did you have four demon mongrel kids tied around your focking neck? My sister got shot rescuing you from your baby sitting job, asshole! Don't tell me those were your focking kids!"

"Take it easy, sister." Keala sits up sideways and changes the ammunition magazine in her pistol. "Just turn right at the next street. Don't worry about the stop sign, nobody's stupid enough to be on the road during this storm. Look, they're having a hard time back there. That's why they can't catch up. Ok? Just relax and drive safe. We'll be alright."

"Did you know there was going to be kids at the party? I never had a child give off a vibe like that." Alana swerves the truck along the road even though they are shrouded from the storm's violence. "Still yet, I just shot a child. Cursed or not, that was a young child I just shot. And actually, how the hell did I shoot the damn rope? I tried to shoot the little monster in the head and he jumped up to take the bullet in his own freakin' neck! That little devil knew I was aiming at his head and managed to get free from his leash. The fockah went sacrificed his own neck just so it could go fetch a machete! That was one mean keiki!"

Akila wipes the blood off of Alana's face and speaks calmly near her ear, "Anxiety is thought without control. Flow is control without thought. Just concentrate on driving down the road and let us take care of this other stuff. Slow your breathing down, deep breaths. Ok? I'm going in the back to help Lono throw some spears." Akila slithers out the back window and pokes his head back through, "Eh. You like me wake up Kaleo? Maybe we can ask him some questions."

Alana realizes she is grinding her teeth. She loosens the grip on the steering wheel and reaches to hold her sister's hand. "Eh. Seriously, did you know that dark vibe was coming from the kindergarten class? That shit was more horrible than the creature with yellow eyes." Alana gasps, "Those weren't Kaleo's kids were they? They were his! That's why you said we weren't doing slavery! Because that yellow-eyed demon wants us to pump out his demon spawn. Is that what's going on here or what? Give it to me straight, wench!"

"Well, I don't think that's the half of it." Keala puts her foot on the seat and pulls her left knee up to pinch the bloody towel on her hip. "Behind

292

that vibe of death, you didn't sense a little kanaka maoli (full-blooded Hawaiian person)?"

"What?" Alana glares over in disgust, "What-choo-ma-sayin'? He went da kine (*the kind* - phrase with universal application for an implied meaning) one wahine (woman) already, went spawned one litter of hapa (mixed race) demon mutts! Hooo, I like shoot his focking balls already!"

"Look, I'm sure he's abducting all kinds of wahine, probably from anywhere he can sail his ship to." Keala holds onto her sister's hand for warmth, "But it's the cloning shit that bothers me. So, if they're already cloning fish, don't you think it's possible that they could be cloning these keiki devils from the DNA of kanaka's?"

"What? Our kanaka's?" Alana glares back mortified.

"Ya. I think that's why old yellow-eyes wanted Ikaika-them to stay as his guests. Eh? So he could vampire their DNA. Ikaika-them all had the bambucha (big) mana that night in Alaska. Their bumbacha (big) mana brought his house honor. Ya? Like what he said. He values that power and I bet that he is trying to clone that power. And it would seem that the opposite of mana, our mana... is his vibe of dark dread. And those little bastards were sure the fock full of it." Keala watches the boys hold Kaleo over the tailgate for vomiting.

"And Tiki..." Alana looks back over for a moment and gives a wince. "Somehow, I like the idea of Tiki out of his body for experimentation a little better than him shagging concubine skanks for demon spawn."

"Wait, what da fock?" Keala calculates that thought for a moment, "You don't think that since Ikaika-them are conscious in their bodies, that they are actually banging the skanks?"

"I'm not saying all that..." Alana regrets steering the conversation in this direction, "Although, I was reading a bit of guilt from lolo Kaleo back there... But seriously, our kanaka could not have created something like those little bastards. Not even if they was tag-teaming the skanks with the yellow-eyed bugger. They must be cloning them because you cannot have two fathers. Ya?"

"Hoo, fock. That was all confusing. I don't like this conversation." Keala watches the boys pull Kaleo back into the truck, but quickly hang him over the tailgate for continued heaving. "Boy do I got some questions for Kaleo." She yells out the back, "Try give him some apple juice!" Keala points ahead, "Eh, go right on Kuhio. Follow the shoreline all the way to town and then we roll right up into the emergency room where the ambulance stay. Guarantee somebody can help us. Now, you're doing really good. But maybe try go a little faster. I think the fockah's is catching up."

Alana peers into the rearview mirror and sees Lono pouring apple juice over Kaleo's face. Everything past that is swirling darkness. She scans the road ahead and slows down for the right turn. She yells, "Hold on everybody!" After carefully turning onto the two-lane highway, Alana speeds up and glances in the rearview. She watches Akila lay Kaleo down flat on his back while Lono dumps out the ice cooler all over him. Choppy waves crash over the rocks and gush onto the flooded street. The sheltering sphere around the truck clears the storm surge from their path, leaving a nearly dry road for Alana. Everything outside their shroud of calmness appears as a violent grey blur. She glances again at the rearview and sees the boys instructing Kaleo on how to hold a bundle of long spears for them. "Eh, can you see where that van is? Are they still following us?"

"Maybe you could drive a little faster. They're actually right behind us." Keala yells out the back, "Eh! Kaleo! Was those your kids? No? Was they Ikaika's kids? No? Eh! Kaleo! Who's kids was those? What-choo mean they came out the jar? Eh? What, test tube kind? Then how do you know they was not your kids? What-choo mean you still got the lava? Oh, stay in your blood from Alaska. Eh? So what, not compatible in the chop suey? What? Who? When? Nah! What? Oh nah! Where he stay? Where the ship stay? Oh nah!" Keala turns to Alana, "Eh, the kids say if you don't go faster, they're gonna hit us."

"I can't go faster! Cannot see more than ten feet in front of me! I thought you was gonna shoot them, eh?" Alana pleads.

Keala shrugs, "Only if they come from the side, then I can shoot 'em. The kids stay in the way, that's why."

Alana finally sees the car's silhouette at the edge of their bubble and accelerates wildly in panic, "Eh so what, who's kids was those?"

"Oh, you don't want to know." Keala is fascinated at the speed of the spear after it leaves Akila's grip. It blasts through the front windshield of the black car and impales the passenger to the seat just before he can fire his gun.

"Say it! What the hell did Kaleo just tell you?" Alana swerves the truck to keep the car from entering their bubble.

"Don't make me say it." Keala yells out the back window, "Get the driver Lono!" She sees the desperate look on her sister's face, "Ok. Ikaika-them aren't compatible for the cloning process because of their transformation in Alaska. Tiki on the other hand..." She watches her sister concentrate on the drive along the rocky coastline. "So was just like you said, those clones were made from Tiki because he never transformed with the lava like the others. And they're the test tube kind so he's probably not shagging the skanks. Plus, he's not even inside his body, remember? He's just on a ship somewhere. They abducted Kaleo and him and Ikaika went to the ship and loaded up the clones." She yells out the back, "Lono, didn't you just harpoon the driver? How is he still driving? Someone from the back seat? How many people are in that fockin' clown car?"

"Poor Tiki." Alana swerves to the ledge trying to lure the black car to close to the rocks. "But, why were they tied around Kaleo's neck like that?"

"Eh! Kaleo!" Keala yells out the back, "Why was the keiki's tied around your neck?" Keala translates the muttering to Alana, "To torture Kaleo. Their aura's clash big time with the clones. They bet Kaleo would not survive and the keiki's would actually rip his head off. But it turns out, the clones really clashed with Lono and Akila even worse.

Hmph, I guess they would be Lono's brothers, and Akila's cousins. Evil quadruplets, how's that? Kaleo says he promised Tiki they would go back for him. Eh! Kaleo! You can find Tiki or what? Kaleo said Ikaika can find him. Eh! Kaleo! Where Ikaika stay? Kaleo said Lika can find him. Eh! Kaleo! Where Lika stay? Kaleo said they are all on separate ships out at sea. He said he can only find them when he's, you know the kind, *receptive*. How mental is that?"

"I guess that's why we had to save his lolo (crazy) okole (ass)." Alana swerves just as the black car smashes into their bumper. "Lono! Put a spear right in their steering wheel!"

Keala watches out the back window at Lono finding the balance point of another spear. Lono crouches and braces his knee against the tailgate for support. Several shots rip into the side of the truck as if they were aiming for the tires. Alana swerves away from the ledge to avoid a collision with the car. Lono heaves his spear, driving it through the windshield, through the steering wheel, and into the new driver sitting on the lap of the old, dead driver. Unable to turn the wheel with the spear locked inside, the impaled driver can only sail the black car over the cliff and onto the rocks below.

"Holy shit! It worked!" Keala suddenly looks to the side and sees the van careening towards them from the mauka (mountain) side of the road. Keala spins to the other side and fires off three shots at the other driver before the van slams against the side of the truck. "Son of a bitch! You gotta get in front of them so Akila can put a spear through their window!"

Alana panics. She gasps trying to fight the truck from hitting the rocks on the maka'i (oceanside) ledge. "I can't! Their pushing me off the road!" Alana stomps the brakes causing the van to skid across their front fender. The van grinds past their front bumper and spins onto the rocks at the ledge. Alana cuts the wheel and rolls back onto the road. "Fock those fockin' fockah's! How much further to the damn hospital?"

Keala spins to the back and looks down at the boys crumpled up against the cab. "I'm having deja vu right now..."

Alana turns to her and tries to fix the bloody towel back in Keala's hip, "How much further?"

"Another twenty minutes." Keala yells out the window, "Eh! What? Kaleo said he's having deja vu right now."

"So what? You smoking the same shit again?" Alana grumbles.

"Listen, all this was for Akila and Lono. They're going to be ok. They're going to find Tiki and Ikaika-them. We've got a different path." Keala holds onto her sister's arm, "We're going to be ok."

"What the shit?" Alana looks in the rearview to find Akila preparing his last spear. She sees Lono sitting Kaleo up, holding his shirt against the blood coming from the top of Kaleo's head. "What the hell were you supposed to tell me about this situation? What have you seen?"

Keala checks the count left in her clip and then wraps her arm around Alana's neck, "Akila! Give mommy a kiss." Akila pops his head through the back window and gives her a peck. "Kiss auntie."

"Eh, keiki..." Alana gives a quick smile to him, "What was Leo's deja vu?"

Akila kisses her cheek, "Kaleo said you're taking us to the bridge. And that he's not worthy and wants to jump out the truck. He's pretty messed up."

"That's the guilt I was reading!" Alana glares to her sister, "The sad warrior is all messed up with guilt and regret!"

Akila pets her hair and tucks some behind her ear, "He's messed up when you slammed on the brakes and he hit his head. He's mumbling some crazy shit right now." Akila ducks away, then returns. "Child of the owl, child of the shark... He wants us to throw him over the side before it's too late." Akila dips to the back.

Alana turns behind them, "Are they still coming? Anybody see them? Too late for what? I'm taking you to the hospital, what bridge is he... Mom's bridge? That's why you didn't want me to drive! Fock that! You think I'm going to drive us over the cliff like her? Well you know what, if they come up and hit me like that again, I will drive off the damn cliff! You gotta kill them!"

"I will! They are going to die. Not us." Keala gives her sister a kiss and wipes the tears from face, "Ok? All I'm supposed to tell you is that the boys will bring the kanaka's back home. Don't be scared for them because I've been shown this. Mom's bridge? Our bridge. We can learn to live in two realms at once. That's what the creature learned to do. And that's where we kill him."

"Wait. What-choo-ma-focking saying?" Alana scans the mirrors and then peeks out the side window behind them. Returning to her seat, "We're going to kill him in the spirit world? You saw this?"

"Nah." Keala kneels on the seat facing the behind them and leans back against the dashboard. "The spirit world is the bridge. There's another realm on the other side."

"Wait! Is this where Tiki is?" Alana detects movement in the blurry storm behind them. She floors the gas pedal, "Did they pull Tiki out to this other realm?" She demands, feeling puzzle pieces align.

"Ya. I think he's using Tiki as a bridge. I think he tapped into some kind of mana of his own and is using Tiki to bring it back here. He's cloning Tiki with this dark mana. That's the opposing charge we were feeling from those little demon bastards. We cannot coexist with that dark energy." Keala clutches her pistol with both hands and points it out the passenger window. Without looking away from Alana's glare, "Don't worry. In the other realm, you will be the one with great vision, and I'll be the warrior who doesn't know what the fock is going on."

Alana catches a glimpse of Akila loading the heavy spear far behind his sturdy stance. Lono has Kaleo tweaked in a headlock, wrestling him down from the tailgate. She gazes back to her sister. They lock eyes as Akila hurls the spear with a mighty thrust. The black van emerges from the blur of the dark mountainside. It enters their bubble with screeching tires. Akila's spear splashes through the driver's side window and rips into the chest of the driver. Lono heaves Kaleo and slides him up to the cab, tackling Akila

298

on top of them.  Keala begins firing shots into the heads of the two men visible in the front seat of the van.  Without breaking their stare at each other, Alana glimpses out their side window at the cloud of blood swirling throughout the inside of the van.  Alana can feel the tears running down her face as she watches the tears run down Keala's face.

She cannot even brace for the impact as the driverless van collides into their passenger door.  Keala is thrust towards Alana.  She catches her sister in her arm, still clutching the steering wheel.  Their eyes still locked, still holding hands.  Alana finally breaks the stare and watches the boys hurl into the air.  Akila spins off above their bubble as the storm's rage whisks him away.  Lono continues his headlock on Kaleo, flying out over the rocky cliff.  Their truck rotates in the air as Alana sees over the cliff from the back window.  Lono vanishes from her sight as the truck continues to spin towards the rocks below.  The van crumples across the rocks above and tumbles down the cliff after them.  Their truck strikes the side of the cliff and bounces off towards the ocean.  The truck rotates for Alana to catch a glimpse of Lono sailing through the air above the stormy sea.  Lono catches her stare and gazes back for an instance.  He tries to give her a smile and holds the stare until he reaches the water's surface.  Alana squeezes onto her sister, staring at her son through the back window.  Just as Lono hits the water, still clutching onto Kaleo's neck, the image of her son freezes in time and suddenly ignites into a fiery blaze.  Alana loses the feeling of her sister's grip.  She is pulled away from the connection of all her senses.  The vision of Lono suddenly becomes blinding white and the frozen image gives way to nothing in the pure blackness.

"I knew you would come."